Court of Deadly Whispers

The Mowbray Chronicles - Book 2

Mette Holm

ISBN-13: 978-87-971343-1-3

DEDICATION

to my readers and all those who faithfully devote their time and energy to creating their own worlds full of wonders.

Beyond history lies reality.

ACKNOWLEDGMENTS

What is a book if it is not written, read and edited ferociously? It is an idea that perhaps, if fair chance is at play, will endure and enjoy. It is my great fortune that I need not wonder if this book is worthy of your eyes. Several people have helped in the process and I owe each and everyone a great thank you.

Thank you to my editor and friend, Steve, who never lets a poorly constructed sentence or strange straggling sentence go amiss. Without your determination the end result would be meagre.

Thank you to the fantastic women who endure my endless post-its and notes that encroach every nook and cranny of a workaway. I hope you will be part of my journey for many years to come.

Thank you to my enthusiastic and wonderfully critical proof-reader who helps me weed out all the little linguistic rascals that inevitably lurk in the dark corners of any manuscript.

Thank you to my amazing graphic designer who once more managed to sort through my chaotic input and create the cover I had in my head. You are a true artist and an exceptionally patient human being.

Thank you to model Ruca Angel and photographer Aage Møller Pedersen for allowing me to play around with what was already a work of art. Such generosity is rare and heart-warming.

Thank you from the bottom of my heart to my family and friends who ceaselessly support and encourage me to keep going. You are the pot of gold at the end of every rainbow.

And finally, a great big thank you to my husband for never doubting me, even if I do. I love you.

GALLERY OF CHARACTERS

HOUSE MOWBRAY

John Mowbray, Baron of Mowbray ✝1368 — Elizabeth Mowbray ✝1368

Margaret b. 1361	Joan b. 1363	Eleanor b. 1364	John b. 1365 ✝1383	Thomas b. 1367	Argyle b. 1368
m. 1380 Sir Reginald de Lucy	m. 1382 Sir Thomas Grey	m. 1385 Baron John de Welles		m.1383 Elizabeth le Strange ✝ 1383 m. 1384 Elizabeth FitzAlan	m. 1397 Isobel Trothby

HOUSE PLANTAGENET

Edward III
✝1377

Edward ✝1376
The Black Prince

b. 1367
Richard II

m. 1382
✝ 1395
Anne of Bohemia

m. 1396
Isabella of France

John of Gaunt
Duke of Lancaster

b. 1367
Henry of
Bolingbroke

Edmund of Langley
Duke of York

Thomas of Woodstock
Duke of Gloucester

OTHER KEY CHARACTERS

Stephen Smith [Master of Arms at Beauworth]

Lady Celeste [French lady in waiting]

Mistress Prudence [lady-in-waiting]

Mistress Catherine [lady-in-waiting]

Lady de Cousy [chief lady-in-waiting]

Lady Mortimer [chief lady-in-waiting]

Thomas Holland, Earl of Kent [half-brother of King Richard]

John Holland, Duke of Exeter and Earl of Huntingdon [half-brother of King Richard]

Thomas Holland, Duke of Surrey [son of the Earl of Kent and nephew to King Richard]

John Beaufort, Earl of Somerset [half-brother of Henry of Bolingbroke]

Thomas Beaufort, Duke of Exeter [half-brother of Henry of Bolingbroke]

Richard FitzAlan, Earl of Arundel [father-in-law to Thomas Mowbray, Lords Appellant]

Thomas de Beauchamp, Earl of Warwick [Lords Appellant]

John Montagu, Earl of Salisbury [English nobleman]

Master Tucker [Master of Coin]

Captain Brook [White Hart]

George [Squire]

Brian Northwoode [Page]

Prologue

16 September 1398 - Coventry

Knights, bishops and visiting foreign dignitaries flocked through the natural opening to one side of the wide field. Here they met many of England's greatest nobles as well as thousands of common folks who had been there since daybreak.

Argyle ducked under a low-hanging branch and paused to untangle his cloak when it caught on a wild rosebush, a few startling red petals shone against the wilted bare branches. He had been trying to persuade Thomas to let him plead with the King most of last night but, for once, his brother seemed determined to see something through to the bitter end.

Today, two great dukes of England were to undergo a joust of war in front of the King. By the end of the day, either Bolingbroke or Thomas would probably be dead. The victor would be vindicated; the realm would have witnessed one of the great chivalric occasions of the age.

'Sir Argyle. Come to see your brother win the day?'

Argyle turned to face the King's half-brother the Duke of Exeter, John Holland, who was staring with contempt. 'No. I have come to try to stop this madness. Unfortunately, my brother still has his honour.'

'Really? Mowbray thinks he has a chance against one of the finest jousters in all of England?' Exeter's surprise was plain on his face.

'I cannot say.'

Exeter snorted and then winced when Argyle gave him an icy stare. Looking around to find someone to relieve him, Exeter found a saviour and threw a parting word over his shoulder. 'Best of luck to your brother.'

Argyle unclenched his fists and drew his cloak close together, no longer caring about ripping holes in the fine cloth. The morning was cold and damp and although the sun was out, it struggled to burn away the thick carpet of dew. Of course, Argyle did not for a second think Thomas would win the joust. If he was very lucky he might escape with his life, but he would be banished from court and from England. That much was certain.

To one side near the Mowbray tents, Argyle spied Stephen stomping his feet to keep warm in the cold morning air.

'No luck?' Stephen asked.

'No. I confess I had hoped he would see reason. Or even allow that I spoke to the King on his behalf.' Argyle was exhausted - it had been a long night.

'You still could, M'lord.'

Argyle smiled sadly. Too much had passed between Thomas and him for that to be an option. 'He wishes to fight this battle on his own.'

Stephen looked around. 'Then is it wise to be so close to his tents?'

'He will not even notice me here,' Argyle said. 'He is beyond all that.'

'M'lord, he does understand fully the consequences of this day?' Stephen rubbed his hands together to get warm.

Resting a hand briefly on Stephen's shoulder, Argyle silenced his friend. Of course Thomas knew. He had simply played every card in the deck and now he had nowhere to go but onto the field to settle an old quarrel in a joust of war.

Across the field, Eleanor caught his eye; she was pale as a pearl, shivering in the damp. Locking eyes with her, Argyle knew that his sister too feared for their brother's life and what might happen to them when Thomas fell before Bolingbroke's lance. Would all of the Mowbrays fall from favour with him?

Argyle could not help but wonder how he had ended up in this chaos? How had he let it all slip away? Although he was miles away from the sea, he could suddenly taste the spray of salt on his lips and hear seagulls scream overhead …

Part 1

Blinded

CHAPTER 1

30 October 1395 - At sea

Argyle rested his hands on the slick, salty railing and stared into the horizon. It was a clear day, and the ship took the waves to the stern, making it roll comfortably. The sails flapped listlessly from time to time, and the men busied themselves clearing the decks and manning the helm or coiling rope that had come undone during the hasty departure. They appeared pleased with the prolonged journey brought on by the calm weather and had plenty of work to do readying the ship for the journey back.

Argyle ran a hand through his hair; it was moist and coarse to the touch. Every day since they had departed, he had stood here, staring out over the sea, and every night he had gone to bed with sea spray in his hair and salt on his lips.

She would be waiting; he knew it. She would be waiting all her life - even if she had betrayed him when they had first met - he was certain that she had loved him too. When he had left her, his heart had been torn still beating from his chest and left to wither on the sand beneath her orange walls. There it still lay, beating slowly - ever more slowly - declaring his love to her every single day by every single beat. He knew some day it would fade and stop, but even then his love for her would go on, pure and eternal. She had been his first love, and she would be his last.

'LAND AHOY!' the call came from the crow's nest.

Argyle was jolted back to a time not long ago when the same call had sounded from another lookout, and he had rejoiced. Today, the words seared his soul and wiped all thought from his mind. He half expected there to be another call from the stern that they were being chased up by some ship, calling for them to stop and turn about, but of course there would not be. Not this time.

This time, there would only be land ahead and no ships behind. Argyle knew he should be happy, and yet he could not even muster a smile. He had dreamed about the moment for so long, had planned it in his head a hundred times over. To have it ripped apart and drowned beneath the black waves was almost too much to bear - even now.

He looked up again, as the captain joined him at the bow. 'We'll be there in a few hours time, Sire.'

'As you promised,' Argyle said.

'Aye, there'd be Hell to pay, if I didn't!'

'That there would.' Argyle looked at the captain, a young man with auburn hair and squinting grey eyes. 'The wind is dying down.'

'We'll row the last few leagues. Needs must we get to port today.'

'They will be waiting.'

The captain looked wearily at Argyle. 'Still not …'

'No,' Argyle said.

The ship's mate shouted for the captain to return to the helm. 'Whatever you've done, they'll understand,' the captain said.

'They will not.'

The captain's hair was tied with a weathered piece of rope to keep most of it from his handsome, square face. He frowned - a picture of the man he would turn into if God and the sea were kind to him - and then gave Argyle a hard pat on the shoulder before he turned to the helm to relieve the ship's mate, who ran down the length of the ship to the stern, shouting commands as he went. Soon oars would sprout from the ship like strange legs on a sleek sea-creature, and they would drive the ship to shore.

They will be waiting, not just for me, but for him too, Argyle thought and looked down at the bow, cutting its way through the topped waves. They will make demands and ask questions, and my answers will not please any of them.

His chest was being squeezed by a giant's hand, crushing his ribs and driving the shattered bones into his lungs. He had to survive this - he had to be strong. It was his own decision, and he had to live with it, though for how long he did not know.

Why did I ask, he wondered for the thousandth time as the coast came ever closer, I could have outrun them - I could have at least tried.

The ship shot forward as the oarsmen began toiling; Argyle felt the deck roll, and the bow bite into the waves, chewing away towards the shore. They were making good speed.

'It'll be good to step foot on English soil once more, eh Sire?' a seaman said.

Argyle just stared ahead as the white cliffs slowly grew larger and more ominous like the looming wings of an avenging angel. He wondered if any angels were waiting for him - or just the Devil.

30 October 1395 - Dover

'BE CAREFUL!' the harbour master called as six seamen carried the large crate between them. The gangway was almost too narrow for them, and Argyle felt his heart crawl into his throat every time one of the men slipped or tottered under the weight of the consignment.

'Nothing can happen to it,' he said to the captain who nodded; he understood full well what precious cargo they were carrying, and he was eager to get it off his ship.

'It won't, my men are sure of foot and know what they're about.' The captain turned to Argyle. 'You'd be wanting off the ship too, I'll wager?'

'Yes, but not here,' Argyle said. 'Anywhere but here.'

'Too bad this is our final destination then,' the captain said. 'I'd offer you a cabin, but those men look like they want you to come down - soon!'

'So they do.' Argyle looked down at the men assembled on the quay, most of them wearing a white hart on their doublets. 'Best not keep them waiting.'

The captain nodded for the ship's mate to lead the horses down the gangway. The six seamen were carefully placing the crate on a long wagon drawn by two black dray horses. While Argyle's chestnut hunter walked steadily off the ship, two of the other horses neighed and rolled their eyes when a couple of soldiers tried to pull them onto the swaying gangway. Argyle felt just as the horses, no good could come from walking down that gangway. And yet it must be done.

If I try to leave again, my family will be destroyed, he thought.

That was what the message from the royal cog had read. If he continued to Jerusalem and ignored the King's command to return, his family would perish. Argyle had read Thomas' note, wondering whether the smudges on it were just seawater or whether the were his brother's bitter tears. Not much could move Thomas, but the destruction of his family - his legacy - was bound to make even the strongest man weak of heart.

'Off the ship, Sir Argyle!'

The captain glanced down at the dockside where several more men had gathered. 'I'll help the men get the rest of the horses off the ship. You must go now.'

Argyle recognised the concern in the captain's voice and understood it well. The longer the captain harboured him on board, the more likely it was that the crew would be heavily fined if not worse - the ship moored at the King's pleasure. He pressed a pouch into the captain's hand and thanked him for the crossing.

'Maybe we'll meet some other time, Sire,' the captain said by way of parting.

'Maybe.'

Argyle walked down towards the four soldiers in the King's livery who had gathered around the planks. He briefly wondered how the King might have found out that he had gone and came to the conclusion that either he had spies at Beauworth, or some message from his family or from court had reached the manor just as Argyle had left, leaving Stephen with no choice but to pass on the message Argyle had written to explain his absence. He refused to consider the third option - that Stephen had sent the message as soon as Argyle had departed.

'Sir Argyle, how good to see you,' the Duke of Surrey, Thomas Holland, said, smirking around at his men. He was dressed in all the splendour of a royal prince, and Argyle noticed several large golden rings glittering on his fingers. 'You are to come straight to court by order of my uncle, the King. Best you ride with the body - and not on a horse that might spook,' he paused, 'and carry you off.'

Argyle nodded briefly, regret mingling with increasing anger and decided to say nothing.

'Do you know who it is?' Surrey asked and tossed his head at the crate.

'Yes, but he should have been left where he was.'

'No doubt the King wanted his old friend to return.'

'No doubt, the King wanted his old friend to return alive,' Argyle said. 'Be grateful the weather is cold - or the stink would be unbearable. He has been dead at least three years!'

Surrey tried to hide his discomfort, gave the command to fall in and led the strange little convoy away from Dover, from the sea and from Argyle's dreams. He heard them crushing on the swell, rolling out to sea to be swallowed up and forgotten.

'You were unwise to leave without asking the King's permission.' Surrey fell in beside the wagon.

'Would he have given it?' Argyle grumbled.

'Since you failed to ask, we shall never know,' Surrey said, 'and now no one else dare do anything before asking the King. He is drowning in petitions ranging from those wanting to go on pilgrimage to those merely asking if they can visit relatives in Calais.'

'You think I brought this on you?'

'Yes. But most of all, you brought it on your family.' Surrey rode on a while in silence, now and again stealing a glance at the crate on the wagon. Finally, he spoke. 'I would be humble before the King, if I were you. He held you in such high regard, but now …'

'I have brought home his friend,' Argyle said, trying to ignore that the hard wooden seat was already biting into his thighs. 'He can ask for nothing more - I did as he ordered.'

'Yes, but he had to send the order a good deal further than he imagined.'

And I still wonder who told him exactly how far, he would have to send word to reach me, Argyle thought. He turned to Surrey, sure that the King's nephew would be well-informed and asked, 'What news from court?'

'Besides your sudden departure?' Surrey said. 'There is peace in the land, the King is proving a deft hand at ruling, and Gaunt is letting up on his demands that the King marry.'

'Marry?'

'He needs an heir, would you not say?' Surrey glanced around and leaned towards Argyle. 'He needs one badly, for the King's grandfather's will has emerged - and his Majesty does not like what he reads!'

'Is that so?' Argyle was curious despite himself.

'Best I not say too much,' Surrey said and spurred his horse into a canter.

The rest of the way to London, Argyle was left to wonder what would happen once he was inside the court's stone walls - and what it was the King had discovered about the succession to turn his temper foul.

CHAPTER 2

3 November 1395 - Westminster

The King loomed above the crowd, his crimson coat spilling down either side of the throne and onto the top step of the dais. He looked down. 'Sir Argyle! You have disappointed your King!'

Argyle knelt before the dais, feeling the ogling, angry stares of the many nobles, courtiers and knights gathered in the great hall, burning into his back. The King's strange order to bring back a certain man's remains and his threat that if Argyle did not obey, the Mowbray family would be brought to their knees, was still very much a mystery to him. Not for the first time, Argyle wondered if his decision had indeed made any difference.

'It is an offence to the King to leave England without a royal permission!' the King boomed, the stone walls enhancing his voice. Although the room was packed with nobles and courtiers, Argyle would have sworn that not a single soul drew breath in the silence that ensued.

'Majesty …' Argyle began, but the King drowned him out.

'SILENCE! You have not only disappointed ME, you have brought shame on your family!' The King's temper was rising quickly. 'Do you care so little for anyone else?! You swore your allegiance TO ME!!'

'And I am your Majesty's loyal subject. But I …'

'YOU DARE INTERRUPT YOUR KING?!!' The King's voice climbed another octave. 'You WILL be quiet and hear my judgement upon your actions, and you will take whatever punishment I see fit to dispense! I will have you cowering before me like the dog that you are. If only I had known how little loyalty I could expect from you, how disappointed your former master would be in you, I would never have let you inherit. I would have thrown you out! You are not fit to be a knight! You are not fit to be anything but the lowest of beasts! Selfish, cruel creature! Swine would turn you from their mud pits and fleas would not deign to bite your traitor back! I should have you thrown in the wettest cell in the Tower to ROT!'

The crowd of men cheered and more than a few no doubt nudged each other. Argyle was about to steal a glance at the King, when a familiar voice spoke up. 'Your Majesty! How can you punish a man for wanting to go on pilgrimage? You who are the most pious man in all of England.'

The great hall grew quiet and the atmosphere tensed. Where before there had been cheers, now there was only a thick, horrible silence. Argyle turned his head to spy Bolingbroke standing near the dais, his fingers hooked in his belt, a sombre look on his face.

'Cousin, you speak for Sir Argyle?' The King's voice wavered. He seemed to shrink before Bolingbroke's calm gaze. It was almost as if he knew in advance that he would not win this power struggle.

'Yes Majesty, I do.' Bolingbroke's voice was clear, his manner calm but somehow forced, Argyle thought. Never breaking eye contact, Bolingbroke continued, 'I speak for all men who would go to find salvation in the Promised Land! Let me be the voice of every soul that might wake one morning and decide to travel the length of the world to behold the wonder that is God's own creation. For they too must be of a most pious disposition and must now fear their Christian imaginings.'

Argyle was surprised to hear Bolingbroke speak in his defence; the two of them had a feeble relationship at best, and he knew that Bolingbroke was indeed speaking not just for him, but for all men. If the King decided to punish Argyle for being pious, then no man in England would be safe.

The King seemed to come to the same realisation and his tone became grudging. 'Very well, I shall consider your plea, cousin! Sir Argyle, stand before your King and explain yourself.'

'Majesty.' Argyle rose and met the King's eye. He was surprised at how easily Bolingbroke had stumped the King. Bolingbroke had opened a tiny door to redemption for Argyle, and now he fumbled to turn the handle and escape. 'I had not thought that my leaving would give you cause to complain and for that, I humbly apologise. Of all men, I believed you would sanction my choice to return once more to the Holy Land. As soon as word reached me that you had a task for me, I immediately obeyed, and I have delivered - I believe - what you desired.' Argyle's words were flat as he struggled not to reveal the extent of his anger at the blatant humiliation. He might apologise, but he would not be repentant.

The King shot Argyle a spiteful glance, before addressing the rest of the people present. His voice shook with fury. 'Indeed you have - though reluctantly, I suspect. You are not to leave court until I have come to a decision!' The King looked about the room, men dropping to their knees when his eyes swept past them. 'Your brother will be your gaoler!'

Argyle bowed his head in unwilling submission.

CHAPTER 3

7 November 1395 - London

The church was quiet but for a few sniffles and coughs; the people gathered were wrapped in warm clothes, and many drew their cloaks closer together around their shivering bodies as if trying to shield themselves from the sense of foreboding that engulfed the church room. Their breath was turned to puffs of white by the icy air, and the few candles lit along the walls flickered in their struggle to stay alight. The courtiers' wives, usually ornamental in their bright dresses, wore all black, their subdued faces white above the black collars. Their husbands looked restrained and anxious. No one even dared whisper to each other.

The King stood before a massive coffin resting a bare hand on the top, his face working constantly, the grief in his eyes burned even stronger than when he had buried his wife the year before.

Argyle shuffled his feet restlessly, earning disgruntled looks from the other bystanders. He was uncomfortable at the scene about to play out and even more uncomfortable that Thomas and several other noblemen were openly absent. Argyle had thought Thomas would revel in playing gaoler to his younger brother, but not even that seemed to have cheered him up. Rather, he had avoided Argyle for the past four days, and now he was avoiding the ceremony too.

Argyle reflected on the elaborate coffin that had replaced the common crate, he had accompanied back from Calais. It seemed the

King had decided that the body of his long lost friend should rest forever in a tomb almost as overwhelming as that of the late Queen.

When de Vere had been driven from the King's service and from England, he had faced the nobles and managed to keep his throne only because his cousin Henry of Bolingbroke had decided to make peace at the very last minute. Since then, the King's hate of the nobles and his despair at not being able to bring back his favourite, de Vere, had grown every day. Some said that by now, the King's memory of de Vere had turned him into a saint, a golden youth whose exile had consumed and eventually killed him. The King imagined that de Vere had wasted away longing only to return to the English court and once more taking his rightful place as the King's best friend. Ordering his body exhumed and freighted back to England to receive an almost royal burial had paralysed the King's council.

Now, the selfsame noblemen who had once tried to unseat the King were openly absent from their old enemy's resplendent interment.

Argyle had accepted his role in this charade only to protect his own family. And that family was absent too. He knew that the King had noticed, how could he not? The church was filled to be sure, but the benches closest to the altar were empty but for a few men and women who looked oddly forlorn.

'What is he doing?' asked the Earl of Kent.

Thomas had persuaded Kent to bring Argyle to the church that he might obey the King's order to be present at the interment. Kent had been only too glad to offer his services and reaffirm his allegiance to his half-brother the King.

'Saying goodbye to a beloved friend, as you well know.' Argyle felt weary to the bone, and the silence frayed his nerves. 'And putting on a show, he enjoys putting on a show.'

'To be sure! My brother is always fond of a little spectacle,' Kent agreed and grinned with malice. 'Remember the Queen's funeral? What a day, even …'

'Even if we do not count the incident with Lord Arundel and the blood spilled on sacred ground?' Argyle whispered well aware that their voices were carried far by the deadly silence in the church. 'Yes, it was a spectacle, as is this, but it is more than that.'

'What then?' Kent asked, bowing his head when his younger brother Exeter sent him an angry look, Exeter was not a man to be trifled with. 'What do you think, he is wanting to achieve?'

'It is a demonstration of power,' Argyle said. Kent was clearly baiting him. 'Though I cannot imagine why.'

'You sound like your brother.' Kent turned his head away. 'Be careful what you say and to whom. This is his Majesty the King we are discussing. But I see your point and you are right of course, but then the lords had it coming, did they not?'

'How so?'

'How can you ask? You who were raised in the household of another beloved friend!' Kent's eyes darted around the church. 'Driving away de Vere and forcing the King to exile him for life was the dumbest thing any lord ever did.'

Argyle secretly agreed with Kent; theirs was not a King to forget and certainly not one to forgive. He opened his mouth to reply, but the Bishop of London rose from his seat and spread his arms towards the congregation. 'OH LORD! We give unto you the body and soul of a true and loyal Englishman, a peer of the realm and a most trusted friend of the Crown!'

The King stood still as a rock throughout the sermon, his back demonstratively turned to the church room forcing everyone else to keep standing as well. By the end of the first hour, Argyle feared that several of the old men and women would fall over from fatigue, and then the King did a most curious thing; he turned to the room and beckoned for two of his guards to step forward.

After a brief exchange of words, the two guards lifted the lid of the coffin. Argyle felt his stomach churn when the whiff of embalming fluid stole through the stifling cold air, dousing the assembled crowd in its sickly sweet scent.

'Beloved friend! Finally, I look once more upon your face,' the King said, his voice quavering with emotion. 'That we should not meet in life again is more than I can fathom. I have prayed for your safe return to England since the day you departed!'

Kent cleared his throat and the sound rang through the tall church room, momentarily breaking the spell of his intense expression of grief. Argyle shot Kent a sideways glance and saw him colouring under the glare of his brother Exeter. Kent might be the oldest, but Exeter was the Holland brother to recon with, his ties to the King much stronger than

Kent's.

The gathered mourners quickly fell silent once more when the King resumed his speech, bending over the coffin. 'I cannot part with you once more without giving you the gifts you should have had by right.' His voice was no more than a whisper, but in the quiet church room, it tolled loud as a bell.

From the left side of the room, Argyle had a clear view of the King and the coffin. Argyle was distressed and astonished to see the King carefully take one of de Vere's hands in his own and slip several golden rings on the corpse's fingers before, just as carefully, lowering the hand again. He proceeded to do the same with the other hand, his body trembling when he kissed de Vere's decayed flesh.

Argyle's stomach turned at the affectionate act, so much a lover's last kiss. He wondered briefly if the King had indeed been infatuated with de Vere in more than a common sense, just as many noblemen had thought and had reacted upon, in the past, to safeguard the kingdom and the King. Perhaps he did indeed resemble his ancestor Henry II more than anyone dared voice.

'Do you know, why the lords are not here?' Kent's whisper broke Argyle's train of thought, and he shook his head while the choir began singing. He was still puzzled that Thomas dared openly defy the King in such a way considering how hard he had worked to stay in the King's good graces these past many years.

'Because they still have not digested their hatred of him,' Kent continued and nodded towards the coffin. 'Some indeed know how to hold a grudge. De Vere's influence ended when he was exiled and certainly no one has pleaded his case in Parliament, not even the King himself. Why not attend today, if nothing else then to ensure that he is truly dead?'

'Either way their absence will have repercussions,' Argyle said, rubbing his cold hands together. 'Absence is always noticed.'

Kent nodded, his face grim and drawn. 'Yes, it always is. And my brother has turned holding a grudge into an art.'

ꕤ ꕤ

'I am ordered to take you before the King,' Kent said when the ceremony was finally over, the choir of boys singing out the mourners with a new hymn dedicated to the memory of de Vere who would now be interred, bathed in the King's tears and anguish. 'It seems he has decided what to do with a man who dares to claim loyalty to both the King of England and to God. It cannot have been an easy deliberation.'

Recognising the sarcasm, Argyle thought; is this why you accepted Thomas' task so readily? Whether he wanted to or not, Argyle would soon be before the King, entirely at his mercy. The notion was sickening.

Kent grabbed him by the arm with a slightly apologetic gesture. 'Best it looks as if I am carrying out your brother's task to perfection.'

'Will Thomas be present?'

'I was going to ask you the same,' Kent said. 'Lord Mowbray has said nothing to me of his plans, I thought you would know.'

'We have scarce spoken these past days,' Argyle admitted and thought; Thomas is very keen to distance himself from me, but I wonder if it is so very clever of him to stay away from both the interment and the King's judgement all in the same day.

He let Kent drag him along to create a show that the King might enjoy, but the King's face was cold and dark when they entered the room. Argyle knelt beside Kent in front of the dais, thinking how wondrous it was that every time he came to court, the King seemed to tower ever higher above the crowd.

'My dear Kent! You bring forth the prisoner!?'

Kent rose and cleared his throat. 'Yes Majesty, I come on the bidding of Lord Mowbray.'

'Oh, he is busy?' The King's icy voice cut clear across the room.

'I would not know, Majesty,' Kent muttered perhaps understanding that his favour to Thomas displeased his royal half-brother.

Argyle kept his eyes fixed on the floor, thinking back to the very first time he was in the presence of the King. When Argyle had first met the King, who was only a year older than he, the King had seemed a glorious young man, and Argyle had been in awe of his ease and benevolent manner. He wondered where that magnificent young man was now.

'Rise, Sir Argyle!' The King stood towering above Argyle, staring down at him with contempt. 'You dared to defy your King. You plotted to leave England without my leave. While I might commend you on a pious act, if you were indeed going to the Holy Land, I cannot ignore your blatant demonstration of disregard. It seems I was right to presume that only a threat to your family would persuade you to return - but not to repent. That is clear to me now!'

The great oak doors let in a gasp of cold air along with someone who was tardy for the King's judgement, and he broke eye contact with Argyle, a whisper of concern gliding across his face. Argyle tried to spy who it might be, but only glimpsed a dark cloak disappearing in the assembled crowd.

The King seemed to steel himself and turned back to Argyle. 'Another man might ask you to explain yourself, Sir Argyle.' The King drew breath. 'But not I! Until I have further use for you, you will return to Beauworth and stay there in house arrest at your Majesty's pleasure. You will be allowed to ride about your estates, but you shall always bring a royal guard. All of your earnings will revert to the Crown for the time being! Should a royal summons reach your house, you will respond immediately and obey any order your King might issue!'

A few of the men gathered glanced at Argyle and whispered together.

'You shall leave London tomorrow at dawn!' The King swept down the stairs pausing briefly next to Argyle to whisper: 'And if I hear of any troubles, Beauworth will be awarded to someone else! The only reason I have not stripped you of lands and title is because of your old master, may he rest in peace. My cousin's words had nothing to do with my decision! Defy me again, and I will have your head on a spike!'

ഗ ര ഗ ര

CHAPTER 4

3 April 1396 - Beauworth

'There are rumours at court.' Thomas swished his wine around the glass.

'There are always rumours at court,' Argyle said dismissively. Thomas' visit was as unexpected as it was unwanted. His brother had never visited Beauworth before, and now that he was here, Argyle wished for nothing more than to see him leave.

'I thought you might be interested,' Thomas said. 'Now that you are holed up here.'

'I can think of no better prison.'

'I grant you, the view is fair, and you can ride far and still be within the bounds of your own estate,' Thomas said and glanced at the royal guard by the door, the King's emblem of the White Hart prominent on his chest. 'But you can hardly enjoy it?'

'I cannot complain.' Argyle stood to close the window, a mild spring drizzle was wetting the rush matting on the floor. He was sure that beneath the guard's disinterested manner, he was spying for the King. Surely all of the royal guards posted at Beauworth were reporting back to court.

'No, I should wager you cannot - even if you wanted to.'

'Why have you come?' Argyle was both curious and eager to get Thomas off his lands. 'Are you here at the King's order?'

'Surely a brother can visit?' Thomas asked.

'Yes, but you never have,' Argyle said, replenishing Thomas' wine and his own, putting the pitcher back on the worn, low table, the top ringed from years of use as a makeshift serving table. 'Which does rather beg the question, why now?'

Thomas caught the guard's eye and dismissed him with a haughty wave. The guard scowled as he closed the door, this too would get back to the King. 'Have you heard from Eleanor of late?'

'No, but then you would know, the King did make you responsible for any communication to me.' Argyle hated the thought of Thomas reading all his letters, deciding whether or not to send it along or keep it to himself.

'Perhaps a letter or two went astray and ended up here?' Thomas said.

'I doubt it, brother, and it does not explain, why you are here.' Argyle took a swig of the wine and tasted some of the sweetmeats fresh from the kitchen.

'Margaret wrote to me.'

Margaret, Eleanor, what are you doing to me, brother, Argyle thought to himself, are you weaving a web too big even for you to control, Thomas?

'She demanded I visit you, since I am still your gaoler.' Argyle heard the sour note in Thomas' voice; he hated being pushed about by Margaret, and yet, he never told her to mind her own business. Perhaps Thomas too saw Margaret as some kind of mother figure, after all she was almost seven years his senior. Or perhaps, the two shared some strange secret that bound Thomas to obey her.

'How kind of her,' Argyle said. 'You must thank her for me. Perhaps you will permit me to send her a letter, if I write it while you are here and put it into your own hands?'

Thomas snorted from his seat. 'You can try. But do not think you can trick me with coded messages.'

'Never, brother,' Argyle replied. 'I leave such tricks to you.'

Thomas rose from his seat and joined Argyle by the window, resting his hands lightly on the damp stone. 'Even in the rain it truly is a fair view.'

How many turns do I have to take with you before you tell me, why you are really here? Argyle thought.

'But back to the matter at hand,' Thomas said in his unsettling way. 'The King has sent me.'

'Oh?'

'He says that you are to be released from house arrest by the end of May,' Thomas said.

'That is good news, brother! And kind of you to bring it in person.' Argyle tried not to let his gratitude be dampened by speculations at what cost he might regain his freedom.

Thomas fingered his cup and looked at the rain that was now coursing down the windowpanes. 'He did not want any of it to be sent by messenger.'

'So he commanded you to come here?' Argyle saw Thomas' face curl; he did not like being called a messenger.

'I offered.'

'Come June, I am free?' Argyle could not imagine that the King would willingly give up the revenue from the Beauworth estate. Certainly the King would demand a high price in return.

'Yes,' Thomas said. 'In so far that you are not to leave England without the King's expressed permission. If you still want to go on your little pilgrimage by this time next year, you can petition the King, and he may well look favourably upon your request.'

Argyle was baffled by the King's change of heart; just a few short months before Argyle would have sworn that he would never have permitted the subject of a new pilgrimage to be broached again.

'What was it that could have destroyed our family?' Argyle had thought about little else since the royal cog had hailed them at sea, scattering his hopes and dreams on the cold sea breeze.

'Does it make a difference?'

Yes, you fool! It makes all the difference in the world to me. If I was called back because of a trifling, I would never forgive you! Argyle thought but aloud he only groaned.

'Eleanor needs to learn to hold her tongue,' Thomas said and Argyle sensed an all too familiar twinge of fear. 'She has been saying things that ought not be said - and to all the wrong people!'

'What has she been saying?' Now that he might finally know the secret that the King had dangled over Argyle's head last summer, he suddenly did not care.

'Never you mind! I cannot repeat her words; they are too foul. Know only that as long as you do the King's bidding, it will go no further,' Thomas snapped.

'Further than where?'

'Where it is now. The King got wind of our sister's carelessness.

Fortunately, she is still high in favour, but even her luck may some day run out.' Thomas went back to his chair. 'The fire needs tending.'

Then tend it, you know how! Argyle's inner demon screamed, but he went to feed the fire nonetheless. 'Carelessness?'

'She revealed a secret that was not hers to share.' Thomas' face was a stone mask, betraying no emotion and Argyle dismissed the idea of pressing the subject. Better to be kept in the dark.

'But the King knows?'

'Yes.'

Argyle shook off his sense of foreboding. 'And he can use it?'

'Anytime he likes,' Thomas said, stretching his hands towards the flames as they took hold of the new wood and started devouring it.

'Something that can destroy our family?' Argyle asked.

'Yes.' Clearly, Thomas was done with the subject. 'The King is considering a new Queen.'

Argyle hated the way Thomas bounced from one topic to the next, closing down any conversation he disliked. 'Is that not what the entire council has been begging of him since Queen Anne died?'

'Yes, and as one of his councillors, I am happy that the King understands his responsibility.'

'But?' Argyle said watching his brother intently; something was amiss.

Thomas looked into the flames a moment longer. 'He wants a French wife.'

'That would make sense, he is looking to secure the peace he has negotiated with France. He is no warmonger, he prefers to have allies not enemies,' Argyle said. 'I thought that you would be happy he is courting a new woman?'

'He is not courting just any woman - in fact he is not courting a woman at all,' Thomas tapped a finger on the arm of the chair, the noise a rhythmic ticking.

'Is he courting a man?' Argyle had not laughed since he had returned to England, all but in shackles, but now he had to bite his tongue not to laugh out loud.

Thomas turned abruptly and glared at him. 'NO! He is considering a child! What say you to that? Our King, a man of 30 who should have at least half as many children in the nursery as I do, is planning to marry a girl of 7!'

Argyle's face faltered. 'A child? You must be mistaken.'

'Princess Isabella of Valois is his favourite - although there has been talk of other child brides!' Thomas slammed his hand down on the armrest. 'He will not even look at prospective women who are of a child-bearing age, although that would give him less grief - they are easy enough to get with child!'

'What say Gaunt?' Argyle knew the King's uncle would have voiced an opinion.

'That the King can do as he pleases.'

'Nothing more?' Argyle asked and thought: that sounds nothing like Gaunt. Something is most definitely amiss.

Thomas shrugged and began to prowl Argyle's study, rumbling his letters and scattering his papers. 'He is hiding something, I know he is.'

'Gaunt?' Argyle watched Thomas rifle through a stack of letters of conveyance. He would find nothing but broken royal seals requesting that Argyle send more money and grain to London.

'Gaunt, the King … all of them have secrets,' Thomas said, apparently studying a sheet of paper with sudden interest.

'You too, brother?'

Thomas turned on Argyle, grabbing him by the collar. 'What is that supposed to mean?'

Argyle took hold of Thomas' arms and put full force into his grip until Thomas let go. 'Nothing, only that it is peculiar that you of all people would begrudge others their secrets.'

'There are secrets that must be kept, and secrets that cannot be kept,' Thomas murmured, rubbing his arm.

'And then there are royal secrets,' Argyle said. 'The kind that all the world must know but no one can speak of?'

'Yes, such as the King taking a new wife.' Thomas had returned to his cool, measured manner. 'The King should know that something as important - politically - as marrying anew cannot be left up to his own devices. He must be made to see that marrying a child would be the worst possible decision!'

'And who is to show him that?' Argyle asked.

'I had thought Gaunt,' Thomas admitted, pouring more wine for himself and letting the pitcher drip on the tabletop when he put it back on its tray. 'He has always been at hand to …'

'Offer advice?'

'Avoid catastrophe,' Thomas finished. 'I cannot imagine why Gaunt is not more invested in finding a suitable bride.'

'A French princess of the blood must be suitable,' Argyle said.

'Suitable in age as well as breeding,' Thomas said, taking a swig of wine. 'She must be a woman grown, and the King must do his duty by his country and sire a son! Am I alone in seeing this?'

'The King is in good health, his grandfather lived to a ripe old age. There is plenty of time for him to sire sons,' Argyle said, but he agreed with Thomas, marrying a child was a terrible idea. 'You may be surprised, brother, but I think as you do. The King ought to marry a woman grown, but if none is to be found that would satisfy everyone's ambition, is it not better to secure a marriage that will seal the peace with France? Even if the King must wait longer for an heir?'

Thomas nodded absentmindedly. 'Perhaps. But I rather suspect that the King never looked very far. An allegiance with Spain or even the Low Countries would position us just as well as with a French bride.'

'But King Charles would see it as a slight, and a way to start the war anew,' Argyle said. 'His Majesty's first marriage was made for politics, and it was a happy one.'

'But not blessed with children,' Thomas said sourly.

'Not for want of trying, I believe.' Argyle was beginning to lose patience once more. 'Why are you telling me this? There is hardly anything I can do about it; the King has made his position clear where I am concerned - I am his subject, not his advisor or his friend.'

'The time may come …' Thomas stopped.

'What time?'

'A talk for another day, I think,' Thomas said. 'I am hungry; when is dinner? Do you think there is more sucking pig tonight?'

Argyle let the thought of pressing Thomas on the subject go, he would never win at this game. 'I think there will be, many of the pigs are soon ready to farrow once more, and there are plenty of suckling pigs in the stalls, curtsey of the mild winter.'

In truth, Argyle had had no say in any household matters since his disgraceful return from London. Not even what to prepare for his few guests. The King governed his life with an iron fist.

'The same is true in Nottingham, Elizabeth sent word that our livestock is living like kings and barons, feasting on the fresh pastures and rejoicing in the warm winds,' Thomas said. 'I have been blessed to have a wife who is such a good landlord - and who does not mind my long absences.'

'You are happy then?' Argyle asked and immediately regretted it when he saw Thomas' wily looks.

'Yes, and you could be too, brother! I have found you another prospective wife; it took some convincing since your current situation is nothing to boast, but the King's message that you will be forgiven in May made my enquiries easier.'

'I am sure it did, and yet I cannot imagine ever marrying if I cannot have …' Argyle could not make himself even think her name. He had tried and failed to bury the memory of the love he had to leave behind once more, half a year ago. Any English woman, however good her pedigree might be, could never replace her, and he felt no urge to accept a wife handpicked by his brother. 'If I ever marry.'

'If?' Thomas snorted. 'You must marry brother!'

'IF I ever marry, I shall choose my own bride.'

'Do you not care for women?' Thomas asked staring into the fire, where the log Argyle had fed it had turned to orange embers.

You have no idea, Argyle thought, no idea how much I care for one woman. So much I braved the sea and the King's wrath, and I would not have gone back for anything less than my own family's undoing. He shirked the painful memories. 'That is not the point.'

Thomas stroked his pointed beard. 'Of course not, but you must not look to be disinterested. Take a mistress, if nothing else! Make sure rumours reach court that you have dalliances with maids or whores, I care not. Anything that might stifle speculations …'

'And I care not for speculations, whatever they might be about!' Argyle decided to end the conversation. 'I shall choose a bride when I am good and ready.'

'I might speak to the King, once you have knelt before the Crown in June.' Thomas had clearly not given up on the idea of marrying off Argyle. He would have an easier time of it, if the bride was settled before Argyle was once more a free man. 'He will be in a good mood - he likes a good apology, and you must strive to make yours so memorable that he never has cause to doubt your affection again.'

'Apology?!' Argyle was thrown.

'Oh yes, did I not mention? The King will release you from house arrest, if you make a public apology before the throne, on the first day of June.' Thomas looked away from Argyle's angry stare. 'I had to promise him you would do it, or you would be stuck here forever.'

'And you need me somewhere else?' Argyle bit back.

Thomas merely smiled. 'Of course. I need you back in the King's favour! I shall help you design an apology that he cannot but admire and accept. It is the least I can do.'

'Yes,' Argyle thought, 'especially since you did not speak for me when the King sentenced me to house arrest - since you did not even deign to be at court when he humiliated me, and Bolingbroke spoke in my defence.'

Argyle had often wondered why Thomas had not been at court that day, surely he would know what the King intended to do. Surely, even Thomas had more care of family and obligation than to ignore a brother's troubles. Unless of course, as Argyle suspected, it was Thomas who had informed the King of Argyle's journey - by means of a spy in his household. If that was the case, he had to wonder why Thomas needed him back in the King's favour when he was high in favour himself?

'I need some air,' Thomas' voice cut through Argyle's wonderings. 'I shall be in the stables.'

'The stables?'

'I brought a new horse; I want to make sure she is tended properly,' Thomas said. 'That new stable master of yours, is he any good? He looks young. Strong and fine, but young.'

'He is 20 and has much experience with horses,' Argyle said.

'Good age.' Thomas left Argyle to sort out his jumble of emotions.

Marriage, children, secrets and humiliation. What gifts my brother comes bearing, Argyle thought wryly while he watched Thomas cross the courtyard to reach the stables, the rain pelting down on him. In the stable door, Thomas clapped an arm around the stable master's shoulder and led him into the stables, out of view.

CHAPTER 5

30 May 1396 - London

To an outsider, it would appear that the King of England kept a merry court. But if you overstayed your welcome or went sniffing around the dark corners, you would soon discover that it was all show. The tension in the great hall slapped Argyle's face when he entered it, walking three paces behind Thomas.

'Remember what you rehearsed,' Thomas whispered as they cut through the crowd, most courtiers only deigning to move when they realised it was the mighty Lord Mowbray leading his ill favoured little brother before the King. The assembled people thirsted for a show.

'How can I not?' Argyle said to Thomas' back. He had been reading and rehearsing his speech since April, Thomas constantly sending revised versions, honing every word to achieve perfection. And it was perfect. Argyle did not doubt that the King would be flattered and pleased, but even a pleased King was no guarantee that he would walk out of the great hall redeemed and released.

The hall hushed when Thomas pushed through the last throng of people and stepped into the open space before the dais, the King high above his subjects, scowling here and there, courtiers and ladies kneeling in submission.

'Majesty, I bring to you my brother, Sir Argyle,' Thomas began. 'He has come to repent and seek your Majesty's forgiveness for his folly.'

The King slowly turned to look upon Thomas, who dropped

elegantly to one knee, signalling for Argyle to follow suit. Argyle saw two guards, the White Hart prominent on their broad chests, walk towards him.

'Oh?' the King said, his voice disclosing no emotion.

'Majesty, Sir Argyle has prayed on his insolent behaviour and comes before you today a man changed,' Thomas said. 'I only ask your Majesty to hear my brother's words, no more.'

His last sentence was delivered so smoothly that Argyle half suspected Thomas had made such a speech a dozen times before, always sure to get what he wanted. Apparently the King had signalled for Thomas to stand, because he did and stepped aside, leaving Argyle kneeling before the dais - alone.

'Well, Sir Argyle, what have you to say?' the King asked.

Argyle made to stand, and one of the White Harts pushed him back down on his knees. It appeared the King wanted a grovelling subject.

'We are waiting,' the King said, his voice laced with malice. This might not be as easy as Thomas had promised it would be. Argyle rather began to suspect that he would have to work very hard to get back into royal favour - not that it was what he wanted. What he did want was to be released from his house arrest, to be free to roam England at least, and to visit his sisters. There was nothing for it but to give the King a show.

'Majesty, I come before you repentant of my insolence. I understand now how much I offended your Majesty by leaving without first seeking your guidance and solace. I beg your Majesty to forgive a poor subject, who knows not what he does, nor can explain what came over him but folly and …' Argyle chanced a glance at the King, but one of the guards pushed his head back down.

Eyes on the floor, Argyle thought and continued his well-rehearsed speech. 'Majesty, I besiege you to display your outstanding kindness and unyielding forgiveness. I know I deserve no such acts of kindness! I know also that if your Majesty does not forgive me, I shall forever be praying that others will take heed from my mistake and not offend your Majesty, as I have done. I bow before your Majesty, humbly asking to be released from my punishment and delivered by your compassion.'

The crowd of courtiers, lords and knights held their breath; Argyle heard a woman cry, and another whimper as she most likely swooned into the arms of some young man. The room was full of actors ready to put on a show for the King. Argyle kept his head down and ignored the pain in his knees.

'I am a compassionate King! And you are right to plead for my forgiveness. What you did was not only folly, it was an offence against the Crown of England, and your anointed King!' the King said, his voice clear and loud in the silent room.

'Forgive me, and I shall never disobey your Majesty again,' Argyle whispered according to Thomas' instructions; he had judged that submission would be best displayed by a hushed voice that might even indicate that Argyle was close to tears. He was not.

The King must have risen, because all around him men and women fell to their knees; even the two guards at either side of him knelt, pushing him down hard on the stone floor. Argyle bent his head even lower and allowed himself a brief prayer.

'I should think not!' The King was standing above him. 'I should think you would have learned your lesson! That you will always be loyal to me - and me alone!'

'I am yours, Majesty,' Argyle said, trying to sound meek and submissive. 'I pledge my life and service to you.'

Argyle glanced to the side and saw Thomas kneeling, a satisfied smile playing at the corner of his mouth. If nothing else, Thomas was pleased with this blatant humiliation. Argyle bit the inside of his cheek to choke the anger that threatened to rise and spoil any chance of his release.

The silence dragged on, everyone on their knees before the King. Argyle began to wonder if the King had even decided upon releasing him or not, or if he was simply toying with him before throwing him in the Tower. There was no way of knowing which way the King's mood would turn.

'Very well! I shall be compassionate and benevolent!' The King clamped a hand on Argyle's shoulder and invited him to stand, the sea of people rising as a rippling wave.

'Sir Argyle - I forgive you!' The King smiled as the crowd cheered him on and he drew Argyle into a hard embrace. 'You have come to me with a pure heart and true devotion, as I always knew you would. Your words have touched my heart and stilled my worried soul.'

Argyle bent his head and saw Thomas smile openly at the courtiers and lords around him. The show had gone according to plan, the King had played his part beautifully, and now, he was rewarded by the admiration of a simpering court. Argyle could not wait to get away. The room had lost all its lustre to him, it was an empty shell filled with the smell of fear.

'As a sign of my gratitude and our rekindled friendship, I invite you to stay at court, until I have announced my future bride,' the King announced and released Argyle. 'And you will accompany me when I go to bring her home!'

The room exploded in false cheers and glee. Argyle gave Thomas an empty look, which he did not return, but Argyle knew by Thomas' frown that whatever bargain he had struck with the King, it had not been fulfilled.

CHAPTER 6

8 August 1396 - London

The cobbled courtyard rang with the sound of hooves and riders, sending a tide of stable boys from their daily chores to tend to the tired horses.

'Make sure they are watered and fed - they've earned it!' one of the riders yelled.

Argyle surveyed his Beauworth men as they dismounted, slung their saddlebags over their shoulders and made their way to the kitchens and outbuildings. The dust swirled in the dwindling sunlight, the air thick with sweat and the sweet smell of horse manure.

He noticed how tight he still held the reigns and loosened his grip, he would need to control his temper before he went to Thomas and from there, no doubt, to the King. Argyle started at the sound of a seagull, screaming as it swerved over the rooftop and returned to the river. Would that he had ignored the calls just last year, would that he could go back and change it, convince the sailors that it was seagulls screaming and not the hailing of an English vessel, commanding them to stop in the name of the King.

'M'lord.'

Stirring from his dreams, Argyle turned towards the cracking voice of his aging steward. 'Mills. Is the house ready?'

'Yes, M'lord.' Mills said. 'I hope all is in order, the note arrived only yesterday that you were to come here.'

The unspoken question hung limp in the air for a moment before it drifted away. Argyle patted his hunter on the neck biting back a spiteful response that would serve no purpose. 'Then you are not the only one.'

'The quarters are set up, but if more are to come, I fear we cannot accommodate all the men here.' Mills gestured to the men chatting and calling out for water and stable boys to take the horses to the stables.

'This will be all of them for now, Mills. Make sure they are fed tonight, I shall be at court.' Argyle said tersely.

Argyle still wondered at the King's change of affection to him; after all, the King had forgiven him in June before all the court, but once the announcement of the King's marriage had been made, their parting in July had been cold. Argyle had even entertained hope that the King would have changed his mind about Argyle being part of the retinue sent to fetch the future Queen of England.

෴ ෴

'What took you so long?'

'Brother.' Argyle closed the door to Thomas' chambers. As ever, the tables were strewn with papers, maps and charts. In the sunlight, dust danced slowly in intricate patterns, their grace a stark contrast to Thomas' dreary interior. Argyle often wondered why Thomas had never filled his rooms with lavish furniture when that seemed otherwise to be the norm at court.

'We have no time for courtesies. The King is quite beside himself. I would not have called upon you unless it was of the utmost importance. Leaving me to wonder whether you would come or not …' Thomas pressed his thin lips together, clearly frustrated.

'I sent word back immediately,' Argyle replied icily.

'All the same. I had already promised his Majesty that you were on your way.' Thomas sounded exasperated. 'He has been waiting anxiously for your arrival, we must go at once.'

'No, brother. First you will tell me what is going on. You send word that I am to make for London, but your information was scant at best. Do not send me into that viper pit without more knowledge.' Argyle leaned against the wall of his brother's castle apartment and crossed his arms over his broad chest. Despite the warm June air outside, the wall was cold beneath his thin shirt.

Thomas gave him a sour glance but relented. 'Very well. It has come to my attention that the King conspires to get rid of his uncle.'

'Which one?' Argyle asked although he had a pretty good idea, which uncle the King wanted to dispose of. He also knew why, as he had himself been instrumental in directing the King's attention towards this particular uncle.

'Do not play clever with me.' Thomas pointed a shaking finger at Argyle. 'Woodstock of course! Ever since the debacle at the late Queen's funeral, the King has been harbouring a deep-seated hate towards several of the Lords. Chief among them Woodstock.'

'This is hardly news,' Argyle said and thought: if he is harbouring hatred for the Lords, is he looking to you too, dear brother?

Thomas glared at Argyle before opening the door. 'We are late for the King! Will you come or must I have his Majesty call upon you here in my quarters?'

Argyle gave a wry smile. 'Lead the way.'

Following Thomas' hunched figure down the galleries, Argyle was soon lost in thought, oblivious to the splendour all around him. It seemed to fade against the uncertainty he always felt when at court. Although the King had never forgotten the slight at the Queen's funeral, he had succumbed to his uncle Gaunt's pleas to make peace. If he was indeed holding on to old grudges, and the King was prone to such temper, surely it would come as no surprise to any of the Lords. Their absence at de Vere's interment was still the tastiest gossip at court. No one would let the King forget their slight, especially not his closest friends, who secretly feared that they might share de Vere's fate. Argyle thought they were wise in their fear but not in their actions.

'His Majesty insisted that you enter alone.' Thomas failed to hide his displeasure.

'Then I shall not keep him waiting.' Argyle nodded at the guard outside the King's private chambers. The door swung open, and Argyle stepped forward.

'Sir Argyle, what news from the countryside?' The King's voice was warm but it had a steely edge to it. Argyle bowed low before approaching the throne, conscious of how hollow his footsteps sounded on the bare floor. In the past, the King had always been surrounded by his friends, but now he seemed to prefer solitude. Only a few guards stood by the doorways, and the tables and low chairs scattered about the room were all empty.

'What did he say?' Thomas asked, his face alight with impatience.

'The King was happy to see me,' Argyle said, his blood bubbling at Thomas' demanding tone. 'Asked about the journey and other general matters.'

'Yes, yes, but what did he say?' There was greed in Thomas' voice as well as impatience.

Argyle surveyed his brother's uneasy looks. 'Even if I wanted to tell you, I could not. The King made me swear to keep our conversation between us. I will not break my oath, not even for you, brother, you know my situation with the King is frail.'

Thomas made an effort to restrain himself, and then he simply gestured towards the gallery and stomped away. Hiding a sardonic smile, Argyle followed. He was tempted to stop and speak to anyone who might pass, but very few people did and they looked preoccupied and withdrawn.

Once the door to Thomas' apartment closed, he turned on Argyle. 'Why are you so slow? I must know all the King said!'

'I thought the two of you were such great friends,' Argyle said. 'Perhaps you should tell me what it is you think the King of England would say to me that he does not wish to share with you. Then I will judge what to share with you.'

'I keep on top of all court gossip,' Thomas said offended. 'Most of it is idle, but a few weeks ago I overheard a couple of the King's servants commenting on an incident from a council meeting that, unfortunately, I could not attend. It was their conversation that prompted me to call you here.'

Argyle bit his cheek to keep from shouting at Thomas - court gossip; he had come all this way because of court gossip!

'Before you think the journey wasted, think again brother.' Thomas still had an eerie ability to read his mind. Perching on the edge of a worn oak chair, Thomas put the tips of his fingers together. Argyle thought he had about him the look of a hawk ready to take flight. 'The Lords were up to their usual trickery, making the most of matters for themselves and cheating the Crown of money, land or some such. Quite frankly, it makes little difference.'

Argyle did not believe his brother for a second, but rather than engage in a fruitless discussion about ambition and duplicity, Argyle simply waited for Thomas to go on.

'Apparently, this time the King took offence,' Thomas said.

'Impressed upon them the need for taxes and rents to ensure that the treasury had means if a war against the Scots or Wales should break out again. His own Cheshire army is growing vastly, of which you are no doubt aware.'

'I have heard rumours.' Argyle leaned back in his chair; the pillow was so thin that he could feel the worn seat through the stuffing. 'Is he funding his own army with resources from the Crown?'

The King's private army had been the reason why Bolingbroke had turned to trickery and deceit to get back from Jerusalem to England, and he had decided that Argyle was too dangerous to leave behind. Bolingbroke had been right to bring Argyle, but wrong to assume that Argyle was part of the King's army. Today was the first time that the King had asked Argyle to join the White Harts. Surprisingly, the King had accepted his refusal, and Argyle still wondered how long he could avoid the draft.

Thomas snorted with disdain. 'As I said before, the Lords are uneasy. The King seems ever more bent on breaking with them. Taking all the lands, forests and rents for himself could be his first measure.' Since the debacle of La Fontaine's death, Thomas had been vigorous in his support of the King. Now, he looked ready to turn his coat once more.

'Do not speak out of turn, brother.' Argyle gave Thomas a warning look. 'If the King asks me, I shall have to relate our conversation. I hoped you were done with rumours and gossip.'

Thomas returned to his story. 'A row broke out, in which more than one Lord lost his temper. Including his Majesty. It seems it took all of Gaunt's efforts to calm the council down.'

'You cannot have liked missing out on such a show,' Argyle said.

'That is beside the point.' Thomas jumped up. 'What does matter is that I got wind of it when I was making my way to the great hall.'

'Servants openly discussing the King's private matters?' Argyle followed Thomas' frantic pacing around the room. 'I find that extremely hard to believe.'

'I like to take my daily constitutional through the cellar passages. I do my best thinking there,' Thomas said, wringing his hands.

'I see,' Argyle said. The dark agrees with you, brother, he thought.

'The servants were in a state of alarm. Apparently, the King had come to his private apartments in a blinding rage, shouting, screaming and making a great spectacle. His closest followers were at hand to fuel his anger and, ere long, the King spat "will no one rid me of this turbulent man". Allegedly such a champion would be richly rewarded.'

Argyle snapped for breath. 'You are sure the King said this?'

'It is not the first time, the King has spoken such about Woodstock.' Thomas' face was ashen, and Argyle felt his anger slowly subsiding. Would the King truly wish his own uncle dead?

'Why does the King want rid of Woodstock? And if he is so outraged, could he not simply banish him from court?' Argyle asked. If one great lord was on the wrong side of the King's good graces, the others were probably not far behind, and how many of them knew that they were about to be called out?

'He has attempted it but Gaunt is always there, ready to speak for Woodstock,' Thomas said, his voice dripping with malice. 'In all this, Gaunt has never wavered in his loyalty to the King, and he still has his ear. But his influence is dwindling.'

'It has been a long time since anyone has been able to tell the King what to do, but surely, he will listen to reason,' Argyle said. 'Do you think anyone would be foolish enough to take the King's words of rage to be an order?'

'There are always fools at court. Not all of them wear motley.' Thomas snorted a cold laugh that chilled Argyle to the bone.

'You think Woodstock in danger?' Argyle asked.

'I think all of us in danger, but yes, him more than most.'

'And now, what is it truly you would have me do?'

'You were close to the King before; rekindle the friendship,' Thomas said, clearly pleased that Argyle finally seemed to understand the situation. 'Gain his trust and then advise against foolish behaviour. Perhaps it will come to no more.'

'He no longer trusts me, as you well know. I am only here because he told the whole court I would ride with him when he goes to fetch his blushing, young bride,' Argyle said with regret. 'I think he does not believe he has my undying loyalty. Although he does.'

'You think too little of yourself, brother,' Thomas insisted, 'you always have. He could have forgotten, quite conveniently, to call for you. And yet here you are. Give him time and never let him doubt you. Help him forget your mistake, erase your former misstep and he will see you as the loyal subject you say that you are. He will come to trust you again. You must make him!'

Argyle walked towards the door, keen to get away. He was less than convinced that he even wanted the King to forget.

'Argyle,' Thomas said. 'The King's choice of wife is … difficult. It may bring with it dangerous times.'

Argyle left Thomas' rooms deep in thought. The King had announced his marriage to the Princess Isabella of Valois, the daughter of the French King Charles. Argyle feared that the King's choice was upsetting the fragile balance at court, in the land even. The Crown needed an heir, and Thomas was right; marrying a child could prove dangerous.

ꕥ ꕥ

CHAPTER 7

20 October 1396 - Paris

Not for the first time, Argyle wondered what it would be like to live here. Would Paris simply swallow him up? Perhaps if things had played out differently last year, would he have been able to live here with Najeelah? It would be the kind of city she might have come to love, the climate warmer than England although no match to the stifling heat in Jerusalem. Around every street corner, he imagined them living in one of the small houses, secluded but happy, perhaps in time even housing beautiful blonde children with black eyes and olive skin.

Paris certainly was a fine city, the river cutting through it and the island palace in the centre of the town were wonderful sights. The royal palace had a certain rich, deep feeling about it; its rooms brimming with furniture, the thick stonewalls hung with heavy tapestries to ward off the permanent moisture trickling down the stone. Only its distinct smell gave away the current state of disuse. King Charles had chosen to house and entertain his English visitors at the old royal palace, although these days, the royal family dwelled in a newly built residence near the mighty Bastille fortress.

Argyle shook his head; surely it was safer to live in the middle of a river than right next to Paris' great prison? He had been sitting too far away from the dais to hear but broken words of the conversation between the King and King Charles, and thus, he did not know why the French King had chosen to move. When the word rebellion had wafted past Argyle, he had looked up to see the two Kings exchange a knowing look.

Now that Argyle and the rest of the English entourage were once more clattering through Paris, he thought the town felt alive, as a great beast with its own pulse. Trying to shake the ominous feeling, Argyle fell in behind the Duke of Surrey and nodded to the Earl of Salisbury who was riding behind the King.

'How do you find the Princess?' As usual, Surrey kept close to his royal uncle.

'She is a fine little girl,' the King said. All through the negotiations to finalise the marriage, the King had laid to rest any concern for the Princess' age by saying that each passing day would remedy her youth. Argyle could not decide whether that was clever on the King's part, or simply a rouse to ensure he did not have to do his royal duty any time soon.

'And besides,' the King continued, 'I am ridding Charles of a very costly girl!'

The King laughed heartily, making many around them look and grin although they did not know why. Argyle nodded. It was no secret that the King had pushed the limits of the dowry. The Princess came with a staggering 100,000 pounds to her name - money that England desperately needed. In return, King Charles had the King's signature on a treaty that would ensure peace as long as his precious Isabella was Queen of England. The King was free to use the dowry as long as it was not to raise an army against France.

'I am sure the Princess is eager to come live with her husband,' Surrey said as they turned onto a broad avenue, the castle now in plain sight, its turrets mirrored in the murky waters of the Seine.

'Most certainly. At first, she will reside at Windsor, and I shall make regular visits. Naturally, she will come to court as often as she wishes,' the King added to the French ambassador.

Surrey grinned broadly and probably thought, as Argyle did, that the little Princess thought her husband very old. He wondered if she knew that, in the eyes of the King and most of the court, she was little more than a token of peace? She might well become a very important bargaining chip, in case King Charles decided to turn on the peace treaty that was sealed by the marriage.

'When do we ride for Calais, Majesty?' Argyle asked when he caught the King's attention.

'In a day or two. Are you desperate to return to England already, Sir Argyle?' the King smiled and was rewarded by numerous sniggers. Most all of the King's retinue knew that Argyle had come but reluctantly. 'I should imagine that you would enjoy being free of the yoke of family for a change - as most of us do.'

ꟹ ꟹ

At night, Paris' worn beauty and pretty ornaments that made the streets picturesque vanished with the dwindling daylight. Now the city was teeming with rowdy, bawdy men dressed in gaudy clothes sporting long daggers or short swords in their belts, and raunchy women with their bosoms bared to any who would even glance at them. Thieves, scoundrels and lowlife mingled to turn Paris into a place of violence and debauchery.

Once more, Argyle caught himself clinging to his sword; he felt that everyone stared at him. Why had he agreed to go? He had never cared for whorehouses or taverns, he had no desire for the licentious women of Paris, and he knew that most of the King's men would rather he had stayed in the palace. Once the King was preoccupied by a pretty, buxom young woman, Argyle had been quick to sneak away, momentarily blessed by the kiss of the cool breeze that crept through Paris.

Now, he was certain that someone was following him. The feeling had increased when he had turned from the large avenue into a narrow street, the middle filled with dirt, filth and waste all waiting for a downpour strong enough to push it into the Seine. Argyle caught a shadow for a flicker of a moment and now, he walked steadily along straining his ears for any sound that was out of place.

He had a distinct feeling of not being alone. Last time, he had felt this way, was years ago in Jerusalem, and he had been right then, although on that occasion his silent stalker had turned out to be fairly harmless. There was something deathly silent about the shadow following him tonight. Even the street seemed to sense it, quiet as it was, all the windows shuttered up against the clammy October air.

So this is what it is like to be hunted, Argyle thought as he worked hard to remain calm; this must have been how Lockley felt, those months in England, when we hunted for him.

Lately, Argyle had thought more and more about the dealings he had had with Lockley, a knight turned rogue, who now lay in a cold, unmarked grave with no tongue to tell his tale in the afterlife. Argyle was certain that Lockley was in purgatory and that he would be there for a very long time. He often wished that Lockley had been sent directly to Hell. No amount of masses being sung for him would save his murderous soul.

The shadow stole across the street behind Argyle; he only just caught a glimmer of a dark cloak before it disappeared into the darkness beneath the overhanging stories of a long building. Best to get it over with, Argyle decided and stopped in the middle of the street. The only light was from the waning moon when the amassing clouds rushed past and left it momentarily exposed.

'Who goes there?' Argyle said.

The street was quiet, too quiet. Argyle looked around slowly, promising himself not to act rashly as he had done in Jerusalem. He never regretted his decision back then, not even now, but resorting to the sword was a bad idea, especially in a town still celebrating the marriage of a French princess to the King of England. It would be even more foolish if his stalker turned out to be French.

'Who goes there?' Argyle repeated in French. He thought he heard someone move to the left where a narrow path cut into the alley. A perfect hiding place, Argyle thought.

'Coward,' he muttered under his breath, fingering the sword hilt and began moving again. He was anxious to get out of the alley and back onto one of the large avenues. He reluctantly admitted to himself that, somehow, Paris was a lot more daunting than Jerusalem had ever been, perhaps because, for all its faults, Jerusalem had also held promise and possibilities. Paris, by comparison, was a haunted, snarling place.

A scream from behind sent shivers down Argyle's spine, and he slid his sword a little way out of its scabbard. A cat ran past him, hissing and spitting before it jumped a low wall and disappeared into the night. Argyle could see flickering lights escaping shutters at the end of the alley, a tavern perhaps, although he could not make out if there was a sign outside the door or not. Someone drew breath.

Argyle spun around, sliding his sword back in its scabbard and grabbing his dagger from behind his back. In front of him stood a slim figure, the hood was drawn to hide the face.

'I said, who goes there?!'

The figure made the tiniest move, and a blade glittered as the moon suddenly flooded the alley in milky light. The blade seemed almost to dance in the hooded figure's hand.

'Answer me!' Argyle's fear was supplanted by anger. 'Who are you?'

'I could be a foe … or a friend,' a deep voice said in flawless English. The blade still danced about. 'Your next move will decide.'

'Decide what?'

'If you will ever know the truth about La Fontaine's death.'

Argyle froze in place, catching his dagger by pure reflex before it dropped, his fingers clutching the top of the hilt clumsily. 'What?'

'You decide if I live or die. I have seen you kill before; you are good with a dagger and even better with a sword. I would be no match to you, but I would try to defend myself.' The hooded man took a tentative step forward. 'And you would be left in another alley with another dead body, only this time there would be nowhere to run.'

The man was right, if they fought, and he won, he would be left in a Paris street with a dead body and almost certainly a host of hostile Frenchmen ready to throw him on the King's mercy. Not his King's though but that of the mad, French King. Argyle knew the King would have to denounce him to take home his new bride, something Argyle knew that he would do without blinking.

'That there, is a tavern; the ale is lousy but the wine is decent,' the man ventured. 'It is just far enough away from the castle that no one will know you, and just close enough that you could slip out and get back unseen.'

'Why?'

'It is also dark,' the man said. 'I like dark.'

'Why should I trust you?' Argyle asked, although he had already made up his mind.

'Because everyone else who might know the truth is either dead or an enemy,' the man said, his voice strangely familiar. He let the blade hang down, swinging it slowly. 'Your choice, of course.'

Never think yourself safe, Argyle thought before nodding to the hooded man. 'You buy the drink.'

The man led the way to the tavern, Argyle taking the measure of the slim figure. He was still uneasy about his decision, but he had to know. If nothing else, the tavern was just the kind of place where a knife might accidentally end up in someone's gut. He glanced around the room as they entered; it was indeed dark, only a few candles giving off more smoke than light burning their way down to the raw tabletops. No one in the room seemed to notice them. Argyle spied another door, leading off to the back of the place, probably to a kitchen or storeroom. It might be used as an exit if needs be.

The man pointed to a table in a corner with a couple of dinghy benches, all pushed up against a greasy window probably overlooking the avenue. Argyle scowled before making his way over, hearing the shadow order two cups of wine and coins being pushed across the serving hatch.

'The finest vintage the house has to offer.' The hooded man took a swig and made a throaty sound. 'I'll wager that it'll knock your block off, if you down it in one go.'

Argyle grabbed one of the cups. 'Who are you?'

'Does it matter?'

Maybe not but I would like to know who I might be killing a little later tonight, Argyle thought but held his tongue. Let the other speak, and then he would judge if it was the truth.

'I am not the enemy!' The man seemed to have taken offense to his silent treatment and, somehow, the reaction eased Argyle's speculations.

'You stalk me halfway across Paris and you would have me believe you are not an enemy?' The man too relaxed a little and raised his cup. After their silent salute, they both took a sip and winced at the sour grapes. 'Thank God, you did not buy the cheap wine!'

'Aye,' the man said and suddenly pushed back his hood, revealing a mop of grey hair and a beard to match. 'We have met before.'

'Have we now?' Argyle immediately recognised him and resisted an overwhelming urge to punch the man in the face. This was the rogue who had captured Stephen in Vienna and turned him over to Lockley.

'Not formally, but then I prefer a life in the shadows.'

'So I have noticed.' Argyle tested the wine again before setting the cup aside. 'Why are you here?'

The grey-haired man smiled. 'Our King is to be married. Of course I am here! Where else would you have me be, Sir Argyle?'

'You have my name, I should have yours.'

'It is not important.' The grey-haired man glanced about.

'Let me be the judge of that.'

'Better you do not know, then we can go on pretending we do not know one another when we are both back in England.' He too tried the wine again, swirling it in the cup before drinking. 'Besides, you should be more interested in what I have to say about La Fontaine than what my name is.'

Perhaps it is better I do not know who I might end up skewering, Argyle thought, sliding out his dagger and resting it in his lap. Better to be safe. 'Very well, tell me then.'

'There was poison on the blade that killed La Fontaine,' the grey-haired man locked eyes with Argyle. 'But you know this of course. Lockley never could keep his mouth shut!'

'He did where the King was concerned. Not a word they got from him, and I saw him on the scaffold, he could not even stand on his own.' Argyle wondered if the grey-haired man had been there in the crowd that day.

'The King has a taste for forcing things,' the grey-haired man agreed with a grudge. 'But Lockley could not say it, could he? That he thought the order came from the King, although he all but told you that too. Tell me, how was your last visit to the Tower? Pleasant?'

Argyle leaned back, feeling the sticky backboard cling to his cloak, how did this man know he had gone to see Lockley? Not even Thomas knew that. 'Not as informative as I had hoped for.'

'Lockley was a pawn, a fool who only knew how to follow orders. The bigger the seal on the order the better. Perhaps he truly thought he was acting out the order of the King himself.'

'But he was not?'

Half of the grey-haired man's face was lit by the weak dancing flame of the little tallow light that flickered on the table, his expression impossible to read. 'Of course not, again something I believe you already knew.'

Argyle was fast tiring of the company. 'Tell me what you meant to tell me or go away! If you are just here to tell me what I already know, why should I not end this tiresome night and your life in one stroke?'

'Rumour has it that the King is blaming Woodstock for the death of La Fontaine. But he is wrong.' The grey-haired man shrunk into the shadows as the door opened, then relaxed when it was just a whore come in from the cold. She was picked up by a burly drunkard who began pawing her, nervous laughter filling the room.

'The document did bear the royal seal, but it was not from Woodstock's time. He may be responsible for much and more, but no one can put this crime on his head.'

'The King might,' said Argyle his mind racing. 'Then who?'

'You are aiming too high. The document fell into the hands of a much lower creature, someone who held a grudge against La Fontaine,' the grey-haired man emptied his cup. 'Someone who knew …'

The door slammed open, and a guard of four soldiers wearing King Charles's livery spilled into the room. The whore pried herself away from the drunkard and hurried through the back door while the rest of the people in the tavern stared at the soldiers.

'Search the place!' the captain commanded. He turned and caught sight of Argyle, who recognised him as one of the captains who had escorted the royal party into Paris a few days ago. 'You! Englishman! What are you doing here?'

Argyle half-rose before he noticed that the grey-haired man was gone. 'Having a drink.' He cursed the French disturbance and sat back down. 'Surely that is allowed?'

The captain muttered something, then made his way to Argyle's table. 'Of course, Sire.' He stared at the extra cup on the table. 'Who were you drinking with?'

'Myself. This is my second drink,' Argyle said, hoping to be rid of the French soldiers and that the grey-haired man would return once they had gone. 'Who are you looking for?'

One of the soldiers whispered something to the captain that made him curse. 'Best you leave with us, Sire. This is not a safe part of Paris, on any night.'

'Surely …'

'Do not make me drag you out, Sire,' the captain said quietly. 'I shall have my men escort you back to the palace.'

Argyle nodded, he might have considered taking on one man, but four soldiers was too much, especially in this crowded room. He saw the door to the storeroom swing open once more, the whore staring back at him with big eyes and a knife to her throat. He recognised the blade instantly.

'Thank you, Captain, that is most generous!' Argyle made sure to block the view of the storeroom while the soldiers and he filed out of the tavern.

'This way, Sire,' the Captain said stiffly. 'You have a wedding to attend tomorrow.'

Argyle felt rather than saw a slim figure slide from the side of the tavern to be swallowed up by the dark. With any luck, he would have another chance to speak to the grey-haired man before they reached Calais. Providing he really was part of the English retinue.

Flanked by the soldiers, Argyle made his way back to the palace, which shone in the centre of town like a ship alight in a black sea. Inside, the future Queen of England would be sleeping soundly, surrounded by women twice her age. Her father was probably with one of his many mistresses and the King of England, the happy husband to be? Hopefully still in a whorehouse somewhere near the Seine, being seduced by a French maid, unawares of the dangers of Paris.

Argyle longed to be on English soil once more.

CHAPTER 8

1 November 1396 - Ardres, France

As they neared the grounds of Ardres, Argyle could hear the clamour that always followed camp life. King Charles had decided to accompany his precious daughter to the formal ceremony in Calais and had staked his camp in Ardres.

Yesterday had been a day of pomp and show, the King of England magnificent in his robes of crimson and gold, the French Princess delicate in her dress of purple and silver with her majestic father, King Charles, by her side. It had been a tableau of royal splendour that had left the people of Calais blinded.

While the city recovered from the theatre that was the English court, the King had been invited to pay a visit to his father-in-law. When they came upon the first tents in the outskirts of the camp, the King signalled for Argyle to join him. 'What do you make of this, Sir Argyle?'

'It seems all of Paris has travelled here.'

The King gave a wolfish smile. 'I should hope not, there are a few people I should not like to see again.'

Argyle looked around and saw the Princess's carriage, her ladies in waiting trailing behind it on their horses. 'How do you like your new wife, Majesty?'

'She will make a fine woman - some day,' the King said. 'Now, where do we go from here?'

Argyle spotted the captain who he had come across in Paris.

'Captain, would you take us to King Charles' tent?'

The captain bowed stiffly and led the way through the camp glancing up at Argyle every once in a while with an inscrutable look on his face. Argyle willed him to keep quiet about their little run-in in Paris the night before the King's wedding to the Princess.

'Does it look familiar?' the King asked, demanding Argyle's attention once more.

'Nothing like the camps I have been in before, although I would know where to pitch my tent,' Argyle said looking around. 'Not there!' The King followed his gaze and laughed at the sight of the latrines being dug.

'This no pilgrimage, Sir Argyle, you need not worry about pitching your own tent on this fine journey.' A little malice glittered in the King's eyes.

Argyle smiled. 'Old habits.'

'They do die hard, I hear,' the King said. 'Charles has offered that we stay here tonight, he wishes to have one final evening in the company of Isabella.'

'She must be something special,' Argyle said.

The King seemed pleased. 'She is. She will bring peace between England and France. Perpetual peace.'

Quite a feat for such a young girl, Argyle thought as he fell back, I only hope she is not daunted by the prospect.

The King proceeded to greet King Charles who was standing outside a massive tent. Argyle had yet to formally meet the Princess; he had seen her at the ceremony and on occasion in the grand palace in Paris, but he had never even bent his knee to her. He had a feeling that the whole of England would be commanded to do so when the couple returned.

'Your Grace.' King Charles smiled. 'I am delighted you agreed to be my guest once more. I hope this will be to your satisfaction. I have left a few tokens of my affection within.'

'Magnificent.'

'My Lord, I too have left a token of my affections. I hope it pleases your Majesty.' Somehow the little Princess had made her way through the crowd to appear at her father's side. To himself, Argyle admitted that the child impressed him even more up close.

'Thank you,' the King said and bent to kiss her tiny hand. 'I am spoiled to have such an affectionate wife.'

The Princess offered a sweet, little smile, averted her eyes and looked directly at Argyle for the briefest of moments. Then she turned around and lead her ladies towards a third glorious tent situated a little further afield, the crowd splitting before her, French soldiers and courtiers bowing low to her.

King Charles drew breath. 'I will leave you to rest. Until tonight.'

'Until tonight.' As the King entered his grand tent, he sent a brief nod in Argyle's direction. Clearly, the King was not done with him yet. 'Will the English like the girl, do you think?' There was a touch of danger in the question.

Argyle inclined his head. 'Most certainly. She has been taught well, and will soon learn more. If …'

'Yes?' The King looked around the tent, clearly pleased with the decorations and ornate gifts.

'If she is allowed to keep her natural sweet disposition, I believe the English might in time grow to love her.'

The King smiled, throwing off his heavy cloak and sitting for a servant to remove his boots. 'I believe they might. Although she is so very different …'

'Majesty?'

'Memories, Sir Argyle,' the King sighed. 'Of course she must be different. There can never be another Anne.'

Silence ensued leaving Argyle to ponder if the King would ever even consider loving the Princess once she came of age. The servant finished his work on the boots and left the tent bowing all the way through the flaps. The King roused. 'Tonight we feast, my little wife and I. What fun we shall have.'

'Majesty.'

'I wonder if there will be any fun once the Princess is whisked off to her own bed?' The King rubbed his neck. Argyle let the remark slide. Certainly, if the King required fun of another kind than food and drink someone else could procure it. 'You can leave me, Sire. I expect you attend the feast and keep an eye out.'

'For what, Majesty?'

The King looked at him with wonder. 'We are in France, what do you think?'

'Majesty, you are here at the invitation of King Charles himself, married to his beloved daughter. I hardly think …'

'I do not require you to think!' The King gestured. 'I have one Mowbray for that, and I left him in England! I just need your vigilance.'

'Certainly, Majesty.'

'Good. And I expect your men to join my White Harts to guard my tent. So many tokens of affection might turn even loyal men into thieves.' The King picked up a splendid golden cup and moved it this way and that, the light from the brazier catching in the gemstones.

'I shall pick the best of them,' Argyle said.

'Very well, you are released for now, Sir Argyle. Keep in easy distance, yes?'

'Majesty.'

Stepping back into the warm, autumnal afternoon, Argyle could hear the King rummage through the many gifts in the tent, clapping his hands as a happy child would. Argyle walked away, picking out a few of his most trusted soldiers in his thoughts.

'Mowbray is your name?' Argyle started at the soft voice and looked up to meet two sparkling blue eyes.

'Yes, my Lady.'

'I am required to escort you.'

Before Argyle could ask why, the young woman turned and began weaving her way through the throng of tents, people, horses and hounds. Only once did she look back to ensure that he was following her. Argyle kept a modest distance and looked around to see if anyone was watching. It seemed not to be the case, but he knew that a camp was full of eyes and ears.

'Alors, here I must leave you.' She pushed away a hidden flap in the side of a big tent, and Argyle stooped to enter.

Within, candles lit the vast expanse revealing cots, chairs, tables and decoration pieces. Several braziers heated the tent, though only one was currently in use. A pleasant scent of rosemary stirred distant memories.

'Lord Mowbray?'

'I am Sir Argyle, my brother is Lord Mowbray …' Argyle's voice trailed away. Before him the little Princess had emerged. She had already changed for the evening's events it seemed. Clad in cloth of gold and blue, she was a promise of the woman, she might one day become.

'Sir Argyle.' The Princess inclined her head, as Argyle quickly bowed deeply before her. 'Come sit with me.'

'Your Grace, this is an honour.'

'Ah … First you must 'ear me, Sir Argyle. Per'aps you shall not then think it such an 'onour.'

Taking a seat on a low stool a short distance from her grand and massive oak throne, Argyle looked at the Princess. She sat with ease and poise, her hands folded in her lap. 'I 'ave been informed, you are the King's loyal servant?'

'Yes, your Grace.'

'Then you are the right one for me to address with my concerns.' She looked intently at Argyle. 'I shall leave for England with but a small group of trusted advisers and ladies. I expect the King will 'ave chosen my 'ouse'old for me. Generous of course.'

The Princess took a sip from a silver goblet seemingly to compose herself. Argyle waited, almost entranced. This was certainly no ordinary child of 7. When the Princess spoke again, it was in her native tongue. 'You are to be one of my advisers?'

'No, your Grace.' Argyle was acutely aware of how crude his French was.

The Princess plumped the cushion on her throne. 'Why not, if the King thinks highly of you?'

'I would not go that far, your Grace. In any case, I leave the dealings of court to my brother,' Argyle said.

'Ah … an older brother, I presume?' Argyle inclined his head and the Princess glanced about. 'I have little time. It is imperative that I know whom to trust. I am to leave for a strange land to live with a man old enough to be my father. What does his Majesty require of me?'

'In time, your Grace, I believe he desires a family,' Argyle said.

The Princess waved her hand impatiently; she was born and bred with the purpose of delivering heirs, preferably by the dozen. She fixed Argyle's eyes in an entrancing gaze. 'What can I expect of life at court?'

'Your Grace is more experienced with life at court than I am, surely.'

'Vite, vite, we have little time!' Her demanding voice betrayed a hint of fear.

'Life at court is difficult, your Grace,' Argyle said. 'There are factions - and there are those who believe that this peace treaty, signed and sealed by your marriage, is not enough to keep France from attacking.'

'Who can I trust? I must know, and you are rumoured to be honest.' She wrung her hands.

'The King and his closest advisers. Those you can trust.' Argyle wondered what rumours the Princess had heard and from whom.

'And the King's family?' the Princess asked.

'Always have a care of in-laws, your Grace,' Argyle said. 'My aunt taught me that.'

The Princess giggled and wrapped her arms around herself, all at once looking like the child she was. 'And you?'

'And me,' Argyle said.

'Good. Oh, someone is coming, quickly bow before me.' The Princess stood, folding her hands demurely before her gown, hiding a sly smile just in time as two of her maids bustled through the main flaps, exclaiming loudly at the sight of Argyle on bent knee before the Princess. 'Rise, Sir Mowbray, and thank the King for 'is concerns and care. I am quite ready to see 'is Majesty again this evening.'

'Your Grace.' Argyle stood up, and the maids gasped as he towered over their tiny Princess. One of them shot him an appraising look; nudging the other when she thought, Argyle was not looking. He bowed once more to the Princess, and quickly escaped the tent.

He still had to muster men for the King's tent and hoped for no more distractions.

ꕥ ꕥ

That night the food was plenty and the wine flowed in abundance, ensuring that the entire camp was merry and in high spirits. King Charles showered the King with lavish gifts, receiving particular joy when he revealed a series of large golden model ships decked in jewels and pearls, glittering in the firelight. The ships looked so life-like that several courtiers endeavoured to entice the King to try and sail them down the river flowing nearby.

In turn, the King presented his wife with a beautiful set of gold and silver necklaces, brooches of amber and sapphire and a massive gold ring with a ruby the size of a dove's egg. As he slipped the ring onto the Princess' tiny finger, it tilted and she grabbed for it, her tinkling laughter filling the tent.

The King took her hand in his, pondering its size. 'My Lady must grow into this, I fear.'

'I have every intent of doing so, my Lord.' The Princess patted his hand gently. The King offered a warm smile and let the little Princess hold his hand for a while. 'I am so happy. Are you not too, my Lord?'

'I most certainly am.' The King bent towards her with a conspiratorial look. 'But now we are husband and wife, we should call each other by our given names.'

'Richard.' The Princess tried the name cautiously, frowning at the sensation. 'I think I must practice this for some time, before I am comfortable calling you Richard. After all, you are a King and I a Princess.'

'Ah, but I shall change all of that soon enough. I shall plan every detail of your coronation, you will not be disappointed, Isabella,' the King said.

'See, much easier for you to say my name!' she exclaimed this with a child's ease and humour, laughing and clapping. The King seemed very pleased with himself, beaming and smiling at all the guests. Standing behind the King, Argyle hid a smile; perhaps this match was not as foolish as Thomas had thought.

A short while later, the Princess was sent off under the pretext that this feast should not be overtaxing for her. Many of the young ladies went with her, leaving the men to carry on feasting.

The King hooked his finger in Argyle's direction. 'Sir Argyle, fetch me Surrey.'

'Majesty.'

'I find that I am in dire need of some talkative company, and you will not do.'

In Paris, Argyle had made his opinion of brothels clear, and the King had accepted his refusal to accompany him. Now it seemed that the King had settled on his nephew to seek out female companions while they were in France. Surrey was a handsome young man whose easy manner and charm seemed attractive to many of the French women in the large, royal entourage. Argyle looked out over the many guests and saw Surrey engaged in conversation with two blushing maids. He made his way over to Surrey, glad to pass on the message and be free to return to his tent. 'My lord Surrey, the King has need of you.'

'Not enough for him, Sir Argyle?' Surrey turned, and the two maids giggled. He had an arm around either girl's waist and a look of satisfaction on his face. By sunrise these two girls would have traded their innocence for first experiences.

'Not in this matter.' Argyle wondered which of the girls the King might favour. 'His Majesty finds himself in need of your special skills.'

Surrey barked a harsh laugh and pushed past Argyle. When one of the girls brushed up against his arm, she glanced up at Argyle and gave an enticing smile. Perhaps they were not as innocent as Argyle had assumed. He watched them weave their way to the low dais where the King was waiting with an eager look on his face. On the left side of the dais, the French King Charles was engaged in conversation with a voluptuous woman's bosom and did not seem too concerned that his new son-in-law familiarised himself with some of the young women at court.

Shaking his head, Argyle went into the bright, cool night in search of some fresh air.

&
'My Lord.'

Argyle turned around to find the blue-eyed woman from earlier standing a few feet away. His eyes were drawn to her blond hair that spilled across her shoulders almost down to her waist. The ghostly glow of the moon made her look otherworldly.

'I am not a Lord, my Lady,' Argyle said. The stifling heat in the tent had made his head ache, and the crisp air was a relief.

She stepped closer. 'Celeste is my name.'

'Though I suspect not your family name?' Argyle said.

'No.' She laughed lightly. 'My family name is not important.'

Despite being out in the open fields, Argyle felt trapped. 'Why is it then that I feel it may be?'

Celeste cocked her head a little and her hair brushed away from her shoulder to reveal a perfect little black birthmark in a sea of cream. 'The Princess sent me.'

Argyle drew breath, but Celeste stopped him, resting a hand lightly on his chest. 'Not like you think. The Princess has gone to bed. She sent me … in case you needed some company.'

'My Lady.' Argyle felt heat crawl up his neck.

'Celeste,' she said.

'The Princess …' Argyle took a step back.

'Is generous. And I come willingly enough. The other maids have been talking.' She sent him a sly smile. 'I admit, when I was first sent to fetch you, I did not concern myself with your looks. But the girls convinced me that you are worth looking at. And I now find they are right.'

'You …' Argyle shook off her compliment. 'It is very kind - of you and the Princess, but I am exhausted.'

'That can be cured.'

He smiled down at her. 'How?'

'That is my concern. You are released from your duties?' She looked around.

'Yes, I think the King and his friends would rather I that do not return to the feast,' Argyle said.

'That makes you sound dull. Are you dull?' Celeste looked up at him with her sky-blue eyes. Argyle was suddenly acutely aware of her presence; the hand on his chest sent a flood of boiling water washing over his skin.

'And if I am?'

'I have a cure for that too, my Lord.'

ꕥ ꕥ ꕥ ꕥ

'So it is true … still waters run the deepest.' She rolled over, her soft hair spread across the coarse covers on his cot. 'Your wife is very lucky.'

'I will be sure to tell her, once I get one,' Argyle said blinking away sleep.

Celeste's eyes widened. 'Not married yet - how can that be?'

'A long story, tiresome and old.'

'We have a little time before the sun breaks.' Celeste walked naked to the tent flap and pushed it open. Argyle cleared his throat. She might have come willingly, sent by the Princess or not, but he wanted her visit to be kept secret. 'It seems, we have a lot of time, my Lord.'

'Then let us not waste it talking nonsense.'

'But I like nonsense. Especially, when I find that a handsome man of a certain age is not yet married. If I did not know any better, I would think you did not like women,' Celeste said. The light from the brazier turned her skin to gold.

'Thank God you know better.' Argyle reached for her, but she slipped away and poured two cups of wine before she returned to his cot.

'To long nights.'

Argyle raised his cup to her. 'And new friends.'

He gently pulled her closer, smelling her soft hair. Celeste turned her face away, this time it seemed he would have to work for his reward. Argyle pushed her hair to one side and slowly traced his fingers down her spine. She arched her back a little, her skin running goose bumps as he progressed. Celeste sighed quietly and grabbed his hand drawing it to her mouth. Kissing one fingertip at the time, Argyle felt every single brush of her plumb lips stirring his body back to life.

She turned and pulled him closer, brushing her breasts against his chest and moving to position herself better on the narrow cot. When he had her again, she was ready.

Celeste did not leave the tent until the moon fell beyond the horizon.

ꟸ ꟸ

2 November 1396 - Ardres

Argyle could smell meat cooking over a fire, the succulent scent wafting on the crisp breeze of late autumn. He stretched and pulled a woollen robe over his head, his squire was still sleeping soundly in his small tent right next to Argyle's, the snoring unmistakable. Argyle wondered if the lad had been up till the early hours listening to the tall tales of soldiers and perhaps even drinking a little too heavily. He smiled, better that than if the boy had been in all night, he would no doubt have heard what went on in Argyle's tent. He certainly had not slept and yet, he felt reborn.

All around him, the camp sprang to life, boys running messages from tents to the cooking area and guards changing before the King's great tent. Argyle relished the memory of honeyed hair strewn over his pillow.

'Sire.' A small boy in the King's livery looked up at Argyle.

'Yes?'

'The King wants to see you, Sire.'

Argyle sighed, it seemed breakfast would have to wait. He followed the boy into the King's tent to find him in his massive chair, dispatching orders and waving a cup of mulled wine about.

'Majesty.' Argyle knelt before the King.

'Ah, good, there you are, Sir Argyle!' the King said. 'I wondered where you had got to yesterday …'

Argyle briefly considered if there was a latent insinuation in the words but pushed the thought aside. 'Once you dismissed me, Majesty, I made my way back to my tent.'

'Alone?' Argyle nodded unconvincingly, but it seemed enough to satisfy the King, who continued; 'We are preparing for a grand day! Charles and I will meet this morning to discuss the final arrangements to take home Isabella. Charles is not too happy to part with her, which tells me he favours her, which is good news for me and England! Politically, I mean.'

Politics, Argyle thought, if only we could live in a world, where a marriage could take place without politics!

But aloud he only voiced his happiness at the King's good fortunes.

'You will accompany me to break my fast with the French. I have it on good authority that Charles has a very interesting proposal for me,' the King said. 'If I am correct it will also be of great interest to you!'

Argyle stepped aside to let the King's servants finish dressing him in a loose crimson gown and a pair of woollen breeches. While the King spent some time choosing his rings and finally a heavy chain of gold and rubies, Argyle pondered what the French King might have to propose.

When the two servants were done pulling on the King's black boots, they were sweating profusely. The King glanced once more in the polished copper disk that served as a makeshift mirror and straightened his chain. 'Come, Sir Argyle, the French await!'

Only a few paces from the King's tent, the reception tent was already brimming with food and crammed with people, but when the King arrived several left to make room for his men. They sat about the tent where there was a place to be had, and only Argyle was ordered to follow the King to the dais where King Charles was presiding over the breakfast.

'Charles!' The King smiled and clasped hands with King Charles before settling down to a mighty feast. 'You said there was something to be discussed?'

'Please, eat!' King Charles waved for more food to be served. Argyle's mouth watered at the sight of the roast pig, boiled eggs and vegetable broth, but he had to wait for the King to dismiss him, which he did not seem disposed to do for the time being. Until then, he had stay standing behind the King's throne. Argyle acknowledged the French soldier behind King Charles' throne a nod, which was gratefully returned.

The King picked out dishes and sent a few Surrey's way; he nodded his gratefulness but only prodded the food. Apparently drinking, and God knows what else, with the King all night was hard for a man to recover from. Argyle, on the other hand, was famished from his nightly adventure.

'Delicious, but you cannot distract me with food, Charles,' the King said, fat from the bacon running down his chin. 'Come now, before the tent is overrun with women, and I have to turn my attention to my new bride.'

King Charles leaned in. 'I have been communicating with the Pope.' Both men crossed themselves. 'His Holiness is contemplating a new crusade.'

'Oh?' The King cracked an egg and sucked out the liquid golden yolk. 'Where?'

'Against the Turks!'

The Turks! In a flash, Argyle saw Jerusalem's bazaar and Najeelah dancing in the teahouse - then she was gone again. He stifled a low groan, and the King gave him a curious glance before turning back to King Charles.

'It sounds magnificent, Charles, but why now?'

'His Holiness has decreed that it is God's will that the infidels be put in their rightful place, and the Holy Land returned to those of the faith.' King Charles washed down his breakfast with mulled wine and winced. It was well known that he had bad teeth and that he was too vain to have them pulled so he preferred to live in constant pain. 'I wondered if we should not offer to take up arms together and fight the wretched Turks in God's honour?'

The King bit into a succulent piece of roast meat and pondered the proposal while he chewed. Argyle knew the King had an aversion to warfare, but surely he would rise to the occasion if the Pope himself wanted the Turks banished. What the King lacked in bloodlust he more than made up for in piety. The opportunity of travelling once more the breadth of the world, to gaze upon the red walls of Jerusalem, was almost more than Argyle could handle. He had to go!

The King wiped his greasy hands on the tablecloth. 'That is an offer worth contemplating. Certainly it is.'

'What is there to contemplate, Richard?' King Charles waved his empty cup in annoyance. 'It is merely a matter of accepting, finding the best soldiers in the land and riding at the head of a grand army, a united France and England ready to wage a holy war!'

Obviously, King Charles was of a more bloodthirsty disposition, and Argyle wondered if perhaps he should petition the King to join the crusade and fight for his father-in-law. King Charles would need able soldiers and knights, and Argyle had both in abundance.

'I must first pray on it, Charles,' the King said in a slick tone.

'Pray on it?'

'His Holiness has great knowledge of God's will and ways, I do not protest it, but I too am called to God,' the King said and rubbed his temple. 'I am sure that I will find the same as the Pope; that the infidels must be purged from the Holy Land and that I shall join in the holy quest.'

King Charles closed his eyes for a moment; Argyle wondered if it was in silent prayer for strength, and looked intently at the King. 'I am sure, you will find as I did - and the Pope does. The Turks must be rooted from this most holy and sacred place in Christendom.'

'Of course …' The King wavered a little. 'It is a grand prospect. Will you really ride at the head of your army?'

'Naturellement! What else would a crusading King do? What would your own ancestors do?!' King Charles was flattered by the King's words, but Argyle had picked up on the fear in the King's question. 'How can one command an army, if one is not at its head? Constantly inspiring the men to be bold and to defy death?!'

The King's hand shook ever so slightly when he picked up his cup. 'To the future!' he declared and all of the men in the tent rose, saluting the two kings.

Argyle saw the King steady his hand before drinking and give King Charles a discerning glance. If King Charles noticed, he hid it well. 'As I say, I shall pray on it,' the King insisted.

'We will let the diplomats discuss the details,' King Charles decided.

'They too must earn their keep.' The King sighed much as a man escaping impending doom. 'I am sure they will come up with very agreeable terms and then you and I will wage a war. Although …'

King Charles grabbed the ornate armrest of his throne and gave his reluctant son-in-law a weary glance. 'Yes?'

'While you have many heirs, I have none …' the King said. 'Perhaps it is unwise to ride so far away from my new wife.'

'It will be years before she is of a childbearing age!' King Charles looked angry, but his voice was smooth. 'By then we will have conquered the Holy Land and have you safe back in England to put a child in her belly!'

'Of course …' The King looked defeated but then perked up. 'She will be thrilled when I tell her that you and I are to go on this grand voyage together!'

King Charles fiddled with his knife, pushing his leftovers around the silver plate. 'I am not sure …'

'She must know!' the King insisted. 'I cannot keep anything from my wife!'

Argyle saw King Charles cringe and understood at once that the King had won the argument. His stomach lurched, and not from hunger, most likely there would be no crusade for the English army.

'Perhaps you should wait until you know God's plan for you?' King Charles' tone was casual but cold.

'Yes, what good advice you give, Charles,' the King said. 'I shall pray on the crusade and what to tell Isabella, and you will know as soon as God answers my prayers.'

Argyle decided that he would approach the little Princess first with his wish to join her father in his holy war. If the King was intent that he should not participate in the crusade then perhaps the Princess would acknowledge that sending one of his knights and a company of his men would be a brilliant gesture that the King of England supported the endeavour wholeheartedly, even if he could not go himself.

'Sir Argyle!'

Argyle started and bowed low to King Charles. 'Your Majesty?'

'See that my daughter is well fed - and entertained!'

'Yes, see to my wonderful Isabella!' The King dismissed Argyle with a little disdainful wave; clearly he took great offence that his father-in-law gave his men orders.

'Yes, Majesty.'

Argyle headed out of the stuffy, cramped tent, glad to get away from the smell of too many unwashed men and the two Kings' painful power-struggle. He had lost his appetite. Lost in thought, he made his way through the camp, and his mind wandered to how to approach the Princess and when.

'Sir Argyle!'

Argyle blinked. 'My Lady?'

Celeste tugged at her skirt. 'You were lost in thought I think.' She smiled but there was a distance in her voice.

'Yes …' Argyle moved and saw Celeste frown at the dirt on the hem of her skirt.

'The Princess is asking for you.'

'The Kings have just sent me to her,' Argyle said and saw Celeste's eyes shine.

'The Kings?' she laughed. 'It took two Kings to send you off?'

Apparently so, Argyle thought and returned her smile. 'They were both anxious that the Princess be well looked after.'

'Really?! I have served her for years, and suddenly, two men are going to tell me how …' Celeste shook her head, releasing a single lock of golden hair. 'Not your problem, I am sorry.'

'Not at all, my Lady,' Argyle said. 'Perhaps you can escort me to the Princess' tent?'

'You have forgotten where it is?' A mischievous smile played on her full lips. 'Do you know, I have quite forgotten myself … where is it? This way, I think!'

Argyle knew he had little time to waste and yet, he let Celeste lead the way to the edge of the woods not far from the Princess' tent. The back of the camp provided easy cover for a little excursion, none of the tent-openings faced that way.

'I think we have gone too far, my Lady.'

'Not at all, I just remembered how the Princess loves fresh nuts … and I happen to know there are some just on the other side of those trees.' Celeste slid her hand around his arm. 'If you go with me, we can carry at least twice as many, and then no one can complain of my attention to her desires!'

'Or your desires?'

Celeste drew him into the thicket.

CHAPTER 9

7 November 1396 - Eltham Court, England

'I still wonder ...,' Argyle said.

Margaret sat at her husband's desk. She had been writing a letter when Argyle arrived, but now it was hidden from view under a neat pile of papers. 'About what?'

'About La Fontaine's death.' Argyle brought her a cup of ale. She looked very much at ease in Sir Reginald's chambers. In fact, they looked to have been fitted out for her, not her absent husband.

'Oh Argyle, why press the matter? The King was satisfied that Lockley was guilty, and now he is dead. Why cannot you too leave it at that?' Margaret looked weary.

'There are too many unanswered questions, Margaret,' Argyle said remembering his interrupted conversation with the grey-haired man in Paris whom he had not seen since. 'What about the poison that laced Lockley's lance? He knew that La Fontaine would die if only he grazed him. He would have said it was his own idea if it was, and from what I learned about him, he might have been loyal and even a good soldier, but clever, he was not!'

Margaret shook her head, and Argyle noticed strands of white cut through her long dark hair when it brushed across her back it was unusual to see her without her hood. 'It makes no difference, Argyle, leave it be.'

He walked behind her chair to get to his own seat. 'It haunts me.'

'Find something else to occupy your mind. What about that French lady everyone is fawning over?' Margaret said, looking earnestly at Argyle. 'She seems interested, why not …'

Argyle laughed. 'Margaret, I never …'

'I know what may turn a man's head to more pleasant things.' Margaret lifted a warning finger. 'I think it would be wise that you began to seek out her company, Argyle. She is close to the Princess, and we all know that the King already dotes on her.'

'Yes, as a father would a daughter,' Argyle said.

'Beware what you say! She will one day bear his children - would it be such a terrible thing if you were married to her friend and confidante by then?' Margaret leaned back in her chair, considering Argyle over the brim of her cup. 'She is pretty.'

'It may surprise you, dear sister, that beauty is not all I care about,' Argyle felt himself shrink under the watchful gaze of his eldest sister.

'It never hurt anyone.'

'Are you sure?'

Margaret's look turned exasperated. 'Really, little brother, do take heed of my advice for once in your life. God knows John never did! You have been too long without a woman, rumours are surfacing at court - and elsewhere, I would have you know - that you do not care for women at all!'

'You must know that is not true.'

'Then pick one - anyone!' Margaret tuned into her well-rehearsed scolding. 'Thomas says he has offered several and none will do!'

'I want to choose for myself,' Argyle slid off her remark. 'I do not wish to marry whoever Thomas might see fit that I marry. You may not have noticed, but I am man grown.'

'And a man grown needs a wife!' Margaret slapped her hand against her thigh, the sound sharp and crisp. 'Or at least, he needs to prove that he likes women. Bed her, if you will not marry her. Or you could accompany the King to the whorehouses and find some wench there who will tell the tale of how she had Sir Argyle between her sheets.'

Argyle crushed his rising temper and gave Margaret a wry look, but she had a way of wearing him out with her calm gaze. In the end, he could not hide his irritation. 'What is it with this family and marriage?'

'What is it with you and marriage?' Margaret returned. 'Before you left for Jerusalem, you promised Thomas that you would marry upon your return. Then you wanted time to mourn La Fontaine. Well, you have now mourned him for years on end and still, you have no wife, no children to show for it. And you have scorned half the English nobles by refusing their daughters. Beware that most of them could have settled for better prospects, but for some reason women are infatuated by you.'

'So I should say yes to the next woman Thomas finds? Heiresses must be scant at best,' Argyle knew that he sounded like a petulant 5-year-old.

'No, you should find a woman before Thomas offers up yet another girl. You are right that there are few girls of an age, but there are several child brides awaiting a man of noble stock, and you might just find yourself in the same situation as the King - though not by choice,' Margaret straightened the stack of papers in front of her.

'Thomas would marry me off to a child?' Argyle could hardly believe his sister's insinuation. Her hard words were a stark contrast to the soft décor of Sir Reginald's rooms, the room faintly scented with dried rose petals.

'What would you have him do? You have refused all the grown women he has paraded before you. So yes - if that is what it takes for you to marry, he would.'

Argyle could hardly argue with Margaret and yet he did not want a child bride either. In truth, he still clung to the hope that the King would decide to go on crusade with King Charles, although that hope was slipping through his fingers with each passing day. 'Desperate measures.'

'Desperate times.' Margaret closed the lid on a little ornate box containing fine sand used to soak up excess ink. She seemed to consider her words carefully. 'Make sure you are spoken for, before Thomas drums up another prospective bride; that is my advice to you. If French she must be, make her pretty - if English, make her from noble stock.'

Argyle leaned back. 'French it is.'

9 November 1396 - Eltham Court

Celeste walked gracefully across the great hall, her mere presence made the surroundings look old and faded. Her smile shone as a rare diamond resting on a beach among ordinary pebbles. Argyle was sure she knew that half of the court was pining for her, and he could see unadulterated hate in the other women's eyes when they were passed over by their husbands in favour of her.

'Now there is a fine French filly, if ever I saw one,' Thomas said, quite out of character. He even looked a little flushed.

'Thomas!' Margaret shot him a flinty glance. 'You are as bad as the rest of them. I swear, as soon as there is a new woman or two at court, you all dream of getting between her legs! I wonder what you would find there, if you ever got so close.'

Argyle smiled lightly, he knew, but he was not likely to tell his brother. Margaret caught his smile and returned it before turning her attention back to Thomas.

'Now, tell me why you have summoned us here!' Margaret said, as Celeste and the rest of the Princess' ladies-in-waiting slipped from the hall and the many courtiers recommenced their conversations. Some of the splendour seemed to have vanished with the ladies and the great hall looked darker than before.

Thomas sighed. 'I would rather not discuss such delicate matters here in the great hall, Margaret.'

'Well then, you had better invite us to your private rooms,' Margaret said, poking Argyle hard in the ribs. 'But first, I think you should escort me to the ladies rooms, that I might be properly introduced to the Princess.'

'Why Argyle?' Thomas felt the snub.

'Because he has already met the Princess on more than one occasion, and I have it on good authority that she has taken a liking to him.' Margaret smiled thinly. 'The big, blond knight … who would not take a liking? Sometimes I think you are something out of a fairy story.'

'Sister - that is no way of speaking of your own brother.' Argyle coloured a little. 'The Princess was kind enough to speak with me briefly in France, and on the journey home, but I cannot say I have any particular …'

'Never you mind that,' Margaret said looking around the room. 'Take me there, and then we will both go to Thomas' rooms and let him explain himself.'

'Very well, if you like your big, blond brother better than me …' Thomas said, balling his fists.

'I do not.' Margaret briefly patted Thomas' arm. 'I just know that Argyle can get us in and out of the Princess' rooms with little fuss.'

'Margaret. Argyle.' Thomas gave Argyle one last displeased look. 'I will see you in my rooms within the hour.'

Margaret nodded and dragged off Argyle. 'Tell me all I need to know before I meet the Princess.'

Argyle smiled. 'She is a child, I doubt you will disappoint her. She is scholarly, she reads a lot, I saw that on the journey across the sea, and she is fond of music.'

Margaret nodded along, seemingly making mental notes of everything. 'And her ladies?'

'Her ladies?'

'Yes, the wonderful French fillies …' Margaret's voice soured. 'What are they like? Besides their ability to turn English heads. Are they all like your special friend?' She turned down another gallery, the walls hung with tapestries to ward off some of the November cold.

Argyle followed her, suppressing a laugh. 'Why Margaret, I do believe you are a little jealous, which I cannot begin to understand, given our talk the other night.'

'Do not be silly!' Margaret snapped and stopped with such force that Argyle had to quickly sidestep to avoid bumping into her. Her lips were a little blue from the cold of the gallery, but her cheeks burned red. 'I am not jealous! Although I cannot imagine that any married woman would like it too much if her husband suddenly was all eyes and - well - if her husband could speak of nothing but the fine French women at court. Your situation is different.'

'I am sorry, Margaret, please forgive me.' Argyle tucked Margaret's hand back into the crook of his arm. 'I never meant to be rude.'

'You never do.' Margaret let herself be dragged along the gallery, the rush matting rustling beneath her silk shoes. 'And if one of those French women had any sense about her, she will prey on you until you relent.' She winked, a gesture so unnatural for her that Argyle could not help but laugh out loud.

The next turn delivered them before the Princess' doors, which were immediately flung open and light music spilled out to embrace them. Argyle bowed low before the dais, where the tiny Princess sat surrounded by her ladies-in-waiting, chief among them the radiant Celeste who looked up from whispering in the Princess' ear. Petitioners lined the room, talking in groups or standing alone, rocking to the musicians' tune.

'Sir Argyle and Lady de Lucy!' the herald announced, and the Princess looked up, a big smile lighting her pretty face.

'Sir Argyle!' she said happily. 'I had begun to think you had forgotten about me.'

Argyle knelt before the throne, noting how the red paint sparkled. It had been made especially for her. 'Not at all, your Grace. I hope you will allow me to present my sister Margaret de Lucy, wife of Sir Reginald de Lucy.'

Margaret swept a low curtsey that made several of the ladies-in-waiting look quite jealous. What his eldest sister did not have in the way of looks, she more than made up for in grace and posture.

'My Lady de Lucy,' the Princess said with much dignity. 'What a pleasure it is to meet you.'

'The honour is all mine, your Grace,' Margaret said in a sweet tone, which made the Princess smile and stand up.

'Please, will you not join me and the ladies?' The Princess swept an offering hand towards the low stools near a big window, which allowed plenty of light for the ladies' sowing and writing. 'We are making shirts for unfortunate orphans.'

Margaret coloured with pleasure. 'I would be honoured, your Grace.'

'Celeste, some wine perhaps?' the Princess said, and Celeste obliged.

Once seated near the musicians along with Margaret and several of her ladies in waiting, the Princess ordered the musicians to play some of her favourite songs. From his place near the smouldering hearth, Argyle smiled at his sister; she was clearly made for life at court, her disposition demure but proud, her French flawless, and her ability to foresee what the Princess wanted was astounding.

Argyle started when he felt a hand on his back. 'We meet again.'

As he turned, he found Celeste standing before him, far too close for Argyle to think clearly. 'My Lady.'

'I had thought you had forgotten all about me.' Celeste mimicked the Princess, but when she bit her lip lightly her words sent an expectant shiver up his spine. She leaned in and whispered, 'I thought you had found someone else to entertain you.'

'Not at all, these days have been busy …' Argyle stammered. 'I would never presume …'

'Presume all you like - Argyle.' Celeste took hold of his hand, hiding the gesture from view by turning a little. 'I think her Grace can do without your company for a little while; she is so engulfed with your sister. This is your chance to make good on being absent. Help me fetch the wine.'

Argyle's blood course fast through his veins and his mouth was dry. 'My Lady, surely …'

'Surely, she can spare us. Surely, she can spare you - and me? She will think that I have gone in search of more wine, after all, the carafe is empty.' Celeste had to stand on tiptoe for her lips to brush against Argyle's ear. 'Surely, you are running out of excuses?'

Argyle nodded, he was running out of excuses, and his body was telling him to shut up and take Celeste on her word. Since the Princess had arrived, the whole court had been in love with the French women, most of the courtiers had been hard pressed to find any suitable flirt at court since the late Queen died. Now, here were plenty of beautiful young women for the courtiers to enjoy, and the finest of them all had singled him out. He watched Celeste slip behind a curtain and out the side door it hid; Argyle looked around and found Margaret deep in conversation with one of the other ladies, the two of them pouring over some cloth or other. The Princess was clapping along to the music, and the rest of the women seemed as preoccupied as she was. He pushed the curtain aside.

Only the last rays of dazed sunlight lit the narrow corridor behind the door. Argyle looked around in search for Celeste and found no one. He was about to turn back thinking she had been summoned or asked for something when he felt her warm hands slide around his body to rest on his chest.

'You are happy to see me, I think.'

'I am happy to feel you.' Argyle could not deny that her presence aroused him.

'Oh good … You see, I feel the same.' Celeste kissed his neck, her hands fumbling with the string on his breeches.

Argyle's pulse quickened and his breathing grew shallow. 'Celeste … I do not think …'

'Even better, thinking makes fools of most people.' Her hand slipped inside his breeches, slowly caressing him as it went, and he gasped. 'But doing, now that is something quite different. That is to be alive.'

Argyle swallowed hard, turning around so fast that Celeste made a little muffled cry when he pinned her to the wall behind her. He felt the cold stone scratch on his knuckles as he picked her up, sliding her back up the stones. Celeste lifted up her skirt and moaned. 'Please … we have little time and I … I want you, I need you!'

She moved, sliding her hand up his thigh and then guiding him to that heavenly place inside her. Argyle shivered as they joined, relishing in the warm, soft feeling.

'I have not been able to sleep …' Celeste flung her arms around Argyle's neck, arching her back, slowly building a rhythm. 'I have been looking only for you … needing you.'

Argyle sought her mouth, and she responded willingly, opening her soft lips as she had opened her body to his, the two of them quickening the pace, the wall behind her growing warmer. When they broke the kiss, Celeste smiled, her eyes hungrily searching Argyle's face, her fingernails digging into his shoulders. Urging him on with kisses, smiles and a low groaning, Celeste increased the rhythm and bit his neck. Argyle recoiled a little but the bite also spurred him on, and he crushed her tighter, holding her up with his hands, he buried his face in her bosom, biting her breasts lightly, struggling to prolong the pleasure.

Argyle felt her tensing; he looked into her sky-blue eyes and saw nothing there but pure, unadulterated pleasure, her mouth slightly open, her cheeks flushed. Then she cramped around him, and he closed his eyes to give way. Release was instant, both of them surrendering to the moment, her head on his shoulder, his hands locked around her thighs.

Argyle slowly released Celeste, but she clung to him, her hands still around his neck, her quick breathing warming and cooling his cheek. She kept him inside her, and he was powerless to move. When her breathing slowed, she looked into Argyle's eyes. 'I do believe you have needed me too.'

'I have,' Argyle said, his hands still holding her thighs tight.

Celeste finally let go of him, and Argyle stepped back, reluctant to let her go, reluctant to go back into the Princess' chambers and see his sister sitting there … His sister!

'Margaret.' Argyle felt blood rush back into his brain, firing it up.

Celeste looked offended. 'Not me you needed after all!'

'No … well, yes.' Argyle grasped for her hand trying to explain. 'Margaret, my sister.'

'You are not making your case any better.' Celeste brushed away his hand and shook her skirt into place, her pretty face sour and dark.

'No, I mean my sister, Margaret, is with the Princess. I introduced her just now,' Argyle said, confused that Celeste had not noticed, who he had brought. 'She will be wondering where I am. I promised her, I would escort her to my brother's apartments after her audience with the Princess.'

Argyle pulled Celeste in, and she warmed to his caresses. 'Oh, I see. I was so delighted to finally see you, to know you had not gone from court, to know you were here that I did not hear her name. I did not know if you were happy to see me or not …'

Argyle released her again, feeling blood rush through his veins, colouring his neck. 'My Lady, please forgive me …'

'There is nothing to forgive. We are two people who wanted each other, who needed each other.' Celeste smiled mischievously, her hand caressing Argyle's upper thigh. 'Perhaps we will need each other again soon?'

Argyle leaned forward, cupped Celeste's face in his hands and kissed her deeply. When their lips parted, her breathing had quickened again.

'We had better get back - and if your excuse is to be made true, you must find some wine to bring with you.' Argyle caressed the curve of her breasts with a finger. 'Although, you are very tempting.'

Celeste laughed loudly, and Argyle scanned the gallery to see if there was anyone there. 'Do not worry, I may have been overcome with joy and passion, but I kept an eye out,' Celeste said, pulling the top of her gown back in place and replacing a couple of loose pins in her hair. 'Our secret is safe.'

'Then you had better find that wine.' Argyle felt a sudden urge to slap himself for not making sure they were alone before letting his desire get the better of him.

'Will you stay long at court?' Celeste asked. 'We go all the time to and from Windsor. I think the King prefers to dote on the Princess from afar, but she will not be put off.'

'I could not tell you,' Argyle said. 'But for the first time, I hope so.'

Celeste rewarded him with a soft kiss before she walked down the gallery and out of sight.

Argyle pushed the side door open and slid back into the presence chamber to find Margaret still sitting with the ladies and the Princess talking to a petitioner. He did not think Margaret had seen him stealing away, but now she looked up and locked eyes with him. Argyle nodded at her, they could go whenever she wanted.

The Princess released them shortly after with a warning that if Argyle did not visit again soon, she would have to ask her husband to demand Argyle's attendance at her Windsor residence. He smiled dutifully and promised it would not be long before he would call again - perhaps to introduce his other sisters.

'Very well, Sir Argyle, if they are half as charming as Lady de Lucy, I shall be delighted,' the Princess said with a pleasant smile that made Margaret beam. 'We shall see each other again soon!'

ꕤ ꕤ

'You waste little time,' Margaret remarked as they left the Princess' chambers.

'What?'

'I saw you.' She looked around the gallery and lowered her voice. Argyle coloured; he had thought Margaret had not noticed his little excursion. When they stepped outside to cross through one of the small gardens, the thin layer of snow on the gravel path soaked Margaret's shoes. For once, she seemed not to notice.

'She is still willing?' Margaret asked as they weaved their way back towards Thomas' apartments, avoiding the great hall.

'Hardly a question you can expect me to answer.' Argyle kept his voice down although there was no one around but them. The weather had everyone else staying indoors, warm light glowing in the narrow coloured windows.

Margaret's voice shook from the cold. 'I think it does.' She approached a door at the end of the garden and a guard opened it for her.

Argyle bit the inside of his cheek for a moment before answering. 'Yes, she is willing. Before you ask, I will say no more on the subject, and I ask that you do not tell Thomas - or anyone - of this!'

Inside the hall, the hearths worked hard to keep the cold that rushed through the open door at bay. The warmth felt as a blanket, folding itself around their shoulders, and Margaret's lips regained their colour.

'If there be gossip, it will not come from me,' Margaret drew Argyle into a window bay overlooking the river, her fingers still icy. 'But I am glad you took my advice. I think you will be richly rewarded for it.'

'How so?' Argyle was curious about this new side of Margaret; she seemed a woman transformed now that she was more often at court without her husband.

'Do not make me say it.' It was Margaret's turn to colour, and she turned her back to a pair of passing courtiers who glanced curiously at her and Argyle in the window bay.

Argyle laughed. 'Margaret, I always had you pegged as one with little interest in the pleasures of the flesh …' He too lowered his voice inside the palace walls had ears. 'But yes, I am sure I will be rewarded. I only wonder if she will be interested in more than a dalliance.'

'A dalliance will do for the time being, just make sure you are always in her mind, even when you have to go from court and back to Beauworth. Invite her to come if you can and make sure to see her before anyone else when you come here. That will make her yours,' Margaret said as they continued along the corridor.

'Very well, but do not think I will ever speak of she and I to you again, you nosy woman!' Argyle smiled; she was as a mother to him and he wanted more than anything to make her happy.

'Better to me than to Thomas.'

'He may find out soon enough,' Argyle said with a grudge, 'if court gossip is anything to go by. You knew - so I assume one or two other ladies saw me leave too and noticed how long Celeste was gone. Although until I know her better …'

'How much better would you know her?' Margaret turned back into the hall. They were close to Thomas' chambers now, and more servants carried trays and pitchers - and many courtiers walked past on their way to or from meetings.

I do not know, Argyle admitted to himself, but a good deal better. It is one thing to be in the grip of passion and lust, and quite another to truly know a person.

Margaret opened the door to Thomas' chambers and walked in, Argyle trailing behind. She looked around and pursed her lips as she always did when she was displeased. 'He orders us to come directly here, and he is not here to greet us?'

'He must have been detained.' Argyle wanted to leave. His brother's rooms were as sparse and dark as ever, the meagre fire burning in the hearth sent puffs of smoke but hardly any warmth into the room. Argyle bent to stoke and feed it, and the flames began devouring the wood hungrily. 'Perhaps he has better things to do than wait for us.'

'Then he should have sent word, he knew where we were.' Margaret leafed through the piles of papers on Thomas' desk, gathering them in neat stacks. 'Our brother is a busy man.'

'And I intend to keep it that way,' Thomas said, and Argyle nearly jumped out of his own skin. Margaret just looked up from her rifling, a piece of paper in her hand.

'This is what you wanted to talk to us about?' She sounded appalled as she waved the paper at Thomas. 'You know better than to listen to idle gossip.'

'It is hardly gossip.' Thomas snapped the paper from Margaret and glared at her. 'This is serious.'

'Dangerous.' Margaret sat down in his chair. 'You need to make a clean break.'

'How can I?' Thomas said. 'The King is erratic. It will not be long before …'

Argyle felt as though he was just an innocent bystander about to be unwillingly dragged into some new conspiracy that he could not escape. He flinched when Margaret slammed her hand into Thomas' desk, her neat stacks falling once more into disarray. 'It is plotting, dear brother. I thought you had got past such childish games years ago!'

'The King wants full control, he is saying that the Lords are not to be trusted,' Thomas mumbled.

'He says so in front of you because he is testing your loyalty. You need to stand firm. You need to be his man, not theirs.' Margaret rearranged the papers, her hands working furiously. 'This has gone on long enough, Thomas! Let it be.'

'But …' Thomas tried again and Margaret cut him off.

'No, Thomas! If the King is souring about the Lords Appellant, best to keep far away from them. Burn the letters they send, or better yet, show them to the King. Let him know that you are beyond reproach.' Margaret turned to Argyle. 'Do you not agree, Argyle?'

Argyle gave Margaret a dark glare that was completely ignored. 'I am loyal.'

'Yes, you are!' Margaret tipped her head at Argyle and Thomas stared. 'And so should we all be. No more words exchanged with Warwick or Woodstock. I suppose Lord Arundel cannot be avoided, he is your family, but otherwise, Thomas, I warn you …'

Argyle looked in wonder as Thomas cringed before Margaret and bent his head resembling an obedient boy. 'Yes, Margaret.' She smiled at him, and he looked relieved. He sat on the edge of his table, looking intently at her. 'Now about this letter, do you believe it to be true?'

'That Gaunt is plotting to put Bolingbroke on the throne? Of course, why else would he insist on always being near the King?' Margaret turned the ruby ring on her finger. 'The question is what are you going to do about it?'

Argyle stiffened. Had they not just agreed that there was to be no more plotting? Thomas merely stroked his pointed beard apparently waiting for Margaret to go on.

'You have to get to the root of it, Thomas,' she said. 'Before Gaunt does something that cannot be undone.'

ଌ ଓ ଌ ଓ

CHAPTER 10

27 November 1396 - Windsor

Argyle visited the Princess as often as he could both for the pleasant and easy company of the King's child bride and to be near Celeste. The Princess was delighted to see him and always asked that he would stay longer than any of the other courtiers, something he knew was being whispered in the King's ear, but for the time being it appeared the King was pleased with Argyle's attentions.

'What do you think, Sir Argyle?' the Princess said when the music stopped. She was sitting on her bright red throne; he was lounging on a stack of cushions at her feet. Several of her ladies-in-waiting were sitting at tables near the windows playing dice or speaking softly. The apartments had a sweet, childish feeling to them.

'A beautiful ballad, your Grace.' Argyle pushed himself up to look at her.

Her face lit up. 'I thought so too. It is made by my husband - he has composed the music and written the poetry himself.' She smiled. 'I think he is fond of me, Sir Argyle. I think, in time, the King may even love me.'

Argyle heard the plea beneath her composure and settled back on his cushions. 'I am sure, he will, your Grace. You are the breath of fresh air he needed, and he is very fond of you.'

'Good. I am to dine with him tonight, you know. I always look forward to it; he will have little presents for me, and all my favourite foods. I especially like the sweets at the end of the meal, and so do you, Celeste, n'est pas?' The Princess held out her hand to Celeste who was seated to her right on a low stool, a beautiful embroidery with silk and gold thread lay in her lap.

Celeste took her hand and smiled. 'Yes, your Grace, they are delightful.' Argyle caught her eye, as she glanced towards him for the tiniest of moments.

'You must tell me which you like the best, your Grace, that I might bring them to you,' Argyle said and got up.

'Celeste will tell you,' the Princess giggled. 'I shall retire to change; I must look my best for the King so that he will be pleased with me. He must always be pleased with me. He must learn to love me, and I shall never disappoint.'

The Princess rose, and Argyle swept a bow to her. 'His Majesty is very lucky to have so dutiful a wife.'

'Angling for praise, Sir Argyle?' The Princess tried to keep her composure but burst into laughter. 'No, not you, you need no praise, you are a true knight!' She offered her hand and Argyle kissed her ring, the one the King had given her on the night of their betrothal. It had been sized down as soon as they had returned to London and rumour had it she never took it off. The ruby looked as if it would swallow up her tiny hand. 'Celeste, tell Sir Argyle what sweets we like best. You are released until tonight. Make sure you are ready for me when the bell tolls.'

The Princess left the room, five ladies-in-waiting trailing behind her.

As soon as the party had left the room, the musicians began putting away their instruments and the audience chamber quickly emptied. No courtiers would stay behind when the principal focus of their attentions had left to prepare for an evening with the King.

'Coming, Sir Argyle?' the Earl of Salisbury, John Montagu, asked. 'We could make it to the tavern and back in time for dinner, I am sure!'

'Not today, my Lord. I am invited to dine with my family and must not keep them waiting,' Argyle said careful to keep his tone light.

Salisbury shook his head. 'You should have a care not to be always so serious.'

Argyle smiled in return. 'I shall go with you next time.'

Salisbury inclined his head to Celeste, who had been collecting the sowing from the windowsills and carefully placing the bright, thin silk threads in the little, ornate cases. She smiled in return, and Argyle saw Salisbury flush slightly before turning away.

'The whole court is in love with you.' Argyle suppressed an urge to grab Celeste and draw her close. 'Sometimes I wonder how you stand it.'

Celeste laughed. 'Stand all the love? That is a strange thing to say. You are not jealous, are you?'

'Not at all.' Argyle was hurt that she had hit so close to the mark. Perhaps it was not exactly jealousy, but certainly he would be most pleased if some other beauty would arrive at court and steal away Celeste's many suitors. 'But you must admit that you, an available, eligible French lady should be looking to secure a husband. The Princess must be making matches for you?'

Celeste looked thoughtful. 'You want me married off?'

'No, I …' Argyle was painfully aware that there were still people in the room. 'I just know what it is like to be part of a noble family.'

'That is true, you do. And yet, you are not married.' Celeste stepped a little closer, clutching one of the little boxes tight. 'Why is that?'

For a moment, Argyle considered telling her about Najeelah. But he thought better of it, this was a part of his history that he buried, why rip open the wound? Instead, he bent down, pretending to pick something off the floor. 'My brother had made a match, but I convinced the King it was better if I made my own decisions when it came to marriage. Since then, Thomas has not let up in his efforts to secure me a wife but …'

Celeste stepped closer, lifting her skirt ever so lightly, her creamy ankle clearly visible. Half a world away, a dark woman had showed herself almost undressed, and oddly, this ankle was almost more enticing to him.

'I pity the woman, who did not manage to catch you.' Celeste crouched before Argyle, bringing their heads level. 'I pity all the women who do not work tirelessly to secure you.'

'Are we alone?' Argyle's throat felt dry.

Celeste shook her head slightly; one of her blonde curls falling out of place and sweeping across her chest. 'No, but they are busy, and none of them can see your face … which I think is good, for it is showing your heart's desire.'

Argyle breathed deep, slowly lifting a hand to brush back her curl, grazing the top of her breasts. He felt Celeste yield to his touch, her cheeks flushing a little and her breath quickening. 'So is yours,' Argyle said getting up and offered her a hand.

'But really, why are you not married?' Celeste said, perhaps to divert her desire. She turned her back to replace the little box and began folding the half-finished embroideries that the ladies had been working on.

'It is a tiresome tale.' Argyle began to feel annoyed at the interrogation. 'I have not yet found the right woman. Some days, I think that soon all of the court will begin wondering if I like women at all.'

Celeste's shoulders shook, and Argyle thought she might be crying. Looking around, he saw there was no way he could even put a hand on her shoulder let alone pull her tight and tell her that perhaps she was the right woman. The musicians were terribly slow at clearing their instruments away. But when Celeste turned around, Argyle saw that she was choking back laughter and felt desire and anger surge through his body, the two feelings racing to see, which would win the day.

'If they only knew,' she finally managed to say, tears in her eyes from soundless laughter. 'They would never say that you do not like women, most likely they would say that you like them too much.'

Argyle bit his tongue to prevent an irritated outburst and fixed Celeste's gaze. 'Too much, my Lady?'

'Ah yes, Sir Argyle,' Celeste teased. 'There are rumours at court that every day a new woman warms your bed. That every night you prowl London and bring home scores of women, all eager to please, all ready to serve you any way they can. And yet, you do not marry …'

'This is not funny.' Argyle was a little surprised that he was so provoked by her words. 'Tell me it is not true, and that you are just teasing me because there are other people in the room …'

'Not at all. Those are the rumours.' She stepped so close that Argyle could feel the heat from her body, the bottom of her skirt caressing his boots. 'Though of course, I know better.'

Argyle reached for her, one finger tracing the lining of her dress, following the intricate pattern on the front just beneath her breasts, slowly moving towards the pointed piece of fabric that joined with the full skirt.

'I think you have to leave, Argyle,' she said. 'Go out by the side door. I will divert the musicians and send them on their way. Wait by the door for my knock.'

Argyle made a shallow bow towards Celeste and walked briskly towards the side door, pulling at his long jacket and hoping against hope that his neck was not red from desire and temper. He pushed the door open and leaned heavily on the stonewall cooling his forehead while he felt his pulse go down again. Celeste had an eerie way of affecting him, so very different from what he had known in Jerusalem. So different from any English woman he had ever courted or even just desired. Every time he saw her, Argyle felt torn between passion and doubt.

The knock was so quiet that if he had stood on the opposite side of the narrow gallery, he would not have heard it. Argyle paused, what was he thinking? Going into the Princess' presence chamber to see her lady-in-waiting and then what? To make love with her right there on the dais? To take her roughly up the wall next to the musicians' instruments? He shook his head; surely this was folly.

The door slid ajar. 'They are gone. I told the guard, I was last here and that I would go to her Grace once I was done, so he could lock the door, and he has.' Celeste smiled.

'Celeste …' Argyle was caught off guard, as Celeste drew him through the door and forced a hard kiss on him. He gave in and felt her eager hands exploring his clothes, soon they would reach their destination, and he would be lost. Breaking the kiss, Argyle slid sideways away from her grip. 'Celeste, we must talk …'

'I have little time, but I …' Celeste stopped, her hands clutching her skirt, which was already halfway up her thigh. 'Talk about what?'

Argyle cleared his throat, the enticing promise of her creamy leg cluttered his head, and he needed it to be clear. 'If what you say about the rumours is true, then I fear it will not be long before someone finds out that I am not prowling London or seducing every woman at court. Someone will speak out, someone who feels slighted …'

Celeste dropped her skirt and gave him a wry smile. 'And what? You would make an honest woman of me? It is a little late for that, is it not?'

Argyle gestured, he had not really thought that far.

'It is too late,' Celeste said. 'Too late for you to make me yours.'

'What?!' Argyle was taken aback. 'What do you mean?'

'The Princess has not made a match for me, because I am already married.'

Argyle had reached for her, but now he could not move, his hand hung limb in the air. Celeste stepped close, folding his arm around her waist and looking up into his eyes. Even with the shock she had just given him, Argyle felt his body surrender to her presence. 'You are married?'

Celeste slid her left hand up Argyle's arm, her fingers curling into his hair when she reached his neck. She pressed against his thigh, her right hand coursing up and down his back. For a while, Argyle gave in to her caresses. She was tantalizing, her breath quick and her lips so desirable that he could do nothing but kiss her in return, when she reached up for him.

Panting, Argyle pulled away, holding Celeste at arm's length. 'How long have you been married?' He hardly recognised his own voice.

'For years,' Celeste said. 'The match was made when I was 14. One day, I was simply put in a litter and carried off to a grand house. Within were my parents, a priest and an old man - my husband. We were wedded and bedded before I knew what had happened.'

'Old man?' Argyle asked incredulous.

'Rich, old man,' Celeste said. 'We might be nobles, but we were poor and my parents did not like being poor. The duke paid handsomely for my hand in marriage, my parents could hardly refuse, and besides, they thought he would not last long.'

'How old?' Argyle refused to believe that life would be so cruel as to once more cheat him out of a chance of love.

'He is almost 70 by now,' Celeste said. 'I have not seen him for years. The King called upon me to wait upon the Princess, and when the Princess was married to your King, she asked me to come. I think partly out of pity, partly because she knows.'

'She knows?!' Argyle was shocked to think that the Princess should know of such adult matters.

'I cannot steal out of her service whenever I choose unless she knows.' Celeste paced back and forth, wringing her hands in despair. 'I have not said it is you though she suspects it to be so. It is easier that way. For all I know, he might have died, and I have simply not been informed yet.'

'Celeste!' Argyle stopped her pacing and drew her close. 'We cannot … I cannot …'

'But I want nothing from you. Is that not easy? If I were free, I would want marriage, I would want honesty, I would want it all, but I am not free, and so all I want is you.' Celeste looked up, her sky-blue eyes bright with tears. 'I just want you.'

'What if …?' Argyle dared not ask.

'What if I get with child?' Celeste finished his question. 'Then I will go home, I will birth the child and love it because it will be half yours.

My husband will despise me, but last I heard he was living openly with his housekeeper as his mistress, letting her sit at high table and entertain his guests. He will have nothing to put past me, and I will have the future Queen of England to vouch for me.'

Argyle nodded, Celeste was hardly the first young woman to be thrown into the arms of an old man, nor the first woman to suffer that her husband preferred someone else. Tears began spilling down her cheeks, and he pulled her into a tight embrace where her tears bled through his shirt. He looked down at her feeling her pain and despair.

When she finally looked up, Argyle kissed her soft lips forcefully, and she threw her arms around his neck. He carried her around the side of the dais, which was flooded in twisting shadows from the candles illuminating the red throne and the steps. He ran his hands down her lacing, finding the ends and pulling hard at them until he felt Celeste's dress give way. She released her grip just long enough to shrug off the dress, and Argyle drew breath at the sight of her.

Celeste gasped as he grabbed her hard, hauling her up and positioning her up the side of the dais, her naked body ready for him. As he slid inside her, Celeste moaned and Argyle felt no regret that he was at this moment having another man's wife. If that man had any sense, he would never have let Celeste go, no matter who had demanded her attendance at court; if her husband was so foolish as to send her off to join a young court, he must have known this might happen.

Argyle felt ripples of joy and desire chase through his body, he felt Celeste shiver and quicken the pace, the two of them joining to be one, to be free of the world, of court, of duty and responsibility. Celeste came first, her jerking movements and muffled cries urging Argyle on, until he too felt sweet release. He slowly fell to his knees, Celeste sliding down the dais wall with him, her thighs tight around his waist, her hands buried in his hair, her lips blindly seeking his. They kissed for a long time, not wanting to let the moment go, not ready to be untangled.

Argyle could smell her sweet sweat, the scent of orange blossom in her soft hair. The heavy scent of her womanhood was so powerful that he felt instantly aroused again. Celeste smiled as if to say that she too was ready, and that they could go on forever, and that he was all she ever wanted.

'I was right when I first met you in France.' Celeste sighed. 'I was right when I said that the still waters run deepest.'

'And I was a fool.' Argyle buried his face in her hair, kissing her ear.

'I was a fool not to know that a woman this beautiful would be married.'

'I will not spoil the moment,' Celeste insisted. 'I will be free here and happy, and I will have all our moments to treasure. I want more moments, I never want them to end.'

CHAPTER 11

30 October 1396 - Westminster

The King and Princess sat on the high dais, sending dishes around and speaking amicably to each other. Next to the King, his uncle John of Gaunt loomed crouched over his food with a tired look on his face. Rumour had it he was working day and night to keep the peace in England, a task few if any envied him.

Argyle accepted a dish from the Princess, saluting her with his cup before tasting the delicious venison. The hall was buzzing with laughter, talk and servants coming and going. He had been keeping an eye on Celeste, the afternoon from the day before was still vibrant in his mind. He felt no remorse, but he had to admit that being a married woman's lover, exciting though it was, was not what he wanted. Margaret had thought he might marry Celeste and he had begun to think it a real possibility. Now that option was gone.

Bolingbroke came into the hall, resplendent in bright green and purple, bowing swiftly to the royal couple and nodding to his father. Argyle noticed Bolingbroke scan the room as though he was looking for someone in particular. As he made his way across the room, Argyle got up and walked around some of the trestle tables towards the windows. It was an uncommonly warm October evening and he suddenly felt the need for some air.

When he skirted one of the smooth pillars, he saw Celeste walk along the wall towards him. Argyle smiled at her, but she had not seen him, she kept her pace but her eyes were fixed on something else, her face turned away. Argyle looked around and saw Bolingbroke approach.

Argyle slipped into one of the window bays, the heavy curtains halfway drawn to allow in the fresh air but prevent too much of a draft. Celeste stopped short of the window bay and was joined by Bolingbroke. Argyle frowned, he had no idea the two of them knew each other, although Bolingbroke would certainly have noticed the beautiful woman just as the rest of the court had.

'My Lady.' Bolingbroke grabbed Celeste's hand and kissed it.

'My Lord.' Celeste let Bolingbroke hold her hand. 'I thought you would not join the court.'

'Certain matters demanded my attention.' Bolingbroke stepped closer and slid his hand around Celeste's waist. Argyle felt a surge of uninvited anger and willed Celeste to step away, but she kept still, accepting the embrace.

'How interesting, my Lord.' Celeste graced Bolingbroke with a winning smile. 'I was sure you would return to Pontefract and oversee your father's affairs.'

'And why would I do that, my Lady?' Bolingbroke released her and looked around the room.

Celeste moved a little closer. 'Duty, my Lord?'

Bolingbroke laughed, his eyes still darting around the room. 'There is duty and there is blood, the two are not necessarily the same, my Lady. As you may well know.'

Argyle saw Celeste stiffen. 'Whatever do you mean?'

'That I know what you have been up to at court while I have been away,' Bolingbroke said softly as he grabbed her arm tight. 'And I do not like, what I hear. I do not like what I hear at all.'

Celeste stepped further into the shadows, drawing Bolingbroke with her. They stopped just short of the window bay Argyle was hiding in, his anger now mingling with worry that they might stumble upon him.

'I thought we could trust each other,' Celeste said, her smile forced. 'I thought you and I understood each other.'

'Oh but we do, my Lady.' Bolingbroke pulled her close enough for them to kiss. 'We understood each other perfectly - and then you went and found yourself a lover.' Celeste recoiled, but Bolingbroke fixed his grip on her. 'You should not have done that.'

'I think you forget yourself, my Lord.'

'No, it is you who forget yourself.' Bolingbroke's smile never reached his cold, calculating eyes. 'And of all the fools at court, you could have chosen, you go and pick the one person, I could not endure. I told you, I could keep you safe, in the palace and in the country. That I would house you if it came to it, but you defy me, and that I cannot bear.'

'What will you do?' Celeste asked, her voice masking the fear that was plain on her face. Argyle held his breath.

'Nothing for the moment,' Bolingbroke said. 'Actually, I will ask that you keep up your little charade for the time being. It might prove useful to me - and to you.'

Celeste pulled free, staring at Bolingbroke with disdain. 'And what if I tell the Princess and ask her to release me that I might go home and tend to my old, sickly husband?'

'We both know that your old, sickly husband is half the reason that you are here in the first place, my dear,' Bolingbroke said. 'Do not for one moment think that you can deceive me. Perhaps your charm works on all others - and pulling up your skirt certainly does - but I know you for what you are.'

Bolingbroke stepped close, and Argyle pushed as far back into the window bay as he could. He could see Celeste now, her face so close that if he reached out, he could touch her hair, but luckily, she could not see him, her face was turned towards the hall.

'The Princess needs me,' she said, trying to get away.

But Bolingbroke moved quickly, grabbing her arms and drawing her in. 'She can wait, but I cannot. Come and see me tonight that we might discuss matters further. I insist.'

'Very well,' Celeste sneered. 'I will come tonight, my Lord, but the Princess will know who I am visiting.'

'Oh, you would not want to distress the Princess, my dear,' Bolingbroke said. 'Best if she is kept innocent.'

Celeste turned abruptly away from Bolingbroke, and Argyle just managed to keep out of sight when she brushed past his hiding place to reclaim her place among the ladies-in-waiting. Bolingbroke smirked as he walked along the wall, never glancing into the window bay.

His mind whirling with thoughts, Argyle excused himself at the table, and signalled for his squire that it was time to go. Whatever was going on, there would be just one way to find out, and Argyle did not like the idea at all, but he also did not like thinking that Bolingbroke knew about his affair with Celeste.

One way or another, Argyle had to find out just how much Bolingbroke really knew.

ꕤ ꕤ

Later that evening, Argyle was making his way from the stables of his London house when the sound of hooves stirred him from his deep thoughts. It was late, who might come at this hour?

'M'lord!'

Argyle looked up at the sound of a familiar voice. 'You are a long way from home, George, and it is late.'

'I have been riding all day, and I got lost …' George bowed his head. 'I have never been to London alone before.'

'You are here alone?' Argyle did not like the sound of that. For a boy, London might be an adventure during the day, but at night it was dangerous to roam the streets alone.

'Master Smith sent me to give you a message,' George clambered down from the horse. 'He says it can't wait, M'lord.'

Argyle called for a stable boy and patted George on the back. 'You are here now and in one piece. Where is Smith's message?'

'I was asked to deliver the message verbally.' George looked strained and tired, so Argyle steered him towards the house.

'If that is your task. You could probably do with some food?' Argyle was curious to know what Stephen wanted. He held the door open for George. 'What news?'

'M'lord.' George stopped before the fireplace in the hall, holding out his hands to the flames, his boots were thick with mud. 'Master Smith asks that you come to Beauworth as soon as possible. You are required to take care of a serious dispute concerning a young woman in one of the villages.'

Argyle wondered why Stephen could not handle it himself. The many men gathered at Beauworth did sometimes need to blow off steam; it would hardly be the first time a young woman was caught with one of his soldiers. Usually, it was resolved with a purse of silver and a promise to find a suitable husband for the girl. He opened the door to his study and smiled when George followed him, sighing with pleasure at the warmth of the room.

'She has been accused of witchcraft.' George coughed and wiped his nose on his sleeve.

Argyle's smile faded. 'By whom?'

'Her own husband and several of the men in the village. Now they say, she has spellbound one of your soldiers.' George squirmed. 'She is with child.'

'What of it?' Argyle did not like the sound of George's tale one bit.

'Her husband wants her tried and punished as a witch, before she births the babe.'

Argyle shook his head slowly - without doubt, the boy had got it wrong. Why would any man ask that his own wife be tried as a witch? There was something menacing about the matter.

'Smith did right to send you.' Argyle paused to consider what to do. 'I must send word to the King that I have to leave court.'

George fidgeted by the fireplace, and Argyle noticed that the boy looked thin and worn. 'Go and get something to eat and a good night's rest. Tomorrow, we ride for Beauworth. You did good, George.'

Argyle pointed George in the direction of the kitchen and the boy shuffled down the hall while Argyle went back into his study. The King would understand, and he could but hope that when he sent word to the Princess of his departure, she would tell Celeste. He wondered when he would see her again and if, perhaps, it was not better to be called from court than to stay and fall in love with a woman who was not free.

A witch at Beauworth, Argyle thought as he sat down at his desk and drew out a fresh piece of paper. He had never truly believed in witches but knew that most others did, and that they believed witches were dangerous creatures. He would have to resolve the matter quickly before it got out of control.

Argyle finished his message to the King and decided to dispatch it first thing in the morning along with a message for the Princess at Windsor. Despite the troubling news from home, the conversation between Celeste and Bolingbroke still weighed heavily on his mind when he went to his bedroom. What was their connection? Could she be having an affair with Bolingbroke too? Argyle threw off his clothes and paced the room. She claimed to love only him, but could she be trusted? A woman who cheated openly on her husband?

But if it was not an affair, what might tie Celeste and Bolingbroke together? Argyle pushed away the dark and sinister thought that perhaps Bolingbroke was forcing Celeste to spy on the Princess - or worse, the King. Surely she would refuse to do such a thing. Unless Bolingbroke knew something that he could use to force her?

Argyle lay back on the bed and closed his eyes. He would have to deal swiftly with the witch. For the first time, he actually wanted to stay in London. His troubled mind ran wild that night, pelting him with old, distorted memories and visions of Celeste, swooning in Bolingbroke's arms, burning pyres and blood trickling down stone walls.

He woke in a sweat, no more rested than when he had gone to bed, and he spent the rest of the night walking restlessly around his bedroom. He decided to return to court before Christmas at the latest. Matters must be resolved.

PART II

Betrayal

CHAPTER 12

9 November 1396 - Beauworth

Argyle had expected his journey back to Beauworth to provide some rest and time to consider Bolingbroke's connection to Celeste, and not least to contain his infatuation with her. However, as he clattered into the courtyard at the head of his retinue, his concerns had grown rather than diminished. Stephen met him in the courtyard and asked that they might speak privately as soon as possible. It was clear that the allegations of a witch in their midst had taken a heavy toll on him, his eyes darted constantly around the courtyard and his voice was strained.

Putting his own speculations aside, Argyle agreed to meet the same evening, which gave him precious little time to tuck away his obsession with Celeste in a dark corner of his mind and turn his attention to the matter at hand. Now both Stephen and Argyle sat in his study nursing cups of ale and staring blankly into the air.

Argyle finally broke the silence. 'What news, Smith?'

'We have had a few problems with the new men, but they are settling in nicely now. It is always a little difficult to secure an easy transition from one house to another.' Stephen skirted the matter that had brought Argyle home, and he decided that perhaps it was better to wait.

'Yes and from one master to another. How many have come since I have been away?'

Stephen counted in his head for a moment, making sure not to miss anyone. '12, most of them very green but I see promise in some. One or two may decide they're better off serving God. Thank the Lord, we've several churches in such easy distance.'

Every year, a few of Argyle's new recruits decided against the fighting life of a soldier and gave up their romantic dreams of tournaments and knighthood substituting them for a position in the church. Some decided to become monks but those of noble blood had their families pay for an education in the clergy.

'That is always the case. Let them figure it out in their own time.' Argyle circled his desk to the pitcher of small ale and a couple of crude pewter cups. As he poured, he took in the view from his narrow window overlooking the training field and further on one of the small villages. The peace of Beauworth never seized to amaze him.

Argyle turned to offer one of the cups to Stephen. 'Thank you. Being your steward is thirsty work.'

'I should like to think so. Never underestimate the mountain of work I carry out while you are in the training field, cuddling the recruits.' Argyle stretched. It would be much easier to enjoy his return to Beauworth if he was not seated in front of the clutter on his desk. 'Sometimes, I wonder if you have the easier life. How is Bessie?'

'Beautiful as ever. Lucky for her, I like my women plump.'

Argyle smiled. Stephen had settled down with a sweet woman who had proved very fertile. They already had two strapping boys to show for it, and now Bessie was with child once more. It seemed as good a time as ever to broach the matter they had avoided thus far. 'This witchcraft business.' Argyle said. 'What is your view?'

Stephen scratched his neck and then began working his right shoulder as if it was stiff from a day of fighting. 'It's a serious accusation.'

'Certainly, and should not be taken lightly. Have you found out anything?' Argyle asked.

'Not much. The village is in uproar and have ousted the young woman. If she's a witch, there'll be Hell to pay.' Stephen took a swig from the cup. He had nowhere to put it in Argyle's sparsely furnished study.

'But surely you are mistaken that her own husband has not spoken in her defence?'

'No. He names her witch too,' Stephen said. 'He claims that she's taken his manhood.'

'I hear he is old.'

'Not that old.' Stephen moved a little in his seat, looking into his half-empty cup. When he looked up again, his eyes were grave. 'I don't like it. If she's a witch, we must rid ourselves of her. If she's not …'

'If she is not, how can she prove it?' Argyle knew that the young woman's prospects were bleak. 'How many have spoken against her?'

'Half the village, and more come forth every day,' Stephen said, balancing the now empty cup on his knee.

'And in our house?' Argyle hoped George had been wrong about that part of the message.

'Bonfrey. I just can't figure out why he didn't speak up sooner,' Stephen said.

'Perhaps he did not know any better.' Argyle rested his elbows on the smooth oak tabletop trying to remember what Bonfrey looked like. He had been away too long the men's faces were a blur to him. 'What do you think?'

'The truth? I think Bonfrey was infatuated. When she denied him - for whatever reason - he felt the slight enough to side with the husband - and the other men,' Stephen said.

Argyle grabbed the edge of the table. 'Other men?'

'Several have come forth stating that she's bewitched them.' Stephen got up to replenish his cup. 'She's pretty, I gather, but if that's a crime then we're in dire trouble.'

Half the world would be infested with witches, if looks were enough to condemn them, Argyle thought. Still, something had to be done. 'I shall have to hear this matter as soon as possible, it will not keep until May, when the Marshal is next in town.'

'No, it won't.' Although Stephen tried to keep his tone energetic, the dark circles around his eyes betrayed exhaustion. 'If you don't react right away, they'll judge her on their own, and then you'll have murder on your hands.'

'Send word to the villagers tomorrow that I am back, and that I will hear their case this coming Monday,' Argyle decided. 'If you have not already seized the woman, do so right away. She is not safe in the village, and if she is a witch, the village is not safe either. Find a room somewhere here for her but not in a cell. Until I know more, I will not have her treated poorly.'

CHAPTER 13

14 November 1396 - Beauworth

'My Lord, surely you recognise that this is a petty, belittled man?' There was fury in the young woman's voice as well as pleading.

Argyle leaned back and returned the woman's fiery glare. 'I have heard little to convince me that your sister is not a witch.'

'Then you have failed to listen!' Her words whipped around the great hall, which had been stripped of its furniture to make room for the hearing. It was crammed with people but quiet as a tomb apart from her voice. 'If you had, you would know that all of these men are fools. They swoon at a simple smile thinking they have a right to a woman because she is kind. Then they do with her as they wish, and she is left the villain?' She spat the words as her sister cringed, folding her hands in a protective gesture over her swollen belly. Some of the men at the opposite side of the room even took a precautionary step back.

Argyle rested his hands lightly on the arms of the great chair that he had ordered to be placed on the dais in place of his usual bench. Acutely aware that everyone was watching him, he fixed her with his gaze. 'I shall have words with them later. But why would all of them name her a witch if they have no proof?'

'It is easier to conceal your own crimes by accusing someone else of something worse than to own up. This is what is happening here. If you ask her, my sister would not even be able to tell you, which of the men is the father of her child. They have all had their way with her so many times it beggars belief.' She gave him a sharp look. 'And right under your watchful eye!'

Argyle could not deny that the men had their own crimes to own up to. Just as he thought to speak, the accused woman's husband protested. 'She's a whore, a slut! She gave herself to anyone who'd have her!'

'Clearly, she did not give herself to you, since you are so quick to lash out!' the sister spat.

'Why'd I sully myself in her flesh?' The old man did not waver. 'She'd mate with the Devil, if he asked her - Hell, she's probably already had him too!'

His young wife began to cry and slid to the floor, folding over as if trying to vanish into her own womb.

Argyle scowled at the crowd. Before either party could speak another word, he held out a warning hand. 'Enough!'

The sister caught her breath, but Argyle silenced her with a stern look. Her jaw working, she appeared to hold her tongue by sheer effort.

'You all agree that she is a witch?' Argyle asked the men who nodded in unison. Only Bonfrey, Argyle's soldier, paused and looked troubled before he nodded too.

'You will have her tried?' Argyle asked.

Another uniform nod from the crowd, as a sob rose from the woman on the floor. Her sister moved to stand protectively before her. She was clearly furious. Argyle squared his shoulders and breathed heavily, he did not like what came next, not at all.

He rose and, nodding to the village priest, passed judgement. 'Tilly, you shall be handed over to the church to be questioned and tried for witchcraft.'

The young woman began to wail, curling onto the floor and gripping her sister's hem tightly. The look Argyle received from the sister was one of utter disbelief and fury. Then she fell to her knees and hugged her sister tightly, glaring at the men.

Argyle cleared his throat. 'All of you will be asked to make your statements to the priest. Including you Bonfrey. One way or another, we shall have the truth of what has passed here.'

Without another word, Argyle turned and left the room, his hands icy and his ears burning. It was not over yet.

By evening, the great hall was once more set up with tables and benches, the smell of stew and freshly baked bread wafted around every time the doors from the kitchen corridor opened. Stephen joined Argyle on the low dais surveying the men while they ate. The hall rang with laughter.

Argyle was brooding over his supper, pushing a piece of meat around with the tip of his knife. 'Why do I feel that I have been manipulated?'

'There was nothing you could do but hand her over to the church. If she is a witch, the priest will know what to do,' Stephen said.

'Really?'

'You think that she is no witch?'

Argyle pushed away from the table. 'Walk with me. This hall has prying ears.'

Stephen followed him out of the hall and into the study across the narrow passageway, looking round before closing the door firmly. Argyle closed the shutters on the biting November cold. 'The woman is hardly a witch. I suspect the men are covering for each other.'

'How so?' Stephen asked.

'Her sister claimed they had all had their way with her. Against her will.' Argyle felt sick at the thought.

Stephen, who had not been present at the hearing, looked disgusted. 'And the husband allowed this?'

'That is what I do not understand. He is old enough to be her father, but to allow young men to take his wife … what kind of man would do that?'

'One eager to be rid of her!' Stephen's voice was thick with outrage.

Argyle clenched his fists to contain his anger. 'Fetch me Bonfrey.'

✧ ✧ ✧ ✧

'Tell me true. Are you bewitched?'

The young soldier stood straight as an arrow in front Argyle who was seated in the massive oak chair behind his desk. Bonfrey gulped. His big eyes screamed with fear of being summoned and commanded to explain his conduct. Stephen crossed his arms and glared at Bonfrey.

'Well?!' Argyle pushed for an answer.

'I … She was enticing …' Bonfrey mumbled.

'Women are,' Argyle said dismissively. 'That does not make every woman a witch.'

'She … When I look at her, my mind goes blank. I cannot think as I should, I do not know what to do.' Bonfrey seemed to gain momentum and pushed on. 'She would bring me little gifts at first. Charms and herbs, oils she had made herself. It seemed harmless enough. She would lean in and give me this … look. You see, I suffer from headaches, and she said that her oils could make it better. So I used them. Rather than getting better I began feeling sick. My head would hurt worse than ever before. I would wake up in places, I didn't remember going to. More than once, I found myself in her bed.'

Argyle motioned him on, best to get it over with.

'She would sit on the edge of the bed, caress my temples and sing.' Bonfrey stared at his feet, his ears red. 'I could not make out the words. I would watch her through half-closed eyes as she moved around, picking out herbs and strange things, pounding them together and rubbing them on my forehead.'

'That sounds more like the workings of a wise woman.' Argyle tapped his fingers on the desk.

'She is a witch,' Bonfrey whispered while looking intently at Stephen, perhaps trying to find an ally. 'She is a witch, and I want to se her punished. One day, her husband came in. He threw a fit, hitting her and screaming at me to get out. My head was splitting, and his words cut through my body like knives. What if she had enticed me to have relations with her? I didn't even remember going to her.'

Argyle found this hard to believe. 'Not even once?'

'The first time, perhaps. One of the other soldiers told me she had cured his toothache.' Bonfrey shuffled his feet. Clearly he had not intended to let this slip, and Argyle gave him an inquisitive stare. 'I forget who,' Bonfrey muttered.

'Best you remember. For the sake of all of you,' Argyle warned him.

'All of us, M'lord?'

'If you think I will send an innocent woman through a trial of the church, then you are sorely mistaken! Who told you?' Argyle asked trying to conceal his sense of foreboding. He had been too long at court.

That night, Argyle spoke to more men than he had wanted to and learned much less than he had hoped for.

1 December 1396 - Beauworth

Bonfrey withdrew his accusations, Argyle had a feeling the young man would soon turn to the church; he was not cut out for a life as a soldier. The other men in the village stood their ground, and the husband got his way. His wife was tried for witchcraft. Argyle went to the church every day to hear new crimes laid before the bewildered priest. It seemed the entire village had decided that the young woman was guilty. Her sister sat by her side throughout the whole ordeal listening to one horrid accusation after another.

The village women claimed that she had lured them into the cemetery at midnight to dance and call upon the Devil. They told tales of children born with their intestines on the outside, cats that gathered before her door, young men driven mad by her. The men were quick to agree, naming her a seducer and a sorcerer. Even children stepped forward and claimed that she had revived dead animals and made them do her bidding.

Throughout the grizzly trial, the young woman seemed to waste away. Every day she looked thinner and more haggard than before. She trembled when anyone spoke and, towards the end, she could hardly stand. Her swollen belly looked abnormally large on her scrawny body.

Finally, the village had had their say. Argyle witnessed as the priest stuttered his way through the evidence, finding it hard to look at the young woman, probably because he was worried she might bewitch him too. Throughout his speech, the church room was quiet as the grave.

'Tilly, I sentence you to a trial of water,' the priest declared. 'If you sink, you are innocent! If you float, you are guilty! Do you take God as your witness and repent that he might aid you?'

Tilly's hands and knees were raw, her dress dirty and her hair mattered. She did not stir even when the gathered villagers began to jeer and insult her. To Argyle, she seemed to have given up. But her sister had not and she put up a fight.

'My sister has nothing to repent!' Her voice seethed at the injustice. 'Other than choosing such a lousy husband!' She spun around, raising a finger shaking with fury. 'And all of you, may you rot in Hell! That is where you belong! Tilly was good enough when you needed someone to help you birth a babe or bind a wound. She was good enough when you wanted something to ward off more children. But you could not keep your husbands from her. Drunken, filthy whoremongers! You raped her!'

The priest tried to silence her and only succeeded in bringing her burning resentment down on his head instead. 'And you! There is a special place in Hell for priests who do others' bidding! You mark my words …'

'QUIET!' Argyle cut her short. The way she was calling out curses, he might end up with a second witch trial. She was momentarily shocked by his commanding voice; but recovered fast. Argyle continued, raising his voice to drown hers out. 'Father, I handed the matter over to the church, and I have been here every day, listening to everyone's concerns. I know you have little choice in the matter but to put her to trial, and yet I will vouch for the woman! Until I am satisfied that the claims against her are true or false, she will be my prisoner!'

The villagers were clearly thrown by Argyle's decision. Some began to argue, but settled down when he gave them a stern look. For all that he had just cheated them of the spectacle of a witch's death, they dared not argue with the man who governed their lands and lives and, if he saw fit, could turn them out to a beggar's life. Their disgruntled murmurs quickly dwindled under Argyle's withering stare. He was grabbing the rail before him so tight, he heard the wood creak beneath his fingers.

'I have asked for a royal marshal to review the evidence,' Argyle snarled. 'His verdict will be final. That is my decision! All of you - go home to your wives, children and husbands. Go home and be satisfied that if Tilly is a witch, she is locked away and can do you no harm.'

As two soldiers marched the young woman out of the church and towards the Beauworth stronghold, Stephen fell into step with Argyle. 'I know of no such message being sent, M'lord.'

'Then you will know soon enough.'

ꟷ

A week later, the royal marshal came for Tilly. As she walked out the door, she squinted at the low sun and clutched her belly tightly, her arms and legs were thin as sticks.

Argyle made sure that he had a moment alone with the marshal, before they left.

ꟷ

CHAPTER 14

15 December 1396 - Beauworth

Argyle was leaning heavily on his table, discussing with Stephen, which new recruits to take on when a servant opened the door. 'M'lord, a visitor for you.'

'Can he wait?' Argyle pushed a couple of documents aside to make space on the cluttered desk for the stack of papers concerning the men they would accept.

'It is a woman, M'lord.'

The two men looked at each other, Stephen's brow furrowed.

'Let her wait in the hall, until we are finished,' Argyle said. 'It will not take long.'

'She is in the kitchens.'

Argyle looked at the flustered servant. 'Then I will find her there.'

As the door closed, Argyle turned to find Stephen looking at him with a crooked smile. 'A woman?'

'You know as much as I do.' He wondered if it might be Celeste, and part of him hoped so. It had proved impossible to go to court for Christmas and the more Argyle had thought about it, the less he wanted to return to see Celeste and Bolingbroke together again. He had had little enough time to contemplate what the two of them might share and, lately, he had to fight off vivid dreams of Celeste and Bolingbroke in hard embraces, her skirts hiked up and his cold smile at her willingness.

'Then it is a great mystery. This will keep, if you want to …' Stephen ripped Argyle from his speculations.

'No, let us get this out of the way,' Argyle said and swept a gesture at the desk, 'then you can send the messages out today.'

ꕤ ꕤ

Argyle found his visitor in the kitchens, sitting close to one of the ovens. Her cloak hung by the side, dripping from the sleet outside, the hem crusted with dirt. She had her back turned to him, a slender figure with a long auburn plait. He was reminded of another woman thousands of miles away and blinked to clear his mind.

Just then, one of the cooks looked up in surprise, and the woman turned around. 'My Lord. How kind of you to see me.'

Argyle felt a surge of surprise. It was Tilly's sister, though for the life of him, he could not remember being told her name. 'Of course, Mistress. Follow me.'

She gathered up her wet cloak and walked behind him up the narrow staircase to the main hall. Argyle instinctively turned towards his study, before changing his mind and leading her into a parlour on the opposite side of the hallway.

Inside, she perched on the edge of the chair Argyle offered her beside the hearth. Flames licked slowly over the logs, and one of the servants had sprinkled the wood with pine needles, which gave the room a sharp, comfortable scent. Argyle pulled up another chair and offered her some refreshments. Once the servant had poured mulled wine into two cups, he left the room.

She sipped the wine. 'I wanted to apologise.'

'What for?'

'My behaviour in the church … and before then.' She sounded a little insincere. 'I was concerned for my sister.'

'And justly so.' Argyle had not liked the way the trial had ended, but a witch was dangerous to have around - even if he believed that Tilly was just a wrongly accused woman.

'Why did you send for the marshal?' Her voice summoned him back.

'Some things are best not left to the church. They see demons even where there are none.'

She looked surprised. 'You speak from personal experience?'

Argyle just smiled. Many things could be left to the church, but some matters were better left in the care of those who understood the law of the land. However she took this smile, she concealed it. 'My sister was found guilty. I was told someone pleaded her case but in vain.'

'I am sorry. You may rest assured that the men in the village have paid for their crimes.'

'She was not a witch, you know?' she said passionately. 'She just understood herbs, our mother taught her - taught both of us. They put my sister to the stake for being able to cure a headache.'

'Whatever the case, it is done now,' Argyle said uncomfortable with the truth in her words.

She stood, the fluent motion sending a ripple through her heavy skirt. Moving around the room, she traced a finger over the edge of the table, the back of a chair, the windowsill. Argyle was reminded again of another time and place with another woman. In the half-dark of the small parlour, her hair was almost black, though when she returned to the firelight, it took on the colour of copper and gold.

'You understand my … actions?'

'Of course. We all love our family, even if they sometimes stray,' Argyle said and rose to turn his back on her.

'Stray?'

Laughing a little, Argyle poured another cup of wine for both of them. 'I spoke out of turn.'

'It sounds interesting.' She watched him. 'Perhaps we could speak out of turn again, some time?'

'Why did you come here?' Argyle put down the pitcher.

'You tried to save her by sending for the marshal.'

'To no avail.' Argyle forced an image of the scrawny woman burning on the pyre from his mind. Against his better judgement, he had felt compelled to be present at her execution, so it seemed had half the village. He still remembered Tilly's husband standing so close to the flames that the soldiers had to push him back, his gaze had been mad. Argyle closed his eyes and sighed.

'It was out of everyone's hands. I still bear a grudge to the villagers.' Her voice was level, free from emotion.

Argyle motioned her to sit, and once more she made that fluent motion. 'They were scared.'

Handing her one of the cups, he felt an unexpected jolt when her fingers brushed against his. She caught his eye. 'Of a woman?'

'Of something they did not understand,' Argyle said and cleared his throat. 'They know that, in the end, they will all be tried in the greatest courtroom of them all.'

'God's?' She sounded bemused.

'Yes. We must all stand before God and be judged.'

'You believe this?'

'I once travelled a great distance to see our Lord saviour's tomb. It makes an impression.' As Argyle turned towards her once again, he noticed her smile for the first time. Little dimples in her flushed cheeks, her eyes twinkling. Argyle broke eye contact and sat down. 'You will stay as a guest, I hope? I should like to know more about your sister. And I should like to know your name.'

'Isobel. Tilly was my half-sister.'

CHAPTER 15

Christmas 1396 - Beauworth

In the days of December, Argyle doled out even more food to his tenants than usual, ensuring their loyalty by filling their bellies, just as La Fontaine had taught him. Every night, Stephen and the head cook would count the barrels of salted fish and pork, the bushels of grain and sides of bacon. Argyle approved the spending without much concern; his mind was preoccupied with his visitor.

He had been watching Isobel with the servants and observing how she got on with the soldiers. Argyle already knew that she could hold her own but he wondered what others made of her. Especially since Isobel had gained quite a reputation during her sister's trial, but his household seemed not to mind her presence.

'Remarkable woman.' Stephen was chewing on a baked apple. He shot Argyle a smirk before continuing. 'How's she settling in?'

'Why do you think she is settling in?' Argyle asked.

'Put it this way; if you have eyes for her, better make it known now, before someone else beats you to it. Women like her don't go without a husband for long.' Stephen finished off his apple, licking his fingers.

Argyle sighed in despair. He had thought his interest in Isobel was a secret. He did not even know exactly what kind of interest it was. Perhaps it was simply the thought of having a woman at Beauworth that was enticing. 'What would you do?'

'Tell her. She's still here, even though her sister was burned as a witch - condemned to death in your village.' Stephen glanced at Isobel. 'Clearly, she doesn't think you're so foul that she'd not consider you.'

'Thank you for that.'

'I think highly of what you did, but even you can't have thought that it'd save her sister?'

Argyle shrugged. 'Maybe not, but I had hoped it would have saved the babe.'

Stephen shook his head. 'They never do, they're afraid she'll give birth to the Devil's child. Better to burn it with its mother. Perhaps they're now reunited in Heaven, I won't believe she's a witch or that she's dancing in Hell now.'

'You believe in Heaven?' Argyle asked.

'Yes. And I believe it's full of women.' Stephen winked at his plump wife, Bessie who was hauling in plates of food for the hungry men. 'Thank the Lord, I don't have to wait until Heaven to get me one!'

Argyle laughed, as Stephen danced away, grabbing Bessie by her hands and swinging her about merrily. She seemed well pleased to be dancing with a man who had half a baked apple in his beard.

'My Lord.' It was all but a whisper in Argyle's ear, yet it sent a tingling through his body, his hairs rising ever so slightly. He could smell Isobel's sweet breath and almost feel the warmth from her body. Carefully, he turned his head; her face was inches from his. She looked out over the crowd. 'I do not think, we will be missed.'

ꕤ ꕤ

Argyle closed the door gently and then turned towards the room. The only light came from the fire in the hearth, the wood crackled in the flames. But then a candle lit, and another. Isobel was working her way around the room, lighting the candles as she went. Argyle increasingly thought of the parlour as her room, he would often find her sitting in there staring into the fire or out of the window, occasionally clutching a book.

Argyle cleared his throat to speak, but Isobel put a finger to her lips. 'Sit.'

He was curious what she wanted. Once Isobel had finished, she threw the thin smouldering stick into the fire and sat down opposite him. 'You have often asked for my forgiveness. And I have forgiven you; you acted only as you had to. But there are things in my past you must know, things that might make you see me differently.'

Even she knows that I have been watching her, Argyle thought. He once more cursed his own ignorance and looked at her. 'You owe me no explanation.'

'No,' Isobel said. 'But I offer one. If we are to chance a life together, you must know. It is what I want.'

Argyle was caught completely off guard at her speaking openly of a possible future together, although he had entertained the idea, it had only been to divert his thoughts from Celeste. Not once had he thought that Isobel would consider him for a future husband - given their history together. What woman would marry the man who sentenced her sister to death? Even if he had tried his best to save Tilly. Stephen was right of course, not even Argyle had truly believed he would be able change the sentence.

He tried to appear composed. 'Very well.'

Isobel locked eyes with him. The intimacy of staring into her eyes made Argyle's pulse quicken. 'Ask me anything.' Her whisper made his head swim.

Leaning back, Argyle took in the sight of her, the light of the fire casting shadows on her face and dress, her eyes glittering. She wore her hair up this night, her long, creamy neck exposed. His mind had gone blank. 'What do you want to tell me?'

'Anything you want to know. Everything.'

'Then begin wherever you choose.'

'There must be something you want to know?' she said.

Argyle thought for a moment, his head finally clear again. He had been disappointed once before - best to get it out of the way. She spoke of a future, but was she free? 'Are you married?'

Isobel's eyes darkened for a moment, her face grew sombre and tense. Argyle could see her shoulders shiver a little, and she crossed her arms as if to protect herself. 'No. But I have been.'

'What happened?'

'We fell in love.' Isobel looked into the fire. 'At least, I fell in love. He was beautiful, a little older than me and I thought he was much wiser than me. He was from an important family, free to choose whoever he desired. I was naïve. The family claimed I seduced him. I was just a servant girl, the daughter of a farmer. His station was well above mine. Now I know it was the other way around, and he soon became the object of my every desire. I could not breathe, think, eat, if I did not see him. He said that he felt the same way, and that we must be together. That he would marry me, if I gave myself to him. I struggled to resist. I was in love,' Isobel said gripping the armrests tightly.

'He had his way, in the end. Most men do, I suppose,' she continued. Her jaw worked. 'Not the way the villagers violated my sister; I gave myself freely. Perhaps it was a mistake, but at the time, it seemed the wisest choice I had ever made. My father found out and confronted his father. Before we knew it, we were before a priest saying our vows. I was dizzy with love.'

Isobel kept staring into the flames, seemingly lost in her memories. 'His family did not care for me. He had been destined for a great match, he was nobility and should have married an heiress, it was all but a given when my father turned up and demanded that he marry me. He said that he did not care that he only cared for me and that we would be happy. I believed him.' She cleared her throat; her eyes were bright with tears.

Argyle went to fetch some wine. When he turned around, Isobel was looking steadily at him. 'You think me weak.'

'No,' Argyle said. The longer she had spoken of her former husband, the less she looked to miss him. But he wondered how a farmer could have persuaded a nobleman to let his son and heir marry a servant.

'Silly then? Marrying above my station,' she insisted.

'No.'

'He was cruel,' Isobel said flatly.

Argyle did not know what to say. Had she not just declared the two to be in love? Isobel seemed to read his mind. 'I was in love. He was not. He had thought that he could have his way with me and still marry the other woman. As it turned out, he had never wanted me but for entertainment. I almost think I could have forgiven him if he had been honest. At least then, I could have been spared what came next.'

'You do not have to tell me, if …' Argyle said.

'You need to know.' Isobel gathered strength from somewhere deep inside. 'He had other women. He would flaunt them openly before me, asking me to take them into my service. Little, silly girls who would swoon over him and giggle when he passed and smacked their backsides. He would parade them past my door at night, laughing loudly at their stupid words. Yet, all this I could have endured, I think.' Isobel clasped her trembling hands in her lap. 'When he saw that his adultery did not cower me, he began tormenting me. Hitting me for no reason.

Yelling at me and calling me names. Foul, despicable names that no woman should ever have to hear from her husband - or any other man. He would come to my bed at night and force himself on me, putting me to the belt - or worse - if I struggled. He would burn me under my feet and then have me dance for hours the next day while he laughed and glared. I thought he might be touched by the Devil.'

Rage surged through Argyle's body; he wanted to say something, but she stopped him with a willowy hand. Tears had begun running down her cheeks, but her voice was oddly detached. 'One night, he came to my bed, drunk and in a rage. He pelted me with words and fists, grabbing me by the throat and cursing me for tying him to a wretched life. Anything he could think had gone wrong, he blamed on me. When he was finally done, lying heavily on top of me, I decided that I would take no more.' She paused. 'The next night, I lay ready, pretending to be asleep, when he entered my room. He pulled the covers back and forced himself on me. Right then, I looked him in the eye and stuck a dagger in him.'

Isobel looked at Argyle with cold, defiant eyes. 'He bled to death in our bed. The next morning, I pretended to wake up and find him dead. I screamed and screamed, but not because I was sorry or felt remorse. I screamed because I was free. Then and there, I decided that no man should ever have a hold over me again.'

Argyle felt as if she had punched him. 'How did the family react?'

'They thought he had died from a rupture in the gut.'

How could they not see that the man had been killed? Justly or no, a dagger leaves a mark.

Isobel gave a cruel smile. 'I stuck the dagger up his arse. And I held it there, slowly twisting it, while his eyes bulged, and until he drew his last breath. He could not even scream. He just lay there, staring at me as I took his life.'

'You killed him.' Argyle fought not to be repulsed. Isobel's hate contorted her beauty and made her almost unbearable to face, and yet something about her demanded his sympathy. Part of him wanted to get up and leave, but he could not move.

'He would have killed me,' she said.

They sat staring at each other for a while. Isobel's eyes glazed over and distant. Argyle's mind churned, the image she had described kept surfacing, Isobel washed clean by her husbands blood.

When she spoke again, her breath was shallow and pained. 'No man will ever take my life again.'

But you told me, and I may turn against you and do just that. Take your life if I tell anyone, Argyle thought. Why had she chosen to tell him?

CHAPTER 16

6 January 1397 - Westminster Palace, London

Argyle looked around the vast presence chamber for Thomas, but there was no sign of him. The room was still decked in Christmas decorations; servants were replacing some of the old decorations made with fir and bright ribbons were being packed in heavy baskets. The fresh fir mixed with yuletide spices filled Argyle's nose, making his mouth water. The walls were covered with thick tapestries, some faded and others startling new, their colours almost an assault on the eyes. The light of hundreds of candles bounced off the jewels and fine clothes of courtiers, lords and ladies, making Westminster's halls glitter like sunlight bouncing off the surface of the sea.

Argyle had received a royal invitation to the King's 30th birthday and had reluctantly returned to London. Still troubled by what Isobel had told him, Argyle had briefly considered staying at Beauworth and making up some excuse or other, but his fragile freedom meant that he could not ignore an order that was only scantly veiled as an invitation. So, Argyle had made his way in the frozen landscape, his cloak pulled tight against the biting winter storms, hoping that the journey would shed new light on the decision he had to make.

Standing at the far end of the room, Argyle saw Isobel so vividly before him that it took a while for him to realise that the woman who was looking at him from afar was not Isobel come to plead her case again. It was Celeste. Resplendent in a gown of deep green with long, bright blue sleeves, she commanded a presence like few others in the room. Argyle could not read her expression, but when he looked at her, she quickly turned her head.

He did not know if the Princess had told Celeste of the reason for his sudden departure, but he had not seen her since her whispered words with Bolingbroke, words that still haunted him. In a weak moment, he had written to Margaret, asking her if Bolingbroke might know that Argyle was Celeste's lover. Margaret had denied it and written that she was almost positive that Bolingbroke thought it was someone in the royal family. Argyle had wondered why.

Now here was Celeste, walking slowly through the crowd, which parted before the Princess. Although surrounded by women grown, her regal manner made her look right at home rather than out of place, slight though she may be.

'Sir Argyle!' the Princess exclaimed with delight, holding out her hand for Argyle to bend over and kiss her ring. The thick purple silk of her sleeve rustled, her ruby was cold against his lips.

'Your Grace. You look remarkably well. I hope your first Christmas in England was good?' Argyle asked.

'Oh, most certainly. The King was very generous - and you sent me that beautiful brooch, it was too much, Sir Argyle!' The Princess glanced down at her flat chest where the little silver and pearl broche gleamed. She gestured for Argyle to walk with her. 'I was sad that you were not able to return for the celebrations. Of course, I understand that the matter that forced you to Beauworth was not a simple one. But I had hoped it would be quickly resolved.' She looked anxious.

'I beg your forgiveness for my absence, your Grace, it was indeed a difficult matter,' Argyle said, he had only relayed a little of the case, not wanting to worry the Princess.

She put her tiny hand gently on Argyle's sleeve and looked up at him with her big brown eyes. 'They say she sang when she burned, sang for her unborn child,' she whispered. 'How frightful! Let us not speak any more of this sad subject. You must come to my apartments, tonight.' The Princess noticed Argyle's worried looks. 'I can assure you, Sir Argyle, the King knows you were to come to my chambers the moment you got here, and that I needed to see you. He will be there too, it will all be quite proper.'

Her ladies-in-waiting let out a peal of laughter at the Princess' words, and she beamed. 'I am practicing how to flirt.' She tugged at Argyle's sleeve to make him bend down towards her. 'It is much more difficult than I thought, but I will learn.'

'Anyone can flirt, your Grace,' Argyle said returning her honest smile. 'But very few do it so easily.'

The Princess slapped his wrist and giggled. 'There, you see, you are much better at it than me!' Argyle noticed a few courtiers' resentful glances. Being favoured by the Princess was an honour that came at a price.

'Perhaps, Sir Argyle was being honest, your Grace.' Celeste's honeyed voice said behind Argyle. 'I do believe he may be the most honest man at court.'

Argyle kept his focus on the Princess. 'Thank you, my Lady, you are most kind.'

'Even I know that that was NOT flirting,' the Princess said trying to scold him. 'So you will come tonight to dine with me? I really must insist. I leave for Windsor again tomorrow.'

'Naturally, your Grace, it will be my pleasure.' Argyle was well aware of the jealous stares from the people around them.

Satisfied that she had achieved what she set out to, the Princess released him to take a second round in the room with her ladies greeting courtiers and noblemen along the way. Her chief lady-in-waiting, Lady de Coucy, gave him a curious glance.

Argyle turned to face Celeste, who had lingered behind. Up close, he noticed that her radiance had faded or perhaps his infatuation had, and he now saw her more clearly.

'We must speak!' Celeste's eyes darted around the room. 'We must speak before tonight.'

'I …' Argyle stopped at the sight of Celeste's desperate look.

'Please! You owe me this!'

'Very well, my Lady, if you wish.' Argyle looked over her head rather than into her still enticing sky-blue eyes. 'Where?'

'The gallery at three,' Celeste said and grazed his hand before turning to rejoin the Princess.

Argyle looked after her, worry churning in the pit of his stomach; she looked pale and scared. He wondered what might have happened to her during Christmas; perhaps he would find out this afternoon.

'Sir Argyle!' Bolingbroke's voice broke Argyle's trance. 'Lurking in the shadows? Is that not what your brother usually does?'

'My Lord Bolingbroke.' Just as the Princess, Bolingbroke had an undeniable regal presence. Today, he was dressed in green, an intricate pattern in silver thread on his chest. Argyle forced a thin smile. 'Visiting your father?'

Bolingbroke grimaced. 'What is that supposed to mean, Sir Argyle?'

Argyle gave Bolingbroke a curious look. 'Nothing, my Lord, merely that perhaps you were here to visit your father. I heard you were not at court for Christmas.'

Eleanor had sent Argyle a letter detailing a rare, joyous Christmas at court and listed who had been absent, probably because that list would be much shorter than relaying everyone who had been present. Argyle remembered that Bolingbroke had been absent and that he had wondered, at the time, if perhaps the relationship between the King and his cousin was still as strong as it had seemed just half a year ago.

'No. That is to say, yes I am now visiting my father - and no, I was not here at Christmas, but then I heard that neither were you,' Bolingbroke said. 'My daughter has been unwell, I chose to spend Christmas with her.'

'I hope she is better, my Lord?' Argyle asked and wondered who had told Bolingbroke that he had been absent.

'The physicians do not know what ails her,' Bolingbroke complained, stroking his pointed beard. 'I sometimes miss that Muslim physician, what was his name? The one that mended you in camp. I am sure he knew much more about medicine and cures than our own physicians.'

'Marsal.' Argyle cleared his throat when Bolingbroke looked at him. 'The Muslim physician's name was Marsal.'

'Ah, yes. He was good, was he not?' Bolingbroke asked. He brushed his sleeve and looked around the room.

'I still have all my limbs,' Argyle said, pushing away a painful picture of Marsal in the cellar. Even after all this time, every second of that fateful night in Jerusalem was as vivid as if it had just happened. He fought an urge to shudder and looked up to meet Bolingbroke's eyes.

'I suppose we must make do with what we have here. Perhaps prayer will suffice,' Bolingbroke said, an uncommon softness in his voice. 'Time will tell. Ah well, I shall be off, Sir Argyle.' Bolingbroke walked a few paces and turned. 'If you are looking for your brother, you look in vain. He left court before the New Year.'

Argyle nodded in response, curious what Thomas was doing that took him away from court, and even more curious why Bolingbroke would stoop to be the messenger.

ꕥ ꕥ ꕥ ꕥ

Celeste was waiting for him in the gallery behind the Queen's chambers. She looked refreshed in a pretty, pale blue dress that brought out her eyes and a simple string of pearls around her elegant throat, but her face was red and puffy rendering her oddly unattractive.

'My Lady.' Argyle bowed to her but kept his distance.

'Sir Argyle,' Celeste said in a tone that made him flush; why was she so formal? 'I am sorry to …'

'Tell me what it is you wish me to know, my Lady, or release me,' Argyle said mirroring her detached manner. Once more he wondered if the Princess had told her why he had left London in November. If she had, why was Celeste so distant?

'You seem to think I have some kind of hold over you.' Celeste mistook his meaning, her voice little more than a whisper. 'But I do not, I believe it is the other way around and that it is you who must somehow release me. But I hope you do not …'

Argyle shuffled his feet uncomfortably; he had worried about meeting Celeste, and now it seemed she might once more make a play for a future for the two of them. Though he had tried to push the idea from his mind, he now admitted to himself that his interest in Isobel was but a meagre substitute for the fantasy he still entertained. He felt his hope surge, perhaps Celeste was finally free? Her old husband dead?

'I am afraid,' Celeste said out of the blue, yanking Argyle from his thoughts.

'Afraid?' Argyle asked.

'I think maybe the King's cousin is not a noble man.' Her eyes glittered with tears.

'You made your choice,' Argyle said icily, all his dreams about a future with Celeste blew away on the January gale that whipped around the thick castle walls.

Celeste looked startled. 'What do you mean?'

'I saw you with Bolingbroke.'

'When?' Celeste's face was a white mask, but her blue eyes were burning.

'In November.' Argyle said and saw her face fall. 'I heard your whispered conversation, and I knew you could be trusted no more.'

'But I …'

'You chose,' Argyle repeated with contempt. 'You chose the one man that no one can truly trust. You are betraying the Princess, the King and England. I do not even care …'

'Care that perhaps you shared me with him.' Celeste fought to maintain some pride. 'Well, you did not! Whatever you think you saw in November, you are mistaken!'

'I know what I heard! And it sounded as if he had some hold over you, and that you were bending to his will.' Argyle bit back his rage. 'If that was so then you should have come to me or to the Princess. You have plenty of people around you who would happily protect you, but you chose Bolingbroke.'

Celeste gasped and glanced around but there was no one else in the gallery. 'Be quiet!'

'Why? There can be no secrets at this court of whispers,' Argyle said.

'You think so little of me …' Celeste's cheeks were wet with angry tears. 'Now that I know what kind of a man you truly are, perhaps I can get on with my life.'

'How?' Argyle felt his rage drain away.

'I cannot believe I asked you here because I thought that you could protect me,' Celeste said, her face drawn, all of her beauty gone. 'That I believed the Princess was right about you, that you were a champion of the weak.'

Argyle felt her words sting. 'Her Grace thinks too highly of me. And you are hardly weak.' He grabbed her hands. 'Celeste, if you truly are in danger, you can tell me.'

'What would you do?' Her hands were cold and trembling but not from fear. 'You think all I crave is a man - well, you are wrong!'

'Tell me,' Argyle insisted even though Celeste fought to be released. 'What is he asking?'

'He wants me to spy.' Celeste wrenched free. 'He wants me to tell him what happens in the royal chambers, he is worried that … well, he wants to know all that goes on.'

'Spy?' Argyle stepped back. The cold air in the gallery was seeping into his body. 'You have to tell me what power he has over you! What is he dangling in front of you?!'

'You think I can be bought? That I have no honour?!' Celeste said sourly, but Argyle could see he had struck a cord. 'If I tell you, you will only run and tell the Princess, and that will release the hounds of Hell! I have to keep her safe! And perhaps he has good reason to worry.'

'You have agreed?' Argyle felt numb.

'I have been avoiding it. I tell him that we rarely see the King, and that we are always at Windsor,' Celeste said. 'The King never even looks at me.'

'You say that Bolingbroke is worried.' Argyle ignored Celeste's nervous hiss. 'What about?'

'I cannot say it - it is treason'!' Celeste sounded desperate. 'He is wrong … oh God, I hope he is wrong!'

Argyle drew Celeste in, stroking her back gently to calm her down. Every meeting with her was like a battle with a secret enemy, tempers flaring, swords crossing and then suddenly; the realisation that you are fighting yourself. Slowly, Celeste stopped sobbing and shaking and began relaxing in his embrace.

'I have to ask …' Argyle felt Celeste shake her head at his chest. 'I have to, Celeste! If I am to help you, to keep you safe, I have to know: is he conspiring with the other lords?' Argyle felt her go limb. 'Is he?'

Celeste shook her head slowly as if in a daze. 'No … I do not know … I …'

'It is important,' Argyle said and felt Celeste stiffen in his tight grip. 'I understand that your loyalties are divided, and that you are afraid. But I must know all that you know.'

Celeste pulled free and pushed a strand of hair back under her hood, her face guarded. 'I know only that he wants reports from the royal chambers.'

Argyle cupped her chin in his hand. 'Keep it that way and tell him nothing of consequence.'

'He will know. He probably knows we are meeting now.'

'Probably,' Argyle agreed. 'And you can tell him that you turned me away - or I you, whatever you want, but you have to keep him at arms length.'

Celeste let out a cold, strained laugh. 'That could prove difficult!'

'Keep him in the dark,' Argyle said. 'Do it for the love you bear for the Princess.'

'Not for you?' Celeste asked. 'If you had never heard our conversation, if you had never seen me with him … would it have changed anything?'

'No.' Argyle could not shake the feeling that she was hiding a great secret, that Bolingbroke had offered her something, she could not refuse

- did not want to refuse. 'As soon as you told me of your marriage, I should have let you go.'

'But you did not!' Celeste moved into his arms once more. 'Say you will reconsider, say you will think on it and meet me tomorrow night, at the feast. Whatever you decide tomorrow, I shall accept it, I shall be graceful and ask no more.'

Against his better judgement, Argyle agreed, his body acutely aware of hers and his mind whirling with what little she had told him. He knew that the longer he stayed at court the bigger the temptation of her willing nature and her enticing manners would be, but he also knew he had to make the decision final and never look back whatever that decision was.

Pulling away from her, he bowed and walked away without looking back. He had no idea if she was still standing there in the dusky gallery when he turned a corner and disappeared from view. Argyle was halfway down the next gallery when he changed his mind and turned back.

For some reason, he paused at the corner and stole a glance down the gallery. Celeste was still there, but she was not alone. She was engaged in what looked to be a hard embrace; her face turned away, her body pinned by Bolingbroke. Argyle felt the poison sting of deceit, had Bolingbroke been lurking in the shadows all along? Had she told him that they were meeting? Or was their meeting his idea?

Celeste struggled free and slapped Bolingbroke. He recoiled and then grabbed her arm so tight that she screamed, and he had to muffle her cries with his hand. Bolingbroke bent forward and whispered something to Celeste, who winced and went quiet. Argyle was too far away to make out any words but he saw Bolingbroke's icy, angry stare and Celeste's guarded, defiant look before she turned and pushed through the side door to the Princess' chambers, leaving Bolingbroke alone in the gallery, obviously fuming with rage.

Argyle walked slowly away. His passion for Celeste lay dying in the cold dark of the gallery. He knew what had to be done.

ꕥ ꕥ ꕥ ꕥ

Argyle was hovering in a corner; he was already tired of the court and wanted nothing more than to make his excuse to the King and leave. The morning's allure and lustre of Westminster was gone, replaced by a menacing atmosphere that hung in the air, pushing poison down his lungs with every breath.

'Brother.' Eleanor's voice startled Argyle. She was dressed in a pale purple dress trimmed with fur, her golden hair pulled back in an intricate braid, tucked into a net of silver adorned with tiny pearls.

'Sister, what are you doing here? Where is de Welles?'

Eleanor pointed across the room where her husband was engaged in conversation with one of the Queen's ladies-in-waiting. 'He likes the French girls.' She laughed at Argyle's aghast look. 'But he keeps faith with me.'

'How can you be sure?'

'We have an understanding,' Eleanor said and tossed her head. Several young courtiers stared at her, and she rewarded them with a brilliant smile. 'We can flirt, but that is all. He knows that I am an attractive catch to someone at court, as is he. Perhaps more so with our brother so high in the King's favour.'

Argyle followed Eleanor's look to the dais and saw Thomas whispering in the King's ear. 'Yes, he is never far from the Crown. Although I was lead to believe that he was not at court.'

'He returned earlier today. He is never long with Elizabeth; she must be a thoroughly tiresome wife for him to be so often at court. The Princess has little care for our darling brother,' Eleanor said, and Argyle saw the Princess staring stiffly away from the King and Thomas. 'But she dotes on you.'

'She is kind.' Argyle did not like the tone in his sister's voice that suggested more than it ought to. He thought back to this morning and the jealous glances from the other courtiers when the Princess had lavished her attention on him. Yet another reason to leave court as soon as possible.

'Margaret says that you have other interests?' Eleanor glanced about the room. To celebrate her husband's birthday, the Princess' presence chamber was decorated with holly and mistletoe. Silver candlesticks held fat wax candles and all the tables were filled with food and drink.

Does she, Argyle thought, I thought we had agreed to keep it to ourselves. He drew Eleanor further into the shadows. 'What interests?'

'Oh Argyle, really, she just said you were courting some woman or other. I told her she was wrong, but now I am not so sure …'

Argyle coloured slightly. 'I have a lady in mind.' He had not thought to tell Eleanor - or anyone - about Isobel, but perhaps it would divert his sisters and make Margaret forget about his connection with Celeste.

'Really?' Eleanor's eyes widened. 'Oh, how wonderful! Is she here?'

'No.' Argyle smiled at Eleanor's surprised looks, Margaret had told her about Celeste then. 'She is at Beauworth.'

'Beauworth? But I thought …'

'Think again, my dear sister,' Argyle said with a smug smile, relishing in her confusion. 'It is no one you know. I first met her during a hearing of a matter from one of my villages. She was there to … it concerned her family.' Argyle decided it was best to keep secret Isobel's affiliation to a known witch who had burned at the stake in London only a few months ago.

'Are you here to ask the King's permission?'

'Not yet, we must first get to know each other a little better.'

It was Eleanor's turn to smile smugly. 'And until such a time you have her penned up in Beauworth, pining for you while you dance at court with all the pretty ladies? You are a scoundrel!'

Argyle was about to retort when a familiar face caught his eye. He stared into the golden, fussy air of the presence chamber, trying to pick out the man again, but he seemed to have disappeared into thin air.

'I could have sworn …' Argyle said quietly, and Eleanor gave him a concerned look.

'What is it?'

'I thought I saw someone, but it cannot be,' Argyle tried to recover from the shock by smiling, but Eleanor's expression told him it did not work.

'You look as though you have seen a ghost.'

'Maybe I did.'

CHAPTER 17

12 February 1397 - Beauworth

'I believe we enter the world alone, and so shall we leave it.' The finality of Isobel's words struck a nerve with Argyle.

Every time he looked at her, he thought she looked somehow familiar, and yet he could not place her anywhere. He had often been caught staring blatantly at her, trying to work out how her chin, the slant of her eyes or her chestnut hair might fit into his world. The one he had been living in before she arrived in November to call upon his mercy and plead for her sister. In vain.

Her silhouette stood out in the light streaming in, her head slightly turned and for the briefest of moments he thought she looked like … but it could not be. Then she smiled at him at ease in the parlour that now clearly reflected a woman's touch. 'But you did not turn me away. You know all that I am, and you are still here.'

Yes, Argyle thought, and I wonder why? She had taken a life, committed a mortal sin. Was he really ready to overlook that? Was his desire to settle a wife greater than his concern that she seemed almost too familiar, almost too easy a choice?

But rather than voice his concerns, he rose and swept her into his arms, the feeling of her soft cheek warm on his neck, her slender hands resting lightly on his back. In many ways, Isobel was exactly what he should look for and want in a wife, and she seemed happy at Beauworth.

She drew back and looked up at him. 'You are troubled?'

'No …' Even Argyle could hear the hollow ring in his voice.

'You are not sure,' Isobel corrected herself.

'It is just …' Argyle hesitated. 'Thomas has offered up another bride for me, one the King wholly supports.'

'Oh?' Isobel wet her lips.

'If I marry you hastily, I will spurn her - and the King,' Argyle said.

'But you are not interested in her?'

Argyle released her gently and stood to one side, blocking the view of the garden with his broad frame. 'I do not know her, and I suspect that I never shall. But now that the King is invested in the union, it is a different matter.'

Argyle wondered why Isobel was not lashing out in anger; he had all but proposed to her and still the mention of another match left her completely unmoved. Perhaps she was not eager to marry after all.

'Marriage should not be entered into lightly,' Isobel said echoing Argyle's thoughts. 'You might think me cold and unfeeling, but I dare not hope anymore … I did once and I must forever live with that decision and those memories. I fully understand that you have obligations to your family, you are of noble birth …' Her voice trailed away, and she put her hand on his, a warm brush that quickly evaporated.

Argyle thought about his options. Refusing Thomas' suitable bride, who would no doubt be of noble birth, well connected and perhaps even endowed with a fortune of her own. Accepting the proposed girl and marrying a complete stranger who might - or might not - come to love him. Marry Isobel, who stood here before him, flesh, blood and full of promise. Would either of those choices be what he wanted? He dug deeper into his heart, knowing what he would encounter when he came to the centre - a deep-rooted, unyielding desire to flee, to run for a land far beyond the horizon. A glimmer of dark eyes surfaced, and he pushed away from the window. Isobel snapped her hand away, startled.

'I am sorry. I must … I have to think things through.' He laughed a little, the sound brittle. 'Thomas always said that I was slow to make up my mind, I am only sorry you have to experience just how slow.'

For just a second, Argyle was sure Isobel looked neither shocked nor sad but as a snake ready to strike, but then her face smoothed, and she managed a smile. 'As I said, you should not rush into anything.'

Before Argyle could say any more, she turned and walked slowly out of the room, swaying lightly. Argyle reached to close the door and saw her a little further down the hall, her forehead resting on her fist, she visibly drew breath, her shoulders shaking slightly, and she looked down for a moment. He wondered if Isobel was more passionate about the match than she was letting on, and why she did not express her desire, if it was desire. She smoothed the front of her dress before walking slowly down the hall.

Was he mad to turn away the woman Thomas had proposed? How would the King react if he heard that Argyle had taken a wife without seeking permission? Although he thought of himself only as a knight, he was a Mowbray, and his family's close connection to the King meant that he was not free to do as he wished. His stranded adventure was proof that the King intended to meddle a great deal in his life, both now and in future. Should he submit to the King's and Thomas' wishes or should he make one last stand for his own sake?

18 February 1397 - Beauworth

A week had gone by, and still Argyle was torn. He had to act quickly before Thomas sealed the deal with his proposed bride - a match sanctioned by the King. Argyle was ashamed that he could not simply decide and be done with it.

In many ways, Isobel was an obvious choice. She was the kind of wilful and outspoken woman he liked, and she was free, which Celeste had never been. Argyle still had not forgiven her for concealing the truth about her status for so long, for leading him on and keeping him close when she knew they could build no immediate future together. He had also slowly realised that when he was away from court it was easy for him to forget Celeste. It was not love but lust that tied him to her.

But if he chose to ask Isobel, Argyle felt he owed her an account of his past. A barter for her honesty. He leaned back from his table where the papers were strewn here and there. He pushed them around without looking at them. He knew they would have to wait, and yet he was unable to get up.

'M'Lord.' Stephen pushed open the door.

'Yes?'

Stephen paused for a moment before shutting the door firmly.

'What's troubling you?'

'You know me too well.' Argyle gestured for Stephen to sit down. 'I have something on my mind that I have to tell someone.'

Stephen stayed standing. 'Who?'

'Isobel.'

'About Jerusalem?' Stephen asked.

'Yes … Do sit, Stephen.' Argyle sounded more irritated than he had wanted to be.

'I need you in the stables,' Stephen said but sat down anyway. 'There's some trouble with one of the stable boys. What're you going to tell her? Or should I say, how much?'

'All of it,' Argyle said and thought, it will have to be all or nothing.

'Dangerous.' Stephen scratched his chin. 'For her.'

'I cannot marry her without her knowing …' Argyle paused. 'I know her story, she needs to know mine.'

Stephen pushed his red hair away from his face. 'I'd leave some of it out. Tell her about your woman and about why you went, and you should probably tell her who sent you. But for the rest of it, the things I know and the things I don't - leave it out. It's old news, it's bad news, and if she doesn't know, she'll be safer.'

'But …' Argyle began.

'It's my opinion, M'lord, you needen't take much heed of it,' Stephen said. 'Knowing you is dangerous business, so perhaps she should know, but I think it'll keep for now.'

Argyle gave a crooked smile. 'Dangerous business?'

'Wouldn't you say?' Stephen asked.

'I suppose so. Although you got yourself into even more trouble than I ever asked of you. Actually, I remember asking you to stay out of trouble, but you did not,' Argyle said. 'I also have to tell her of more recent events.'

'The French woman?' Stephen asked. Argyle had told Stephen a little about Celeste, careful to keep her name and station out of the tale - and how often he had seen her. But he had told Stephen that she had kept Bolingbroke's company, and now he regretted that decision.

'Perhaps. I cannot begin my married life on a lie. No matter how well intended it might be,' Argyle said, stacking his papers as if that might help him get his thoughts in order too. 'I know that I may be much at court. I would feel better if Isobel knows why.'

'If you're to be much at court, is it wise to tell her about the French woman?' Stephen shifted in his seat. 'Won't she be worrying every time you're away?'

Argyle had not thought about that. 'Perhaps, but Isobel is strong. I need her to trust me - there can be no secrets.'

'But there could be missing information.' Stephen got up. 'Now, I don't think we should keep the lad waiting any longer. I ordered him to muck out the stables on his own - with his hands. He should be tired, dirty and, hopefully, remorseful by now.'

'Or just dirty and angry.' Argyle rose to join him. 'We will soon find out.'

Stephen opened the door and turned around. 'I think, I'll go ahead, M'lord.'

'I am coming …' Argyle said, but Stephen stepped aside to reveal Isobel standing before the two of them. 'Isobel … Yes, Smith, go ahead.'

Stephen bowed lightly to Isobel. 'M'lady.'

'And Smith. I trust you can make a decision on proper punishment for whatever the poor boy did,' Argyle added.

'Naturally, M'lord, just thought you'd like some air. Some other time perhaps.' Stephen said and Argyle was glad Isobel had her back turned so she would not see Stephen's worried face.

'Yes, some other time.'

'Oh, I would not …' Isobel looked up at Argyle, her hands fidgeting with the thin belt around her hips.

'Come in.' Argyle stepped aside. He wondered what she might think of the state of his study, it was so unlike the tidy parlour she usually occupied in the daytime.

'I always marvel at all the things men have in their rooms.' Isobel let Argyle lead her to the warmth of the hearth, her hand resting lightly on his arm, and she settled on one of the low stools. 'My father would never let me into his study.'

Argyle drew a second stool close to Isobel and sat down. 'Why not?'

'Not a place for a girl - and later, a young woman.' Isobel wrinkled her nose. 'It always made me think that he was keeping something secret behind his door, some monster or a great treasure that he did not want any of us to know about.'

'Now that would be a wonder, but I rather think he wanted to spare you all the boring paperwork,' Argyle said.

'If his study was anything like yours, certainly! He would have been better off simply inviting me in,' Isobel said. 'I would never have asked a second time.'

They both laughed, looking around. Argyle's eyes lingered on a chest in the corner that contained his letters from court. 'Were you looking for me?'

'I rather thought you were looking for me.' Isobel turned slightly to face the fire and stretched her hands out as if to warm them, although Argyle had felt the warmth of her hand through his shirt, just moments ago. Sometimes she seemed almost to read his mind.

'You have been honest with me, you have trusted me with your story, and I …'

'That was my decision.' Isobel reached out and took hold of his hands for a moment. 'And I think a very good one. But you should not feel obliged to return the favour. We will get to know one another, in time.' At least she seemed sure that he would choose to marry her.

'I want you to know before … You said no secrets.' Argyle felt tension wash into the room, the walls closing in. He had made up his mind. Once he had said his piece there was no turning back.

Isobel gave him a scrutinising glance and leaned back. 'Tell me.'

'You need to know that I travelled to Jerusalem. You need to know who I met, what I did and why I did it.' Argyle noticed the desperation in his voice and felt it resound in his heart. 'And yet I need to keep you safe!'

Isobel stiffened a little. 'I am safe with you.'

'Smith would disagree.'

'Why?'

'He was there; he knows what happened and how it has affected me - both of us. Once you know, it will affect you too.' Argyle got up to fetch some wine, his hand trembling as he poured. 'I fear it may cast a dark shadow over our union.'

'I understand.' Isobel took the cup he offered her and wiped the trickle of spilled wine on the base with her finger. 'Tell me about Jerusalem. Leave nothing out.'

ഗ ര ഗ ര

CHAPTER 18

19 February 1397 - Beauworth

In the grey, pearly dawn, Argyle stirred the fire and fed it a few logs, watching as the flames slowly came to life and ate away at the dry wood. Revisiting his journey to Jerusalem had opened a door to other, more sinister memories that had haunted his sleep. Najeelah had visited him, Marsal too, but most disturbingly, tattered memories of La Fontaine had surfaced, for the first time in years. When Argyle woke in a sweat, he had abandoned any hope of more rest.

While the light slowly crept in, he emptied the pitcher of ale and opened the window to let in a cold breeze, which seemed somehow to always soothe him. Refreshed by the air, he pulled on some clothes and then walked slowly towards his study, his boots slung over his arm. He enjoyed the silence of the house, and the haunting sound of the owls in the nearby forest.

As dawn turned to day, Argyle sat down at his desk and began drafting a letter to Margaret. He would write to all his sisters to formally announce his engagement with Isobel. Why was his mood so dark? Why could he not rejoice in the decision he had made?

A light knock stirred his troubled mind. 'Yes?' he said without looking up.

'M'lord.' Stephen pushed the door open. 'I saw the light in your window. You're up early.'

Argyle motioned for Stephen to come in and put away the rest of the papers. The letters would have to wait. 'You too.'

'Waiting for a long time in the stables and then being scolded by Bessie when I came home late'll do that to a man,' Stephen said with a faint smile.

'I hope you came to terms?'

'We did.'

Argyle rose and walked around the desk. 'I was just about to write to my family to announce my plans to wed Isobel.'

'Congratulations!' Stephen gave Argyle a hard pat on the back. 'You told her?'

'About Jerusalem - some of it, yes. The important parts anyway. I left out some of the more gruelling details, about …' Argyle bit off the rest of his sentence, some parts even Stephen did not know. 'She knows that the King sent me.'

'Ah …'

'None too pleased about that,' Argyle said and led Stephen from the study. Noises from the great hall revealed that the men were ready to begin a new day.

When they entered the room, Argyle noticed Isobel sitting near the hearth, her face haggard. Stephen made his way to the benches closest to the empty dais and received a rumbling welcome from his men. A few shot stolen glances at Argyle as he turned and made for the hearth.

'You look tired.'

'I had trouble sleeping,' she said. She looked tiny on the big wooden bench, her hands little doves resting on a bed of dark blue.

Argyle sat down next to her. 'I have been writing letters to my family. I would like to announce a date.'

'You have a church, even if the priest is a foul creature,' Isobel's face showed her disdain for the priest who had condemned her sister to death. 'We can wed whenever you choose.'

What an offer, Argyle thought, but do you really mean it? He had wondered if perhaps Isobel regretted accepting his proposal and now feared he would turn into her first husband. Argyle smiled to console her, but it did not seem to work.

'Before we do, I have to gain the King's permission.' Argyle saw Isobel stiffen. 'I cannot marry without his consent.' To himself he finished the sentence; the King will throw me in the Tower if I do anything without his permission.

Isobel drew breath and stared into space. 'Very well.'

'My sisters will dote on you,' Argyle said to soften the intense atmosphere.

Isobel gave a strained smile. 'If you say so.'

'I will speak to my tailor, Romaine, when I go to London. He will know which dressmaker to choose.'

'Be careful you do not spoil me. I might just get used to it, and then I will be of no use to you at all,' Isobel said with affected delight. 'You are lucky to have a family to invite, I have none.'

'What of your father?'

'Dead.' Isobel looked away. 'Tilly was my last relative, and she died with her unborn child. Oh, all of this makes me dispirited when I ought to be happy! I want to be happy. Please, do not mind me, go and inform your family of our union.' She got up. 'And please, make whatever preparations you see fit.'

Argyle watched her walk away, was there something forced in her manner? He too left the hall deep in thought, hoping his sisters would rejoice in his decision, even if he did not himself. Argyle knew for certain that Thomas would be furious and could only pray that the King would take kindly to the petition to marry Isobel.

CHAPTER 19

25 February 1397 - Westminster Palace, London

'You intend to wed?' The King gave Argyle a discerning look, and he was glad that the King had sent away most of the courtiers who had thronged the room when Argyle had entered. He made to step forward, but the King stopped him with a gesture. 'Who?'

Not who you think, Argyle thought and wondered how the King might react to what came next. 'The lady Isobel Thorne.'

'She is not the woman I agreed to with Lord Mowbray,' the King said, his eyes flinty. 'What makes you think you can approach your King and petition to marry some nobody I have never even heard of?!'

'If your Majesty remembers …' Argyle was cut short.

'I do! I should also imagine that you remember what has happened since then.' The King's threat hung between them as an arrow caught mid-air. 'Do not presume to be in any position to change my decision! The lady your brother suggested is an advantageous match - although her father did argue that she was marrying beneath her station. But he has been given to understand that, as part of the Mowbray family, his daughter will be held in high esteem at court. Not thanks to you - but to your brother.'

Argyle nodded, he understood the difficult position he had put both the King and Thomas in. 'Majesty, I pledged myself to you, and I stand by my oath. If you consider Thomas' bride the better match, I shall not deny her. I shall take her down the aisle even if my heart belongs to someone else.'

'Is that so?' The King looked somewhat appeased at Argyle's submissive demeanour. He was not to know that the woman Argyle secretly thought of was not Isobel, but a dark beauty thousands of miles away. While he might fool the King and most around him, Argyle could not fool himself into believing that he loved Isobel. But what he had decided could not be undone, only the King could decide a different life for him, and for once, Argyle was content to leave it in his Majesty's hands.

The King stroked his clean-shaven cheek; a big ring sparkled at the motion. 'What are you not telling me, Sir Argyle?'

'Nothing, Majesty. I met Isobel last autumn and since then, I have spent much time with her at Beauworth.' Argyle noticed the King's knowing smile. 'The roads are difficult to travel and a woman alone is easy prey. I thought it better she stay somewhere safe.' The King's smile widened, and Argyle continued a little more confidently, perhaps the King could be swayed. 'She is the daughter of a landowner near Dover - he died a few years ago.'

'I see.' The King's eyes sparkled. 'She is perhaps in a family way already? That might explain a lot, such as why you would refuse a bride proposed by your brother and sanctioned by me.'

'No, Majesty, she is not yet,' Argyle said with a disarming smile. 'And though I am sure my brother had my best interests at heart, I have not had the pleasure of meeting any of his prospective brides.'

'She must be presented at court. If both I and my wife agree that she is a suitable match, you may marry her.' The King summoned a servant. 'Wine!' The servant scurried away to fulfil the King's demand. 'You are happy with your decision? There is no one here at court you would rather wed if you were free to chose?'

Something about the question bothered Argyle, but he dismissed the idea that the King knew about his affair with Celeste. 'No, Majesty. I have made the right choice and now can only hope that you agree.'

The servant returned with a tray of wine and glasses. The King thrust a glass in Argyle's hand and gave him a keen look. 'Truly there is no one you can think would satisfy your desires better than this Isobel? None at all?'

'No, Majesty. I know of no woman free to marry that I would prefer to Isobel.' Argyle watched the King to see how he might react and thought he caught a glimpse of triumph before the King clapped a hand on his shoulder and toasted with him. Argyle took a deep draught of the wine, relishing in the sweet, sharp taste.

'You must tell me about her!' the King demanded and motioned for Argyle to sit on a low stool. 'Is she fair or dark? Shapely? What is her temper?'

Argyle was glad to turn to a safer subject. The King's reaction to his last comment had him worried, something was awry, though Argyle could not tell what it might be. He forced a smile. 'Isobel is auburn - and shapely. She has spirit, but not too much, and though she appears strong there is something frail about her.'

Greed stole over the King's face, a sly smile lingering at the corner of his mouth. 'If your account is to be trusted, she may prove a most suitable match - if not in status …' The King mulled over his glass for a while before he spoke again. 'Still, I must meet her myself! Bring her to court, bring her for the Princess' coronation.'

'I am honoured, Majesty,' Argyle said, surprised to hear about the coronation from the King and not from Thomas or even one of his sisters. 'When will the Princess be crowned?'

'I am planning it even as we speak!' The King looked about, although the room was empty but for the two of them and the White Harts at the doors, and leaned in with a conspiratorial expression. 'She is a little displeased with me - over a trifling matter - so I decided to surprise her with a lavish coronation. I want Isabella to be my Queen consort and for all of England to attend. I know that she will be pleased if you were to bring her the news - and your own news of course.'

Why would you not tell her yourself? Argyle thought and tried to hide his confusion with a smile. 'What an honour, Majesty. Where is the Princess these days?'

'Oh, she has retired to Windsor,' the King said airily and drank deep. 'Court life can be very taxing for a child.'

'I am sure, Majesty,' Argyle said. 'Would you like me to present the Princess with the news today?'

'No, it can wait. I want to be almost done before she knows. You will dine here tonight and go to her tomorrow. You may find her to be a little low in spirit. But I am sure, she will be delighted to see you, she always is.' The King tried to conceal his displeasure. 'You can tell her that you are bringing a prospective bride - perhaps you can persuade Isabella to sanction the match.'

ꕤ ꕤ

Argyle stepped off the wherry and watched it steer back into the murky flow of the Thames. Whenever he visited London it always brought back memories of his first visit with La Fontaine. How thrilled he had been to see the city, how excited to meet the young King. Sometimes he wished for those feelings to return and that his visits to London might occasionally be more enjoyable.

Tonight had been a tiresome affair, the meal had dragged on, and the company had been surly. The King had appeared in high spirits, but the absent Princess had been the topic of much mumbled debate. Once the King retired, Argyle had left quickly, glad to be away from the strange, uncomfortable ambiance of Westminster. The London air had done little to blow away Argyle's strange mood and now … Argyle stopped at a scratching sound in the shadows. The lane leading up to his house forked a few feet ahead. Did something move?

'Sir Argyle.'

The voice was so low and hoarse that for just a moment, Argyle would have sworn that it was Lockley returned from the grave.

'Show yourself!' Argyle cursed himself for leaving his sword at home.

Out of the shadows emerged a ghost, and Argyle's breath caught. His mind whirled, pummelling long gone memories at him: fire, panic clutching at his throat and the searing pain when he pulled away flesh and cloth to reveal a glistening sword. How could a burned man return unscathed?

'Coxcombe?! We found you burned - in Calais, the fire on the docks in the early morning … I found your sword!' Argyle's brain kept protesting to what was right before his eyes. 'Even Bolingbroke agreed …'

'I was in his service, why would he not play along with you?' Coxcombe spread his arms in mock flourish. 'Yet here I stand, not a mark from the fire on me! What does that tell you?'

That either Bolingbroke is a splendid actor, or you fooled him too, Argyle thought and noticed that Coxcombe did wear a sword, though not the one they had found on the burned corpse in Calais. Irrationally, he wondered what had happened to it.

'I know you spoke with an old friend of mine, in Paris. He needed a little persuading before he would admit to it,' Coxcombe said, tilting his head. 'Fortunately, he was interrupted before he could divulge too much information to you, or so he insists.'

'Fortunate for whom? You? Why would you not want the truth of La Fontaine's murder brought to light?' Argyle's brain was slowly waking from the shock of Coxcombe returned from the dead. 'Why would it matter to you?'

Stepping closer, Coxcombe slid his sword from the scabbard, a silky soft whisper of steel against hardened leather. 'I have a better question for you: why would it not?'

'Because Bolingbroke was involved?' Argyle tried desperately to buy time, to see if he could rattle the truth from Coxcombe. He had dismissed Bolingbroke as an accomplice - had he been too gullible?

Coxcombe laughed, the sudden harsh noise bouncing off the buildings. 'Bolingbroke pays me for my services, such as they may be, but why would you think he is the only one?'

Argyle saw a light flicker in one of the second storey windows behind Coxcombe. If they were to fight, someone would see it and perhaps call for the city guard. It was a long shot, but it gave him some comfort.

Here is a man with no loyalties, Argyle thought, no loyalties at all. He tried again, 'Gaunt then?'

'While they are constantly together, and the son dare do little without his father's approval, they are misers enough not to pay double,' Coxcombe suddenly sounded grudging. 'Look in another direction.'

'One of the other Lords Appellant?' Argyle asked, desperation beginning to take hold of him.

Coxcombe froze. 'They say you are no match for your brother's wit, but perhaps they are wrong.'

'Perhaps.' Argyle smiled, he was on to something, and it might just distract Coxcombe long enough for Argyle to get away. 'Or perhaps my brother is in on it too.'

The wily expression returned to Coxcombe's face. 'You go too far.'

Yes, but I needed to know if Thomas was involved, Argyle thought. He took a step backwards, missing the comforting feeling of a sword by his side. He continued his questions: 'Why not just tell me who it is? What difference does it make?'

'Even conspiring to kill someone, especially the King's great friend, is punishable by death. Imagine what he would say if you offered up another murderer.'

'You should have thought about that before you delivered the poison to Lockley.' Argyle felt a savage pleasure at Coxcombe's reaction. 'He told me.'

'No ...,' Coxcombe whispered clearly confused now. He turned as Argyle slowly began to walk around him. This might be his only chance of escaping. Argyle remembered seeing Coxcombe in tournament melees and knew his skills with a sword.

'Your meeting in Jerusalem,' Argyle said taking another step towards the fork in the lane, 'you were not alone. Hell, you said it yourself, man, no one is ever truly alone in a camp.'

A startled look froze on Coxcombe's face. 'You followed us?'

'No, not I,' Argyle enjoyed having the upper hand for a change. He considered whether or not he would be able to snatch Coxcombe's sword if he could just keep him unsettled. 'But much later, I confronted Lockley with my knowledge, and he told me how it was.'

'Fool,' Coxcombe whispered. 'That bloody fool!'

'We should speak again, under different circumstances. But you will understand that I do not intend to stay here tonight,' Argyle said and saw Coxcombe finally realise what he planned. Dismissing the idea of fighting for Coxcombe's sword, Argyle sped up the side alley, ducking under low hanging signs before turning another corner and jumping over a low brick wall.

He heard Coxcombe swearing as he searched the alley. Argyle considered following him to see if he would return to whoever was currently buying his services but thought the better of it. He was still a sword short of feeling safe and now Coxcombe was alert and angry. He could ask Thomas if he knew anything, but that would set off a whole host of other questions that Argyle would rather be without. He would have to keep an eye out for any sign of Coxcombe while he was in London and never again leave his house without his sword.

Once rid of the shock of Coxcombe's return and the rush a lucky escape still coursing through his veins, Argyle found that he liked the prospect of having something to do while at court. What he did not like was that Coxcombe, whom he had thought burned to death, who he had pitied such a cruel death, was unharmed and that he had even been responsible for a poor unfortunate's death in Calais. He had just earned himself another enemy.

What if Lockley was innocent of the crime? But then why would he take the fall? Argyle thought as he heaved himself over a high wall and landed in the orchard of his neighbour's house. He stole through the little trees and slid out of the gate at the far end of the garden, glad to see a flickering light in the hall window of his own house.

Which of the Lords would have had reason to kill La Fontaine? If not Bolingbroke or Thomas that left three men: Warwick, Arundel and Woodstock.

But if the man in Paris is to be trusted, and Coxcombe's keen interest indicated that he could be, that ruled out Woodstock, Argyle thought, which narrowed it down to two. Arundel, Thomas' father-in-law, and Warwick who was the grandfather of Thomas' first wife. Which put Thomas in the thick of things.

'God's blood, what a mess!' Argyle whispered under his breath opening the door and feeling a welcoming breath of warmth curl around his body. 'Who can I trust then?'

ꙮ ꙮ

'Where have you been?' Thomas' haughty tone pierced Argyle's thoughts as he shut the door to his house thinking he was safe at last.

He whipped his head around, astounded to see his brother in the hallway. 'What are you doing here?'

Thomas looked momentarily unsettled but soon recovered. 'I looked for you at court but they said you had left.'

'Who?'

'The other men at your table. I did not ask their names.' Thomas gave Argyle a disapproving look. 'You look a mess.'

Argyle brushed his clothes and scowled at Thomas. 'It is late, Thomas, say what you came to say and go home.'

'Not here.' Thomas glared at one of Argyle's servants who had appeared when he heard his master's voice. 'In your study perhaps?'

Argyle led the way without looking back marvelling at what might finally have Thomas deign to visit him in his London home. The night was proving full of surprises. He paused inside the door to let Thomas pass before he snapped it close.

'You seem uneasy, brother.' Thomas looked around at the small parlour with a sour expression.

Argyle had decided against bringing Thomas into the study lest he had left some letter or other on the desk that Thomas ought not to see. 'It has been a long, tiresome evening. What brings you here that could not wait till morning?'

'Did you notice the Princess was missing tonight?'

'Yes, but she is not always at dinner,' Argyle said. It was unlike Thomas to pay much attention to the Princess, he had often dismissed her as a silly child, unimportant to matters of state. 'Perhaps she decided to stay at Windsor.'

'She has been absent from court these past three or four weeks,' Thomas said, pulling off his gloves. 'Though the King does not say so in public, he is furious with her.'

'He married a child, what did he expect?' Argyle breathed deeply, he had to get a hold of himself. 'She is bound to find the endless feasts tiresome, even if she was brought up at court.'

Thomas grunted. 'But this is different. She is blatantly disregarding his commands to attend.'

That did not sound like the Princess, which peaked Argyle's interest. 'How do you know?'

'I have my ways.' Thomas waved his gloves dismissively. 'The question you should be asking is why has the Princess suddenly changed her tune? Why does she refuse the King? She will not even have him visit, she sends back his gifts.'

'It is too late in the night for me to speculate, Thomas, say what you came to say and let me go to bed!' Argyle was tiring fast.

Thomas closed the gap between them. 'I want to know why the Princess is acting thus. I want you to find out.' He cringed a little as Argyle stared at him with contempt.

'I will not be your spy!' Argyle slammed his hand down on the table. 'Whatever you think to uncover that might somehow strengthen your position at court - because that must be, what you are looking to achieve - I will NOT help you!'

'My position is strong,' Thomas said, but a glimmer of unease ran across his face, before he regained his composure. 'The King told me you intend to decline another bride - one his Majesty has already sanctioned. Are you really in a position to deny me a favour?'

'This is no mere favour,' Argyle spat. 'If you already know what I have only discussed with the King himself, surely, you have plenty of others to do your bidding. Choose one of them!'

'Yes, but none who once bedded the Princess' most beloved lady in waiting,' Thomas said with a wolfish smiled. 'A lady who, by-the-by, is no longer a favourite!'

Argyle had not been surprised by the Princess' absence; the King had said she was away from court. Nor had he wondered where Celeste had been, since she was always with the Princess. But Thomas' words had an ominous ring to them; if Celeste was not with the Princess and not at court, where was she?

Argyle's silence prompted Thomas to smirk. 'You too are a favourite of the Princess. Do you not think it is time you paid her a visit?'

'If I do, will you leave me alone?'

'If you discover why she is spurning the King, then yes,' Thomas said and opened the door to the hall, making the fire in the parlour dance. 'You know where to find me.'

Yes, Argyle thought, just within reach of the next scandal. But the thought of Celeste fallen from grace gnawed at him all through the night and sleep would not come.

Ʂ Ʂ Ʂ Ʂ

26 February 1397 - Windsor

Argyle rode up the alley towards Windsor, the pretty palace slowly came into sight as the trees subsided and the twisting road straightened to give the visitor a clear view of the beautiful stonewalls. A few early messengers of spring sprouted in the brown and white flowerbeds in front of the gate that led to the inner courtyard.

A guard in the royal livery hailed him as he rode onto the bridge, which could be drawn shut if needs be, although the castle was not protected by a moat, and the portcullis looked as though it had never been lowered. Argyle gave his name and was asked to wait in the courtyard. A stable boy took the reigns of his horse, and Argyle looked around. The castle courtyard was as pretty as the outside, a perfect sanctuary for a Princess who was tired of the bustle at court. Somewhere inside, Lady de Cousy was commanding the Princess' household as chief lady-in-waiting. In reality, she was the one to decide whether the Princess would receive visitors or not, although Argyle suspected the Princess had a way of getting what she wanted.

'The Princess will see you shortly, please follow me,' the guard called from the door. He led Argyle through a massive hall into a small parlour overlooking one of the little gardens. 'Wait here.'

Argyle took in the room, which showed no signs of being the receiving rooms of a child, its walls were covered with wall hangings displaying scenes from the Bible and one wall was covered with paintings of former Kings and Queens. He noticed the striking portrait of a young fair Queen Anne, which took pride of place, and wondered if it would some day be replaced with the Princess' dark features.

'Sir Argyle, the Princess is waiting for you, please follow me.'

Argyle turned, expecting to see Celeste waiting for him but the girl who had spoken was years younger and her English was flawless.

'Thank you,' Argyle said and followed the youth through quiet corridors and passages until he heard the muffled voices of women.

The young girl glanced back at him, her cheeks rosy and her eyes shining. 'Here we are, Sire,' she said a little out of breath. She offered him a sweet smile, probably meant to be flirtatious. 'The Princess is in here.'

Argyle smiled and saw her blush. 'Lead the way, Mistress?'

'Prudence,' the girl breathed, clearly excited to have caught his attention.

'Lead the way, Mistress Prudence,' Argyle said.

The doors to the Princess' apartments opened and Argyle followed Prudence in, bowing when she curtsied low.

'Sir Argyle, how kind of you to visit,' the Princess said, and Argyle straightened to see her sitting on her red throne, her face solemn. Just as the parlour, this room showed no signs of the person inhabiting it.

'Your Grace is most kind to receive me.'

'You are always welcome thought I am curious as to why you have come,' the Princess said and motioned for Argyle to step closer. 'Have you been long at court?'

'Long enough to miss your presence,' Argyle said and saw the Princess frown.

'Oh?'

'I was worried you might be ill.' Argyle had contemplated what his excuse for visiting without a formal invitation should be, and the Princess' health was all he could come up with. 'The King told me you were here, and I have come to present a gift from him.'

'As you see, I am well,' the Princess said ignoring the mention of the King. 'I was just preparing for my morning walk, perhaps you will join me?' Argyle bowed, and the Princess turned to Prudence. 'Show Sir Argyle to the garden, I shall be there shortly.'

Prudence looked equally delighted and shy when she led Argyle through a few passages, displaying statues in high, narrow arches carved into the stone walls. In the middle of a slightly wider gallery, Prudence turned to a glass door that led to a beautifully landscaped garden full of bare hedges. A few gardeners were hacking away at the cold earth in one of the square flowerbeds, no doubt preparing for this years first flower bulbs to be planted. The sight reminded Argyle of his aunt Blanche who had loved her garden and constantly fussed over it.

'Her Grace prefers this garden to all the others,' Prudence said to break the awkward silence. 'She has walked here daily since …'

'Since?' Argyle asked and added a smile for good measure.

Prudence blushed scarlet. 'Since she decided, she needed some time away from the hustle and bustle of court.'

I wonder why that is, Argyle thought and followed Prudence to an old, wooden bench standing to one side of the gravel path. Argyle sat down perhaps a little closer to the young woman than necessary, she seemed willing to trade secrets for an intimate closeness to a man grown. Perhaps this would give her incentive to share more, and at least it would give her something to tell the other ladies. She lowered her gaze and fidgeted with the ends of her shawl.

'Perhaps you should have dressed warmer, Mistress Prudence.' Argyle caught her eye and put on a concerned expression. 'I would not wish for you to fall ill.'

'I am quite warm, thank you, Sire.' Prudence stared back and paused. 'I ... you knew Lady Celeste, I believe?'

'Yes, I met her when the King went to France to marry the Princess,' Argyle said, careful not to commit to an intimacy that most others knew nothing about. He turned slightly, when his knee touched hers she gasped lightly and he deliberately let it rest against her dress.

'You saw her too at court?' Prudence asked in a flustered voice, her gaze now fixed on his thigh. 'Or so I heard ...'

'I did not see her this time, the King said that all the Queen's ladies were with her here,' Argyle said. 'Is she unwell?'

Prudence turned her face up at him, apprehension gleaming in her eyes. 'The Princess has sent her away!'

Argyle tried to hide his confusion adopting what he hoped was a detached expression. 'Oh?'

'They had such a row three weeks ago, and we have not seen Celeste since.' In her distress Prudence forgot her curtsies. 'They were shouting at each other and finally, the Princess ordered her from Windsor and now, neither of us know where she has gone!'

Argyle was about to ask her what she thought might have caused the sudden displeasure with Celeste, when the Princess showed up, ready for her walk. She waved Prudence away and gestured for Argyle to join her. When Argyle looked back at Prudence, her face revealed envy at being excluded; he offered her an apologetic smile that was returned without enthusiasm, clearly she would have preferred to stay seated on the bench, their knees touching, sharing secrets.

The gravel crunched beneath Argyle's boots; apart from a few early birds singing in the hedges the garden was quiet. The Princess' four ladies-in-waiting trailed behind just out of hearing, pretending to marvel at the barren garden and looking at Argyle with disapproval.

He wondered if the Princess was merely being polite and the whole stroll would take place in silence when she cleared her throat. 'Why have you really come?'

'There are rumours at court that you are displeased with the King and refuse to come to court?' He knew that asking the Princess anything was a risk and that she did not owe him any answer if she chose to keep quiet.

'My husband sent you?'

'Yes, your Grace, as I say the King has a great gift for you.' Argyle saw the Princess hunch and stopped talking.

'I am surprised that he sent you, considering what he did,' she sneered. 'He must know that I cannot trust him - or her - anymore!' The Princess stopped near a pavilion, dry wines hanging from the roof, most likely making a pretty sight in the summer but in winter its wilted branches had an ominous feel. She looked around and waved her ladies further away, from their dismayed looks Argyle could tell this would get back to Lady de Coucy.

'What happened, your Grace?'

'I had to send Celeste away,' the Princess said without ceremony. 'He cannot keep his hands off her! I did it for her, for our friendship.'

'Who?!'

'The King of course!' the Princess said blinking away tears. 'I knew that he would have other women, my father said as much, I expected it, but not that he would find them in my chambers!'

The King? Argyle thought, not Bolingbroke? That would explain why the King kept asking, if free to choose, Argyle did not want to marry a woman at court. What would the King have done if Argyle had admitted that he longed for Celeste? He shuddered at the thought.

The Princess wiped her eyes angrily and stared into the horizon trying to compose herself. It was strange to see a child of seven displaying such mature emotions, though Argyle suspected her frustration had more to do with feeling the loss a friend and companion than infuriation with her husband's adultery. Or so he hoped.

'Your Grace, you are sure?'

She whipped her head around and glared. 'I saw them! I asked her, I demanded the truth, and she said that I was right. She did nothing to deny it or try to persuade me it was nothing. Just said that I was right. I had to send her away!' Her voice trembled, betraying her fear; after all she was a child alone at the English court, betrayed by a woman she had loved as an older sister.

Argyle swallowed to get the taste of iron at the back of his mouth away; he did not know what to say.

'You have not seen her at court?' The Princess seemed to have regained control.

'No, your Grace,' Argyle said. 'I have not seen her.'

'Why would he pick her?' The Princess rose, folding her hands inside her wide sleeves. 'And why would she accept him when she is in love with you?'

'Me?!' Argyle had never thought Celeste in love - her passion and desire he had never doubted, but love?

'Oh, Sir Argyle, it was the worst kept secret at court! We all knew! Every time she saw you, she would blush and stammer. Why could you not have loved her back?' The Princess looked up at Argyle. 'Why did you not return for Christmas?'

'I fell in love,' Argyle said, marvelling at how natural that sounded. 'I came here to tell your Grace that if you - and the King - approve of my chosen wife, I shall marry this spring.'

'I suppose he must be pleased! Now that you are out of the way for good, for I cannot in good faith believe that you would keep Celeste as your mistress if you are to be married,' the Princess said and gave Argyle a pleading look.

'No, your Grace, I had given up all thought a future with Celeste before Christmas.' Argyle let the Princess lean on his arm. 'I hoped you might speak up for my chosen bride? The King had sanctioned another match made by my brother, but he is sure to accept the match if you do. '

The Princess gripped his arm, her fingers felt as a tiny bird's claws piercing his skin. 'Those were his words?' Argyle nodded and she forced a weak smile. 'Then of course I shall receive her - and speak in your favour. How can he think to deny me anything at this point? Why would he? Although,' she paused and looked up, 'if I do sanction your match, there is nothing to stop him from pursuing her. Nothing to stop them being together.'

Argyle fixed her gaze. 'Until you come of age, your Grace, nothing will.'

She nodded at the reality and began walking again. 'I am no fool, Sir Argyle. Before my marriage, my father explained the duties of a husband and the instincts of a man. I expected the King to be discrete and find his pleasures somewhere that was not … I know I cannot hide here forever.'

For a while they walked on in silence, the footsteps of the four ladies-in-waiting now closer. Argyle pointed out a little sparrow sitting on a branch, all puffed up against the cold to the Princess, but she only glanced at the bird that took flight as they approached.

In the end, Argyle spoke again. 'And Celeste? Where is she?'

'I do not know. I sent her away, and I have heard nothing from her since.' The Princess looked lost. 'She has not gone home, or I would have been informed. Either she is hiding somewhere in London, or someone has taken pity on her and taken her in. I care not!'

'I could enquire on your behalf,' Argyle said. 'No one needs know.'

The Princess considered his proposal and Argyle glanced at her every once in a while, but she looked lost in thought. 'If you do,' she said suddenly, her clear voice startling Argyle, 'you must report directly to me, there can be no messages sent between us.'

'As you command, your Grace.'

'Is it treason? Do you think my husband will think it treason?' There was something desperate in her questions. 'Because I cannot be thought to be acting against the King.'

'You are concerned for your friend that is hardly treason,' Argyle said although he was not certain that the King would agree. 'And I will take full responsibility, you have my word.'

The Princess gave him a saying glance before walking briskly towards the doors where Prudence and Lady de Coucy were waiting. 'Do come again soon, Sir Argyle,' she said. 'Your visit has been a solace.'

'Please allow me to present a gift from the King before I leave, your Grace.'

'Very well,' the Princess said and folded her hands once more. 'What has my husband sent with you?'

'A coronation,' Argyle said and the Princess froze. 'The King is planning your coronation, and he intends for all of England to see their splendid Queen in all her glory.'

'A peace offering?' She sounded doubtful. 'I thought he had forgotten about his promise to my father to crown me within a year.'

'He had not.' Argyle was certain the Princess was right, and that the King was indeed offering peace in the form of a lavish ceremony.

'You will bring your future bride to the ceremony?' the Princess asked and clutched Argyle's hand. 'I can meet her then? Oh, it would bring such joy! Promise me that you will bring her!'

Argyle bowed low and ignored Lady de Coucy's cold stare. He waited until the Princess and her ladies had gone back inside before he walked around the corner of the castle heading for the stables, his mind whirling with thoughts of the King, Celeste and Bolingbroke somehow entangled. Argyle wondered if the King knew of Celeste's dealings with Bolingbroke and if perhaps this was the King's way of unmanning Bolingbroke. Or had Bolingbroke finally managed to get a spy into the royal bedchamber? Without the Princess' friendship, Celeste was in a weak position where Bolingbroke's demands were concerned.

Once in the saddle, he saw the Princess looking down at him from one of the high windows. He nodded to her but she did not move.

What worried Argyle most was that the King would spurn his own wife by choosing his new bedmate between her ladies. How had Celeste come to be the King's favourite? Did he not see how it might look to the French if the Princess decided to tell her father of her grievance?

Argyle was far from sure that a coronation, however lavish and splendid, would be enough to appease the Princess.

CHAPTER 20

10 March 1397 - London

Isobel had arrived the night before and was still sleeping in her room. It had been a long, weary journey for her, the weather had changed from sun to sleet, and she had told him that she regretted taking a carriage. It had got stuck so many times that Isobel claimed it would have been faster if she had walked. Argyle had laughed until she had shot him a dark glance and had gone to bed without eating. Argyle still found it strange to have a woman in his London house.

'M'lord.' Stephen had accompanied Isobel on her journey. 'When is the event to take place?'

'The day after tomorrow. The King believes that the best way to get all the Londoners into the streets for their new Queen is to have the coronation on a Sunday. They will be out after church, and he is determined that she is to be cheered by every soul in town.'

Argyle had asked for his breakfast to be served in the parlour and had invited Stephen to join him. A tray of empty bowls and half-eaten bread stood by the door, Stephen was picking his teeth with the tip of his knife. 'And more. We were caught in a throng of people riding for London because of the coronation. I think the King'll be pleased.'

'He has certainly planned the event in detail,' Argyle said. 'It may even outshine the coronation of Queen Anne.'

Stephen got up. 'Well, I'll be in the streets to see this Princess you always speak so highly of. She must be something special to be crowned Queen when she's still a child.'

'He is lucky,' Isobel said from the doorway, startling them, she looked at Stephen. 'I cannot eat for fear of being presented at court.' Stephen nodded to her as they passed, he was careful to sidestep the tray. Isobel stayed standing just inside the door, looking around the room, which was small but comfortably furnished.

'You had no dinner last night, you must eat.' Argyle went to her. 'The King is expecting that my bride to be is in good health.'

Isobel rested her hand on his arm for just a moment. 'Oh, and what interest would the King have in your bride?'

'Hopefully not too much,' Argyle said in half jest, he still could not shake the image of Celeste in the King's arms. 'We are summoned to meet the King and the Princess today at noon. Please dear Isobel, take some comfort in the fact that the Princess is determined to like you.'

'Because she favours you?'

Argyle thought he heard a drip of spite in Isobel's words but dismissed it; she was tired, most likely aching from the tiresome journey, and most of all, she was scared of the prospect of being at court. 'Because you are important to me.'

She seemed to soften. 'Then lead me to the table and feed me, my Lord. I shall do nothing to change the Princess' high opinion of you - and of me by association.'

Argyle was fairly certain that the Princess would sanction the match, and completely sure that the King would too, after all, he had much to gain from Argyle's marriage, although no man could ever deny the King anything. Still, the King saw Argyle as a rival to Celeste's affections, and he did not want that role. A married life might just provide the sanctuary from court, Argyle had long desired.

'You may also meet some of my family,' Argyle led Isobel into the hall where many were breaking their fast. 'They will all attend the coronation. I believe Thomas has some great part to play in the ceremony.'

'Oh?' Isobel cracked the shell of a boiled egg. 'Will they be there when I am presented?'

'I do not know.' Argyle regretted that he had not thought to ask. 'I think it is a very formal affair.'

'You do not even know what I am expected to do?!' Isobel's voice was shrill.

'The King's secretary is sending someone to instruct us.' Argyle saw her stiffen. 'I will be by your side through it all.'

'I should expect no less.' Isobel put down the uneaten egg and left the room.

10 March 1397 - Westminster Palace

'Do not leave me!' Isobel clutched Argyle's arm so tight that he winced. The tall doors to the great hall of Westminster were closed to them, two White Harts standing at either side. Argyle remembered being in the chamber with La Fontaine long ago, the two of them waiting to congratulate the King on his marriage to Queen Anne. It seemed a lifetime ago.

'Of course not. You heard the secretary, we go in together, you curtsey and I kneel, the King asks us to stand, and I formally announce our betrothal. If the Princess chooses, she may acknowledge you by speaking to you. It will be over before you know it.' Argyle patted her icy hand. 'Truly, there is nothing to fear.'

Isobel looked up, and Argyle saw that her eyes were welling with tears. He wanted to say something encouraging but the herald announced them to the room, the doors opened and the crowd parted. He felt as if he was half-dragging Isobel along, but when he glanced at her, she held her head high and looked beautiful in her pale green dress, her auburn curls spilling down her back. Argyle knelt before the dais, Isobel curtseying next to him.

'Sir Argyle!' The King's voice resounded in the hushed hall. 'Rise.'

'Your Majesty, your Grace. I have come to present my bride, the lady Isobel Thorne.'

'Lady Thorne,' the Princess' sweet voice rang out. 'It is a pleasure.'

Isobel curtsied again and the hall applauded. The formal presentation was over, but Argyle could still feel Isobel's hand clutch his arm as knights and courtiers came over to congratulate him and glance at her. He wondered why she was so taut and uncomfortable even though the King had held true to his word, and the Princess had been kind enough to speak directly to Isobel without forcing a reply.

'Relax,' he whispered to Isobel. 'It is done and now you can claim a little fame for being a new lady at court, attractive to all the men because you are yet unwed and interesting to all the women, who are jealous at your catching such a fine husband.'

Isobel gave a weak smile. 'I will be happy when we are back at Beauworth.'

'Lady Thorne, Sir Argyle,' the Princess said behind them. 'Please, walk with me.'

The crowd dispersed, and several of the ladies in the room glanced enviously as the Princess took Isobel's hand. 'I am truly pleased to meet you, Sir Argyle has not done you justice.'

Isobel coloured. 'I … thank you, your Grace.'

'I wonder if you might accompany me to my rooms,' the Princess said but was cut short by the King.

'Sir Argyle! What a fine bride you have chosen! I fully understand why you could not let her go!' The King smiled broadly at Isobel, who dropped into a deep curtsey and kept her eyes to the floor even after the King had motioned for her to stand. 'She is a beauty!'

The King grabbed his wife by the hand and tucked it into the crook of his arm. 'You will forgive us, but there is so much to do before tomorrow. I will see both of you there, I am sure.'

The Princess looked back over her shoulder while the King dragged her from the room. Argyle thought she looked almost desperate to be away from her husband, and knowing their sordid secret, Argyle could hardly begrudge her. As soon as the royal couple left, the atmosphere in the room changed, the air seemed somehow cleaner and easier to breathe.

'She is kind,' Isobel said. 'But the King …'

'Is eager that the ceremony tomorrow is a success,' Thomas said and sketched a bow to Isobel. 'I am Argyle's brother, Lord Thomas Mowbray.' Isobel curtsied and let Thomas grace her hand with a kiss. 'It is a pleasure to meet the woman who finally caught my brother in matrimony. I was beginning to run out of prospective brides, and lo and behold, he finds one on his own. And a fine woman too.' Thomas looked at her as he might at a brood mare. 'Very fine.'

Argyle grit his teeth. 'Thank you, Thomas. Have you brought Elizabeth?'

'She is here somewhere,' Thomas said never taking his eyes off Isobel. 'I offered the Princess her company, but she declined. Still, I am to carry the Princess' crown tomorrow and Elizabeth her train. We will have important roles to fulfil.'

'Let us not keep you, my Lord,' Isobel said, a sting in her voice. 'I would like to meet your wife, but it will keep now that I know that you are so favoured by the King.'

Argyle bit his lip to keep from laughing at Thomas' baffled look. Composing himself, Argyle nodded, 'Yes, brother, you should be about your important business, not here speaking to us. Perhaps we might find Eleanor here? Or Margaret?'

'Margaret and Eleanor are not here yet,' Thomas said sharply to Argyle. 'They will be present tomorrow.'

'And Joan?'

'Who knows, she is as fickle …' Thomas stopped. 'I must leave you.' He turned and all but ran from them, the assembled people parting before his stride.

To Argyle, the room had begun to feel claustrophobic, there were so many people crammed into the space that you could hardly move or turn without stepping on a dress or bumping into someone. Now that he knew his sisters were not present, he longed to get back to his own house, and he could tell Isobel felt the same. He bent to ask her if she wanted to leave, when out of the corner of his eye, he saw the crowd parted for a rustling, dark blue dress.

'Argyle!' Joan threw her arms around his neck and kissed his cheeks. 'Isobel! Oh, I was so delighted to see you; the court was so secretive about who was being presented. Imagine my surprise that it was my little brother, finally ready to settle down.'

Isobel looked bewildered and Argyle made a quick introduction. 'Isobel, this is my sister Joan. And her husband Sir Thomas Grey.'

Sir Thomas always had a quiet demeanour about him, perhaps it was his way to balance out his wife's fluttering personality. He bowed lightly and shook Argyle's hand. 'I must see Exeter on urgent business,' he said to no one in particular and bounded off, Joan looking after him.

'Oh! One minute he does not want to go to the coronation and the next, he is thick as thieves with the King's half brother.' Joan turned to Isobel. 'You might as well grow used to it, when your husband is tied to the Crown somehow you never quite know where he is from one moment to the next.'

Isobel blinked. 'Really?'

'Oh, Argyle,' Joan said in a scolding tone. 'Have you explained nothing to this poor, sweet creature?! Really, do I have to do everything myself? Come, Isobel, let us be properly acquainted.' Joan pulled Isobel towards the garden doors that had been opened to let in a bout of fresh spring air. London was glittering in the sunlight, the air suddenly sweet and warm after days of cold and sleet. Isobel shot Argyle a last doubtful glance before she let Joan drag her through the doors and into the garden.

'Sir Argyle.' The King pushed his way into Argyle's train of thought. Although the King had professed to be busy with the coronation, apparently he was not too busy to lay claim to Argyle's time. 'Now that my wife is safe in her rooms, and your future wife is preoccupied, I would have a word.'

'Majesty.' Argyle followed the King who walked briskly into the garden and proceeded around the bend of one of the hedges, which was sprouting fat, green buds, promising to cover the bare, spindly branches soon.

'A fine bird you have caught in your net.' The King plucked at a bud. 'She looks a little familiar …'

'Really, Majesty?' Argyle had the same feeling, there was something about Isobel that looked very familiar, but he could not quite place it.

'I may be wrong,' the King said and let the bud fall to the ground. 'There is the matter of another lady. Isabella confessed that she told you - I suppose it could not be helped. Keeping secrets at court is a tiresome affair. A little like yours.' The King stopped Argyle's protests with a hand. 'But I think you of all men would not deny that she is very beguiling.'

'Certainly, Majesty.' Argyle began to suspect that Celeste had seduced the King; she could turn her charms on and off, as Argyle well knew.

The King began walking slowly down the gravel path, kicking at the small, round pebbles. 'My cousin Bolingbroke is back at court.'

'I had heard, Majesty.' An ominous feeling crept up Argyle's spine and clawed its way into his chest. If the King knew the real reason Bolingbroke was here there would be trouble and danger ahead, but only if Thomas was right and Gaunt was plotting.

'My uncle is not well,' the King said. 'I knew he would send for Henry, after all he is next in line for the Lancaster lands … they will be the death of me. My grandfather was cruel to me in his dying wish.'

'Majesty?'

'He decided that if I was unable to have a child - a son - the throne would pass to my Lancaster cousins.' The King harked a laugh. 'Little did he know what and who they are. How could he do this to me? I am considering putting it before Parliament that they revoke his decision, I have already named March as my successor, and why should I not be entitled to do so without others interfering? After all he is my cousin's son.'

Argyle looked up to see the King staring intently at him. 'The Earl of March is a fine choice.' A child, Argyle thought, another child to be a pawn in court politics and a proof of old grudges. When will this end?

'I trust that you will keep our conversation secret?' The King began making his way back to the palace. The wind was kicking up and drifting clouds were blocking out the sun, stealing away what little warmth early spring had to offer. 'All of it.'

'Yes, Majesty,' Argyle said, remembering his promise to the Princess, which he intended to keep even if it meant asking questions without the King finding out. But he would have to be careful. Soon he would have much more to protect than his own life, and Argyle was certain that if he crossed the King, he would not shy away from punishing everyone Argyle held dear - chief among them his soon to be wife.

Such secrets we all have, Argyle thought and caught sight of Isobel standing alone beside a monstrous statute. She was staring intently at someone, but when Argyle turned to follow her gaze there was no one there.

14 March 1397 - Westminster Palace, Baron de Welles' apartments

'The Queen looked spectacular!' Eleanor sounded thrilled. 'She won the heart of every man, woman and child present at her coronation. She is such a sweet creature!' She twirled around the grand apartment, the de Welles coat of arms prominent above the doors and the fireplace. The gold emblem sparkled in the dim candlelight.

'She certainly is,' Argyle agreed. The Princess had transformed into a Queen consort most gracefully, swearing her oaths in church with confidence and letting the King parade her through the city. The King had swathed her in regal attire and even designed a new crown to fit her pretty, little head.

'And the King! Spared no expense! I dare say he was trying to prove a point.' Eleanor turned and gave Argyle a knowing look. 'Isobel has left?'

'Court did not agree with her,' Argyle said with regret. Isobel had insisted that she return to Beauworth the day after the coronation, claiming that she had to start preparing for their wedding.

Argyle had decided to stay in London, and their parting had been cold. Rather than stay at his own house the first night she was gone, Argyle had accepted Eleanor's invitation to dine with her. Baron de Welles was busy at court and Eleanor hated eating alone.

'It rarely does if you are not born and raised for it,' Eleanor said. 'I dare say that the Queen still has not forgiven the King his misstep.'

'Whatever do you mean, sweet sister?'

Argyle had hoped to avoid the subject, but Eleanor would have none of that. 'Oh please, his mistress! That he would pick her of all the women at court, what a mess. She lives at court now, did you know?'

'I know the Queen sent her away. Are you sure she is at court?' Having had little time to make enquiries while Isobel had been in London, Argyle was in a way glad to know that he would not have to search far.

Eleanor tossed her golden hair, in the light of the fire she looked years younger than her 26. 'Of course, I am sure. Margaret asked me long ago to keep an eye on Lady Celeste, back when …' Eleanor's cheerful tone changed when she noticed Argyle's glare. 'Well, she was concerned.'

'Back when I was having an affair with her,' Argyle said. 'She was unnaturally interested in it.'

'She was just being Margaret,' Eleanor said sitting back in her chair so hard that a pillow dropped to the floor. When Argyle bent to pick it up, Eleanor grabbed his shoulder and pulled him close. 'Celeste is here at court - perhaps the King himself is hiding her in his apartments. Just yesterday, one of my ladies came upon her in the corridors beneath the King's kitchens. She is here! Right here in the palace!'

'Why would the King hide her?' Argyle threw the pillow into another chair. He was halfway pleased that the Queen's lavish coronation had not been enough to appease her wrath. She had returned to Windsor, with the Queen consort's crown on her head and still refused to show herself at court and would not let the King visit.

'But Argyle, what if she is not housed by the King?'

Eleanor's question drew Argyle back to the present. 'What are you talking about?'

'She is said to be affiliated with Woodstock.' Eleanor glanced at Argyle, her face thoughtful. 'Feed the fire, will you?'

Argyle obeyed, relieved that he could hide his face from her. He had thought she would mention Bolingbroke or even Gaunt, why did she point to Woodstock? Why did everyone try to pin blame on Woodstock? Everyone except Coxcombe.

'Where does this gossip come from?' Argyle pushed the glowing embers around the fireplace.

'You know I cannot tell you,' Eleanor said twirling a lock of her hair. 'And I know that you want to think well of her, she is important to you still, I think?'

Argyle let the comment linger and then disappear.

'But she is the King's ... whore.' Eleanor shrugged at his obvious displeasure. 'Perhaps she thought she was doing the Queen a favour, perhaps the King charmed her …'

'But where does Woodstock fit in? Apart from his dislike of all things French, including the Queen, he has never shown any interest in the King's dealings with women. And Celeste is French.' Rather than look at Eleanor, Argyle followed a drip of wax course down the fat candle on the table between them. It was set in a heavy gold candlestick as opulent as the rest of the room.

'Is that not enough?' Eleanor asked.

'Woodstock lives as a recluse these days, I hear,' Argyle said. 'But for the Queen's coronation, the King's uncle has not been at court for almost a year. I hardly think he would harbour a French mistress in his royal apartments - even for the King.'

'Not even if it would hurt the King?'

Argyle gave Eleanor a wintry look that made her cringe. 'Woodstock relies on Gaunt's good graces to even live as he does now, at peace in the countryside. Why risk that?'

'Hunger for power,' Eleanor suggested rising to fetch a piece of paper. 'Thomas writes from Nottingham. He asks that you stay until he returns to court.'

Argyle sighed, it felt as though most of his life he had been waiting for his older brother, never able to shirk his natural place in the family. He wanted to get back to Beauworth and finalise his marriage, not sit here and wait. 'Why has he left court?'

'He does not say.'

'At least he met Isobel, he cannot argue that she is ill-suited when the

King himself approved of her,' Argyle said. 'Does he say when we might expect him?'

Eleanor skimmed the letter. 'In a week or so.'

Then I have one more week to find Celeste and get her to talk to me, before Thomas is back, Argyle thought and hoped it would be enough. He decided not to involve Eleanor, she might look like him, but he was not sure that she was anything like him.

'Is the Queen coming back to court soon?' Eleanor asked. 'I miss her ladies and the breath of youth that clings to her.'

'When I last visited her, she was in high spirits, I am sure she will rejoin court soon,' Argyle said looking out of the window at the grey skies.

'You have spent much time with her.'

'The King has asked that I visit,' Argyle said.

'Maybe he should have chosen another bedmate then,' Eleanor said joining Argyle at the window. 'But that would entail him having to think about someone other than himself …' They smiled at each other, Argyle searching for clues of dishonesty in his sister's blue eyes. All he saw was a reflection of himself.

When he finally made his way across London to his own house, Argyle decided to give his enquiries just two more weeks. He would have to keep quiet about it to Thomas and draw back from Eleanor. And most of all, he would have to get the Queen to come back to court soon.

CHAPTER 21

3 April 1397 - London

Argyle was fuming and riding through London did not improve his mood. Thomas would be back soon, and most likely, he would be in a foul mood when Argyle told him that the Queen was still at Windsor. Adding to his anger was the fact that he had still not seen Celeste, although he had begun loitering in the corridors outside the King's apartments, at all hours.

He spotted a tavern its sign swinging in the April breeze, and on a hunch he decided to go in. He handed his horse to the stable boy and pushed through the door. The room was gloomy, only a few men playing dice. Argyle bought a mug of ale and sat at the far corner, brooding over his failure to find the truth for the Queen. She would expect his report tomorrow, and he had nothing new for her.

The door opened, letting in a gush of spring air that made the tallow candle on his table flicker and smoke. Argyle leaned back. He was at his wits end, he had stalked the corridors, poured money into the pockets of anyone he might think would know something, and yet he had nothing to show for it. In addition, he had made no progress finding out who had ordered La Fontaine's death. More than anything, he was angry with himself.

'Sir Argyle,' a hoarse voice whispered near his ear.

Argyle moved to turn around and felt cold steel on his throat. 'Sir Coxcombe.'

'I have been waiting long for this,' Coxcombe said, turning his dagger to let the flat of the blade rest under Argyle's jaw. 'I am beginning to think that you are a little too dangerous to have roaming the streets.'

'Only a little? You offend me.' Argyle tried to stay calm. 'What do you want?'

'I want to make sure you stop asking questions that you ought not be asking,' Coxcombe sounded a little drunk, his hand shook ever so slightly.

'Not to worry, I have been preoccupied.'

'So I hear. Which put me in mind that perhaps we might strike a deal,' Coxcombe lowered his dagger to rest it on the back of Argyle's bench, just inches from his throat.

'How so?'

'I tell you where to find the King's whore, you give up your other matter,' Coxcombe slurred.

How does everyone know what I am about? Argyle thought and came to the conclusion that his skills in secrecy left too much to be desired, Thomas was the spy-master of the family, and Argyle had never truly intended to rival his position. 'What do you mean?'

'I happen to know where the lady is,' Coxcombe said, dragging out the word lady.

'What is that to me?'

'Besides the King's eternal gratitude that you were able to persuade the Queen to return to court?'

Argyle cursed inwardly. 'And your price is that I stop asking about La Fontaine's death?'

'A fair deal, I think.' Coxcombe's breath was sour and foul. 'Yes?'

Argyle nodded, he needed to know, he needed to talk to Celeste and discover what was going on. He could strike the deal now and break it later. If Coxcombe was drinking heavily, Argyle knew he would win a fight if needs be but he hoped to avoid it, best not to draw attention to himself or his search of Celeste.

'Good,' Coxcombe turned the dagger again, the tip of it punching a tiny hole in Argyle's skin. 'You will receive a message tomorrow. Stay at home until it arrives.'

'Or?'

'No deal.' The dagger was pushed in a little further and Argyle felt a warm trickling down his skin.

'Very well, you have my word.'

The dagger disappeared, and Argyle turned quickly to see Coxcombe's back slip out of the door. Rather than pursue Coxcombe, Argyle got up, ordered another mug of ale and, pulling up the collar of his shirt, he took part in a game of dice for the next couple of hours. By the time he rode into his courtyard, the tiny hole in his neck had clotted, the dry blood sticking to his collar, and he had won a fair few coins. Argyle spent the night prowling his study waiting for morning and the chance of finally seeing Celeste, although he had no idea what to say to her.

Just before dawn, he fell asleep in his chair, his rest was disturbed by whirling dreams in which Celeste danced with the corpse of La Fontaine, who kept giving him disappointed looks while the blood from La Fontaine's shoulder wound soaked Celeste's beautiful sky-blue gown.

4 April 1397 - London

Argyle woke the following day with a heavy head, and the air in his study thick and stale. He threw open a window and called for a servant to bring some food and a basin of water. Splashing his face, he relished in the cold trickle down his chest and winced when he accidentally brushed against the tiny wound on his neck, this could prove to be a long day. He had finished his meal when a messenger arrived in the yard, and Argyle snatched the note from his squire's hand.

'The man is waiting for your reply, M'lord,' the boy said.

Argyle split the seal, the wax cracking lightly in his grip and wondered what Coxcombe could write that would sanction a reply; he was simply to inform Argyle of Celeste's whereabouts. The sight of familiar writing made Argyle grimace, Thomas had returned to court and required his presence this afternoon. 'Tell him I am busy today and will call tomorrow.'

The boy looked as if he wanted to ask something, and Argyle regretted choosing to leave George at Beauworth to bring this young lad. George, at least, knew when to obey and keep quiet.

'Tell the messenger,' Argyle said, his voice hard and cold. 'Go on.' The boy ran from the room leaving Argyle with Thomas' message.

- I need to see you this afternoon on business that cannot wait. I am appalled and shocked at what I have been told upon my return to court. How is it that I cannot leave, even for a few weeks, without the whole world falling to bits? Why did you agree to this silliness? Why did you drag Eleanor into it? Ours is not the task to annoy the King, ours is to keep him happy! -

If it was indeed his task to keep the King happy, why had Thomas left? And how did he know what Argyle was about, unless Eleanor had broken her promise and told Thomas everything?

Well now, here is proof that we might all turn back on our word, just as I mean to do on mine to Coxcombe, Argyle thought and opened the window to breathe in the watery spring air. He knew that Thomas would be furious to hear that he would not come until the morrow, but Coxcombe had been clear in his terms. If Argyle was out, the message about Celeste would not be delivered.

It was well past noon before another messenger arrived, stomping into Argyle's room and delivering a scrap of paper. He stayed until Argyle had read the scribbled address and was paid for his troubles.

Sitting in his chair next to the burned down fire, Argyle stared at the address on the note. The cool spring air had left the room clammy and dismal, and although he had closed the shutters the draft from the cracks made the little note in his hand flutter. He would never have looked for her there; he had not even thought it possible that she would be there.

4 April 1397, evening - Charing Cross

Celeste opened the door and stepped back with a gasp when she saw Argyle. He walked in and slammed the door shut before she could cry out or protest. In the brightly lit room, Celeste was not alone, two girls, her ladies-in-waiting Argyle assumed, were picking through her chest of dresses most likely trying to choose which dress to put her in that night. Through the half-open door at the other end of the room, Argyle spotted a large four-poster bed, flowing silk curtains drawn and a woven carpet on the floor. The luxury of her bedchamber was undeniable, as was the sparse almost tawdry furniture in the front room. Clearly her lodgings had been made up hastily, emphasis put on her inner sanctum. She was not housed here to host evening parties; she was here to entertain one man in only one capacity.

Eying the girls, Argyle asked, 'A word alone, my Lady?'

'This is not a good time …'

'Now, my Lady!'

Celeste bit her trembling lip but seemed to decide that it was better to give Argyle what he wanted than risk the girls overhearing their words. 'Leave us.'

'But my Lady, the King …,' the red-haired girl protested.

Celeste gave her a dark frown that stifled her protests and sent the two from the room with a wave. They dragged their feet, the red-haired girl glancing back at Argyle several times, before they left by a door at the back of the room, the glimpse of opulence disappearing when they closed the door.

Hunching her shoulders, Celeste retreated behind a big chair placed near the hearth. Argyle tried to see past her hostile looks to find the woman who had seduced him in France, and who he had once entertained dreams of marrying, but she was gone. Perhaps it was for the best, it would make his mission so much the easier. 'Celeste …'

She interrupted. 'How did you find me?'

'I made a deal with a man I thought to be ... it does not matter.'

'It does to me,' Celeste said, 'I was promised that I would be safe here.'

'You are safe. I have only come to plead with you on behalf of the Queen who still wishes to be your true friend.'

At the mention of the Queen, Celeste looked ready to faint, and she grabbed the chair tight enough for her fingers to turn white. 'The Queen? She is a Queen now?'

No one told you? Argyle thought but pressed on with his well-rehearsed speech. 'She is on the brink of despair; her only true friend has left her and has seduced her husband. She cannot trust a soul in her household. I simply do not understand …'

Celeste looked away. 'Why do you think it was I who seduced the King?'

Because I know you, Argyle thought, and because I know the King. But clearly there are secrets between you, if you did not know he had her crowned. Argyle wondered how she could not have known when all of London had turned out for the Queen, the church bells tolling in celebration and the streets decorated with silver and purple. Celeste must have been packed off for the coronation to ensure nothing would go wrong.

'Tell me what happened that would make you turn against your Queen,' Argyle demanded, stepping close enough for his knee to touch the seat of the chair. This close, he noticed the lines around her eyes and her mouth, clear signs of the strain she was under.

'He approached me,' Celeste said through gritted teeth. 'Said he had noticed me right from the start but that you had beat him to me and that, since you were a loyal and honest man, he would not come between us.' She looked Argyle in the eye, tears glistening. 'Imagine his relief when you left for Beauworth in the fall and did not return to claim me. Nothing stood between him and me then.'

Argyle let out a breath he did not know he had been holding, his suspicions of the King's selfish desires having affected his decision to accept Argyle's petition to marry Isobel had been true. Had the King feared that faced with a choice, Celeste would have chosen Argyle? What might have happened if his petition had been for Celeste? If she had been free?

The prospect made him shudder and he held out a hand to Celeste, but she shied away, using the chair between them as a shield. 'You abandoned me.'

'You were married - you are still married!' Argyle said a little resentment sneaking into his voice. 'You knew how I felt. And to thwart your Queen, your friend, so!'

'Better me than some random tart!' Celeste snarled when she continued. 'The Queen should be happy he is with me!'

'Happy that her husband is whoring with her friend?!' Argyle shook his head. 'Why?'

'She should have kept me nearby,' Celeste said, her face white. 'Then she would know that I do not love him and that I did this for love of her. That there was no need to send me away; she merely had to ask her husband to find his distractions somewhere else. Would he dare defy her, do you think, when you know what political power she embodies?'

'Love of her?'

'She is in many ways family ...,' Celeste said. 'Would you not do anything to protect your family?'

She had hit the mark; Argyle had done almost anything to protect his family, and if his union with Isobel was blessed with children, he almost dreaded the lengths he might go to, to protect his family. He stepped back. 'Yes. But how are you protecting her?'

'Would that I trusted you enough to tell you,' Celeste said. 'Family makes you do remarkable things. Things you would never have considered if the stakes were not as high as they are.'

'The Queen will return to court soon,' Argyle said wondering at Celeste's final remark. 'She will be devastated to find you on the King's lap.'

'I only see him at night.' Celeste gave Argyle a grudging look. 'No man would ever openly show me off at court.'

'Bolingbroke might,' Argyle regretted his words the moment he spoke them. He turned his back to her and went to the door, resting his hand on the handle, the iron ring cold to the touch.

'So he might.' Celeste said and Argyle glanced back to see her smile. 'And you can ponder that on your way back to the Queen.'

5 April 1397 - London

The next morning found Argyle in front of Thomas' ornate door. Drowning the deep desire to turn away, Argyle gave a quick knock before entering. The cluttered room was dimly lit, Thomas sitting in his chair by the low fire. For just a moment, Argyle thought he was sleeping, but then Thomas stirred. 'What took you so long?'

'The Queen wanted a word,' Argyle lied.

'She is quite taken by you,' Thomas said and beckoned for Argyle to sit. 'But perhaps other, more pleasurable attractions keep you near?'

Argyle ignored Thomas' insinuations. 'What was so important that it could not wait?'

'I have a bit of news that might interest you.' Thomas eyed Argyle keenly. 'About Bolingbroke.'

'Margaret and you may scheme as you desire, but leave me out of it!'

'I thought you would be interested,' Thomas said and stretched towards the fire, rubbing his brow. 'After all, it has to do with the little Queen.'

'No.'

'Are you sure? You who claim to be such a great friend of hers.'

Argyle rose, the room felt stuffy and claustrophobic with its piles of papers and dingy furniture. 'As I said, you may scheme with Margaret, she seems to enjoy it, but leave me out of it.'

Thomas waved at him. 'Very well, if you want to be kept in the dark, so be it.'

'I do!' Argyle shut the door on Thomas; for once he would have the last word.

But on the ride home, his mind whirled with thoughts about what Bolingbroke might possibly have to do with the Queen, and Argyle half regretted not listening to his brother. Did Thomas know who harboured Celeste? The thought filled Argyle with fear.

6 April 1397 - Windsor Castle

'What does she take me for? A common fool?' the Queen bristled when Argyle told her what Celeste had said. 'I do not see how his being with her is better than his being with any other woman. Actually, I can only see it being worse!'

Her ladies-in-waiting pretended not to hear her angry words, but Argyle could see them lapping up every savoury morsel. He wondered why she had not dismissed them when he had knelt by her red throne to whisper in her ear that finally, he had seen Celeste.

'Majesty, the Lady was very upset,' Argyle said. He knew how weak he sounded. 'I let her know that you would return to court soon, and she said that the King only sees her at night. I know you had hoped she would throw herself on your mercy, but she did not. Perhaps she cannot.'

'So, I am to sit by his side and smile while she waits for him to come to her?' Argyle was surprised at her passionate tone and her pained looks. The Queen was only eight years old, and hard-pressed Argyle would have sworn that her love for the King was that of a child for her father and not the kind that would warrant such anger or jealousy.

'She was adamant that she is protecting you, Majesty,' Argyle repeated. 'Now that we know where she is housed, I can try to speak to her again, see if I can persuade her to change her mind, although ...'

'Although if she does, she risks angering the King,' the Queen said in a hushed voice. 'Oh Sir Argyle, if it had only been any other woman!'

One of her ladies turned to see the Queen gripping Argyle's arm tight, tears spilling down her face, and the lady frowned nudging the woman sitting next to her. Argyle noticed them exchanging a glance and wondered what they were going to say to Lady de Cousy when he left.

'Majesty, I shall do anything within my power to make Celeste see reason,' Argyle promised and gently made to remove her hand, noticing that the shiny red colour of the throne was already flaking.

The Queen clung to him, for a moment, staring into his eyes. 'Please do.'

Again, Argyle caught the two ladies-in-waiting exchanging glances. 'What is best is for you to rejoin the court. Let the King see what he is spurning. Let him know that his peace with France rests on his relationship with you. After all, of all the Princesses in Europe, he chose you. He made you his Queen.'

'I shall return to court this coming Saturday,' the Queen announced to the room. 'His Majesty has long requested my presence, and I find that the succour of a quiet life is wearing thin.'

In the clamour of her ladies exclaiming their happiness, the Queen leaned in and made Argyle bend his head to hear her words. 'Do whatever it takes and I will reward you richly. Very richly!'

When Argyle straightened up he saw one of the ladies looking intently at him and snap her head round when their eyes met.

Argyle left Windsor to ride to the King and finally announce his success in persuading the Queen to return to court.

What games we play on each other, Argyle thought, the King believes I am solely about his business, and the Queen believes I am her man. I wonder how Thomas navigates these dangerous seas day in and day out without crashing against the rocks?

7 April 1397 - Westminster Palace

Argyle had been waiting outside the King's chambers since daybreak, hoping to be among the first to get an audience. When the bells tolled for Sext and the sun was high in the sky, Argyle had given up any pretence that his message would be prioritised above those of the nobility or the King's personal friends. Apparently, he was no longer either.

Eleanor appeared at his elbow. 'How long have you been waiting?'

'I came before the sun was up,' Argyle said, offering her a seat on the hard bench set up against the wall. From here he had a good view of the room and the doors to the King's chambers that opened and closed at regular intervals. 'I think perhaps the King no longer believes that I can bring him good news.'

'But you can?' Her eyes widened a little.

'You might as well know,' Argyle said deciding to test her loyalty. 'But you can tell no one until the King makes his announcement!'

Eleanor nodded, staring at one of the White Harts guarding the King's door rather than meeting Argyle's eye. 'The Queen will return to court this Saturday.'

'What wonderful news!' Eleanor gave a brilliant smile when a courtier bowed to her from across the room. She raised a hand in greeting and the young man winked. 'She has forgiven him?'

'It may be a while before she does, but she grows weary of her solitude,' Argyle said. 'Even if it is self-inflicted.'

Eleanor grabbed his arm, finally turning her blue eyes at him. 'Well done, little brother. I never doubted that you would be the right one to get the Queen restored to her usual happy mood.'

Really? Argyle thought, because I did not think she would ever forgive either the King or myself.

'Well, well, would you look at that,' Eleanor cut through his thoughts, her attention focused on the centre of the vast room. 'I thought he was away in York.'

Argyle followed his sister's gaze and saw Bolingbroke standing in the middle of a large crowd of courtiers and noblemen. He appeared in high spirits, the gemstones on his clothes and fingers flashing when he gestured animatedly, causing laughter and raised voices.

'Sir Argyle, the King will see you now!'

Eleanor turned with Argyle, her face serious as she leaned in. 'Be careful, you are not out of the woods yet.'

The herald gestured impatiently, and Argyle felt Eleanor let go of his sleeve, a little smile on her face. He noticed that Bolingbroke's crowd had gone quiet, all eyes on Argyle as the doors swung open for him. Before he entered, he bowed to Bolingbroke but his expression was as always inscrutable.

'Sir Argyle!' The King's voice boomed across the chamber, and Argyle bent his knee. 'Rise and come closer!'

Argyle noticed that the King was all but alone in the chamber and wondered where all of his usual followers were. Did the King know that his cousin was holding court just outside his door? Argyle walked to the foot of the dais. 'Majesty, I come straight from the Queen.'

The King motioned him closer, and Argyle scaled the steps to the dais where the King leaned forward on his great throne. 'What did my little wife have to say?'

'That she will return to court this Saturday,' Argyle said and was relieved to see the King smile. 'She grows tired of the Windsor quiet.'

'Does she now?'

'Yes, Majesty. She is fully rested and cannot wait to join you here at court.'

'Well, she must still live at Windsor,' the King said quickly. 'But I am happy that she has decided to come back to me. I have missed her.' The King got up and led the way down the back of the dais and through the door to his private chambers. Two White Harts stood guard either side of the door, swinging it open for the King to enter. He walked across the richly decorated carpet on the floor, and Argyle followed him with a sense of foreboding.

As soon as the door closed behind him, the King turned, his face sour and angry. 'I hear you have been asking questions that are none of your business!'

'Majesty?' Argyle forced a calm expression.

'Celeste had an unexpected visit from you. She was very displeased!' The King stepped close, his breath hot and laced with wine. 'So am I! I asked you to sweet-talk the Queen, not to go poking your nose in where it does not belong!'

'The Queen …' Argyle protested but a glare from the King silenced him.

'I do not care, what the Queen asked you to do! You are to do as I command, not she! She is a child!!' The King took a deep breath. 'You are not to go near Celeste again!'

'You will continued to see her, Majesty, even if the Queen …'

'The Queen will behave, and you will NEVER question me again!! Is that clear, Sir Argyle?!' The King grabbed Argyle's collar. 'I asked you a question!'

The guards at the door stared ahead with vacant expressions; undoubtedly they were not going to intervene. Argyle adopted a crestfallen attitude. 'Quite clear, Majesty, please forgive me.'

The King's grip loosened. 'Good - that is good. I hope you do not feel that you have to choose between my wife and I - for loyalty at least.'

'I am but loyal to you, Majesty,' Argyle said staring at the floor.

The King sat down on his throne. It was smaller than the one in the presence chamber but its pattern was much more intricate, little wooden faces peered out over the shoulder of the King. He seemed to ponder what to say next and in the silence, Argyle heard one of the guards clear his throat.

'I cannot stop seeing her.' The King spoke so softly that only Argyle could hear it.

'Majesty?'

'Celeste,' the King said; a flush brought colour to his white cheeks. 'She has bewitched me.'

Dangerous words, Argyle thought, for Celeste if not for the King. He decided to keep quiet; sometimes it was best to let the King lead the way.

'When the Queen comes of age, I shall do my royal duty by her,' the King's voice wavered a little. 'Of course I shall, it is for the good of England. But I do not think, I can ever live without Celeste …' The King looked at Argyle with a savage grin. 'I do not understand how you could give her up so easily and settle for another! Even if your bride is a fine, English woman.'

'Celeste was married,' Argyle said the fire of resentment kindling inside. 'She still is.'

'Luckily, I need not worry about such a trifling matter,' the King said in a mocking tone. 'Neither should you. But then I suppose you could not wait for her ancient husband to die? No, eventually your brother would have brought a prize too great to turn down! For the family if not for yourself.'

Argyle felt his neck burn and struggled not to take the bait. 'Your Majesty has sanctioned my marriage.'

'Yes! I would have been a fool to argue with you, after all your intent to marry cleared the path to my heart's desire,' the King said cheerfully. 'To think I would ever consider you an opponent. What would you have done, if I had insisted that you let her go for me?'

'We shall never know, Majesty,' Argyle said the fire inside drowned out by a rush of clarity. If the King had ordered Argyle to give up Celeste, he would have; he would have chosen his own life and freedom almost without hesitation, for certainly refusing a royal order of any kind would land Argyle in the Tower.

'No. Though I think you would have tried to intercede.' The King leaned back in his chair. 'For love of the Queen.'

Argyle felt his throat tighten and merely nodded.

'Good, she too needs someone to love her,' the King said. 'Let it be you who would never do anything but admire from afar.'

How tiresome and little you are in the face of someone you fear another would choose instead of you, Argyle thought.

'I have no further use of you for now, Sir Argyle,' the King said stealing a glance to a side door that was slightly ajar, a warm golden glow flickering within. 'You have done your duty well, now forget the lady this was all about and go home. Your marriage can go ahead, your bride must miss you greatly.'

Argyle bowed quickly and left the way he had come in. He saw a figure move behind the half-open side door and knew it must be Celeste; after all there was a subtle scent of orange blossom in the air.

CHAPTER 22

21 April 1397 - Beauworth

'Where is Thomas?' Joan's voice was laced with irritation as she surveyed the bright green forest view. Argyle had invited all his family to the wedding, and his sisters had accepted at once, excited that their little brother would finally marry. When Thomas finally deigned to write his letter had been spiteful and angry.

'He is busy at court,' Argyle said, arranging more chairs around a low table to one side of the room. Isobel had insisted he try to make the grand parlour grander, which apparently meant moving as much furniture into it as possible. Right now, Argyle felt he could hardly move without stumbling over something, but he wanted Isobel to be happy and would cram in another hundred chairs if that would help him achieve his goal.

'Busy?' Joan was livid. 'Too busy to visit his brother and meet his bride?'

Argyle held out his arms to his sister. 'Life at court is not always at one's own disposal, you know that. And he has already met Isobel.'

'Do not take his side!' Joan spun around violently, knocking over a small table, all the things tumbling on the floor, clanging and rattling. Eleanor slipped into the room, her eyes wide at the commotion.

'How could you possibly be content that he is not here?' Joan demanded, brushing a strand of her dark hair back into her glittering hairnet.

'Because if he had come, he would ruin the wedding.' Argyle bent to pick up a candlestick and put the table right.

'So he did write?' Joan kicked the candle stub and it rolled across the floor, coming to rest before Eleanor's silk slippers.

'In the end, I got a message from him, yes.' Argyle still had not forgotten Thomas cold reply. 'I am happy you are here, and Eleanor and Margaret too. If Thomas had come, I would have welcomed him. But I have defied him too many times, and I did not expect him to ever forgive or forget.'

'He is mostly angry because you are marrying someone of lesser birth.' Eleanor sat on the edge of the oak table. Dangling her feet, she looked at the two others. 'You know it is true.'

'Yes,' Argyle said, Thomas had doled out his disapproval in the angry reply to Argyle's invitation, but he was as likely to be angry because Argyle had refused to be his spy any more, something his sisters did not know about. 'He even dared to protest to Isobel being a widow, although the same is true of his own wife.'

'He is blinded by ambition.' Joan stomped her foot, puffing up the rushes and sending a sharp scent of lavender and pine wafting around the room.

'He has chosen well for us though,' Eleanor said.

'But his latest choice for you would never hold a candle to Isobel,' Joan said, and Eleanor waved the candle stub, nodding in agreement; apparently the two of them had met his latest prospective bride.

Eleanor smiled. 'You would have turned her down.'

'How do you know?' Argyle asked.

'You need a strong woman. You do not need a brood mare to bear your children.' Eleanor turned to Joan. 'Remember Thomas' first choice? Argyle had just conquered half of Europe, and Thomas thought he would settle for a delicate little flower bereft of wits altogether? Who knows what he did once out of the country? Had a string of women pining after him no doubt.'

'He is too kind,' Joan objected. 'Argyle would never leave behind broken-hearted women. Not willingly at any rate.'

'But would you leave behind any unwillingly?' Eleanor wanted to know.

'We will never know,' Argyle said sorrow clutching at his heart. 'On the way out, I was too busy experiencing the world, and on the way back, I was too busy trying to keep up.' Another lie easily told.

'Will you ever tell us what really happened on that pilgrimage?' Eleanor now sat in the massive chair by the hearth, stretching her feet towards the flames, her pointed slippers glittering in the firelight. Darkness was creeping in through the windows.

Argyle grimaced. 'No more than I already have. Which is quite enough.'

'I still think it was all a little too peculiar,' Eleanor said.

'Think what you like,' Argyle said. 'You will get no more out of me.'

The sisters began chatting among themselves, conjuring up vivid scenarios in which he fought the Turks for their father's memory, romanced women in every town and even had visions of God at the Holy Sepulchre. Argyle was happy to leave them to speculate; he was much more worried about the ceremony tomorrow than why Thomas was not here or even what stories his sisters might dream up. His prolonged stay at court had sparked increasing concern at the prospect of marrying Isobel.

Until death doth part us, Argyle thought - it somehow seemed unreasonable to both of them.

22 April 1397 - Beauworth

The bells tolled loudly, announcing their marriage. Argyle smiled at Isobel, hoping she did not see the grief he was desperately trying to hide. She looked beautiful in her tailored dress; her chestnut hair had been pinned to her head in an elaborate style, little diamonds sparkling when the sunlight hit them. He should be out of breath from the sight of her, but she was not what made it hard for him to breathe. They were tied together now until death, and he was uncertain whether she was any more pleased about the prospect than he.

'Are you happy?'

Argyle blinked. 'Are you?'

Isobel offered a weak smile. 'Not really an answer is it, husband?'

'Yes, I am happy.' Argyle tucked her arm in his and began walking the length of the decorated courtyard towards the house, turning to face the crowd to hide his insecurity. 'How can I not be? With such a beautiful wife.'

The crowd cheered although Argyle noticed a few angry stares too, especially from the villagers who had condemned Isobel's sister to burn forever in purgatory. He knew Isobel had paid for masses to be said for her sister's soul and that his own priest had declined her wish that he too say mass for Tilly. The ceremony today had been a painful affair for all parties involved but Argyle was almost certain that his sisters had not thought anything amiss.

'They remember me.' Argyle followed Isobel's gaze and saw half a dozen villagers turn their backs and walk away. 'I told you they would!'

'Forgetting the woman who cursed them would be too much to ask,' Argyle said. 'Give them time, and they will see that what was said in anger and despair is not all that you are.'

'I was angry, but I knew full well what I did.' Isobel's grip tightened. 'I would do it again.'

Argyle gave her a sharp look, but she simply smiled at the crowd. If she was not willing to let the past rest, how would that affect their lives? He saw his sisters and their husbands standing by the door, Joan and Eleanor smiling, Margaret inclining her head ever so slightly. Were they truly pleased with his choice?

As they passed the family on the stairs, Margaret leaned in. 'I need a moment of your time.'

'Tomorrow,' Argyle said.

'The sooner the better.' Margaret stepped back, smiling at Isobel. 'Congratulations! I am certain my brother could not have made a better choice.' Argyle was sure Margaret was struggling not to add, 'for a country wife'.

He gave a strained smile and almost dragged Isobel into the shadowy hall, garlands of flowers hung all around the room. She looked up at him, smiling in earnest this time. 'I hope I do make you happy, I really want to. You make me feel safe, which I am not accustomed to, and I want you to trust me.' Isobel paused. 'I want this marriage to work, and I will do anything to earn your affection.'

'You have it,' Argyle said and felt a stab of pain in his chest. 'I hope I make you happy too.'

'We will weather any storm together,' said Isobel, 'promise me, Argyle, that we will always have truth between us.'

Argyle heard the plea in her voice. 'I swore before God, and I meant every word.'

ꟈ ꟈ ꟈ ꟈ

Argyle saw Isobel standing in a corner. It was strange to think that his new wife was hiding from her own wedding. All around them the guests were deep in their drink after feasting for hours on course upon delicious course. The whole hall smelled of baked bread and roast pig wrapped in herbs and spices that lent something exotic to the air he breathed. A servant passed by, and Argyle put his cup on the tray, he had had enough wine to last a fortnight. Nodding to a couple of knights who were busying themselves trying to impress a young women, Argyle sat down keeping his eyes on her corner.

Isobel's face was hidden in the darkness, only her hands visible before her dress. They kept twisting and turning, sleek pale fingers intertwining and releasing, intertwining and releasing in tune with the rhythm of the music.

'Come dance with me, brother!' Eleanor was out of breath, her cheeks flushed and her hair had come undone, falling down her back rich as a river of gold. 'You cannot sit here brooding on your wedding day, people will begin to suspect you do not want a marriage at all!'

Although her voice betrayed laughter, her eyes shone with concern, and Argyle gave her a bright smile. 'I was going in search of my wife to see if she might dance with me.'

'I have not seen her, perhaps she has gone for some fresh air.' Looking about, Eleanor seemed not to spy Isobel's writhing hands in the corner. 'Shall I see if I can find her?'

'You are probably right, she will need a little peace and calm from all the debacle of meeting her in-laws,' Argyle said and grabbed Eleanor's hands. 'There will be other dances for her. For this one I am yours.'

As they took the floor, Argyle stole a glance at the corner and saw Isobel now in the company of Stephen. He looked to be telling a story with his entire body, leaning in and waving his hands. Isobel was smiling and it made Argyle relax. They had both been tense all day, and he had worried that their whispered words in the courtyard earlier on had caused Isobel to regret her decision. If Stephen could lighten her mood and make her feel better then Argyle was well pleased.

'I wish Margaret would stop scowling,' Eleanor twirled around Argyle and caught his hand. 'It does nothing for her waning features, and she looks twice her age already in that dreary dress. Really, you would think she would make an effort for your wedding.'

'She is displeased,' Argyle said and lifted Eleanor from the floor, marvelling at how light she was despite the layers of heavy fabric covering her body.

When they were children, Argyle had been forced to dance with his sisters and had always struggled to find their hands in the long flowing sleeves that were popular years ago. Now that the sleeves were buttoned tight around Eleanor's wrists, it was so much easier to grab her hands at just the right time. A flicker of the Queen's thin arms hidden by wide flowing sleeves crossed his mind, for some odd reason she seemed best pleased with the old ways.

The music stopped and Argyle joined Eleanor and the other dancers in applauding before slipping from the floor with Eleanor's hand on his arm.

'Perhaps you should … oh, there she is!' Triumphant, Eleanor dug her nails into Argyle's arm and began crossing the room, weaving between the other guests. 'How drunk everyone is getting! Just look at Joan's husband, he looks fit to be bundled off to bed! Look out! You tread on my hem! Really, Argyle who are all these people?' Eleanor jabbered as she craned her neck to keep her eyes on Isobel.

'M'lord,' Stephen said at Argyle's elbow. 'A word?'

'Not now, Smith!' Eleanor snapped but softened her words with a brilliant smile. 'Tomorrow, he will be your Lord again, but tonight he must cater to his wife. How would it look if he favoured your company to hers?'

Stephen smiled at Eleanor before turning to Argyle. Concern lurked in the corner of that smile. 'Your sister's right, of course, M'lord. It'll keep until tomorrow.'

'Are you certain?' Argyle saw something in Stephen's face that he did not like.

'Really, Argyle!' Eleanor clicked her tongue. 'I have a mind to summon Margaret and have her give you a right scolding! Smith says it can wait, and I say that Isobel cannot! Come along!'

Before Argyle could object, Eleanor tore at his shirt and he stumbled along to the sound of Stephen laughing loudly. Whatever he wanted to ask Argyle it could not be so very important since Stephen found the time to make merry on his master's behalf. Trying to catch Stephen's eyes in the crowd, Argyle bumped into Isobel and flushed.

'I am … I hope … You …'

'No harm done,' Isobel said with a shy smile. Eleanor quickly released her grip and thrust Argyle's hand forward for Isobel to take it. Her touch was cold despite the heat of the room, her fingers barely resting on his skin. 'I was looking for you.'

'How lucky, I found him for you then,' Eleanor said with a satisfied smirk. 'Now you can dance with him and my aching feet can get some well-deserved rest.'

'I did not step on you once, sister,' Argyle called after her.

'Did I say that you were the culprit?' Eleanor teased and danced away. 'Beware his big boots, Isobel, I may have taught him to dance, but it seems he is a little rusty!'

Isobel looked up at him. 'Am I quite safe with you, Sire?'

The teasing glimmer released the knot in Argyle's stomach. 'Only one way to find out, my Lady.'

When he led her into the next dance, Isobel was light on her feet and smiled brightly whenever he looked at her. How could any man in the room be but infatuated with that face? How they must all envy him his beautiful wife, her comely shape, her wonderful eyes.

Panting, they retreated from the dance and crossed the room to escape out the side door that La Fontaine had so often used to get quickly from the hall to his study. Argyle held the door open for Isobel to slip out and for a second, he felt watched. Looking around, Argyle locked eyes with Margaret. She looked to be fuming with rage; her lips pressed tightly together, her hands clasped by Eleanor's whose back was turned. Margaret looked to be hissing something to Eleanor, and then

Joan appeared from out of nowhere and interceded. She glanced up and smiled at Argyle, breaking the spell.

'Are you coming?' Isobel's voice soft in his ear.

'Yes, of course.' Argyle let himself be guided by her from the door through the dark hall and out into the now all but empty courtyard.

'This is a relief.'

Although summer was fast approaching April could be fickle and tonight, the air breathed cold on his skin. 'We could have saved half the candles in that room and it would still be too hot to bear,' Argyle said, sliding an arm around Isobel's waist. 'How do you find your wedding, Lady wife?'

'To tell truth, I was concerned when I woke this morning.' Isobel leaned into his caress. 'But once the words were said, and you smiled down at me, something fell into place. I am content. I find my wedding is just as I wanted it to be, full of life and joy and music.'

'And good food.' Stephen stepped out from the shadows. 'I needed some air too, it's melting in there! I've been to the kitchens. Bessie's keen to get off her feet soon, but I've convinced her she's to award me a dance before she does. And one for you, M'lord.'

'Let the poor woman rest if she needs it, Master Smith,' Isobel said and fidgeted with the silk covered buttons on her dress. 'If she is so very tired, and who can blame her, then she does not need you ordering her about.'

'No one orders Bessie about.' Stephen grinned at Argyle. 'She pushes me about all the time, M'lady. Just this once, I'd like to have my way.'

'Is this true?' Isobel glanced at Argyle. 'Am I to take on a house where the cook will not listen?'

Argyle kissed the top of Isobel's head, relishing in the soft smell of roses. 'I am sure you have already come to terms with her, my love. After all, you have spent hour upon hour in the kitchens these past days and both of you are unscathed.'

Extracting herself from Argyle's embrace, Isobel stepped close to Stephen, her skirt swishing on the steps. 'You are right, husband. Bessie is a kind woman, you are lucky to have her, Master Smith.'

Bowing to kiss Isobel's hand, Stephen winked. 'You're right, M'lady. Quite right. I'm blessed.'

'You may leave us, Master Smith.' Isobel turned towards Argyle, her cheeks a little flushed. 'I would have a quiet moment with my husband.'

'Won't be long before they come to take you to bed, M'lord.'

Argyle saw Isobel stiffen and smiled to relieve some of her tension. 'I thought we agreed that no one would be putting us to bed.'

'We agreed that M'lady'd be spared.' Stephen sidestepped smartly. 'You failed to mention yourself, M'lord! Best be off!'

When Stephen opened the door to the hall, light and voices filled the courtyard for a moment before the oaken planks swallowed the noise once more. The constant humming from the house resounded deep inside Argyle's body. How strange it was to be the centre of the party and yet be able to slip away so easily. He suspected his sisters might have something to do with it.

'I have a present for you, wife.' Argyle beckoned Isobel to his side. 'It can wait if …'

'You will find that I can never have too many presents,' Isobel said and put her hands on his chest. 'I do not like surprises, but I do favour presents above all else.'

'Are they not two sides of the same thing?' Argyle drew her hands to his mouth and kissed her palms. 'Surprises and presents?'

Isobel contemplated his question while he slowly drew her across the courtyard to the stables. 'There is a difference to me. Presents are planned and should be given only if you know the receiver will appreciate your efforts.' She stopped when Argyle opened the stable door. 'Surprises have a way of sneaking up on you - and rarely harbour good news.'

It was dark in the stable, the smell comfortably warm and earthy. Something moved in the corner and one of the stable boys stuck his head out from a pile of hay blinking his bleary eyes. 'M'lord?'

'Go back to sleep.' Argyle motioned for Isobel to follow him. 'This is for you.'

Eleanor had picked out the mare on Argyle's specifications. He wanted a horse that was Isobel's, a gentle mare that was used to sorts of people, a gentle steed. Eleanor had delivered the most beautiful and delicate chestnut horse, its hide a perfect match to Isobel's hair.

'Oh, its wonderful,' Isobel breathed. 'I have nothing like this for you, my Lord.'

'It matters not. I wanted to give you something that was all your own.' Argyle bathed in her smile. 'I know what it is like to be far from home with nothing but what you can borrow to get by with. Now, you never have to wait for someone to come back if you want to go for a ride. She is yours.'

'If this is the kind of gifts you mean to bestow upon me in the future, I can ask for nothing more.' Running her hands over the mare's neck, Argyle thought Isobel looked completely relaxed for the first time that night.

'I do mean to make a good husband, Isobel.' Fervour stole into Argyle's voice. 'I do mean to always do right by you.'

'That is a mighty pledge. Beware you do not promise more than you can control.'

In the soft darkness of the stable, Argyle could not make out her expression.

ꕥ ꕥ

The room was dark but for a few candles and the banked fire, Isobel moving in the shadows. Argyle sat on the bed, his shirt hanging on the screen that separated the bed from the small altar, wondering what this night might be like.

Isobel slid between the sheets, tucking at the blanket he was sitting on. 'Come to bed.'

He heard anxiety in her voice; this would be difficult. 'I am in bed.'

'No, you are on it and still half-dressed.' Isobel put her hand lightly on his shoulder. 'I know … this might not be the night you were dreaming of, but …'

'Why do you say that?'

'I am not blind, Argyle,' Isobel said. 'All day you have looked to be in agony. I know that I might not be your first - or even natural - choice, but I am here, flesh and blood …'

Argyle turned and grabbed her hand kissing it hard. 'Never say that again. You are my choice - or you would not be here, in this room tonight.'

She went a little rigid at his caress and forced a smile. 'I know. Now come into bed.'

For the first time, Argyle felt awkward undressing in front of a woman. With Najeelah it had been natural and with Celeste he had given it no thought. But in front of Isobel, with her wide eyes and pale cheeks, he was acutely aware of his many scars and bruises, and conscious that her previous experiences in the marriage bed had been far from kind.

When he threw back the sheets to slip in, she clung to her side of the blanket trying to smile but failing. Argyle knew he would have to tread carefully with her. A quick flash of defiance ran across her face before she relaxed her grip, letting the sheet fall away from her breast.

Argyle's breath caught at the sight of creamy skin and dark brown nipple. Isobel was breathing quickly, although he suspected not from desire or anticipation but rather because she was reliving nightmares of the past. He gently drew the blanket up again, brushing against her shoulder, his fingers slowly traced their way to her neck, relishing in the feeling of her soft hair that smelled sweetly of roses. Isobel sat completely still, when Argyle caressed her cheek before cupping her chin and turning her face towards his. Looking into her eyes, he bent to kiss her. Isobel drew away ever so slightly before relenting.

They broke apart panting, Isobel's cheeks now flushed but her fear seemed to be gone.

'I will do nothing that you do not wish,' Argyle said. 'If you are not ready, we will wait.'

'What if I am never ready?'

'Then we will live amicably without …' Argyle could not finish, he wanted her to want him, to forget her spiteful first husband and to be happy, and yet he knew that if she said that she did not want him in her bed, he would get up and leave immediately, and that he would be relieved.

Isobel turned around slowly, her hand resting on his thigh before she began to undo her braid. Argyle stopped her. He gently pushed her arms down, his hands momentarily lingering on her wrists as he leaned forward and kissed the nape of her neck. Isobel went taut.

Argyle began loosening her braid, her auburn hair spilling down her back. When he stopped, Isobel leaned back a little, turning so that he could see her face in profile. Her cheeks were still wet but she seemed more determined somehow and enough at ease to draw his arms around her. They sat like that for a while, letting the sound of the crackling fire fill the room.

'I mean it, Isobel,' Argyle said into her hair. 'I will do nothing that you do not wish.'

Isobel took his hand and drew him down next to her, staring into his eyes when they kissed again. If she was searching for something, he hoped she found consolation. Slowly, Isobel guided Argyle with her body and hands, and finally, Argyle slid into her. He felt her clench and felt even more aroused while she gave a startled look. When he did not move, she closed her eyes and breathed deep before she moved again. Argyle let her set the pace, moving along when she quickened and pausing when she went rigid. Her fear seemed somehow stimulating, and he wondered if that was why some men went violent in bed. Perhaps they could not help themselves?

Finally, Isobel quickened her pace, kissing him with unexpected passion and arching her back, pushing his face towards her breasts. When he sucked on one, she moaned and rewarded him by bearing down, entirely enveloping him before she cried out, muffling her voice by pressing her face into his chest. Argyle groaned in ecstasy.

He raised himself up to claim a kiss and was rewarded with a faint smile and a gasp, when he took her breast in his mouth. He moved on to kiss her most intimate parts and lingered there, letting his tongue explore her, feeling her go wet. He sucked harder and slid two fingers inside her. Isobel panted and pushed up against him to spur him on, her hands shifting between pushing his head away and drawing it back in until she gave way to her own pleasure.

Argyle looked up at her, a smile playing on his lips and her taste in his mouth.

'What was that?' Isobel sounded as if she was waking from a dream. 'Where did you ever …?'

Argyle pushed himself up on one elbow running his index finger down the centre of her chest from her neckline to her navel. 'Do you really want to know?'

ꙮ ꙮ

23 April 1397 - Beauworth

Margaret was waiting for Argyle when he came down for breakfast. Isobel was still fast asleep, her scent the faintest whisper in the air when he left the bedroom. In the morning light, he noticed that the garlands of flowers were already withering. He looked around to find a servant and order that the decorations be taken down. Margaret cleared her throat.

'Margaret, can it wait?'

She pursed her lips, and Argyle showed her into his study, the only room in the house not affected by the festivities of yesterday. Inward, he cursed himself for letting her have her way so easily; after all, they were not children any more. Closing the door on the bustling hallway and the many people hurrying to and from the hall carrying trays of food that smelled delicious, he offered Margaret a chair next to the fireplace, but she did not accept.

'How did you get the King to accept your marriage to … Isobel? What did you have to offer in return?' Though Margaret's tone was hard, Argyle did not care. He was free from the King and from Thomas' eternal prompting that he marry. Now that he had a wife, he could hardly believe why he had not married sooner - there could be no more demands, no one could complain, and if they did, they could all go to Hell.

'Nothing. In truth, I think he could not care less.' Argyle found that lying was fast becoming a habit.

'You are wrong! Why did you choose her, Argyle? Was it to spite Thomas?'

'Why do you ask? You pushed me into the arms of a seductress. Surely Isobel is the better choice,' Argyle snapped. Margaret was out of line.

'Because your choice in wife, how ever kind and pretty she is, is a bad one.' Margaret wrung her hands. 'You should have accepted one of Thomas' prospects, you should have listened to him.'

'And live in an arranged marriage controlled by Thomas?'

'One way or another, little brother, yours is an arranged marriage!' Margaret hissed. 'It may well have been arranged by yourself, although I think you were persuaded to accept Isobel by other means …'

'She did not seduce me, if that is what you are implying.' Argyle clenched his fists, his nails digging into his palms, why was Margaret …

'Nor I her. This is a good match! Isobel is my choice.'

Margaret turned white. 'How can you say that? Do you not know what they are saying at court?'

'Most likely they are not singing my praises. As long as Thomas is in the thick of things, no one will ever sing our family's praises, sweet sister.' Argyle saw tears well up in Margaret's eyes and went to comfort her; she was stiff in his embrace. 'But no, I do not know what they are saying. Truly Margaret, I went into this match with open eyes, I know what I have done and I know Isobel.'

Better than anyone, I should wager, Argyle thought as he released Margaret. 'She is the right choice for me.'

'So you keep saying. Are you trying to impress the notion upon yourself, now that the deed is done? Now that you are stuck with her for the rest of your life?'

'Careful, sister.' Argyle's blood began to boil.

Margaret breathed deep and seemed to summon control from deep inside. 'I have nothing against Isobel personally, I do not know her, and I am sure - really, I am Argyle! - that you made your choice for all the right reasons.'

'But?'

'Did it ever occur to you that the gossip is not about you?' Margaret leaned on the desk; she looked faint. 'I have to know what the King said when you approached him.'

Argyle resisted the urge to please his eldest sister; why was she so determined that the King had demanded anything from him? 'I learned my lesson when I went to Calais without the King's permission,' Argyle said. 'I asked his approval, and he gave it freely. We both know why!'

'Nothing the King sanctions comes without strings attached.' Margaret sounded bitter. 'Nothing ever has and nothing ever will. If he simply accepted that you marry a woman of no position, no breeding, just to get to Celeste, I should be very surprised.'

'Watch what you say, Margaret.'

'What about Celeste?' Margaret cut across Argyle's thoughts. 'Is she nothing to you?'

'It is too late. The whole court knows about her and the King - and the Queen seems to have accepted the situation.' Argyle looked into the fire. 'Celeste is not my responsibility!'

'Really?' Margaret's tone turned cold once more, the older sister telling off her youngest brother. 'I implored you to keep Celeste close. I even told her that you would help her - God save me - if she needed protection. And you left her! At court, alone!'

'Celeste is a woman grown - married too! - what she does is her own affair.' Argyle fought to keep his voice down. He could hear servants and guests pass by the door, the steady drone of voices from the great hall a buzzing backdrop.

'Not when she is sleeping with the King, then it is everyone's affair!' Margaret sounded exasperated, her tone very like that of Thomas whenever Argyle was slow to grasp something 'Thomas saw her one morning stealing from the King's room to Gaunt's. Did you know?'

'Thomas should mind his own business.' Argyle had told Celeste to stay away from Bolingbroke and Gaunt too, he had pleaded with her, but it seemed she was simply not to be trusted. He was sure that she was spying for Bolingbroke, and by extension Gaunt too.

Something inside Margaret seemed to snap, and she slumped forward. 'You knew?'

'Knew what?' Argyle turned away from her to stir the fire.

'Knew about her connection with Gaunt?'

'If I did?'

Margaret rose slowly, her dress rustling as she moved around the desk, her soft footsteps on the flat rushes that needed changing. Still, he almost jumped out of his own skin when she put a hand on his shoulder. 'How could you not tell any of us?'

'To what end?' Argyle heard how hollow his own words were. 'I asked her to stay away from Bolingbroke, warned her that he was dangerous, but I did not - I still do not - command another's life. I could not tell her what to do - it was not my place. Either way it has nothing to do with my marriage to Isobel.'

'It has everything to do with Isobel,' Margaret said. 'Do you not see, Argyle? Now that you are married you are no longer …'

'An option to distract a tiresome, French woman?!' Argyle lost his temper. 'What the Hell is wrong with you, Margaret?! She was fine to be my prostitute but not the King's?!'

Margaret backed away looking hurt and angry. 'They are saying at court that you married to free yourself from the jumble of being a suitor to the King's whore! They are saying you would have married anyone, that you DID marry anyone, to avoid the King's fury. Is that the case, Argyle? For if it is, then I can understand your choice!'

'Why I married Isobel is none of your business! Let them say what they will at court, it is nothing to me!' Argyle grabbed Margaret by the arms, and she winced. 'Let me tell you this, sister, I will not be named the villain by my own family!'

'I promised Thomas …'

'Stop making promises, you cannot keep!'

Isobel opened the door. She stared avidly at the scene, and Argyle released Margaret who shrunk away. 'Argyle, what …?'

'Margaret slipped, and I caught her just in time,' Argyle said, plastering on a smile that stretched thin on his face. 'I must clean up more often that there be less danger when entering my study.'

Margaret went along with his lies, offering a false smile that never reached her eyes. 'Yes, it really is high time, little brother. I must go to my rooms and oversee the packing.'

'You are leaving?' Isobel looked confused.

'Yes, there is so much to be done, and I promised my husband …' Margaret shook her head. 'I hope you are very happy here, I have told my dear brother to be kind to you.'

Isobel blushed. 'Thank you.'

Margaret walked stiffly from the room without another glance at Argyle, and he knew that Thomas would be informed of all that had happened this morning. He reached out to Isobel. 'Are you hungry?'

CHAPTER 23

10 August 1397 - Beauworth

Argyle read the letter once more. What the few lines contained was so unsettling that he hardly knew how to feel about it. He was certain that the letter would soon be followed by either a royal order to go directly to court, or a demand from Thomas to get to London immediately. Neither held any promise of a peaceful summer.

'M'lord, any word to take back?' Argyle had completely forgotten the messenger, who was standing in a puddle of water amassing from his dripping cloak and hair. The summer rain had been coming down hard these past days, turning roads to mud and threatening the crops.

Dismissing the man with a wave, Argyle went to the window where fat drops of rain chased each other ceaselessly down the glass panes. A reflection betrayed that someone had entered when the messenger left. 'Husband, what is it?'

'Unsettling news from court.'

Isobel joined him by the window. Argyle smiled down at her, and when he graced the curve of her belly with his fingertips she offered a small smile in return.

'You need not worry though,' Argyle said to reassure her as much as himself.

'Which is exactly why I worry,' Isobel said. 'Every time a messenger arrives, I hold my breath and hope you do not have to leave. It will not be long before I come to hate the sound of hooves in the courtyard.' Isobel sat in Argyle's massive chair. 'When are you going?'

'It was not that kind of message. It was news, nothing more,' Argyle said.

'But unsettling, you say?' Isobel shuffled his papers around, trying to arrange them in neat stacks. She did this every time she was in his study, and somehow, they fell back into a jumble the moment she left.

Argyle crumbled the letter in his hand; he had to soothe her troubled mind. 'The King has arrested Warwick and Woodstock.'

'Oh?' Isobel cared little for court-life, and yet Argyle thought he saw her stiffen.

'Warwick had been invited to dine with the King.' Argyle's voice darkened. 'At the end of the feast, the King rose and ordered Warwick arrested. He now sits in the Tower.'

Isobel flinched. 'The Tower?'

'Yes. Though it should have come as no surprise. He had been openly criticising the truce with France ever since the King married the Queen,' Argyle said. 'Nonetheless, he must have thought himself safe when he agreed to dine with the King. Foolish man.'

'Foolish, why?'

'La Fontaine once told me the King never forgets a grudge. He has since been proven right time and time again.'

'I am afraid you have married a very ignorant woman.' Isobel's voice shook ever so slightly. 'I do not know what grudge you speak of?'

'And just as well.' Argyle took her hand and stroked it gently. 'Eleven years ago, Warwick, Woodstock and Arundel were among the principal aggressors in a rebellion against the King's most trusted advisors. They styled themselves the Lords Appellant. They appealed to the King to send from court all of his young friends and take only the advice of the seasoned Lords, including his uncles. Truth be told, they also felt it was a personal slight that the King sought council from anyone but themselves.'

Argyle released Isobel's hand. 'It all ended with several of the King's closest friends being exiled from court, by the same Lords who had locked the King in the Tower and would not let him out until he agreed to send his friends in permanent exile abroad. A few even lost their heads in the process. Once the deed was done, Woodstock positioned himself as chief advisor to the King and let only his sworn allies near the King. For a while, England was in effect governed by Woodstock and the other Lords Appellant, and not by the King.'

'I never knew,' Isobel said.

'The council was good at hiding the fact and the King was eager to please, for a while at least, just to keep his crown. In time, when the King came of age, he decided to take back power, and the lords saw the young upstarts that they had rebelled to exile return to court, one by one. It seemed the King had learned little from the dispute.' Argyle sat heavily on a low stool next to the hearth. Outside, the relentless rain kept pummelling at the castle walls, the leaden skies reminding Argyle of the day La Fontaine had died. Argyle felt a stab of guilt that he had all but given up on finding La Fontaine's murderer.

'But what has all this to do with your letter?' Isobel wet her lips.

'It seems the King is finally lashing out and getting his revenge for what happened all those years ago.' Argyle frowned when Isobel's eyes widened, why was she so shocked? 'Once Warwick was safely locked away in the Tower, the King wasted no time but rode at the head of an arrest party to retrieve Woodstock at Pleshey Castle. Even as we speak, an armed guard is taking him across the sea to face prison in Calais.'

'Woodstock in Calais?' Isobel bit her lip. 'What about the last one? Arundel?'

Argyle stroked his chin. The stubble scratched the palm of his hand. 'Arundel made to run. He might even have succeeded had not his brother persuaded him otherwise. He is now confined on the Isle of Wright.'

'Why not keep them all in the Tower?' Isobel asked.

'God knows what goes on in the King's mind?' Argyle was more concerned about Isobel's strange manner than the message he had received.

11 August 1397 - Beauworth

La Fontaine took the message from Argyle and gestured for him to shut the door on the bustling corridor. Argyle wondered if La Fontaine had seen the seal on the paper, a crest of rampant lions prominent in the red wax.

'I wonder what the King might want from me this time,' La Fontaine said in a wry voice that made Argyle steal a glance at his master. Since their falling out, they were still establishing a fragile relationship, and Argyle was not sure when to speak

and when to keep quiet.

'It must be important, Sire,' Argyle ventured.

'No doubt it is and yet I wonder if it might be …' La Fontaine broke the wax seal and read the note with increasing speed. He turned his back to Argyle and looked out of the window where the land was coming to life after a long, hard winter. 'How dare he?'

The words were uttered so softly that Argyle thought he must have misheard them at first, but then La Fontaine slammed a fist into the window frame, his face dark and contorted. 'FOOL!'

Argyle shrunk back. 'Sire?'

'He knows full well that I cannot accept!' La Fontaine got up and began pacing the room. 'He knows that the peace is fragile and that we have to be on our best behaviour, then why would he suddenly decide on something so utterly, utterly foolish?' La Fontaine turned to Argyle. 'Do you know what the message says?'

'You broke the seal, Sire,' Argyle said.

'There was no message for you?'

Argyle knew what La Fontaine hinted at and felt a twinge of old regret surface. 'No, I have had no news from anyone since….'

'The King is building his own army.' La Fontaine let Argyle's lost comment float away.

'His own army?' Argyle was dumbfounded.

'Always wanted one, and now it seems he has finally gone and done it.' La Fontaine let out a mighty sigh. 'What make you of that, young master Argyle?'

'The King has but to call upon the Lords of the land to raise their banners and muster their men ... he needs no army.' Argyle's voice betrayed a hint of doubt.

'No, but he has ever desired one,' La Fontaine said. 'And now he calls upon me to be part of it. I and my entire household. On some foolish notion that it will prove my loyalty beyond doubt. As if he has ever had cause to doubt me!'

Argyle bit his tongue and stared at the floor, the King might have no cause to doubt La Fontaine's loyalties, but La Fontaine housed a member of one of the most powerful English families, and Argyle wondered if perhaps his being at Beauworth had something to do with the King's sudden demand.

'I have no choice but to decline.' The words came out heavy and sad. 'You should endeavour to always obey the King, Argyle, and never disobey him, never do it lightly, but this once I must persuade him that he has my full allegiance although I have to deny him.'

'Why?'

La Fontaine gave Argyle a cold stare. 'Because unlike certain others on the King's council, I cannot back both sides.'

Argyle shrank back. 'Of course not, Sire.'

La Fontaine scratched the coarse stubble that shaded his strong jaw. 'Tell the messenger that I shall leave for London tomorrow. I shall speak to the King myself. This is not a message that ought to be delivered on a scrap of paper.'

'Never disobey the King ... never do it lightly ...' The words kept ringing in Argyle's head. Was the King involved in La Fontaine's death after all? Had he done something, commanded something that had led to La Fontaine's death? Argyle did not want to believe it, but he remembered how La Fontaine had looked when he returned from London back then, how angry and haggard.

Still everyone - and everything besides Coxcombe's dubious statement - pointed to Woodstock. Argyle wondered if perhaps the King might be persuaded to send him to fetch back Woodstock. Suddenly, he had questions for the Lord that could not wait.

CHAPTER 24

12 August 1397 - Beauworth

'We need to speak,' Argyle said surveying the dusty grounds and the soldiers drilling, metal ringing as they wielded their swords and mazes. 'The men are working hard.'

Stephen moved a little. 'Yes, they're hungry for battle, though I wonder if most of them'll ever see one.'

'I remember riding the length of Scotland and never seeing a single sword drawn,' Argyle said, circling the heel of his boot in the withered yellow grass; August had been harsh to the land. 'La Fontaine was furious with the King - and for once, he sided with my brother.'

'A rare thing.'

'A unicorn if ever there was one. To Thomas, La Fontaine was a jumped up nobody.' Argyle scratched his neck. 'However, the King lost a great advisor when La Fontaine died. He was always honest, even if his opinion did not agree with the King.'

'I'll take your word for it, M'lord,' Stephen said. Was he a little evasive? Argyle could not tell. 'Remember when we first met? The buck-hunt?'

Argyle smiled. 'Yes, you nearly took down a doe yourself.'

'Aye, so I did,' Stephen said. 'MEN, change positions!' The soldiers took up new stances, a few throwing down the well-worn old straw sacks to replace them for new ones that would face certain death by blade. Stephen spat. 'What'd you want to speak of, M'lord?'

'Calais.'

Stephen rolled his head, his shoulders tight and hunched. He licked his lips. 'Calais?'

'It need not be here,' Argyle said. 'But I must ask you something.'

'Why bring up Calais again? It's over and done with - the crook swung for it.'

'Did he?'

Stephen turned and eyed him sharply. 'What?'

'As I said, it need not be here.'

'Better get it said, M'lord,' Stephen said, and Argyle noticed a touch of insolence in his friend's voice.

They walked towards the tiltyard, and Argyle noticed George mounting a great black beast. He looked out of place in the saddle, his helmet a little too big and his grip on the lance very tight. 'Loose shoulders, George!' Argyle called out and saw George relax a little.

'I saw Coxcombe in London. In March.'

Stephen froze in place, his face white under the freckles. 'Oh?'

They stepped back as George thundered by, his aim too far off to ever hit the plate. Argyle involuntarily winced when the boy's shoulder hit the plate with a loud thud. George slid sideways in the saddle but managed to stay on the horse, though he had to drop the lance. A couple of the other squires laughed.

'Northwoode, you go next! You can use George's horse! ' Stephen yelled. 'That ought to teach him not to laugh at others, he's right scared of the beast, stupid lad,' he said to Argyle

'Is it one of the new horses?' Argyle gave the horse an appraising look.

'Training it to be your new destrier,' Stephen said. 'I thought it looked like good old Noble.'

'Only bigger.'

Stephen nodded. 'You need a big horse.'

'Really?' Argyle grinned a little and some of the tension between them faded. 'Perhaps I do. I will most likely be riding to London soon, but not on that one,' he added when the horse reared and sent young Brian Northwoode flying.

'Take the Queen's horse, it flies like the wind,' Stephen said. 'I never saw such a fine creature as that one. Word is she picked it specially for you.'

'A wedding present,' Argyle said.

'Very generous of her.' Stephen's eyes never left Northwoode who was trying to mount the black horse once more, dancing around it with one foot in the stirrup. The boy fell on his arse, and it took three squires to stop the beast from running off with Northwoode still hanging from the stirrup.

Argyle drew Stephen further from the field, what he had to say next was not for all to hear. 'Coxcombe.'

'He's dead, you saw that, same as I,' Stephen said, a whisper of fear in his eyes. 'Burned.'

'Beyond recognition. All we really saw was a charred body, impossible to say whom it was,' Argyle said. 'He is alive. He put a hole in my neck.'

Stephen choked, pale with shock. Argyle could see Stephen struggle to accept what he heard. 'You're sure? I don't … How? Why pretend to be dead …?'

'We know he pretended to be La Fontaine's friend but was in fact working for Gaunt, and most likely Bolingbroke, for years before the pilgrimage,' Argyle said. 'I know he was nervous throughout the pilgrimage …'

'Because of Lockley!' Stephen balled his fists. 'That bastard made everyone miserable, and continues to even now from beyond the grave! I hope he burns in Hell for his sins!'

Oh, I am certain he does, Argyle thought and asked. 'What if Coxcombe was putting on a show?'

'A show?' Stephen laughed, the sound cold and harsh. 'I think I know true fear when I see it. You could almost smell it on him.'

'We both thought his fear was for Lockley, but what if it was not?' Argyle said. 'I think he killed the man we found burned in Calais. He knows something.'

Stephen turned and glared at Argyle. 'And what might that be, M'lord?'

Once more, Argyle let the insolent tone slide. 'He knew La Fontaine would die at that tournament. What I do not know is if he told you.'

'He left before La Fontaine went to the field against Lockley. He was nowhere nearby when … it happened,' Stephen said flatly. 'I told you so.'

'I believed you.'

'And now you don't?'

Truth be told, Argyle did not know what to think. 'All I ask is that you think on it.'

'I'll think,' Stephen said in a taut voice. 'If that is all, M'lord.' He stalked off leaving Argyle to wonder if Stephen had been keeping secrets all this time, or if he truly believed that the body in Calais had been Coxcombe. After all, they were not the only two to call the dead man's identity - there had been a third man present.

26 August 1397 - Beauworth

Although proclamations had been issued against Woodstock, Warwick and Arundel that they had been arrested for offences against the King's Majesty, most all of the English nobility was in uproar. The King's fervent denial of the arrests having anything to do with the events in 1386 rang hollow, even in Argyle's ears. Was this the King showing his true nature, one that was vindictive and childish?

Warwick, Arundel and Woodstock would have to plead for their lives, and the English court grew ever more dangerous. Somehow Thomas was once again high in favour with the King, and in one of his letters, Thomas doled out equal measures of spite and triumph about the King's latest feat. Argyle suspected that Thomas was mostly relieved that he not joined his three former allies. Once charged with treason, there was little chance of surviving, no matter your affinity to the King. Thomas finished his narrative with a command that Argyle make his way to London immediately. He was to attend the trial and support his brother if needs be.

Argyle slammed his hand onto the table sending paper and quills dancing and a pot of ink spilling over. 'Damn it!' He tried to save as many of the documents as possible, staining them with the ink on his hands. 'Damn it all to HELL!'

'M'lord?' Stephen opened the study door and took in the scene. He quickly grabbed a boy scuttling by and forced him inside. 'Clean this up! Be quick about it!'

The young lad shook as he wiped the floor with a rag and attempted to mop up the ink that was seeping into the wooden tabletop.

'Never mind, boy,' Argyle said having regained some control over his temper. He grabbed the rag and tried to dry the ink off his hand. 'That is quite enough, off with you.'

Stephen closed the door behind the scared boy. 'Bad news?'

'Is it ever good news?' Argyle said.

'Not these days, M'lord.'

'I have to go to London.' Argyle pushed his chair back from the table; he felt an urge to ignore Thomas' order.

'I'll assemble some men for the journey,' Stephen said.

Argyle nodded, it would not do to stay in Beauworth. 'Six will do. It seems that things have gone from bad to worse at court.'

'The imprisoned lords up to no good?' Stephen asked.

'Not the lords. Most likely their sole concern is to save their own hides. No, this time it is very much another and much more powerful man scheming.' Argyle cleared his throat, not quite sure how much to reveal.

Stephen poured two cups of ale, put one in front of Argyle and brought the other to the windowsill. He balanced there while opening the window to let in the dry evening air. The both of them drank deep.

'And your brother?'

'Requires my presence in London.' Argyle's jaw tightened. 'Though I cannot think why, these are his kind of games, not mine. He knows that Isobel is pregnant and that I have little desire to be in London.'

'Still you need to go?'

'Not need, must.' Argyle tipped the cup and a little ale trickled onto the floor, mingling with the leftover ink. Argyle watched it worming its way into the grooves between the floor slabs. At least I can continue my enquiries about the poison. Someone must know something, Argyle thought.

'M'lord …' Stephen was interrupted by a knock on the door.

'Another messenger, M'lord!' George passed on a letter with shaking hands. 'From the King.'

Stephen went to stand by the window with his back turned when Argyle broke the seal and read the message. 'He orders me to come to London. He has a task for me.' Argyle crumpled the letter and threw it into the hearth where the flames flared up. 'I must leave today.'

ꟼ CR ꟼ CR

Isobel was standing at the top of the stairs, the autumn wind pulling at her clothes and hair. Strands of auburn curls had broken free from under her cap and were whipping across her face. From her vantage point the courtyard must look as if in turmoil, but Argyle knew better, he saw everyone moving with military precision.

Stephen had been quick to pick out a few men to go with Argyle and ordered the kitchen to supply food for the journey. The horses were ready, stable boys running around the jittery horses, fastening packages and bundles to the saddles. As the last of the men mounted their horses, Argyle paused with his hand on the saddle and looked at Isobel with concern. 'I will be back soon.'

'So you say.' A single tear coursed down Isobel's cheek, she wiped it away with a furious stroke. 'What would England do without you?!'

'Move on,' Argyle said, though he wondered if it was true.

'Then stay. I feel wretched, something is wrong.'

'It is court, something is always wrong,' Argyle said thinking about all the other times he had been ordered to go to London, but Isobel's cold laugh stopped him, one foot in the stirrup. Why was she being so difficult? By now, she was used to him being away either in London or in the county. Isobel had never asked to go back to court, and when Argyle had last broached the idea, she had shrugged it off.

'Come here, wife,' Argyle demanded.

Isobel walked stiffly down the stone stairs almost reluctant to obey, as if she could stop time all together if she moved slowly enough. Argyle pulled off his gloves and grabbed her hands. 'What is different this time? Is it the babe?'

She turned her face up at him, her eyes big and scared. 'I have a bad feeling about your going. You said yourself that the King is erratic. What if he turns against you?'

'He has no reason to, unless I disobey his order to come directly to London.'

'Then go.' Isobel's cold manner pierced his heart. Argyle wrapped her in a hard embrace then released her and swung into the saddle. The other riders were waiting for his command. 'Ride out!'

When Argyle turned in the saddle, the stairs to the house were empty.

CHAPTER 25

4 September 1397 - London

Argyle pondered the frame of the door in front of him. The massive oak beams arched slightly, the crest on top proudly boasted the Mowbray coat of arms in red and white. He was deep in thought when the door was flung open, and he was almost run down by a fuming Bolingbroke. Sidestepping just in time, Argyle took a blow to the arm as Bolingbroke pushed by, growling as he went.

Thomas stood in the middle of the room, his cheeks slightly flushed, his hands trembling. A cup of wine lay on the floor, the content creating a perfect little red river carving its way through a thin layer of rushes. At the sight of Argyle, Thomas' look turned guarded. 'Come in, brother.'

Closing the door, Argyle took in the scene; a chair and the small table that had undoubtedly housed the now spilled wine were overturned, but the rest of the furniture seemed intact. 'You requested my presence?'

Thomas waved angrily at the door. 'Sometimes, he can be the most infuriating man!'

'Trouble?'

'None of your business.'

Argyle grabbed the chair and pulled it upright and as he turned his attention to the small table, he noticed that Thomas' dark hair had streaks of grey in it. His brother was aging before his time.

'You are to attend Parliament in my place.' Thomas brushed his sleeve, which looked damp. He pushed a few sheets of paper under a large pile of documents.

'Parliament?'

'Yes.' Thomas accepted a fresh cup of wine with a curt nod. Sitting on the edge of his table, he seemed to gather his thoughts and reign in his temper. 'The King has appointed me with the task of fetching home Woodstock from Calais.'

Argyle hid a frown by staring intently into his cup; suddenly the wine tasted sour and his breath had caught in his throat. He had hoped to persuade the King to send him to Calais; why had he not gone to the King before he went to Thomas?

'Calais?'

'To bring back Woodstock for his trial. I will need command of some of your men.' Thomas worked his elbow as if to relieve pain. Argyle stared at his brother, had he just asked to command some of his men?

Thomas gave him an irritated look. 'Yes, some of your men! I must leave immediately, and I have no time to summon enough of my own! Surely, they will be as loyal to me as they are to you? It seems the King and Queen are eager for you to visit. I suggest you go to the King right now,' Thomas said by way of dismissal.

ᘓ ᘐ ᘓ ᘐ

'Sir Argyle, come closer!'

The King's voice boomed across the room and several courtiers turned to stare at Argyle as he made his way to the dais. When the King dismissed most of the people in the room, several of the courtiers exchanged glances of excitement and curiosity. Argyle was sure that those left were careful to keep to the shadows, hoping to pick up a secret or two. 'Now, tell me all the news.'

'What would you like to know, Majesty?'

'Your new wife. How do you find married life?' the King asked, and Argyle thought he heard a note of spite in the question.

Argyle looked up and wondered if the King still met with Celeste every night. He forced the image from his mind. 'Thank you, Majesty. My wife is well and with child.'

'Well done, Sir Argyle! Marriage suits you.'

Argyle forced a smile, and the King led him by the elbow to the inner chamber, the colourful carpet was replaced by rush matting. When the door closed behind them, the King turned with a cold smile. 'Have you seen your brother? I can see that you have. You should be honoured that I have chosen you to substitute him. The trials will be quite the spectacle.'

'Majesty.' Argyle felt trapped, the King was still holding his elbow.

'You really must bring your wife to court next time you come,' the King insisted. 'Or we may be forced to come to Beauworth. The Queen longs for your company - and to see more of your wife.'

'How kind of her, Majesty.' Argyle wondered what Isobel would say to a royal party descending upon her.

'I am instructed to ask that you pay my dear Queen a visit, as soon as possible,' the King said with a smug look.

'Before I go, might I ask a question, Majesty?' Argyle saw the King's eyes widen, but he nodded. 'Why is my brother to go to Calais?'

The King visibly relaxed and a dangerous glitter crept into the King's eyes. 'It is simple. Who would I rather spare, him - or you?'

'Him, your Majesty.'

'Indeed.' The King smirked. 'Though I confess that I have another reason too, but I shall not bore you with the details. Needs must that my dear uncle returns for his trial, and who better to fetch him back but the Captain of Calais?'

'When will the trials begin?' Argyle wondered if the King knew of his own enquiries, and that he did not want Argyle to get the opportunity to speak with Woodstock alone, but since he had never asked to be the one to bring back the King's uncle, these were idle speculations.

'We must first open Parliament. It is a tedious affair, but the commons and nobles do so enjoy a good show, and I am not one to deny them a little theatre.' The King paused and glanced sideways at one of his faithful White Hart men. 'Let us not keep Isabella waiting much longer, Sir Argyle. Go to her and make merry, you and I can speak again at a later time.'

Thomas and Argyle entered the vast banqueting hall together that night. Wearing the de Mowbray colours, Thomas looked every bit the part of a courtier while Argyle had barely had time to wash and change, since the Queen had been overjoyed to see him and had insisted that he stay in her apartments for hours. He straightened the belt at his hips and shook out the sleeves of his long, green shirt.

While they made their way to one of the foremost tables, Argyle felt watched. He looked over his shoulder but saw only a throng of lords, courtiers and servants filing through the doors and spreading across the room.

'You are here.' Thomas was pointing at a table a little to the left of the dais.

Argyle looked down the long trestle table already laid out with bread and wine. 'And you?'

'Over there by the hearth.' Walking away, Thomas gave him a dead stare. 'I expect you to escort me back to my rooms after dinner, brother. There are matters to discuss.' He turned his back on Argyle before he could reply.

The King emerged from his private quarters with the little Queen by his side. 'Let us eat!' The Queen looked pretty in her purple dress, a little diadem sparkling in her dark brown hair. The King smiled down at her and received a smile in return. They did indeed seem to have mended their relationship.

'Sir Argyle.'

Argyle looked over his shoulder at Prudence. Tonight, she was wearing a beautiful, low cut dress, the lace on her sleeves nearly reaching the floor. Argyle thought she looked the complete opposite of her name. 'Mistress Prudence?'

'Her Majesty asks for a private word when dinner is over.' She looked around. 'I will come for you.'

'I shall look for you,' Argyle said and earned a beautiful smile before Prudence left to join the other ladies-in-waiting, Lady de Coucy strangely absent.

'Well now, there is a sweet little flower ready for plucking,' Lord Latimer remarked and the table roared with laughter.

Argyle saw the Queen look at Prudence and receive a small nod. She looked out over the crowd, and her eyes found Argyle's. He wondered what she might wish to talk to him about; it was not two hours since he had left her rooms. The smell of roast meat wafted through the air, announcing the beginning of a long meal.

Later in the evening, the Queen's ladies-in-waiting were dancing before the dais, the King clapping a rhythm and smiling at the Queen from time to time. She sat very still, letting him grab her hand on occasion and offering non-committal smiles. Before long, the King's attention drifted from the dancing women, and he got up to wander around the room, two White Harts walking close behind him.

He met Bolingbroke near the doors to the kitchens and the two of them seemed to engage in a friendly conversation. Bolingbroke gestured wildly and the King smiled, but his manner was forced and cold. When Bolingbroke walked away, the King looked relieved. He began making his way towards the side door across the room. Argyle watched him step out of it.

'The Queen will see you now,' Prudence said. 'Please come with me.'

Argyle rose and Latimer looked at him. 'I thought you were recently married, Sire. You could leave a few of the pretty girls for the rest of us! Some of us have been married for a lifetime, we need the company more.'

Turning his back on the laughter, he grabbed Prudence by the arm. 'Better get us away quickly, Mistress Prudence, before the other lords get hold of you.'

Prudence laughed nervously and wound her arm around his, her hand squeezing his wrist. 'Oh, Sire, they would never care for someone like me.'

Silly girl, Argyle thought, but she is right, she might be sport for them, but no, they would not care.

'Do you know what the Queen might want from me?' Argyle asked, and Prudence blushed.

'No, Sire, I have not her confidence. She very much keeps her own council these days,' Prudence confessed, looking up at Argyle. 'We all think she should be so happy, but she is not, she is sad all the time and she will not tell any of us why. And now, Lady de Coucy is ill …' Prudence clasped her hands to her mouth. 'Oh, I do go on and on, I'm sorry, Sire.'

'Not at all, Mistress Prudence. You are much more interesting company than that, which you just rescued me from.' Argyle hoped that a little flattery might get more information from Prudence.

'They say that Lady de Coucy is to be replaced with Lady Mortimer!' Prudence breathed. 'Was that her husband saying such bawdy things about me?'

'Yes, that is Lord Mortimer,' Argyle said. 'Why is she to replace Lady de Coucy?'

'Oh, I am not supposed to tell …' Prudence looked down. 'Perhaps it is what the Queen wishes to tell you.'

I doubt it, Argyle thought and put his hand on Prudence's. 'The sooner you get me to her, the sooner you will be rid of me - an old married man. You will be free to …'

Prudence blushed more deeply. 'I don't want to be free …'

'Mistress Prudence, what took you so long?' The unfamiliar anger in the Queen's voice made Prudence cringe. 'I told you to get Sir Argyle here quickly, not to parade him around the room!'

'It was my doing, Majesty,' Argyle interfered and earned a thankful glance from Prudence. 'I was trying to keep her from all the bawdy men in the room.'

'All of them?' The Queen waved Prudence away. 'Or just one?'

Argyle ignored her hint and bowed. 'You wished to speak with me, Majesty?'

'Yes, come with me,' the Queen said and pulled Argyle into a window bay, pulling the heavy curtains close behind them. 'I could not tell you earlier for I am hardly ever alone! But here there are so many people, so much noise, I thought it might be done, and now that my husband has left to amuse himself …' The Queen looked away. 'Well, we must still be quick, Mistress Prudence flaps her mouth about.'

'I noticed,' Argyle agreed. 'What may I do for you?'

'This time, it is I who might do something for you.' The Queen beckoned Argyle to stoop so she could whisper in his ear. 'I know where you might find Coxcombe.'

Argyle stared at her in stunned silence. How did she know?

'One of my ladies knows the rogue,' the Queen said, wrinkling her nose. 'I think she is bedding him. And he is a talkative drunk, she says so herself.'

Argyle struggled to gain his bearings. 'What does he speak of?'

'You grew up with a knight named La Fontaine, is that not so?' the Queen asked, and Argyle nodded. 'He is talking about his death and how he helped bring it about.'

'This I already know, Majesty.'

'But do you also know who ordered the death? Do you know how it came to be decided?'

'No, Majesty,' Argyle said, worried that the little Queen was now involved.

'Look to the White Harts!'

The curtain was pulled back and one of the Queen's ladies let out a surprised gasp. 'Majesty!'

'Sir Argyle was helping me close a window the draught was terrible,' the Queen said. 'The curtain must have blown out behind us.'

The lady looked confused, and Argyle knew that she must have seen the two of them with their heads close together.

'I am tired,' the Queen declared. 'Mistress Catherine, summon my ladies, I want to go to bed.'

Mistress Catherine had no choice but to obey the order, but she sent Argyle a suspicious glance before she walked away. The Queen looked after her. 'She will be running her mouth about this, but it could not be helped.' She turned to glance up at Argyle. 'The White Harts.'

Rather than go to Thomas' chambers, Argyle chose to go home. He needed time to think. Thomas' important matters would have to wait.

CHAPTER 26

5 September 1397 - London

Argyle turned his horse from Thomas' house and let it slowly pick its way through the crowded streets. He had been surprised to find that Thomas had left for Calais without sending word to him. Then again, Argyle had ignored Thomas' summons yesterday evening. A sullen silence was perhaps better than an angry message.

The city was teeming with White Harts; the King had decided to gather a large part of his archers for the impending Parliament. Now that Argyle was free from Thomas, he might as well turn his attention to the Queen's whispers about Coxcombe and the White Harts. She had claimed that one of her ladies knew Coxcombe and Argyle decided that if the White Harts proved uncooperative, he would try to single out the lady and see if he could press her for an address.

Argyle hailed a couple of White Harts lounging outside a tavern. 'Where might I find your captains?'

They gave him a curious glance. 'Who wants to know?'

'One of the King's knights,' Argyle said, and they jumped to their feet. 'In the Tower. They'll be watching over some important prisoners these days, Sire.'

Obviously, Argyle thought a little dismayed. The Tower was dangerous territory when you wanted to make enquiries without the King finding out, but there was no two ways around it.

The guards must have thought that his frown meant he was displeased because one of them spoke up again. 'There's also Captain Maydestone. He's at the Clink, isn't he?' His companion nodded.

'Thank you,' Argyle said and turned for the Clink. He was fairly sure he would more easily blend in near Winchester Palace than at the Tower and that there would be fewer people there who might recognise him.

When he turned the last corner, he put his horse in a tavern stable near the Clink, which lay right next to the Bishop of Winchester's vast palace. Argyle walked down the street looking for someone to ask about Maydestone. He grabbed a boy by the shoulder. 'Do you know where I might find Captain Maydestone?'

The boy squinted at Argyle and seemed to decide that there might be coin to be gained. 'What's it worth to you M'lord?' Argyle dropped a couple of coins into the lad's hand. 'Right there, M'lord.'

The boy pointed and ran before Argyle could reclaim his coins. He walked slowly towards a squat man with a bushy beard, a bow slung over his shoulder. 'Captain Maydestone?'

The captain turned. 'Yes?'

'Might I have a word?' Argyle looked around the crowded gate where soldiers, archers and visitors scurried back and forth. 'Somewhere quiet perhaps?'

Maydestone seemed to consider Argyle for a moment before he nodded. 'O'course, M'lord, we'll go in here.' He led the way into the gatehouse and closed the door on the commotion. 'London's a madhouse if you're not used to it!'

'I will not disagree with you there,' Argyle said and sat where the captain offered. The stone wall was cold and a little wet against his back. 'I have come to ask about a man that might be associated with the White Harts.'

'Can't be good if they're sending a lord …' the captain grumbled and stroked his impressive beard. Argyle decided to let him believe he was a lord and not a knight. 'Who?'

'I know the man as Coxcombe,' Argyle said and tried to read Maydestone's face. The beard covered most of it but the captain's eyes looked steady. 'He …'

'He might be a White Hart, might not,' Maydestone said. 'Who's he upset this time?'

'Others have come asking?' Argyle tried to hide his surprise. 'Who?'

'Some fellow in a hood, didn't get a good look.'

Argyle was a little rattled; what if it was the man from Paris, come to London to look for Coxcombe? Maydestone would need some coercing to spill what he knew, Argyle thought. He hoped his smile looked casual. 'Ah, yes, I thought he might. Not the easiest of men to get along with.'

'Nor is this Coxcombe.' Maydestone let his guard down a little. 'He's good at getting into trouble, but not enough to put him in the Clink. Here's mostly debtors and heretics, though the Bishop's been putting up more classy people too.'

I wonder who, Argyle thought and cleared his throat. 'Where might I find Coxcombe?'

'In the Tower.' Maydestone tossed his head noncommittally, clearly he was not well known with the city. 'He's not in a cell though some might like him to be, he's overseeing the care of one of the … prisoners.'

Argyle knew that only Warwick was in the Tower and wondered if the King might be storing other important prisoners in the Tower, but then he was fairly sure that he would have heard about it. The King did love to boast about who had fallen into disgrace.

'Thank you, I shall not take up more of your time,' Argyle said, and Maydestone opened the door on the bustle.

'Glad to help, M'lord, mayhap you'll tell whoever sent you that I was …' Maydestone might have smiled, his mouth was completely lost in his beard. 'Someone's holding a hand over the wretched man. He's been halfway in a cell twice already, and he only just returned before the coronation.'

'Where does he dwell when he is not in London?'

'Dunno,' Maydestone said and looked up when two of his soldiers came barging through the gate, a poor unfortunate between them. 'Damn, that's the third time that lad's been trying to smuggle out his sister.'

Argyle looked out into the yard and saw a pair of scrawny adolescents being pushed back into the Clink. Maydestone shook his hand gruffly. 'They'll never get out now. All they've done is get him in the Clink too. Poor fools.'

Argyle smiled thinly. 'Yes, poor fools. Well, thank you, captain.'

On his way back to the tavern stables, Argyle thought that there was no other way around it but to visit the Tower. He did not look forward to it but hopefully, it would be full of White Harts and he might be able to slip a soldier a few coins in return for an address.

No one needs know, Argyle thought as he trotted back towards the centre of London and the gleaming white Tower. There were rumours that the King had called a staggering 500 Cheshire archers to London. If the King ever wondered why the Londoners did not always take kindly to his whims, perhaps he should consider using the city guard rather than his own army. But then, the King probably never gave it a thought.

ꟿ ꟿ

'Stable my horse,' Argyle said to the boy, who plucked the reins from his hand and led the horse to the big Tower stables. Fortunately, the many archers do not seem to ride, Argyle thought and made his way towards the white Tower.

'Sir Argyle!' The Earl of Kent hailed him inside the barbican. 'What brings you here?'

Argyle had to think fast. 'I am here to see …'

'They are not letting anyone visit Lord Warwick,' Kent said and drew Argyle close. 'They say he cries night and day and has quite lost his wits. I wonder if he even knows that the Lord Arundel arrived yesterday and is housed right below him in the Traitor's Tower?' Kent inclined his head in the general direction of a squat stone building.

'Lord Arundel is here?'

'They are preparing for the trials; it caused great distress that he was held on the Isle,' Kent said with a withering smile. 'I think your brother was dispatched to fetch back Woodstock only this morning.'

'So I gathered when I went to see him,' Argyle said and sidestepped when a regiment of archers marched out of the gate. 'I have never seen so many men gathered by the Tower before.'

'And foul the stench of all of them.' Kent sniffed and glanced about, lifting his costly cloak that it might not be sullied by touching the ground. 'Well, I had better be off, the King wants me at Westminster. He is preparing the speech to be held before Parliament. You must not miss the opening, it will be like nothing you have ever seen before.'

'I will be there,' Argyle said.

'Ah yes, you are substituting your brother, I think?'

Argyle nodded. It was time to get away from this nosy courtier. 'Best not keep you from the King, my Lord.'

'I will tell him I met you,' Kent said, his eyes glittering. 'I am sure he will be surprised that you are here.'

'I thought I might finally get to see exactly how good the archers are,' Argyle gestured towards a group of archers sitting about on the green in front of the white Tower. 'Do you know where they train?'

'Around the side, they have set up a range and are shooting at carcasses. Their arrows go straight through flesh and bone, it is quite a sight.'

'Give my regards to the King,' Argyle said and walked off towards the faint sound of whoops coming from the far side of the Tower. He glanced back just once and saw Kent walk towards the river where a royal barge was waiting. Argyle stopped and bent, pretending to remove dirt from his boot, while watching the barge steer into the current and drift quickly away. He turned and walked towards the Tower.

'Can I help you?'

Argyle looked down at a short man with a thin, lined face. He looked vaguely familiar. 'You are?'

'Felix Tucker, keeper of coin at the Mint.'

'Ah yes, Master Tucker, I have seen you at court some times.' Argyle looked around. 'Might you know where I find the man in charge of the White Harts?'

'My Lord Exeter?' Tucker looked confused. 'He must be at court … Perhaps you could take your query to Captain Brook. He is by the training course, you cannot miss him, a burly, big man with flaxen hair.'

'Thank you, Master Tucker,' Argyle said and hoped he would meet no more court servants. It was bad enough that he had not known that Exeter was in charge of the White Harts while they were in London. 'He will do.'

Tucker bowed and gave Argyle a troubled look before he scuttled off towards the Mint. Argyle made for the training court, the twang of hard strung bows cut through the bustle of the Tower, the closer he came, the more clearly he could make out men shouting.

'Captain Brook?' Argyle asked a youth who pointed to a man almost as tall as Argyle himself. 'Thank you.'

'I'll introduce you, M'lord,' the boy suggested and puffed out his chest, the White Hart prominent on his shirt. 'Captain Brook! A visitor.'

Brook turned and eyed Argyle. 'Another Lord come to see us practice?' he grumbled. 'What'd you think you may learn?'

'That I shall never be a good archer,' Argyle said to lighten Brook's mood. 'I am here on other business.'

Brook dismissed the young White Hart who looked reluctant to leave. 'Damn little bastard! One of Lord Exeter's brats by some mistress or other, Brian the boy's named. Lord Holland wants him trained in archery. He'll never amount to much, he's no stamina.'

Argyle noted Brook's massive shoulders and looked after Brian. 'No, he does not seem to have the right build.'

Brook barked a laugh. 'No! But you do. Too bad you're too old to be trained, M'lord. You may not think it, but I'd make a decent archer out of you.'

Argyle acknowledged the compliment, and they watched the archers practice for a while. 'I am here to find a man.'

'Oh?' Brook looked at a flaxen haired youth whose bow sang louder than the others. 'That's my lad. Best in his year! Best not be him, you're eying.'

'Not at all, though he is doing you proud,' Argyle said a little amused by Brook's direct fashion. 'I am looking for Coxcombe.'

'The fallen knight?' Brook asked and met Argyle's eyes. 'They say he was once high in favour with the King but did something or other to be cast down. Now he works for whoever'll pay him. No loyalties in him.'

'Do you know where I might find him?'

'Probably entertaining Lord Warwick,' Brook said with a sour smile. 'He's set to look out for the old man's wellbeing, but I'd say he's wearing him down.'

Argyle cursed to himself; if Coxcombe was in the Tower there was no way he could get to him without the King hearing about it. It was bad enough that Kent and Holland's boy had seen Argyle here. 'Ah well, it will keep.'

'I think Lord Warwick'd be grateful if someone took away his tormenter.' Brook smiled when his son sent an arrow flying through a pig's carcass. 'But I know where he dwells when he's not in with the Lord.'

'Oh?'

'Wych Street,' Brook said. 'Lives with some whore or other. You can't miss it, the way the girls hang out the windows flaunting their … goods.'

'Thank you, captain,' Argyle said. 'Perhaps we can keep this between us.'

'Oh aye. I've no love for the fallen knight. If he should happen to have an accident, well that'd just make my day.' Brook gave a rough smile. 'Sure you don't want to have a go at the bow, M'lord?'

'Some other time, perhaps,' Argyle said. 'How many archers have you brought?'

'Just neigh on 500. The King's wanting 300 to oversee the opening of Parliament now that it's to be held in temporary quarters.'

'Ah yes, they are working on Westminster Hall, I have seen the structure they have erected,' Argyle said and Brook nodded. '300 you say?'

'My boy's among them, same as me,' Brook said and turned towards the field. 'Best I keep them to it, M'Lord.'

Argyle left the training field to the twang of bows and the soft squishing of flesh yielding to the iron-tipped arrows.

ꙮ ꙮ ꙮ ꙮ

CHAPTER 27

21 September 1397 - London

'Your pardon is revoked, traitor!'

Gaunt's words rang out over the crowd. The silence in the room was palatable. Argyle moved slightly, and the courtiers around him looked over to assess if he was about to protest. In front of them most of the English nobles sat on long benches, their attention focused on Arundel who stood before the council, the scarlet hood of his robe was just visible over the tops of the seated lords. Arundel's whole body shook, although Argyle could not tell whether in fear or anger.

Argyle was still surprised that Gaunt had been chosen to preside over the parliament as Lord High Steward. In this role, he would have to sit in judgement of his former allies and of his own brother, Woodstock.

Although word had it that Bolingbroke was fuming at the spectacle and had refused point blank to participate in the proceedings, Argyle saw him standing in the corner, a dark look on his face.

Bolingbroke's half-brother Thomas Beaufort sidled up next to Argyle who was standing at the back of the room. 'The King's cousin is upset.'

'I thought he would not come?'

'The King commanded him to attend.' Beaufort turned to Argyle. 'You know full well what happens when you go against the King.'

'Your brother did too, years back,' Argyle looked steadily at Arundel. 'So did he.'

'Yes, but unlike the two of you, he is on trial for treason.' Beaufort glanced at Bolingbroke again. 'The King has ordered my brother to speak today.'

'Speak?'

'It is a trial, Sir Argyle, there must be evidence.'

Argyle's stomach lurched, what was the King plotting? And how did Bolingbroke fit in?

'Truly, you lie!' Arundel shouted, all heads turning to him. 'I seek a pardon to silence the tongues of my enemies, of whom you are one. And to be sure, when it comes to treason, you are in greater need of a pardon than I am.'

'Answer the appeal!' the King seethed.

Arundel looked around, his eyes cold. 'All those who accuse me of treason, you are all liars. You are NOT here to act faithfully. You are here to shed my blood! I am NO traitor!'

'Did you not say to me at Huntingdon, when we first gathered in revolt against our King, that before doing anything else it would be better to seize the King?' Bolingbroke stepped forward.

'You lie! I never said anything to you or anyone else about the King except what was to his welfare and honour.' Arundel looked shaken.

'Did you not say to me,' the King said, staring at Arundel with what looked to be avid satisfaction, 'that Simon Burley was worthy of death. And I replied that I neither knew nor could discover any reason for his death. And that even though the late Queen and I interceded tirelessly on his behalf, you put him to his death?'

Arundel's face went white at the mention of the late Queen, whose memory he had sullied when he was late for her funeral. Back then, the King had struck him, and Arundel's face bore a visible scar across the left cheek from the clash. He turned to Bolingbroke, perhaps for support, but Argyle knew he would find none there.

'You have evidence, Lord Bolingbroke?' Gaunt asked, and the attendants all turned to face Bolingbroke who knelt before the King.

'I have, my Lord,' Bolingbroke said, his face tight. 'Majesty, I come to lay before you proof that Lord Arundel plotted to have your Majesty arrested.' The Parliament gasped as one. 'In 1388.'

Argyle was confused. The Lords Appellant had acted against the King in 1387, but here was Bolingbroke saying that Arundel had plotted against the King a year later?

'Was he alone?' Gaunt asked in a cracked voice.

'No.' Bolingbroke looked to the floor. 'He was not.'

'You will have to speak up, cousin!' the King said. 'We must hear the evidence clearly from your lips.'

Bolingbroke looked up with a defiant glance to his father. 'The Lord Arundel was not plotting alone, he sought the support of Lord Warwick and Lord Woodstock. Your own uncle plotted to have you arrested, Majesty.'

'And you?' The King's voice was like silk. Gaunt hunched over.

'I refused him,' Bolingbroke said. 'Our issues had been resolved, there was no need to …'

The King gave Bolingbroke a prompting glare. 'No need to what?'

'There was no need to arrest you, or try to supplant you, as the Lord Arundel dreamed to do.'

Parliament hissed, and the King leaned back with a pleased look on his face. 'Did he?'

'He had tried before, your Majesty, but Lord Mowbray and I changed his mind,' Bolingbroke said. 'When we walked into the Tower that morning in 1387, we did so in unison, all of us had agreed that you were the rightful heir and King. I later learned that Lord Arundel had turned back on his word. He wanted you gone.'

'LIAR!' Arundel screamed and lunged at the kneeling Bolingbroke. Two White Harts grabbed his shackles and pulled him back roughly, sending the old man to the floor. He writhed and screamed. 'YOU LIE! THAT IS A FILTHY LIE TO SAVE YOUR OWN HIDE! YOU WERE IN IT AS MUCH AS I!'

The King gave a wave and one of the guards hit Arundel on the shoulder with the butt of his lance. The old man yelped and stifled his accusations.

'This is dire evidence indeed. Have you any written proof of Lord Arundel's plans?' Gaunt asked, his face a blank mask.

'No.' Bolingbroke glanced at Arundel, who was grabbing his wounded shoulder tight. 'I burned it.'

'Why?' the King asked, curiosity playing in his eyes.

Bolingbroke barked a laugh. 'Because I wanted nothing to do with such treason, Majesty. Because I hoped that Lord Arundel would forget his hatred and bury his plan once he saw how well you governed England.'

'Did he forget?' Gaunt asked.

'I do not know,' Bolingbroke said, looking at his father. 'He never approached me again.'

'Why did you not come to me when he first came to you?' The King looked at Bolingbroke, a little smile fixed to the corner of his mouth. 'You should know better, cousin.'

'I did not want to stir up trouble.' Bolingbroke returned the King's look. 'As I say, Majesty, I never heard more about it, and therefore, I thought he had laid his plans to rest.'

'More to add, lord Bolingbroke?' Gaunt asked and Bolingbroke shook his head, staring at the floor.

'The punishment for treason is death.' Gaunt leaned back heavily and gave the King a quizzical glance.

The King looked at Arundel with unadulterated hatred. 'Pass judgement on him.'

'Lord Arundel,' Gaunt cleared his throat. 'I hereby sentence you to be drawn to the gallows, hanged, beheaded and quartered.' The assembled men exhaled as one, most likely wondering as Argyle was, if the King would be merciful. It was within his power and might just serve to appease the distraught noblemen. When Argyle looked at the King, his hopes faltered.

'Out of regard to your rank, Lord Arundel,' the King sneered, 'you need only be beheaded. Guard, lead this man to the Hill.'

'NO!' Arundel yelled, clawing at his shackles. The two guards pulled him roughly to his feet, bumping his broken shoulder once more to get him to shut up. Arundel looked around in confusion.

A murmur rose in the crowd, no one had expected the court to carry out the sentence immediately. This was proving to be a spectacular day. Argyle let his eyes wander over the men gathered in the room, most seemed out of sorts, some wore sardonic smiles. Bolingbroke stood before the dais, looking at the King in open disapproval and disbelief.

'Your titles and lands are hereby confiscated to be redistributed according to the King's pleasure!' Gaunt declared while the guards dragged Arundel away.

So these are to be the last words one of England's mightiest men will ever hear, Argyle thought. Friend or foe, even Arundel did not deserve such an end, and it seemed that Bolingbroke shared Argyle's opinion for he was staring at his father, but Gaunt did not acknowledge his son's presence with even a single glance. The King smirked.

People pushed to get out of the room; they wanted a good spot on the Hill. Arundel walked to his death, smiling at the many people lining the streets to see him go. The Londoners were faithful to their Lord until the end, Argyle thought and noticed several noblemen sending the commoners worried looks. Either Arundel had gone mad from the trauma of the sentence, or he was even now attempting to evoke rebellion - Argyle could not decide.

The executioner was already at the block; standing next to him was the King's own priest, who looked very uncomfortable. The two of them exchanged a quick word before the executioner went to stand on the left, his hands behind his back. The priest grabbed his Bible tightly.

'Come, Sir Argyle. We must hurry if we are to get at good view.' Argyle stared blankly at Beaufort who was pulling at his elbow. There was no honour in a traitor's death, and Argyle had little inclination to witness it, the trial alone had been enough to turn his stomach.

'You go ahead, I need not see Lord Arundel's head roll.' Argyle ignored Beaufort's glare.

'We must all see the traitor's death.' Bolingbroke appeared by Argyle's side. 'You and I especially.'

Argyle gave Bolingbroke an angry stare. 'Why?'

'We are both out of favour. I for knowing what Arundel plotted,' Bolingbroke said through gritted teeth. 'You for past sins and for your brother's involvement long ago.'

'I had nothing to do with that!'

'No, but the King ordered you to take Lord Mowbray's place at Parliament for a reason,' Bolingbroke said and grabbed Argyle by the arm. 'If you do not go, his Majesty might decide that you know more than you have let on. And as your brother's substitute, you can cast guilt upon him by default.'

Madness, Argyle thought while Bolingbroke dragged him along through the throng of people, pushing men aside. Utter madness!

'How can I be guilty by default?' Argyle asked and wrenched free.

Bolingbroke grabbed hold again, digging his fingers into Argyle's arm. 'Were you not in the same courtroom as I was, just now?'

'Yes.'

'Then you too must have realised that the King can do as he pleases!' Bolingbroke scaled a low wall to get to a good vantage point well above the common Londoner's come to see a great Lord lose his head. 'The King needs to see you and I present for the execution. To him it will be proof that we are innocent.'

'How?'

Bolingbroke turned an angry face at Argyle. 'Because my father has arranged it to be so! He has convinced the King that if we are present to witness the death of a traitor, it is because we are not traitors ourselves.' Bolingbroke stared at Arundel who was still smiling even through his speech to the people amassed to see him loose his head. 'Old fool!'

'Did he really come to you with plans to arrest the King?'

'Does it matter?' Bolingbroke sneered.

Arundel was pushed to his knees before the block, and the priest said a short prayer that was drowned out by the sound of the mob, moving as one great, foul beast smelling blood. The executioner pushed Arundel's head to the block and instructed him to cast out his arms when he was ready.

'MAJESTY!' Arundel screamed and threw out his arms.

The executioner's blow fell so fast that Argyle only saw the blade glitter in the pale sunlight. Arundel's head was split from his body, blood spraying the people closest to the block when it rolled away. Next to Argyle, Bolingbroke growled and kicked the ground. He glared at Argyle before he turned and left.

When Argyle finally found the strength to move, he caught the eye of the King watching him intently. Argyle dropped to his knee and waited until the King had left, his smug satisfied smile was burned into Argyle's memory.

ꙮ ꙮ

CHAPTER 28

24 September 1397 - London

Thomas stood before the Parliament. The hushed assembly looked intently at him, and Argyle could tell that his brother savoured the moment. Today, the King's nephew, the Duke of Surrey, sat next to Argyle and now he leaned over. 'Your brother seems to be doing well again.'

'Yes, he is the King's most loyal servant.' The words were jagged in Argyle's mouth.

'That is certainly one way of looking at it, I suppose,' Surrey said. 'Do you know that many believe it was his doing that the King arrested Warwick and the others?'

'No. It is gossip no doubt.'

'Let me enlighten you. It seems that your brother had words with Warwick only a few days before the infamous dinner. I am sad I was not there to witness it.' Surrey leaned back with a smug air.

Argyle suppressed an urge to slap him. 'I cannot know what might have transpired, but it certainly is quite a tale. It would mean the King lends more trust to my brother than you, my Lord. But I am sure that is not so.'

Surrey narrowed his eyes at the comment, before waving a hand dismissively. 'Not true. I believe there is room for both of us in the King's good graces. Still, I would have words with Lord Mowbray later, if I were you. It seems his prisoner suffered a regrettable accident.'

Before Argyle had a chance to ask what Surrey meant, Gaunt rose and the crowd hushed.

'My Lord Mowbray, you stand before us today to present the traitor Woodstock. Where is he?'

Thomas took a deep breath before speaking, his voice rang clear over the hushed assembly. 'I regret to inform you that Lord Woodstock is unable to attend his trial at Parliament. He died in Calais, only hours before we were to begin our journey back to England.'

Gasps of astonishment rose from the crowd, lords looking at one another in worry. With an effort, Gaunt managed to regain silence before he turned to Thomas. 'What happened, Lord Mowbray?'

'My Lord, Majesty, the prisoner died from apoplexy.' Thomas gestured apologetically. 'Before doing so, he did make his confession to me.'

'A confession?' Gaunt asked.

'Yes, my Lord.' Thomas' eyes glittered in the scattered sunlight. Argyle thought he saw a glimmer of malice when Thomas continued. 'He confessed to numerous crimes that took place in 1387 - and later on too.'

Once more the assembly voiced their disbelief and surprise, and the King smiled coldly. Argyle turned his gaze back at Thomas who stood still as a rock while Gaunt called the gathered men to order. 'Continue, Lord Mowbray.'

'Lord Woodstock felt his end was at hand and decided to go to God with a clear conscience. He confessed to plotting against your Majesty, in an attempt to gain the throne for himself.' Thomas was in his element, enjoying the crowd's undivided attention. 'He would have done so in 1387 but his efforts were smothered, and he felt sure that this time, he would have been victorious. That is until your Majesty arrested him.'

Argyle felt a hand on his shoulder. 'Sir Argyle, you are required to come with me.'

'Now?'

'My Lord requests your presence.'

Argyle looked over his shoulder to see a man in Gaunt's livery. Frowning, he followed the servant out of the room, giving Thomas one last look while he delivered the details of Woodstock's final confession.

For a man on the verge of death, the Duke had been surprisingly clear and talkative.

'This way, Sire.'

ꕤ ꕤ

Pushing open the massive oak door, Argyle was not surprised to see Bolingbroke standing near a window. He looked up and waved Argyle in. A shape lurked in the shadows.

'My Lord?' Argyle stopped just inside the door.

'Perhaps you had hoped to avoid meeting me again?'

'And why would I hope for that?' Argyle asked in a guarded tone.

Bolingbroke barked a laugh and reached for a cup. Wiping his forked beard, he gestured for Argyle to sit down. The room looked much the same as it had done years ago when Argyle had approached Gaunt to gain a place in Bolingbroke's pilgrimage. Gaunt's many papers made the room seem much smaller than it was; after all it was part of his vast royal apartments.

'You did not seem pleased with my father's sentence on Arundel, nor that you had to witness the execution.'

'Neither did you.'

The shape stirred in the shadows, and Bolingbroke turned. 'Meet Clyford Grenteville.'

Argyle was shocked to see that it was the grey-haired man from Paris, but he tried to hide it and only gave Grenteville a curt nod before focusing on Bolingbroke again. 'Is there a particular reason that you would have me come here while Parliament is in session?'

'The King will spare you, now that your brother is returned,' Bolingbroke said. 'Do you believe what you just heard him say? Do you honestly believe that before dying of apoplexy, Woodstock confessed his sins to your brother?'

Grenteville slid silently from the shadows to the window, his slim figure carefully turned to the room and Argyle leaned back. 'I have heard no more or less than anyone else.'

'No, but you will,' Bolingbroke said. 'Your brother has a strange habit of confiding in you, even if he knows you are not entirely to be trusted.'

Argyle balled his hands and breathed slowly to master his temper. 'Why would Thomas think that I cannot be trusted?'

'Can you?'

'Yes.'

Bolingbroke smiled. 'Then why are you here?'

'I am here at your command.' Argyle was annoyed. 'Since your father chose to bind us together for Arundel's trial, how could I refuse your summons now?'

Once more, Bolingbroke laughed, gesturing for Grenteville to bring two cups of wine. As the man handed over the cups, Bolingbroke said. 'Leave us.'

Grenteville looked at Argyle before leaving the room; was he trying to gauge whether Argyle might reveal that they knew one another?

'Silent as Death,' Bolingbroke said.

'Why have you brought me here, my Lord? Certainly not to question my loyalties to the King or my brother?' Argyle tapped his fingers on the cup, but did not drink.

'No. I may accuse you of many things but disloyalty is not one of them. At least, not to the men you just mentioned. Loyalty to me, now there is a different matter,' Bolingbroke said.

'And what reason would I have to be loyal to you, my Lord?'

Bolingbroke smiled. 'Actually, it is my father who demands your loyalty. After all he saved you from the King's wrath just a few days ago.'

Argyle was trapped. Gaunt had indeed saved him, although he had not known he needed it, and Bolingbroke had carried out his father's command very unwillingly. But how could Gaunt expect Argyle to openly declare his loyalty to the Lancaster family? Argyle had once before been asked to divide his loyalties, and he had refused. He held his tongue and let Bolingbroke lead the conversation.

'Three of the Lords Appellant face charges of treason,' Bolingbroke said by way of explanation. 'I was called to give evidence against one of them, and I might be summoned again. Your brother was ordered to fetch Woodstock from Calais, and now Woodstock is dead. What might happen if the King decides that I or your brother are traitors after all?'

'That is for the King …'

Bolingbroke interrupted. 'Yes, but the King is easily swayed. Especially by his friends, those fickle young men who know little or nothing about governing a country. The King is killing off some of the last men who might be good advisors. There is no love lost between us, he is afraid of me and my claim to the Crown.'

'Why am I here?'

'Rekindling an old friendship … it was my father's idea. I told him that you are loyal to a fault, but you are also fair. You would fight injustice even if it was in the face of the King, I believe?' Bolingbroke was leading Argyle down a dangerous path.

Argyle went to the door and grabbed the handle. 'Your point, my Lord?'

'What is more important to you? Family or King?' Bolingbroke asked.

'God willing, I will never have to choose.'

'And if God is less willing?' Bolingbroke was looking intently at him.

Argyle had often wondered if God was there at all, and he felt almost certain that God was not interested in his small matters. 'I could not say.'

'That is all I wanted to hear,' Bolingbroke said. 'Thank you, Sir Argyle, for your time and honesty.'

Leaving Bolingbroke's rooms, Argyle knew they had sprung a trap on him. He had to see Thomas.

ꕤ

'What did you think of the King's choice to open the proceedings the other day? I heard of it upon my return.' Thomas was swirling his wine while staring out of the window, the pitcher standing on a new wooden table that had substituted the one Bolingbroke had destroyed last time the two had met. Argyle moved uncomfortably in his chair; the King's wording had troubled him greatly.

'One King above them all!' Thomas snorted. 'Quite a bold move, I should say. It seems the King is sharpening his battle axe once more.'

Worry snaked around in Argyle's mind. He decided to broach a new topic. 'What really happened to Woodstock?'

Thomas' lips turned into a thin, displeased line. 'None of your business, brother. Suffice to say he needed a little … encouragement before speaking the truth.'

'I see.'

'I do not think, you do.' Thomas said, his voice toneless. 'When the King demands something of you, you do it. And if you cannot do it, then you dig until you find something else he desperately desires.'

'Even if it means …?' Argyle left his question half spoken for fear of uttering the words.

'Yes. I was under orders, and I had no other choice than to carry out those orders.'

Argyle regretted once again that he had not pushed for the King to allow him to go to Calais with Thomas. In a way, he should be satisfied that Woodstock was dead. If he was truly responsible for La Fontaine's death, Argyle would personally have parted Woodstock's head from his body, but there were too many unanswered questions. If Woodstock had nothing to do with the death as Coxcombe insisted, then who ordered the murder?

'Did you see the King when you announced his uncle's death?' Argyle asked. He still remembered the King's amused look; he had looked as if he was struggling not to laugh out loud. 'What did Woodstock say before he died?'

'He named himself, Warwick and Arundel traitors.' Thomas glanced at Argyle. 'I hear that Bolingbroke gave evidence against Arundel.'

'Yes,' Argyle said with a tight voice. 'Though I wonder if he was telling the truth, but the King lapped it up happily.'

'If it was enough to satisfy the King, why should it concern you?' Thomas rounded on Argyle. 'You cannot pin Arundel's death on me, I had no idea that Bolingbroke would be asked to bear witness or what he would say!'

'No, but with Woodstock it is a different matter, would you not say?' Argyle leaned forward. 'I must question your methods.'

'My methods?! You make me laugh.'

'He was in your custody. I find it hard to believe you had no choice what so ever.'

Thomas ran his finger around the cup rim. 'I might have had choice, but I also had my reasons.'

'Not this old song again, Thomas.'

'You are not here every day, do not pretend you understand anything. Sitting in your country house and making merry with soldiers. It must be such a simple life.' Thomas' voice had gone up a few octaves, teetering on the verge of breaking. He cleared his throat, took another swig and turned once more to the window, his shoulders shaking slightly. 'I did not ask you here to comment on my actions, little brother.'

'Very well,' Argyle said. 'Did he say anything else?'

Thomas looked puzzled. 'Confessing to conspiring to remove the King from the throne is not enough for you?'

'As I recall, you all but named him the instigator of La Fontaine's death,' Argyle prompted and Thomas snorted a laugh.

'Not this old song again. You say that I am stuck in the past, but I say that so are you! If he felt remorse about La Fontaine's death, he did not express it to me. Perhaps trying to save his own life was more pressing than admitting to an old crime, not that I thought to ask.' Thomas put down his cup. 'Leave it be.'

'I will leave court then. Now, you are here to take your place in Parliament, there is nothing more for me to do.' Argyle was irritated and tired, it had been a long day.

'No. I have it on good authority that, this Friday, Bolingbroke will plead for his one remaining friend. I want to make sure you are here to see it. Perhaps he will succeed.' Thomas eyed Argyle

'Why?'

'You saw him condemn Arundel to death,' Thomas said. 'Did he look to be enjoying it?'

'No.' Argyle wondered if Thomas had gotten wind of his visit to Bolingbroke this afternoon. He hoped not.

'It seems Bolingbroke is torn. These are his people; they are loyal to him before the King himself.'

Argyle rubbed his brow. 'They are your people too. And Woodstock was his uncle, is it any wonder if he is reluctant to appear once more at court? You were not there to see Gaunt condemn Lord Arundel to death.'

'Sadly no,' Thomas said. 'If Bolingbroke is clever, he will make his peace with what happened, he saved his own skin, but only just. Trouble is brewing, and I intend to be on the right side of it. Although this time, I must choose sides before I know the outcome, and that I do not like.'

'Makes it difficult to turn your coat, brother? In such tight quarters.'

Thomas brushed him off. 'Mock if you wish, I am building a legacy.'

'And the mortar is to be the blood of the King's enemies?' Argyle knew the answer.

'I could not say if they are enemies.'

'But they do have a quarrel with the King of England?'

'Every day that passes they watch from the corners as the King favours other men, men of less noble birth, men with little to commend themselves but an ability to be bawdy and offer ill advice. Is it that hard to grasp that, at times, the nobility of this land question the King's behaviour?' Thomas asked.

Argyle looked at his troublesome brother. 'Not the nobility, but you? Yes, I find that extremely hard to grasp.'

Thomas balled his fists until his knuckles went white, he was furious and barely containing himself. Argyle rose to tower over his older brother, but for once it did not work. Thomas could not hide the anger in his words. 'You speak out of turn, brother. Make sure you do not repeat our conversation to anyone. Just be there this Friday for the final trial.'

28 September 1397 - London

Warwick entered the room, and the Parliament turned to face a broken old man. Gone were his feisty manners and ill-begotten airs and left was the shell of a once great nobleman. Perhaps Coxcombe had succeeded in wearing down the great man, Argyle suspected that the fallen knight had enjoyed his task immensely.

Argyle stood beside Thomas at the back of the room, both of them glowering at the spectacle. Thomas turned his head when his former ally scanned the crowd for a friendly face. 'Look, he knows he is doomed.'

'What did you expect?' Argyle whispered.

Thomas shrugged. 'Perhaps a little more honour.'

'When you have lived as long as he has, seen a great King to his grave and another to the throne, perhaps your last thoughts are not of honour and valour but of saving your own neck.'

Thomas laughed quietly, the sound eerie and unsettling but, when Argyle made to go on, Thomas touched his sleeve. 'No. We shall speak no more of this, it is indeed a sad moment.'

Gaunt stood and the murmur died down. He held out his hands and commenced the proceedings. Argyle feared it would be another short trial ending with the death of one more of the King's old enemies. Gaunt took his place, his old bones creaking, and the rest of the nobles sat down, only Warwick remained standing, wringing his white hands.

'You are called before this court to answer for your crimes.' Gaunt leaned forward resting his chin on pointed fingers.

Warwick broke down in tears. 'Your Majesty, I beg your forgiveness. I beg your mercy. I am but an old man, my bones ache and my mind is not what it once was. If I have offended your Majesty, I apologise. If I did anything to offend your Majesty that you may not pardon me for, please have mercy!'

With a mighty sob, the old man fell to his knees before the King, who looked down at him with cold, calculating eyes. To Argyle, he did not look inclined to pardon Warwick, nor have mercy on him. Argyle felt Thomas move uneasily.

'Your Majesty, I BEG YOU!' Warwick tore at his clothes and hair - he was a man gone mad. Still, the King was unmoved; he just looked at the old man as if seeing him for the first time. Gaunt, however, looked unsettled by Warwick's display, but he called the first witness who took his place before the King and began his explanation. Warwick kept glancing up at Gaunt who ignored him, and Thomas tapped his fingers on the chair; clearly he was not overwhelmed with the witnesses.

'They might have spared him this,' he muttered to Argyle after a while. 'Is it really necessary? He is guilty; we all know that he is. Woodstock named him.'

Argyle saw a figure slide in through a doorway across the room. Bolingbroke.

'Just like him.' Thomas grunted. He had obviously seen Bolingbroke too and it was true that like any member of the royal family he had a flair for drama. The King too noticed his cousin and spoke briefly with Gaunt who motioned his son to come before the court. Bolingbroke obeyed though he looked unhappy at the prospect.

'What say you, cousin?' the King said with a slightly frantic look in his eyes.

Bolingbroke knelt and looked up at the King. Even though Argyle could not see his face, he saw his shoulders tighten. Thomas held his breath.

'Your Majesty, cousin,' Bolingbroke began. 'I come before you to plead for my Lord Warwick's life to be spared.'

The King looked genuinely amused. 'Go on.'

'I know that Warwick has spoken against you in the past, but I do not believe he has ever done so in spite. He has tried to give earnest council, even if it was not always welcomed or even right.' Bolingbroke remained on his knees. 'Warwick too turned away Arundel when he plotted to arrest your Majesty. I know because I was present when Arundel approached Warwick.'

The King rubbed his smooth cheek. 'Were you?'

'Lord Warwick agreed with me that you had been gracious to hear our concerns and that you were the rightful King. He never wavered in his support of your Majesty.' Bolingbroke spread his hands. 'I beg your Majesty, do not pass the wrong sentence on this most innocent man. Do not let old grudges be the undoing of one of your most loyal servants and advisors. I plead that your Majesty remember all the good that this man has done for you, all the times he has given just council and stood by your Majesty's side. I beg your Majesty to be benevolent and fair. I beg you to stop the bloodshed!'

The King seemed to consider Bolingbroke's speech for a moment, but before he could turn to Gaunt, John Montagu, the Earl of Salisbury spoke up. 'Majesty, I besiege you. Has not enough blood been spilled in the name of justice? Cannot you find it in your heart to forgive a man lost?'

The King scowled at Salisbury, but Gaunt raised a hand. 'You wish to speak on behalf of the prisoner, my Lord Salisbury?'

Salisbury nodded, his lips a tight line on his face, and when he turned to the King, he knelt slowly, bowing his head in submission. 'Majesty, for the love I bear for you, please let me speak.'

'Very well,' the King agreed, staring at Warwick who looked up in surprise, his cheeks streaked by tears and his eyes big in wonder. Perhaps he had expected Bolingbroke to speak in his defence, but that Salisbury, so devoted to the King that he had never spoken against him before, would run this risk was more than the defeated Lord could grasp.

When Salisbury made to rise, the King cleared his throat and tapped his fingers on the wooden table before him. Salisbury settled back on his knee at once. 'Speak true, my Lord Salisbury - for the love you claim to bear me.'

'Your Majesty knows that I would never defend a man I thought had betrayed his oath to the Crown, nor his duty to England and to you.' Salisbury's voice was rich and melodious and for a moment, Argyle thought the King looked a little appeased. 'I have known my Lord Warwick since I was a child, and he was a most devoted friend to my late father, who trusted him with his life on more than one occasion. Even your grandfather - God rest his soul - found the advice of Warwick always prudent and useful.' Salisbury looked up and saw the King stiffen. 'I am not denying that upon the demise of your grandfather, Lord Warwick made certain poor decisions that cannot be explained away.'

'No, they cannot!' The King shook in an effort to keep calm.

'However, Lord Warwick returned to your service and regretted his actions, much as other men present here today,' Salisbury said and glanced over his shoulder at Bolingbroke. The King once more cleared his throat prompting Salisbury to continue. 'Much and more has been said and done that shall never be repeated at this - or any other - gathering, Majesty, and I warrant that Lord Warwick has lamented his decisions these many years ago every day until now.'

'As well he should,' the King said and leaned back to consider Salisbury. 'What of it?'

'Majesty, hear my plea this day. For though I have had my doubts about certain men in your service, I have never had cause to distrust my Lord Warwick …'

'But for a single time …' Thomas whispered and Argyle balled his fist.

'… and he has repented, Majesty. Repented and been forgiven once already.' Salisbury drew breath. 'Let the kindness that I know to be in your heart win the day, Majesty! Let Lord Warwick live. I do not pretend to offer any advice on what other punishment he must receive, for surely, your Majesty would never arrest a nobleman if the cause was not just and true! If punishment there must be, let it not be paid in blood.'

Several of the noblemen assembled nodded at each other and the King. Argyle tried to read the King's face, but it might as well have been carved in stone. He revealed no emotion, simply sat before the court, staring over their heads, perhaps summoning strength to resist Salisbury's plea to spare the life of a man, the King had known his whole life.

'I beg your Majesty to spare Lord Warwick's life!' Salisbury's voice burned with passion and his shoulders shook with emotion. 'Please, let not the sun set on another death. Be merciful, Majesty, and your people will reward you with undying love - for all eternity!'

Bold promise, Argyle thought and attempted to gauge the mood in the room. Had it shifted slightly in favour of Lord Warwick? If it had, only God knew whether the King had noticed and if, for once, he would act against his own agenda. Argyle was certain that the King had arrested all three noblemen with the intent of ridding himself of them once and for all. If Salisbury managed to change the King's mind, would that leave the other noblemen assembled in the room feeling safer than before - or not?

The King stared down at Salisbury for a long moment before he nodded to Gaunt and, as soon as the King left with Gaunt in tow, the room began to buzz.

Bolingbroke had delivered another grand speech, but had been bested by the King's most loyal ally and trusted advisor, Salisbury. Would their words be enough to save a man's life?

Thomas leaned in. 'Oh my, what performances. I wonder how long they have been preparing? And how did they get Salisbury on board? I told you Bolingbroke would interfere, even if he was not the one on trial. What a fool.'

'Perhaps he had little choice?' Argyle said remembering Bolingbroke's fury after Arundel's trial. Although Argyle was still perplexed by Salisbury's defence, he could not help but wonder if there was more to this trial than met the eye?

'Please, brother. The last time Bolingbroke did anything like this was when …' Thomas' voice trailed away under Argyle's cool glare. Clearly, they were thinking about the same event, but they would never agree about the outcome. 'You know of what I speak.'

'Yes, and I do not care to be reminded.' Argyle paused. 'Nor should I think you would.'

'Best left unsaid. It all came to nothing.'

'To nothing? You dispersed of all the King's closest friends!' Argyle's temper flared. 'My household was exiled for years.'

Thomas looked away; the result had not been to his satisfaction. In the end, La Fontaine - and many other favourites - had returned to court and the King had let all of them keep their titles, lands and men. Now Argyle held La Fontaine's title, lands and men, and he wondered if that meant that he and Thomas were natural enemies.

Before either could speak again, Gaunt and the King reappeared, their heads close together. The King was nodding and looking at Warwick who had remained on his knees before the empty dais. Bolingbroke had retreated to a corner, his face guarded and concerned, while Salisbury was once more sitting in the front row with an anxious look on his face. He was as much on trial now as Warwick was, and he clearly knew as much.

'Your pardon is revoked!' Gaunt gritted his teeth when announcing the same words that had led Arundel to the executioner's block. Warwick flung himself to the floor and wailed, and Argyle saw Salisbury's shoulders shake.

The room held its collective breath when Gaunt continued. 'My Lord Warwick! You are condemned to life imprisonment on the Isle of Man! It is the King's pleasure that you forfeit all your lands and goods to the Crown.'

A ripple went through the crowd. Warwick looked up struck dumb in surprise and wonder, his face streaked with grime and tears, his clothes in tatters. In the corner, Bolingbroke turned from the room and slid away as quietly as he had appeared while Salisbury received a few appreciative nods. Next to Argyle, Thomas groaned.

'How did it go, M'lord?' Stephen had reached London the day before, but had been out on business while Argyle had been at court. He had been waiting for Argyle to return from Parliament, and having retreated to the small study, the two of them stood looking out over the river.

'Two great lords dead,' Argyle said, resting his elbows on the table.

'Two?'

'Yes, the King imprisoned Warwick for life.'

Stephen looked worried; the flickering candlelight cast strange spasms of darkness over his face. 'That is a good thing then?'

'I cannot say; the man will die penniless and alone.' Argyle felt empty. 'His heirs will have nothing to their name.'

'But they will live,' Stephen said, and Argyle smiled sadly. Stephen would always value life over name and honour.

'Yes, they will live - as outcasts for the rest of their lives.'

'Ah …' Stephen said. 'Not entirely worth it to your lot, is it, M'lord?'

'Not really, no.'

Stephen reached for his cup and inclined it at Argyle in mock ceremony. Argyle grinned in earnest for the first time for weeks on end when Stephen swept a clumsy bow, spilling some of the wine in his efforts. 'M'lord!'

'That is quite enough, Smith!' Calling for a servant to clean up the mess, Argyle motioned for Stephen to sit with him near the hearth, the embers glowing dimly.

'London in September, who would've believed you'd need a fire by now?' Stephen said stroking his beard.

'At Beauworth it will still be warm.'

'When do we return?'

Argyle pondered the question for a while. He had been considering his departure ever since he had arrived and now, he found that he was strangely unwilling to leave the city. There were still questions to be asked, and he had not forgotten the Queen's suggestion that he look to the White Harts for answers to La Fontaine's death. He had been preoccupied at Parliament and had yet to follow the lead that Captain Brook had given him. 'I shall send you and most of the men home soon. If you have finished your business here there is nothing more for you to do.'

Stephen nodded slowly. 'And you?'

'I will return in due course. I fear that I may have to stay here longer than I desire.'

'M'lady'll not like that,' Stephen said.

Argyle grit his teeth. He was not certain if Isobel cared if he came back before or after she had given birth any more. 'How long before she is confined?'

'Bessie said about two months before you left.'

'Then I will return before November.' Argyle said, although if the King ordered it, he could be stuck in London for much longer than that.

'That'd do, M'lord.'

'I shall send a message with you, for Isobel,' Argyle said. 'Put her concerns to rest.'

When Stephen left the room, Argyle went to his desk and grabbed a quill. How much should he relate?

CHAPTER 29

2 October 1397 - London

The King demanded that Argyle stay in London for a certain occasion that he was sure would please him. Now that Argyle was watching Thomas and Bolingbroke walk towards the King's dais, he was concerned. Behind them walked John Beaufort, one of Bolingbroke's half-brothers, he looked a little out of sorts.

Thomas' face was tense and Argyle sensed his brother's fear in his movements. Bolingbroke looked extremely uncomfortable, but he held his head high, probably aware that all of court was staring at him waiting to see what the King had planned.

It was not long since the King had incarcerated three of their fellow lords for treason, two were dead and the last was incarcerated on an island for the rest of his life. Now, the King rose from his throne, and the crowd knelt before him. He looked long and hard at the three men kneeling before him, and then he walked slowly down the steps. A guard stood close by and offered a sword to the King. He took it and seemed to weigh it in his hand.

Argyle swallowed hard before recognising the glittering hilt of the ceremonial sword.

The King laid the flat of the sword upon Bolingbroke's shoulder.

'Rise my Lord Bolingbroke, Duke of Hereford.'

The King moved on to Beaufort. 'Rise my Lord Beaufort, Marquis of Dorset.'

Thomas was last in the line, and the King paused before laying the sword on his shoulder. 'Rise my Lord Mowbray, Duke of Norfolk.'

Argyle applauded with the rest of the courtiers, ladies and lords, but secretly, he wondered what these three men had done to reap such favourable rewards just days after three of their former allies had been sentenced as traitors. While many were falling over each other to congratulate the three fortunates, Argyle found that he could not muster any pride or satisfaction on his brother's behalf. Instead, he decided to make one last stab at rooting out Coxcombe. He would go to Wych Street.

ꕥ ꕥ

Argyle looked up and down the tawdry street, the timber-framed houses with their protruding first storeys loomed over him, making Wych Street dark as well as dank. Right now there was none of the women present that Captain Brook had mentioned but, come nightfall, Argyle could easily imagine the street teeming with life. He was contemplating where to begin, when two men approached him. One of them had a white hart on his coat. 'Looking for something?'

'An old friend of mine,' Argyle said. 'He is said to live here these days, but I have not the exact address.'

'Maybe we can be of some service, M'lord,' the other said, he had on no livery but a vibrant Cheshire drawl. 'Your name?'

'Sir Argyle Mowbray.' This seemed to be one of those rare moments where his family name would make a difference, after all Thomas was now Duke of Norfolk; word would already have travelled through the London streets. 'And you?'

The soldier and his companion bowed and looked bewildered. 'Well, Sire …'

'You are not here on official business?' Argyle smiled and they relaxed a little.

'Well, not exactly,' the Cheshire man said. 'We're looking for a couple of lasses to …'

'Let me not detain you,' Argyle said with a wink. 'I can look for my friend just fine on my own. You are for the north soon?'

'Aye,' the soldier said. 'We're the last company left in the city. We'll be leaving first thing, and this's the first I've seen of London outside the Tower. Drab place!'

'It most certainly is,' Argyle said and pointed. 'That might be the establishment, you were looking for.'

The two men turned and saw a bawdy woman emptying a pale of water on the street. Her bosom could scarce fit into her dress, and her hair was tied high to make the most of what little beauty she possessed. They grinned at each other. 'If you'll not be need'n us, Sire?' the Cheshire man said. 'We might just's well …'

'Indeed,' Argyle said. 'Show them what an archer can do that the rest of us cannot.'

They half-ran down the road to the woman and she showed them in, looking after Argyle for a moment before dismissing him as a customer. Now, all he had to do was wait for a few moments until the two men had found companions, and he could go in to ask his own questions.

While he waited he noticed that there were a few more houses that looked to be brothels. Always work for that kind of woman, Argyle thought, hopefully, one of them remembers Coxcombe.

Behind him a window opened and slender arms crawled around his chest. 'Lookin' for company, love?'

Argyle turned. 'If I were where might I find it?'

'Oh, you're not the kind we usually entertain, M'lord,' the girl clawed at him and pushed her breasts in his face. 'But we'll find someone nice for you. Madam's opened the door 'special for you, come in, you can have your pick, but I think you're already sweet on me.'

This may be as good a place as any to try my luck, Argyle thought and walked towards the door, which was now ajar. He marvelled at how often he had tried to avoid going to whorehouses, and now he might end up visiting every last one in Wych Street.

ꙮ ꙮ

His purse hung almost empty in his belt, his head throbbed and his feet ached. All the thwarted women had been paid for their troubles, and most of them had looked almost disappointed that he did not want to buy their company but rather their words. One or two had even offered themselves for free when their madam was otherwise engaged, but Argyle had refused, and they had been baffled when he did not even want to pay for them to pleasure each other while he watched.

He had been to all the brothels save two, before he finally found someone who remembered Coxcombe. Now, he sat across from a sturdy woman with fleshy arms and a bosom that had a commanding presence. The table beneath his hands was sticky wet and it felt as if it wobbled, although that might just be too much drink.

'When did you last see him,' Argyle asked the bosom.

'He's gone with them archer fellows,' the woman said and smiled when Argyle looked up to meet her eyes. They were deep set in her full face. 'They knew what they were about, but then so do you I'll wager.'

Argyle straightened and pinched himself under the table to keep his eyes on her face. 'You are sure?'

'Ay, you look right for plucking, love!' The bosom jiggled when the woman laughed. 'But you're not interested in women, you say?'

'Well … ' Argyle said and tried to shrug off a young waif who was trying her luck on his lap. 'Not today.'

'Off with you Mina! If he's payin' it'll be for me!' The waif gave the bosom a haughty look before she left. 'No one's got what I do.'

I dare say, Argyle thought and tried to focus on his ale instead. His lap was still warm from Mina's visit and he was not entirely sure, she had not felt his enthusiasm. Shaking his head, he slurred: 'He left? And you are sure?'

'Oh aye, he's gone! All but lodged here for weeks, turned my girls' heads with his tales of valour, but he didn't fool Milly.'

From upstairs Argyle could hear creaks, shouts and rumblings. Mina had found a more willing customer at the corner of the bar and now she pushed the flustered youth up the stairs, sending Argyle a tempting glance.

'Milly?' Argyle asked the bosom, wondering what it might look like out of its tight cage. 'Who is Milly?'

'Millicent, Milly for short,' the woman said and put a finger under Argyle's chin to draw his eyes up. 'And that'd be me.'

'Oh,' Argyle drank deep; he had to stop soon. 'Why did he not fool you, Mistress Millicent?'

She laughed harder. ''Cause he'd no money near the end, did he? If he's a real knight, he'd be able to pay for room and board somewhere nice, not live here with Mina's sister. She's gone too, bless her.'

'The little …'

'Aye, she went quite mad when your knight left, packed up in the middle of the night and went after him.' Milly shook her lank, greying brown hair. 'Poor lass.'

'Do you know where he went?'

'Awful' interested in him … A lover spurned?' Milly smiled kindly and placed Argyle's hand on the crevasse between her breasts where it was almost buried when she spoke again. 'No, you're not the sort. We cater to all kinds, you know? It don't matter if you want a girl, a boy, both or none. You can watch too, if you like.'

Argyle let his hand rest on the soft cushion of flesh for a moment longer and struggled to look Milly in the eye. There seemed to be two of her, a mindboggling sight. 'You are sure he left?'

'Aye. Gone with them White Harts.' She put Argyle's hand back on the table and patted it. 'Any more, and you'll have to pay, handsome devil though you are.'

'Do you know where they went?' Argyle asked, a little sad that his hand was back on a hard, sticky surface. 'I will reward your words.'

She scrutinised his face seeming to decide something. 'Mina says her sister's gone to Ireland. Though why the silly lass'd do that, I'll never know. In truth, pet, your guess's as good as mine.'

Milly refused to get paid for more than her drink, but had him pinch her hard on the ass when he left. 'Good for the little'uns to know I'm not past me prime!'

She squealed like a giddy girl when he pinched her and pressed his face into her bosom for good measure, and he slipped a few coins down her crevasse in return. Argyle left the Lone Sailor a changed man, regretting only that he had not been fast enough to catch Coxcombe and wondering, drunkenly, why the waif's sister had left for Ireland and not Cheshire where the White Harts dwelled.

ഇ ര ഇ ര

CHAPTER 30

16 October 1397 - Beauworth

Beauworth slowly came into view, its beautiful grey walls almost black against the setting sun. Argyle had a sinking feeling in the pit of his stomach; the place usually brought succour and peace to a troubled mind, but today it seemed to tear at Argyle, suffocating him with dark, poisonous fingers that reached out to throttle him.

His prolonged stay in London had shed little light on some of his worries and instead it had brought with it a lot more concerns. In the end, it was Isobel's impending labour that had forced him to return.

The gate was thrown open, the massive oak planks glistening from the afternoon dew. Behind it, the courtyard was plunged into shadow, a gloomy foreboding chasm. Argyle thought his horse's hooves gave off a sinister hollow sound on the cobbles. On the far side of the house hidden from view by the stables, he heard the clamour of men fighting, swords ringing when they met, and the shouts muffled by distance. It sounded too much as warfare today.

Argyle looked around the courtyard as his men dismounted, happy to be home but troubled by all he had seen in London. The trials had been a disgrace, and he still struggled to believe that his brother had killed Woodstock. Thomas might have acted on the King's orders, but

Woodstock was still dead, another link to La Fontaine dispersed of. Most of all, Argyle was disappointed with the King. His behaviour had been shameful.

'Husband!' Isobel appeared next to his boot, looking up at him the fabric of her woollen dress drawn tight over her bosom and her big belly. If her face had not been white as snow, she would have been beautiful.

'Wife.' Argyle dismounted, tired to the bone from the long journey. 'You are well?'

'Thank you, I am. You must tell me all about your trip,' Isobel said with a shrill, forced voice, her smile strained.

Maybe not all of it, Argyle thought and spied Stephen standing at the far end of the courtyard trying to get his attention. Argyle released Isobel whose face had a brief irritated glimmer. 'I shall be right in, I just have to …'

'Of course.' She released his arm and walked off, her shoulders stiff.

Argyle met Stephen in the middle of the courtyard. 'This had better be important, Smith …'

'I thought you might want to know that twice a messenger came and was turned away,' Stephen said, his voice almost drowned out by the commotion in the courtyard. 'And she refused to read the letter, you sent home with me.'

'What?'

'Bessie says M'lady insisted she'd hear the news from you and no one else.' Stephen kicked dirt off his boot and looked briefly at Argyle. 'How much'll you tell her?'

Argyle had not thought he would come home to a household that knew nothing of the King's misdeeds. The cold, grey light of the courtyard weighed his spirit down. 'Have you told anyone?'

'No,' Stephen said. 'When you're not here, she's in charge, and I'm not saying that's a bad decision, only that …'

'That now I have to tell her and everyone else.' Argyle crushed the gloves in his hand. 'What ever might have possessed her to act so strangely?'

Isobel was sitting in the small parlour, the last rays of sun colouring the horizon a deep, bloody red that rattled Argyle. The room was bathed in a darker shade of red, the corners veiled in black, but it still had a distinctive feel of being Isobel's safe haven. He walked quietly towards her and rested his hands on her shoulders; did she jump ever so slightly at his touch?

'Some wine?' Argyle poured two cups and handed her one before pulling a chair close to hers. 'I am sorry.'

'For what? I know that you have duties.'

'Smith had a few issues to settle, I thought it best to do it now, and then I could indulge in an evening with my beautiful wife.'

Isobel awarded his blatant flattery with a thin smile. 'You are forgiven. Oh! Give me your hand!' She placed it on her belly, and Argyle felt an odd sensation beneath his palm, which made him want to both pull away and press down harder. He looked up to find Isobel staring at him. 'He has been moving for some time now, the midwives say it is a sign it is a boy if the baby is restless, but as long as it is healthy and survives its first years, I shall be content.'

'Such an odd feeling,' Argyle rubbed her belly lightly, and she let him for a moment.

'Not nearly as odd as having it happen inside you,' she said, stretching like a lazy cat in the chair, but her face was anxious, the emotion enhanced by the last kiss of the setting sun caressing her skin. 'Will you feed the fire?'

Argyle obliged and settled down again. He took her hands in his. 'How long?'

'Not long now.' Isobel's eyes shimmered, was it sadness, happiness or something in between? Argyle could never tell. She took a sip of her wine. 'Tell me about court - and the trials, were they cruel?'

'Two of the Lords are dead!' Argyle had not intended to tell her so abruptly, but he was still angry and shocked at the King's thirst for blood and revenge. 'Thomas and Bolingbroke survived.' Isobel made no comment, and Argyle rubbed his face, hiding behind his hands for some time to gather his thoughts. It had been a grizzly business, noble lords screaming for their lives, blood spilled, Thomas' hand in Woodstock's death. But most of all, Argyle was appalled of the King's vindictive brutality.

'Lord Arundel was first on the stands. He hardly had a moment to defend himself before he was dragged to the block.' Argyle tried to sort his thoughts. 'Gaunt led the procedures, it must have been arduous for him they - are all his old friends and allies, for God's sake one was his brother!'

Isobel stirred. 'Was?'

'Woodstock died in Calais.'

She stood abruptly and clung to her cup, to Argyle she looked ill. 'What is it, is it the baby?'

'Sometimes he kicks so hard, I have to get up,' Isobel said, her voice both weak and sharp. 'He will calm down if I walk about the room, please go on.'

She was rubbing her belly but Argyle thought that it was not the baby that was causing her distress. 'Are you sure …'

'Go on!' Isobel cut him off. 'I … it is better if I think about something else until it passes.'

'I found out why the King had ordered my presence in Parliament - he had charged Thomas with the task of bringing back Woodstock from Calais. There was some gossip that Woodstock had died in August, but it turned out to be …' Argyle gestured.

'False,' Isobel prompted.

'Yes … He was alive and well when Thomas arrived to ferry him across to Dover and bring him to London for his trial. But before they could go, he took a turn for the worse.' Argyle paused when he saw Isobel go white. 'Before Woodstock died, he confessed to his crimes - old and new - Thomas heard his words himself.'

'And then he simply died?' Isobel sounded distraught.

'Yes.' Argyle wondered if the pregnancy had made Isobel more sensitive and emotional than usual. She looked as if she had lost a beloved family member.

She smiled and wiped away a tear. 'I am sorry, I cry about nothing these days, I think it must be the baby disrupting my humours. The physician suggested bleeding me but I thought better not. Why would I cry for someone that I do not even know?'

Why indeed, Argyle thought, and why did you send away the messengers without taking my letters? What news were you trying to avoid?

'How did he die?' Isobel asked, ripping Argyle from his thoughts.

'Apoplexy. It seemed he had experienced some problems before, a pain in his arm, loss of cohesion, loss of speech. He died in the night.' Although Argyle was sure that was a lie. Only, he still wondered if Thomas' hints that the King had ordered that Woodstock confess whatever the means were a falsehood too.

'Was he ill before?'

'Why do you ask?' Argyle said before he could stop himself. She was acting very strange.

'Oh, my father had some of the same symptoms before he passed …' Isobel said and turned away. 'The physician could give no reason for his death. I simply wondered if perhaps he had died from the same thing.' Argyle was surprised; Isobel rarely spoke of her father. She changed the subject. 'It must have pleased Thomas.'

'Why?' Argyle knew Isobel and Thomas were at odds. Thomas' reluctance towards Isobel was easy to understand, but Isobel's anger seemed more deep-rooted almost like pure hatred towards someone she had met but once. It did not help that Thomas had refused to come to the wedding.

'Now he is one of the senior advisors to the King, is he not?' Isobel tried to sound indifferent, but something in her voice gave Argyle pause. 'I mean, if he and Lord Bolingbroke survived, it must mean the King still trusts them. What of the last Lord?'

'Warwick was spared,' Argyle said.

Isobel sighed and fingered the pitcher of wine, and then picked up an apple. 'I have such a craving for apples!'

This apparently was her peace offering, and Argyle took it, he was too weary to argue about Thomas. 'I must make sure that there are apples in every room.'

Isobel laughed quietly and went to sit next to him, resting her head on his shoulder. 'The baby has settled again, perhaps he just wanted an apple.'

'Perhaps,' Argyle said and resumed his narrative about the trials. 'Warwick will live the rest of his life in house arrest on the Isle of Man.'

'The King does not want him in the Tower?'

'Hardly a place where he can be easily forgotten. On an island, the King can control who comes and goes, and who Warwick speaks to,' Argyle said taking a bite of the apple when she offered, it was juicy and tart. 'He was also stripped of all his possessions. His family is downcast, and he will die penniless.'

'But in a pretty prison,' Isobel said. 'I suppose that is something. Did the Queen beg the King to spare him?'

'No, she was not present. Bolingbroke did.'

Isobel looked shocked. 'Lord Bolingbroke?'

'He made an excellent case, as did Lord Salisbury.' Argyle stroked her hair; it was soft as silk, the curls at the nape of her neck caught his fingers. He admired the deep copper colour and the gold running through it. 'And Gaunt, I think, was also pleading with the King behind closed doors trying to make him see what would happen, if all three died.'

'It seems to me that you believe the King was responsible for Woodstock's death?' Isobel dropped the apple core into her cup. 'Was he?'

'I do not know.' Argyle was not happy to lie to her, but she had acted so strangely that he dared not upset her again with his own suspicions and Thomas' confession. 'The man is dead … Thomas said it was a peaceful death, which I suppose is all any of us can hope for.'

Isobel looked into the fire. 'Hope … yes, we can hope, but to what end?'

24 October 1397 - Beauworth

Since Argyle had returned from court Isobel had been distant. She often took to her bed early in the day, claiming her back hurt or her head ached and once, she even thought the baby might be coming but it was false alarm. They still slept together, but she constantly turned away from him and shrugged off his hand when he wanted to feel her belly. She insisted her body was just preparing for childbirth and that was why it was suddenly tender to the touch, but he frequently saw her maid touch her back and belly, and she never shied away from her. Argyle began secretly dreaming of her confinement. At least when the door closed on the birthing chamber, he would know where she was at all times, and he would know that she was about to be a mother. Perhaps that would settle her mood and calm their strained relationship.

This morning, Stephen was sitting next to him on the low dais, shovelling down bread and eggs. 'Much to do, M'lord.'

Argyle found the food oddly tasteless, the eggs congealing on his trencher of bread. 'I was wondering …'

'What?' Stephen stopped to give Argyle a curious glance before resuming his meal.

'Did Bessie …'

'Did Bessie what?' Stephen focused on his food, sloshing down great gulps of ale between his massive bites.

'When Bessie was first with child, did she push you away?'

'What, more than usual?' Stephen grinned, some egg stuck in his ginger-grey beard. When he caught Argyle's frown, he stopped. 'No, she didn't. She wasn't more affectionate either … though towards the end, she actually began …'

'Thank you, Smith, Bessie must be allowed some secrets,' Argyle cut him off.

Stephen wiped his mouth with the sleeve and leaned back. 'No two women are alike.'

'I know! But …' Argyle looked around. 'She is avoiding me. Openly too. It is as if she cannot bear my touch. Ever since …'

Stephen eyed him. 'Ever since? You've got to speak in full sentences, M'lord, or we'll all think you've lost it.'

Argyle had not really thought about it before now, but she had been acting oddly ever since he returned from Parliament, ever since he told her about the old Lords' destinies. Why would a farmer's daughter care about that?

'Ah … ever since you've come home from London.' Stephen guessed. 'I could ask around, but I haven't heard of anything strange about her - only that she likes her apples and that we're running out fast.'

Argyle was disgusted with himself at his next words. 'Please do, but keep it quiet.'

Stephen nodded, stood and barked a command to the boys and men still in the hall. They were late for their daily training, and Stephen was not one to take such slacking lightly. 'I'll be discrete.'

Isobel passed Stephen in the door and when he bowed to her, she smiled and briefly touched his arm. She continued towards the dais, looking every bit the lady of the house, her green wool dress falling smoothly around her round belly, her cheeks flushed. When she came closer, Argyle noticed that her hair was a little out of sorts. 'Where have you been, wife?'

'In the dairy,' Isobel said, seating herself to his right, just far enough away that their elbows did not touch. 'The cheese is coming along beautifully. I confess I had a bit of a taste.'

Argyle forced himself to smile. 'Apples and cheese?'

'He is your baby too.' Isobel grabbed a piece of bread and some seared bacon. 'It is not long until my confinement and until then, I intend to be out and about as much as I can.'

'No one could begrudge you that.' Argyle poured some weak wine for her. 'Next time, I might come with you.'

She started and looked away. 'No need, I have my maid, and there is so much for you to do.'

'Isobel,' Argyle said, 'what is wrong?'

She had to lean in to hear him over the rumble in the hall of men stomping out and servants clearing the tables. Argyle enjoyed the mingled smell of sweet milk and crisp autumn air in her hair. She looked at him for a long time.

'Nothing, I cannot believe I have changed so much, I feel fat!' Isobel finally said, biting down on a piece of bacon. She licked her fingers. 'I am sure you cannot desire me when I look like this.' Argyle thought that she could not be more wrong, she was radiant - he almost said as much but she continued. 'Once the baby is born everything will be better. I know my mother would often be inconsolable and overly happy within minutes, she almost drove my father mad. I even think I take after her when it comes to the apples.' Isobel smiled when Argyle offered her a plump, red apple. 'You worry about nothing.'

Do I, Argyle wondered, when Isobel left the table nibbling at the apple. She sang a pretty song about the pregnancy but something was off, something he feared no child could mend.

CHAPTER 31

1 November 1397 - Beauworth

Argyle looked at La Fontaine, his eyes cloudy and blood seeping from his mouth.

'Sire?' Argyle breathed, feeling tears stinging behind his eyelids and not bothering to blink them away. He reached over to grab La Fontaine's limp hand; Argyle could almost feel life slipping from La Fontaine's body.

'Do not trust …' La Fontaine struggled, choking on the blood in his mouth, spitting angrily, his eyes momentarily clear and alert. '… anyone.'

Argyle woke with gasp, hardly knowing where he was or what had happened. The room was pitch black. He kicked away the soggy woollen blanket and shook violently at the stuffy, stale air that immediately wrapped its clammy arms around him. His eyes slowly adjusted to the dark room, little by little revealing a chest, a table and one of the bedposts. Argyle shook his head to clear it, feeling the dream wafting away, the images slowly descending back into oblivion. He felt Isobel stir next to him and sat still for a moment waiting for her to settle back to sleep. Only then did he swing his legs over the bedside, relishing in the sharp cold that shot up through his toes and woke his whole body. Hunching he rubbed his sweaty brow before feeling around for his tunic. Isobel loathed it - she had never said as much but he knew, she did - just as she hated the thin, long necklace that clung to his sweaty skin.

Argyle slid from the bedchamber, knowing he would not be able to go back to sleep. Every time he blinked, La Fontaine's gaunt, dying face swam before his eyes, reminding him of a pledge that he had yet to fulfil.

'I gave my report to the King,' Argyle whispered to himself while he snuck down the corridor towards his study. 'I gave a full account.'

But you did not find out, did you? his mind taunted him. You only found what the King, Bolingbroke and your brother wanted you to find! You are weak, you betrayed your promise to a dying man - a man you claim was almost a father to you!

Once inside the study, Argyle finally let out the groan that had swelled inside him, he was weak. He had forgotten what he was, who had made him, and to whom he owed his allegiance. He reached for the wine pitcher but shook so hard that he could not pour the lazy wine and instead, he began pacing up and down the room, crushing the rushes under his bare feet, feeling the lavender stalks prick his soles. He threw open the windows, not caring that the shutters clanged against the wall as the November wind caught them. Argyle leaned through the window and let the wind slap his face and chest, beating the sweat from his brow and cooling his head enough to think clearly. He wondered whether he would feel this way if he had not turned around on the narrow sea between France and England, if he had paced the oarsmen and run from the royal ship. But he had turned around, and he had gone back under royal orders to a court of deadly whispers.

And now, his dreams of La Fontaine grew ever more vivid or more accurately; his dreams about La Fontaine's final moments. Oh, there had been dreams before but none like these. None so clear or which caused so much heartache and torment. It seemed La Fontaine was not satisfied.

'I rode across the world to find a murderer, I found all that I could, and I handed it to the King,' Argyle protested to the dark room, the embers in the hearth pulsing weakly. 'I have spoken to all of London! It is no use!' His last words came out a whimper, and he winced at his own pettiness.

Argyle leaned back in the big, oak chair, feeling as he had done so often these last weeks - Hell, years - completely lost. 'Why did you name me heir?' he asked the encroaching shadows. 'Why me?'

But once more, La Fontaine had said all he wanted to for the night. Argyle's temper flared at the silence of the dead knight. 'The King, you made me swear an allegiance to, is nothing but a worthless liar, vain, petty and self-serving; he is tearing his own kingdom apart. I fear he might even have had a hand in your death! Is this what loyalty is?!'

The room roared back and silenced Argyle. His bedchamber was a safe distance away, but if he kept shouting, Isobel was bound to wake and come to him, one hand on her swollen belly. Could he bear that? 'She loves me,' he tried to reassure himself. 'Of course she does. No two kinds of love are the same, in her own way, she does love me.'

Argyle was sure that Isobel knew he got up at night and did not return to bed until the sun rose. She must know she always slept lightly, for the first many months of being the castle's lady she had woken at the slightest sound. Now, she said that she had tamed the castle ghosts and slept soundly, but Argyle often heard her shallow breathing and knew she was afraid. When he confronted her, she avoided his questions, laughing it off as the follies of a pregnant woman.

5 November 1397 - Beauworth

The sun crept through the narrow windows sending weak rays into the nursery. In the cradle, a little dark-haired boy stirred slightly, squirming in his tight swaddling. The whole room had a dreamy quality from the rocker in the corner to the bowl of water perched on a table near the cradle. Everything was bathed in a wintry, silver light.

Yesterday, he had considered breaking the rules of confinement to steal a moment with Isobel. Argyle knew she would much rather be left alone, and after pacing the corridor for some time, he had left.

Now, he stood in the doorway of the nursery waiting for the wet nurse to return from fetching more swaddling for the baby. Argyle whiled away time contemplating the boy's distinctive dark hair, it was the hair of a Mowbray. Argyle and Eleanor had golden hair and Isobel had chestnut curls. Hopefully in time, the boy would trade his dark hair for a fairer shade.

The child was so tiny. Argyle had been afraid to touch him in case he broke, but the nurse had soothed his concerns, and he had held his little heir, seized by the marvel of life and birth. To imagine that some day this minute creature would grow into a man. He quickly spat over his shoulder to ward off evil convinced that the mere thought that the child would survive his first year would somehow jinx it.

The wet nurse returned and eyed her lord for a moment. It was rare for a man to take an interest in a baby even if it was his firstborn son. Then she smiled at him. 'Would you care to stay while I change him, M'lord?'

Argyle nodded then stepped forward gingerly, soft shoes stirring the rushes on the floor.

'He is perfect. Healthy and strong, and suckling well.'

'And his mother?'

'She is recovering very well, she is eager to be out of confinement already, M'lord.'

Argyle forced a smile. Of course a wilful women such as Isobel would not be kept in close quarters for long. Every once in a while, her behaviour would spark an old, dusty memory of another wilful woman, and a small part of his heart would ache as an old wound.

'It will be a long six weeks,' he said to please the wet nurse. In truth, he had not missed Isobel's recent strange behaviour; she made him feel guilty although he did not know why or what about.

He bent forward to look at the little naked boy waving his arms about and kicking his fat legs. The boy was truly perfect. When Isobel had first told him she was with child, he had been torn. So many women and children died in childbirth, but they had come through it without a worry and his fear had been replaced by wonder. The wet nurse let the child lie naked a little longer than usual before ushering Argyle from the room, the babe must be swathed to his board to ensure he would grow straight and strong.

Argyle stood a moment longer outside the closed door. They had not agreed on a name but he would insist they call him Edmund - for La Fontaine. He was not sure if Isobel would give way willingly, but he would name his firstborn, and then she could name all the others. Edmund would inherit Beauworth - if Argyle could stay in the King's good graces.

CHAPTER 32

2 January 1398 - Westminster Palace

'Sir Argyle!'

On a whim, Argyle had decided to exit the presence chamber through one of the side doors leading off to a narrow hallway. The King was at Windsor visiting the Queen, and Argyle was secretly pleased because it gave him more time to search for Coxcombe. Although the madam at the Lone Sailor had been adamant that Coxcombe had left with the White Harts, Argyle was less sure. He remembered her ample bosom with a faint smile. If Coxcombe was indeed in Ireland as the waif had told her madam, Argyle would have to find another way of discovering what had happened to La Fontaine.

'My Lord.' Argyle looked across the dimly lit corridor at Bolingbroke. 'Back at court, I see.'

'I am back because my father summoned me.' Bolingbroke was dressed in sombre clothes today; only the large brooch on his chest added a little colour. 'Although I did wonder why you were here and your brother so obviously missing.'

'If you are looking for Thomas, I cannot help you.' Argyle leaned against the wall. 'I do not know where he is.'

'I was looking for you. I saw you at court yesterday,' Bolingbroke said.

'Is that so, my Lord?' Argyle felt his heart sink, he knew that if Bolingbroke decided to dig deeper into Argyle's presence at court, he would have a hard time lying about it.

'Not here, these walls have ears and eyes.' Bolingbroke gave Argyle a knowing look, and he followed Bolingbroke down the hallway. They weaved their way through the galleries and halls and eventually wound up in front of Gaunt's familiar oak door.

'My Lord, I hardly think …'

Bolingbroke shot him a dirty look and opened the door. 'Father, I have brought a visitor.' He forced his voice to be light.

Argyle had expected to find Gaunt on the brink of death, but when Bolingbroke stepped aside, Gaunt was standing; his posture even more crouched than the previous fall but his face was still determined, and his beady eyes were alert. At first glance, Gaunt's apartment looked much the same as ever.

'My Lord.' Argyle sketched a bow.

'You have brought me a Mowbray.' Gaunt's voice was splintered. 'How considerate - although I believe, I asked for the other one.'

Bolingbroke laughed. 'Sometimes lady fortune smiles on us, father, and we must take what she offers. I could not find Lord Mowbray and was surprised to see Sir Argyle at court yesterday. When you asked for Mowbray, I thought perhaps the younger could be of some use to us.'

Argyle resented being stuck in the stuffy room with two men who clearly felt so high above him that they hardly deigned to glance at him, much less speak directly to him. However, it did provide the opportunity of looking around the room while the two bantered and exchanged snide remarks.

Gaunt's room was big and ought to be airy with is vast river-facing windows, but the shutters were closed against the cold January and the fire was roaring. Sweat built around Argyle's neck and the first droplets began their slow descent down his spine.

Once his eyes had fully adjusted to the dusky room, he noticed the piles of paper stacked high everywhere, the many strange little glass vials tottering on shelves and tables, and the big rug that lay hastily abandoned next to Gaunt's chair. Despite Argyle's initial thoughts that Gaunt looked well this was undeniably a sick chamber.

'Thoughts, Sir Argyle?' Gaunt's cracking question whipped Argyle back to the present.

'My Lord?' Argyle's brow was wet from the heavy heat in the room.

'You must pay attention, Sir Argyle!' Gaunt sat down leaning heavily on Bolingbroke. 'I asked you what you thought about your brother's disappearance.'

'Not much, my Lord. Thomas is sometimes away from court, I suspect he had some business or other in Nottingham that commanded his presence. Perhaps he is visiting his new dukedom.' Argyle saw Gaunt exchange a glance with Bolingbroke.

'This is disappointing indeed, Henry. This Mowbray is of no use at all!' Gaunt scolded.

'I thought we might have a quiet word with him, father. On a certain matter.' Bolingbroke tried to appease his mighty father.

'Why would Sir Argyle care?' Gaunt asked.

'Because it is his brother telling the tale,' Bolingbroke said, rearranging the chairs to take a seat near his father.

Argyle sat down on the edge of a low stool that Gaunt offered him with a gesture and decided to take the bait. 'What tale might that be?'

'He is accusing the King of wanting to kill me,' Gaunt said without ceremony, and Argyle's breath caught. 'He is saying that the King has grown weary of me and wants me gone and Henry too - for good measure.'

'Why, my Lord?' Argyle cleared his throat.

'Obvious, would you not say, Henry? The King is jealous of my estate, my houses, castles and all my wealth. He wants it for his own.' Gaunt coughed and let Bolingbroke replace the blanket around his legs. 'Thank you, son - I find I am so very cold these days. Your brother is playing a dangerous game, Sir Argyle, one I cannot condone. He is pouring poison into the King's ears and for some bizarre reason, the King is listening.'

'But my Lord, the King only has to …' Argyle stopped, unsure of how to continue. If the King was indeed so petty that he wanted the Lancaster estate to himself, all he had to do was to levy a new tax on Gaunt or command him to relinquish some of his houses or lands to the Crown? Gaunt was famous for his loyalty, he would not deny the King anything. But Gaunt's heir Bolingbroke was another matter.

'The King only has to call the muster, and we will rally our armies for him - and yet he has built his own private army,' Bolingbroke said. 'The King only has to ask for a loan, and we will happily give it to him. He can ask that my daughters marry whomever he chooses and yet …'

'Yet he grows ever more suspicious and dangerous.' Gaunt held out a warning hand when Bolingbroke made to protest. 'No, Henry, it is the truth, and as a sick old man, I can say it. I have spent my life serving first my father and brother and then the King. I have gone where they have asked, battled the Scots over and over again, warred on and negotiated with the French, appeased the lords and the King … all of this I have done, and my nephew only sees a man determined to ruin him - to undo him - on my deathbed?!'

Gaunt fell into another fit of coughing, and Bolingbroke jumped from his seat to fetch some wine. Argyle tried to gather his thoughts; if Gaunt was telling the truth, then this could end very badly.

'Father, you are not well enough for this …' Bolingbroke protested, but Gaunt turned to Argyle.

'Your brother is saying that I mean to put Henry on the throne.'

Argyle swallowed hard, the heat in the room made his head throb. 'My Lord, I had not heard …'

'Whatever you have or have not heard, you will listen now.' Gaunt's breath was jagged and rattling. 'It is true that my father's dying wish was for us to be next in line for the throne. It was an old man's precaution because he had seen his own magnificent son perish, and he was leaving the country to a child, a boy who did not know how to be King. None of us ever believed the King would die without issue, and he still has time.' Gaunt paused to catch his breath, and Bolingbroke eyed him with concern.

'The young Queen was a foolish choice, not for her breeding or her being French, but because he delayed his chances of siring an heir.' Bolingbroke gave his father a grudging look, but Gaunt pressed on. 'No matter what the King decides, I shall always support him. If he decides to set aside the Lancaster-line in favour of the little Earl of March, I shall be first to bend my knee to him, for he too is family. I am not so foolish that I think I will live to see the Queen with child, let alone birth a son, but Henry will, and then Henry will bend his knee to the rightful heir.'

Bolingbroke inclined his head and took over. 'I shall do as my father commands. I shall be as loyal to the King as he has been.'

'Why are you telling me this?' Argyle already knew the reason.

'That you might take it to the King.' Bolingbroke stroked his beard. 'I have been hard at work trying to get the King to listen, but to no avail. For whatever reason, he has decided to listen to your brother and those wretched men he surrounds himself with.'

Argyle noticed the sour look on Bolingbroke's face, and Gaunt's light touch on his sleeve. Bolingbroke breathed deep before continuing. 'Or that you might ask your brother to stop scheming.'

Now they were both looking at Argyle. 'I shall speak to Thomas, although I doubt that he will listen. As for the King, he has little faith in me these days.'

Gaunt smiled. 'Good, then you will not overstep the mark. The King prefers deference to ambition.'

'As you say,' Argyle half-agreed hoping it would be enough to get him out of the thick, sickening heat of the room and away from their conspiring glances.

'My father is tired.' Bolingbroke rose. 'We both thank you for listening, Sir Argyle. Whatever happens next, we know that you will be loyal to England and to the Crown, and we thank you for that.'

Gaunt waved a limp hand at him by way of dismissal, and Argyle went to the door. Pausing with his hand on the handle, he asked one last question, his back to the room. 'What happens if the King dies without issue?'

'If that happens, we will support the rightful heir,' Bolingbroke said behind him. 'All of us in this room, all the nobles and all the lords and everyone in the land will support the rightful heir.'

'Yes,' Gaunt agreed in his splintery voice. 'The rightful heir must claim the throne.'

'Good,' Argyle said and left the room, glad to be away from the illness that lingered in the air, the staring eyes and the twisted words.

Later, Argyle began suspecting that what he had heard had been rehearsed and planned out like a masque in which each player knows exactly how the play will end, except for one, and it is he who will be sacrificed on the altar of ambition.

CHAPTER 33

5 March 1398 - Windsor Castle

'Why have you come?'

Argyle looked around Thomas' chambers. They were sparse but with a pleasant view of the Windsor gardens, the rush matting on the floor was fresh, and he did not look to be suffering too greatly although he was in custody, accused of plotting treason.

'Margaret wrote me,' Argyle said indifferently. 'And Eleanor.'

'Nosy women!' Thomas scowled. 'And you just had to come?'

'No, they told me that you were in custody, nothing more.' Argyle went to the window. 'It was the Queen who summoned me. She was surprised to suddenly be housing my brother.'

'I should hardly call this housing,' Thomas said with contempt.

'Better than a cell in the Tower.' Argyle suppressed a shudder and contemplated the budding flowers in the brown beds. 'What happened?'

'Your precious Queen did not tell you?'

Argyle turned and clamped a hand on Thomas' shoulder. 'I would be careful how you speak of her Majesty, if I were you, and of any of her household and affinity. I am here to get the tale from you, not to listen to gossip of others, but if you prefer, I shall go to Westminster and hear what they are saying there.'

'They will be telling lies.' Thomas cringed under Argyle's forceful grip. 'Bolingbroke took a private conversation between us to the King. I had thought he would appreciate my warnings, but perhaps he saw it as a way to get back in the King's good graces. Though God knows, he has never been there before!'

'The truth, Thomas. I think you owe me that much.' Argyle released Thomas' shoulder and sat by the fire. 'You have endangered our family once more.'

'Bolingbroke declared me a traitor, recreant to the King,' Thomas said looking out the window. 'All lies of course. I told the King as much, but he was not inclined to listen. Not even when I named Bolingbroke a traitor too.'

'So you were both arrested?'

'Yes. Bolingbroke had his family stand bail for him,' Thomas sneered. 'Much more than my family did for me.'

'We have neither the connections nor the money to set you free,' Argyle said. 'You must know that Margaret tried and Eleanor too. Even if we were to stand bail for you, and the King would agree to release you, where would you go? Gaunt is holding Bolingbroke, do you really think the King would simply let you go home?' He did not remark on the fact that Elizabeth, Thomas' wife had not offered her help.

Thomas snorted a laugh. 'No! And Gaunt holding Bolingbroke is hardly a punishment.'

'Tell me true, is there anything to Bolingbroke's accusations?'

'You mean do I hold proof that the King will undo Gaunt and Bolingbroke?' Thomas toyed with the inkwell on his table. 'Yes and no.'

That is neither here nor there, Argyle thought, why must the truth always be so difficult and dangerous to get? He wondered, not for the first time, how many of Thomas' secrets were tied to the King.

'He had me kill Woodstock,' Thomas said. 'He wanted him, Arundel and Warwick out of the way. Once he had achieved his goal, where would he turn but to punish Bolingbroke and I? Bolingbroke is calling me a traitor because he knows that it is his only escape. We are all doomed. Bolingbroke knows that I cannot call out the King on Woodstock's death, it would be my undoing.'

'Then there is no escape for you?'

'No. Either I name the King murderer, and I die before his hand, or I name Bolingbroke traitor, and I die by his.'

'You think it will come to that?'

'The King is plotting something savage,' Thomas said. 'You mark my words.'

ꕥ ꕥ ꕥ ꕥ

CHAPTER 34

29 April 1398 - Westminster Palace

'God came to me in my dreams - he told me that a golden sword of truth would tell the liar from the honest!' The King stood before Parliament his arms stretched out, purple and gold cloth seemed to stream from his body, spilling onto the dais and the massive gold crown of England rested on his golden curls. He still commanded any room, as a King should. 'God shall decide if I have nursed a traitor - or indeed two - at my bosom these past many years!'

The room rumbled, the lords stomping their feet on the wooden floor, sending dust spiralling into the thin rays of sunlight coursing through the high narrow windowpanes. Many of the tapestries had been taken down in preparation for the King's progress, but some still hung on the walls, their bright colours and biblical scenes revealing that they were new, most likely ordered to emphasise the King's piety.

'Hear, hear!' A few bold voices rang out.

The King enjoyed the atmosphere for a while, sending benevolent nods this way and that before resuming his speech, silence settling at once on the assembled crowd. 'The Lords Bolingbroke and Mowbray shall commit themselves to a joust of war!' The King smiled cruelly.

Now the room erupted in jeers and shouts of acknowledgement.

Argyle scowled at the men standing closest to him, but either they did not notice or they simply did not care. Crossing his arms, Argyle refrained from displaying any sentiment and waited for the King to call the Parliament to order.

'My Lords. Until I name the date, Lord Mowbray shall remain in custody!' The King glanced at Argyle who stared back. 'And I trust that my Lord Gaunt will keep his son close. The joust will be a spectacle unrivalled by any seen before!'

As the mass of nobles whooped once more, Argyle elbowed his way to the bottom of the room. He looked for Thomas or Bolingbroke, but could see neither in the crowded room. When he reached to push open the door, the King spoke again. 'I encourage anyone with important information to come before the throne and divulge their knowledge. As your compassionate King, I shall be lenient and kind-hearted.' Argyle felt the King's eyes on his back. 'I shall listen in earnest!'

Sliding through the half-open door, Argyle breathed the fresh air of the outdoor passage deep into his lungs. If the King would truly listen in earnest and be lenient, it would be the first time in over a decade, and Argyle did not believe it to be the case.

'Lord Mowbray.'

Argyle turned to face two of the King's White Harts. 'Yes?'

'His Majesty requests your presence.' One of them gave a half-smile, but it never reached his eyes. 'Now!'

It was a short quiet walk before the guard opened a door to the King's private chambers and ushered Argyle in. The room was empty, the dark throne on the dais stark against the evangelic tapestry behind it. Argyle wondered again how such a devout King might be so cruel.

'Ah, you are here, good.' The King's voice startled Argyle. 'I have a task for you.'

'Majesty.' Argyle dropped to his knee and waited.

'You heard the horrid accusations laid before me,' the King said in a toneless voice. 'Had you any idea of your brother's misdeeds? Or those of Bolingbroke?'

Argyle shook his head and kept his eyes on the rushes. There was a faint smell of orange blossoms in the room.

'Do you believe them?' the King asked.

'No, Majesty.'

'So, they are both innocent?'

Argyle looked up at the looming King. 'I could not say, Majesty, but it seems perhaps both lords had cause to hate one another. Tempers might rise.'

'Whatever be the truth, I intend to have it out of them.' The King sat down on his throne and gestured for Argyle to stand. 'Your brother will remain in custody until such a time as either or both see fit to give me what I want. I am naming you his jailor.'

Argyle felt his hands twitch and clasped them together behind his back. 'As you command, Majesty.'

'You will remain with him at Windsor and ensure that your brother is treated to such courtesy as he is entitled. But no more!' the King said. 'You may visit the Queen, if it pleases her. But you are there at my command. Do not forget.'

12 May 1398 - Windsor Castle

Thomas proved a most difficult prisoner. He was not pleased with the rooms offered to him at Windsor, and he wanted Argyle to ask the Queen to be moved. Argyle refused, which sent Thomas into a fit where he ravaged half his rooms before the Queen's guard came storming in and clasped him in irons. None of the broken furniture had been replaced, and now Thomas' rooms were sparser than ever.

Argyle was weary to the bone, when he stood before the Queen. 'You look tired, Sir Argyle.'

'I bear a heavy burden, your Majesty.'

'So you do,' the Queen beckoned him closer. 'Is there anything I might do to help?'

You will never persuade the King to release me, Argyle thought. Despite his gloomy mood the bright spring flowers in the room lifted his spirits a little. 'You might relay some news from court, Majesty?'

'Something cheerful?' The Queen gave him a doubtful look, her fingers tapping the armrest of her throne. It looked to have been recently repainted, the red once more bright against an inlay of gold. 'Is there such a thing? Perhaps we should walk?'

It was drizzling outside, the countryside almost lost in a thick fog that soaked everything and everyone to the bone. Argyle had crossed the courtyard earlier in the day and his clothes still felt wet.

'Inside, of course,' the Queen added and beckoned to Prudence. 'We shall walk the gallery, you and Mistress Catherine may join us.'

Prudence looked longingly at Argyle for a moment before she called out for Mistress Catherine to join them. She reluctantly gave up her place near the roaring fire and draped the Queen in another shawl. They set off through the adjoining rooms; the women's dresses brushing over the tiles.

'The King has presented me with peacocks,' the Queen said. 'Although you cannot see them right now. But surely you have heard them call out in the garden?'

'Is that what that noise was?' Mistress Catherine said. 'It curdled my blood.'

'Mine too.' Prudence sidled up alongside Argyle. 'Oh, I was so afraid.'

'That is quite enough,' the Queen said and waved the ladies out of earshot. Prudence looked particularly upset. 'She fancies herself in love with you. Thinks she might turn your head while you are here.'

Argyle smiled faintly, he could hardly be less interested. 'She is kind.'

The Queen stopped before a large portrait of Queen Anne. 'The King still loves her, I think.'

'A first love is hard to recover from,' Argyle said and earned a curious look from the Queen. 'He has lived a whole life before you were even born, Majesty.'

'I know. It was your face that gave me pause,' the Queen said and pulled her shawl close around her small shoulders. 'Your wife is not your first love, I think?'

Not even my second, Argyle thought. He shook his head. 'No, Majesty, there were women before her.'

The Queen turned and walked on. 'I know.'

'I am sorry, Majesty, I am not good company today.' The gallery was damp; the little wood stoves' smoke cluttered the air and gave neither much warmth nor light. The old statues in the niches that were usually bright white looked grey and filthy. The surroundings mirrored Argyle's mood.

'We cannot keep ignoring that there is a woman in my husband's bed that we both loved,' the Queen whispered. 'But we need not speak of her today. The King is asking me to go with him on progress to Cheshire. I can hardly refuse.'

'Nor should you, Majesty. Perhaps a little travel would be good for you.'

'That is why I am leaving with all my ladies this coming Sunday.' The Queen turned around and began walking back. Mistress Catherine and Prudence pressed against the wall to let her pass before they resumed their walk behind Argyle and the Queen. 'I will be gone for more than a month. It may be lonely here with your truculent brother.'

'Yes, Majesty.' Argyle wondered why the Queen was telling him of her plans.

'I have petitioned the King to allow that you go home for that month to visit your wife and child,' the Queen said, reaching up to pat Argyle on the arm. 'You must miss them terribly.'

'I hear little enough from them, Majesty,' Argyle admitted. He had only had one letter from Isobel to tell him that Edmund was growing and had turned wilful. Stephen had written a few times with news of the training and lands, but other than that, Argyle had felt almost forgotten at Windsor.

'Since I will travel with the King, I shall not need my guard,' the Queen said, finally revealing her true design. 'I felt sure the King could not object if I order them to guard Lord Mowbray in my absence. After all, he has picked them personally to guard me; they must be fit to guard a prisoner too.'

'Have you heard from his Majesty?' Argyle held his breath.

'He has agreed.' The Queen gave one of her rare, winning smiles that lit up her pretty face, reminding Argyle that she was still only a child. 'You can leave tomorrow too. But you must be back before I return, Sir Argyle, or he will never forgive me!'

23 July 1398 - Beauworth

Argyle was returning from his ride around the villages when Stephen came careering down the road, dirt spraying from his horse's hooves. In the speckled shadows, Argyle could only make out his shape, not his face. But he knew by Stephen's speed that his peaceful summer at Beauworth was at an end.

'M'LORD!' Stephen shouted, waving a hand. He pulled hard at the reins and the horse almost sat down at the sudden stop, patting his horse on its sweaty neck he leaned on the wooden pummel.

Argyle spurred his mount into a canter, it chewed on its bit, clearly happy to see another horse after a day of grazing with cows and skirting pigs. 'What are you doing here, Smith?'

'A message from the King.' Stephen drew out a piece of paper, sealed with the royal crest and handed it over. The two horses greeted each other, snorting and pulling at their reins. 'I rode out early this morning.'

'The royal party must have returned to London, and the Queen to Windsor,' Argyle felt his stomach churn, he had promised the Queen to be back at Windsor by the time she returned, but she had sent no word. He turned the letter in his hand. 'The King must have decided when the duel is to be. Why is it never good news?'

'Mayhap, he's had a change of heart,' Stephen said running a hand through his unruly hair.

'Hardly.' Argyle broke the seal and read the brief message. 'Thomas is to present himself to the King on 2 August - on pain of death. I am ordered to ride directly to Windsor and escort him to the meeting. He is allowed to bring as many as 20 men. When was this delivered?'

Argyle had spent the previous night in a tavern in one of the northern-most villages, in part to get a little break and in part because a case that he had heard the day before had drawn out when one of the parties had arrived late. He secretly relished in the rest, alone and away from the castle, Isobel and the energetic babe. Isobel had reluctantly agreed to name the boy Edmund, and his insisting had put an extra strain on their relationship for some time after the christening. She was finally thawing, and now he would have to leave.

'Late last night,' Stephen said. 'M'lady does not know.'

'Just as well, any royal summons sets her on edge.' Argyle spurred on the horse, and they trotted through the woods towards Beauworth. 'At least, this one is not from the Queen.'

Stephen leaned back in the saddle and closed his eyes. 'How many summons have you had from the Queen?'

'Three,' Argyle admitted. 'But none requesting that I return to Windsor. I have sent the same reply each time. That summer is a busy time, that I am handling new recruits and overseeing the fields, woods and livestock. And that I would return as soon as she commanded it.'

'But a summons from the King …'

'Cannot be deferred.'

ꟻ ☙ ꟻ ☙

CHAPTER 35

2 August 1398 - Shrewsbury Castle

'My Lord, you forget yourself!'

The threat was undeniable and yet, Thomas stubbornly went on. 'I warned you that you and I were in great danger, but you refused to listen!'

'Stop this now, Mowbray!' Bolingbroke shook with anger. 'I warn you that …'

'SILENCE!' the King roared, and Argyle, who was standing behind the King's seat, sent his brother a warning glance. If he did not know any better, the hushed atmosphere would have had Argyle believe that the hall was all but empty. Instead, it was packed with courtiers, nobles and knights.

Thomas was down on bended knee, while Bolingbroke was standing before his cousin, his face white with anger. 'Majesty, I cannot in good faith withdraw my accounts of Lord Mowbray's indiscretions. He has stolen money from the Crown and must be punished. He murdered our uncle, a crime punishable only by death!'

'Ah yes, they are grave accusations indeed,' the King agreed, folding his hands in his lap. 'But you might consider reneging you accusations that Lord Mowbray murdered our uncle Woodstock? If Lord Mowbray is willing to admit to storing away the Calais money?'

Bolingbroke huffed. 'Never, Majesty. I stand by my accusations.'

Thomas remained on bended knee his body shaking with fury. 'It is not true, Majesty. It is Lord Bolingbroke who plots against you!'

'I will have the truth!' The King sat back heavily.

'Majesty, what I lay before you in January is the truth. Lord Mowbray warned me that my father and I was about to be undone by you,' Bolingbroke said in a placid voice.

'And why would you say that, Lord Mowbray?' the King demanded, his voice as dry as the August breeze wafting through the open window.

Thomas stood looking defiantly at Bolingbroke. 'I have no idea, Majesty. My Lord Bolingbroke has many fancies, I would never presume to understand any of them. He most likely mistook what I said to be a threat.'

Bolingbroke shot Thomas a dirty, dark look. 'It is not the first time that Lord Mowbray has spoken against you, Majesty. Whether for fear or folly, I could not say.'

Thomas opened his mouth to rebut, but the King silenced him with a stern look before turning his attention back to Bolingbroke. 'Go on.'

'My Lord Mowbray has been saying for several months that your Majesty's actions last year have proven that no nobleman in England is safe from your wrath. For some ill-advised reason, Lord Mowbray is convinced that your Majesty is looking for any reason to rid yourself and the court of me - and my father. Just as he claims you ordered the death of our beloved uncle, Woodstock,' Bolingbroke said.

'Is he now?' The King surveyed the room with feigned disinterest, but Argyle could see his knuckles turn white from gripping the throne armrests.

'I have warned him many times, Majesty, not to speak against you, but he does not seem to want to listen. In fact, he believes that the pardons your Majesty granted us are worthless, and you have long been plotting to have the entire duchy of Lancaster for yourself.' Bolingbroke cleared his throat and looked at Thomas. 'All nonsense of course.'

The King gave an amused laugh that made Argyle's skin crawl. 'Is that so, Lord Mowbray?'

Thomas looked briefly from Bolingbroke to Argyle before settling on the King. 'I believe my Lord Bolingbroke has it all wrong, Majesty. I have indeed been concerned for my Lord Gaunt, but only because he has been sickly of late. As to the other accusations …'

The King raised a hand and cut off Thomas. 'I find it curious that you think I would plot against my own family, Lord Mowbray. Very curious.' The tone was laced with threats, and Thomas flinched. 'Why would I do such a thing?'

'Majesty, I am saying that Bolingbroke is telling lies, I have never …' Thomas squirmed.

'You have never WHAT?!' The King's eyes bulged and his cheeks flushed red. He strode towards Thomas, who fell to his knees, and Argyle clasped his hands behind his back to keep them from trembling.

'Majesty, I beg of you, it is not true …'

'Beg all you like, Mowbray! This is not the first time your poison words have reached my ears! To think you would speak thus against your own King! You are a thief and a craven!' The King turned on Bolingbroke. 'And you - dear cousin - why is it you are always stirring up trouble? You cannot think that I would believe a word either of you say! Turncoat!'

Unlike Thomas, Bolingbroke had remained standing, and the King was panting in his face. A single bead of sweat trickled down Bolingbroke's face, tracing the contours of his jaw before it was swallowed up in his pointed beard. The King grabbed Bolingbroke's tunic and pulled him close enough for their chests to touch. What the King had in height, Bolingbroke had in brawn, but the King's rage changed the balance of power. 'What have you to say for yourself?'

'Only what I have already said, Majesty.' Bolingbroke had something of a cowed dog about him.

Argyle had never heard Bolingbroke speak this way before, no matter what disputes and discussions he was in, be it with the King or other noblemen, Bolingbroke never lost his nerve. Argyle worried what might happen if the King went completely unopposed.

'That Lord Mowbray is lying?' the King demanded to know.

'Yes, Majesty. That perhaps Lord Mowbray thinks so little of our King that he fears for his life - but that I do not. I know that your Majesty has long since lain to rest any bitter feelings about what happened between us,' Bolingbroke said.

A glimmer of horror raced across the King's face before he released Bolingbroke. 'I see.' He turned slowly to look down at Thomas. 'You believe your King to be so merciless? So vindictive?'

Thomas' voice trembled. 'No, Majesty.'

'I ask you remember the words uttered here today.' The King looked around the room. 'That two of our finest and greatest Lords have turned on each other - that one of them even dare accuse his King of malice and betrayal.'

The assembled men stared angrily at Thomas, even his own men. Argyle's vision blurred from staring unblinking into the distance, he had to keep to his place behind the throne - as a well-trained dog.

'I also ask that you look deep within your own souls and ask our Lord God for forgiveness if you have ever had evil thoughts about me - or my reign. I urge you to remember that God shall judge us all on the final day. If there be truth in your hearts, you need not worry.'

The King turned towards Bolingbroke. 'But if evil lurks there - then I pray God have mercy on your soul.'

As soon as the King had left the hall, Argyle scaled the dais steps to help Thomas to his feet, but before he reached Thomas, he leapt up and lunged for Bolingbroke. 'You vile, evil coward! You know as well as I do that no one is safe in the madhouse! That I ever believed us to be friends … well, now all of you know what kind of man Lord Bolingbroke truly is!' Thomas screamed in Bolingbroke's face.

'Thomas …' Argyle stretched out a hand, but Bolingbroke interrupted.

'No, let your brother speak. He always did love an audience, I only wonder if this audience will love him back.' Thomas stumbled when Bolingbroke pushed him away. 'Go on, Lord Mowbray! Tell them all!'

'Radcot Bridge …' Thomas began, turning towards the crowd of lords. 'The King will never forget the treason at Radcot Bridge.'

If Thomas had hoped for support, he was greatly disappointed. The other lords muttered and moved away from him as a great wave rolling back into the sea after crashing on jagged rocks. The King's rage still hung heavy in the air.

'And who was responsible for the events that took place at Radcot Bridge?' Bolingbroke asked.

The sea of faces turned towards Thomas, who stuck out his chin like a petulant child. 'You.'

'Me?' Bolingbroke laughed but his eyes burned with resentment. 'Oh no, I think you have it all wrong, Mowbray. It was you who was responsible. After all, it was you the King trusted with the fatal order -

and you who betrayed his Majesty.'

Thomas' anger flared. 'And what did you do?! Rush in to save the day?'

'The council was concerned about our young King.' Bolingbroke's face turned hard and cold. 'I acted on the word of a most trusted advisor.'

'What advisor? The one who is short a head? Or the one …' Thomas' voice trailed away.

Bolingbroke stared at Thomas. 'Or the one you killed?'

A gasp went through the crowd, and Thomas turned on them. 'As if you did not know that the King ordered me to get Woodstock's confession, whatever means necessary!'

'My Lord Mowbray, we knew of no such order.' Bolingbroke looked disgusted. 'This is a wild accusation, and I for one shall let no more of your venom drip into my ears. His Majesty was distraught at the death of his uncle - as was I.'

Bolingbroke walked towards the massive doors leading out of the hall, and Thomas screamed at his back. 'None of us are safe! You mark my words - the day will come when the King will kill us ALL!'

'Shut up!' Argyle slapped Thomas across the face and he stared back blankly, reaching to touch his cheek. 'Shut up, before you reserve yourself a seat in one of the damp cells of the Tower!'

'You dare hit me?' Thomas asked, wonder filling his voice. 'You?'

'Yes, me! If you continue your treasonous words then neither I nor anyone else in this room can save you! Or will want to save you.' Argyle gave Thomas a warning look. 'What will it be? Will you continue along this most dangerous path?'

Thomas shook his head, suddenly hit by the realisation of what he had done.

'Good! I am under orders to return you to your rooms, brother.' The lords parted before Argyle, silent shock and anger painted on their faces, but Argyle took little notice, all he wanted was to be as far away from court and Parliament as he could possibly get.

He knew that there was nothing for it now but for Thomas and Bolingbroke to do battle.

CHAPTER 36

15 September 1398 - Coventry, Cheylesmore Manor

'How did it come to this?' Thomas wiped his brow. Thomas had been quick to claim the small bedchamber at the back once he discovered, he had to share his measly rooms with Argyle, who was left to sleep in the drafty parlour. The King had insisted Argyle stay with Thomas and by the second night, Argyle was aching all over from the discomfort of sleeping on the floor.

'You fell apart before the King,' Argyle said. 'You stole from him and refused to reconcile with Bolingbroke while you still had the chance. How did you think it would end?'

Thomas stoked the fire angrily and threw the poker down. There were already several burn marks on the wooden floor from Thomas' exertions. 'You would have me take Bolingbroke's offences and apologise?'

'I am not disagreeing with you about the slight and accusations, but …' Argyle paused. 'You must have known it was your last chance.'

Thomas hid his head in his hands and sighed. 'I truly believed that the King would see that Bolingbroke is lying and trying to pin the blame on me.'

Argyle rose to fetch a cup of wine. 'Are you prepared?'

'To joust the greatest fighter in England?' Thomas' voice climbed an octave. 'I am no stranger to jousting, but Bolingbroke is undefeated! I even heard Surrey say he would never ride uncapped against Bolingbroke, and he never shies from a fight.' Argyle offered the wine to Thomas who took it, his hand shaking. 'What inspired the King to make it a joust of war?!'

Because he is determined to rid himself of at least one tiresome Lord, Argyle thought, but knew better than to say so. 'He will claim it was God.'

'He is vindictive and …' Thomas stopped as a servant entered with a tray, but quickly retreated when he caught Thomas' eye, the tray teetering on the corner of a table.

'Let me plead your case,' Argyle said for the hundredth time, ignoring Thomas' searing glare, and pushed the tray further onto the table. 'I might be able to at least prevent a joust of war.'

'No.'

So definitive, Argyle thought. Thomas had spent most of the past ten years relying on and ensuring Argyle's close affiliation with the King and now, when he might finally be able to help, Thomas rejected him.

'I have sent Eleanor to plead my case,' Thomas said as if reading Argyle's mind. 'I have little hope of her impressing anything on his Majesty, but she is close to the Queen these days, God knows why, and I thought she might charm her way to a result.'

'Eleanor?'

'Has been a constant companion to the Queen since ... since you left,' Thomas said.

'Is that so?' Argyle gritted his teeth. 'And how did she come to be so close to the Queen?'

'I might have encouraged her to see the Queen.' Thomas got up and walked to the window. 'I cannot believe the King would order my lodgings guarded by his White Harts.' Thomas' voice was laced with contempt. 'Where would I go?'

Running into the night to find a ship to take you to safety? Argyle thought and decided to turn the conversation back to Eleanor. 'How did you arrange for Eleanor to become one of the Queen's close friends?'

'Her Majesty was a woman short,' Thomas said and turned his back to the King's guard standing below him, a blatant slight according to Thomas. He was still furious that the King would distrust a Duke in such a fashion as to warrant a royal guard outside his door. 'You know that Lady Mortimer is herself unsafe in her position. I thought the Queen might like a reminder of you, and Eleanor fit the bill.'

'The Queen has many ladies-in-waiting,' Argyle sneered while inside acknowledging Thomas' crafty decision. They were so alike that the Queen would most certainly be reminded of her loyal knight every day she looked at Eleanor, but to what end? 'And the Queen hardly needs a reminder of me.'

'She needed a confidante that was not employed by the King.'

'So you chose Eleanor?' Argyle thought that if he had to choose a new confidante for the Queen, Eleanor would not be his first or even fifth choice.

'Better it is one of our own than one from Bolingbroke's household.' Thomas began pacing the floor. 'It has been weeks since I have heard from her. Has she sent word to you?'

'No,' Argyle said. 'She is with the Queen now?'

'Who knows?!' Thomas slammed his hand into the desk. 'She must know that I need her now more than ever! Why is everything and everyone working against me?!'

'You have spun too many webs,' Argyle said, ignoring Thomas' scowl. 'If Eleanor does not succeed then what?'

'What about you?' Thomas said thoughtfully.

'What about me?'

'Are you truly in a position to risk being out of favour?'

'I do not think I am even on the King's mind these days,' Argyle said. The King had made Argyle Thomas's jailor, but since August, Argyle had had no word from court. He sometimes heard a little something when visiting the Queen in her chambers at Windsor, but it was all idle gossip.

'How could you not be?' Thomas sniffed. 'After all you were the one who bedded his mistress before him. Until the King turned against me, he often spoke of his luck that you had settled on a wife.'

Argyle breathed deep, why would Thomas mention Celeste at a moment such as this? Why was she even on his mind?

'There are rumours that the lady is with child,' Thomas said, and Argyle felt as if someone had punched him in the gut. 'They say the King has grown tired of her. Eleanor told me.'

She seems to know everything, Argyle thought but kept quiet.

'The younger sister of one of the Queen's ladies is in the service of the lady Celeste,' Thomas continued, colour creeping back into his face. 'She says that the lady has been unwell in the morning these past few months, and that the King is not a frequent visitor any more.'

'Will the King be happy?' The question came out quiet and reluctant.

Thomas poured another cup of wine, his hand still shaking. 'Perhaps. He never had any children by his first wife, though not for lack of trying. What is the point of a Queen if she cannot produce an heir? She seemed a perfect fit to him, but she failed in her greatest responsibility. It may well be that this is the good news the King has been waiting for.'

'But not the Queen.'

'He need not acknowledge the child,' Thomas said. 'We do not know if the Queen will be able to conceive, she is still a child herself, and looks to be a small woman when she comes of age.'

Small women have birthed children before, Argyle thought. He moved to find a more comfortable position on the hard chair. 'Perhaps you are right.'

'Of course I am,' Thomas said finally regaining his usual composure. 'Though I have never approved of your choice of wife, you did enable the King to find a woman that might for the first time provide a child. A true heir to the throne. Even if it is born a bastard, the King can always change the succession to suit his own cause. A child might appease him.'

Argyle grabbed his cup so hard that he felt the pewter give way beneath his fingers. 'You seem in higher spirits. You do not need me here anymore tonight, I think.' The King had commanded that he stay with Thomas every night, but not that he could not leave the lodgings if he so desired. The royal guard was there to make sure that Thomas stayed put.

Thomas' face flashed with anger. 'You offered to stay.'

'So I did,' Argyle said, 'but I have changed my mind. Excuse me, brother.' He reached for the door when he heard light steps in the corridor that announced a visitor.

'Good, you are both here!' Eleanor's golden hair glistened in the dim firelight. 'I come straight from the Queen.'

'The Queen?' Thomas hunkered over the desk. 'Not the King?!'

'He is keeping to his rooms seeing no one.' Eleanor smiled at Argyle who thought he saw a glimmer of apology in her eyes. 'Or at least, he is not seeing anyone we may mention.'

'REALLY?!' Thomas exploded. 'He cannot see even the Queen but he CAN see her?!'

Eleanor ignored Thomas' angry stare. 'I can hardly walk into his private chambers without an invitation. I do not know if she is there, but I know he did not dine with the Queen. Who is sad - by the way.'

'Why?'

'She misses your company, little brother,' Eleanor said to Argyle.

'Me? She must know that I cannot leave my family at such a time as this.' Argyle was tired of being caught in the games of court, playing with opponents who were brought up with the game while he stumbled along. He had a royal command hanging over his head, threatening to crush him to a thousand pieces if he decided to ignore it and leave Thomas' side for longer than a night in a tavern.

'Not tonight,' Eleanor said, filling a cup with wine. 'Although I think she half-expected you to come and intercede for Thomas.'

'What could she have done for me?' Thomas asked, clearly angry that he was kept out of the conversation. 'She is a child.'

'She holds some sway over the King.' Eleanor's words were passionate. 'She too has power.'

'Not enough,' Thomas growled and owned a harsh glance from Eleanor that silenced him. Argyle was surprised that Eleanor seemed to have control over Thomas.

'You should not underestimate her, given that she is all that stands between the King and a war with France,' Eleanor said, sipping the wine. 'Are there any sweetmeats?'

Thomas grumbled but went to the door to call for a servant. Eleanor turned to Argyle and pulled him quickly to the far side of the room. 'We have little time. You must go and see the Queen!'

'But ...'

'Not tonight, Thomas is right, even the Queen cannot change the King's mind,' Eleanor glanced at Thomas' back. 'But once the duel is done, you must come, she insisted!'

'If the duel ends badly …' Argyle could not finish the sentence.

'If?' Eleanor drank the rest of the wine. 'Thomas cannot possibly win. He can only hope that the King has a change of heart. We know he is fickle, though this time, I think he will go ahead with the spectacle. You know how fond he is of chivalry and theatrics.'

Argyle rubbed his elbow, feeling the ridge of the old scar from Jerusalem through his shirt. 'I agree with you, and if we are right, I cannot see the Queen.'

'Why not?' Eleanor asked.

Argyle noticed Thomas had returned to his chair behind the desk, apparently unaware of their whispered words. 'Because we will be burying our brother.'

'Family first?'

'I thought that was our family motto,' Argyle said with a grudge.

'Meeting with the Queen may be the one time you have to put loyalty to the Crown before that of your family.'

Argyle's jaw worked. 'When did you become this cold?'

'When the Queen found out her former friend was with child,' Eleanor said. 'And she decided to get her revenge over the King's indiscretion.'

'Revenge?'

'Just visit the Queen,' she said and went to try and comfort Thomas, leaving Argyle to wonder how the Queen would get revenge and how it might, in any scenario, be something he had to be a part of.

ꙮ ꙮ

Part III

BLOOD

CHAPTER 37

16 September 1398 - Coventry

'THE KING!'

Argyle was jolted back to the present by the shout of the herald and broke eye contact with Eleanor when she turned her head towards the sounds of approaching horses. Stephen glanced at Argyle, a look of concern plain on his face, but Argyle ignored him.

The announcement of the King's imminent arrival sent a ripple through the crowd. As the royal retinue came into sight, every man, woman and child went down on bended knee. The King in all his magnificence nodded benevolently here and there, play-acting to his heart's content. Gaunt was riding a few paces behind, slumped in his saddle; he looked worn and sick. When the King lifted the Queen off her horse, the crowd cheered for her and she rewarded them with a brilliant smile.

Argyle felt the dew soak his clothes and gritted his teeth; he was relieved when the royal procession turned before reaching the Mowbray tents. He rose with the rest of the crowd assembled on the far side and turned briefly to see Eleanor clasp her hands, her head turned to the right. Argyle followed her gaze and saw the Mowbray colours moving steadily towards the field. As soon as Thomas came into view, Argyle fixed his eyes on his brother's big, grey mare, decked out in crimson velvet embroidered with silver and mulberry trees.

Nearly an hour passed before Bolingbroke finally made his appearance, his massive white warhorse draped in a livery of blue and green velvet embroidered with gold swans and antelopes. The crowd whooped and cheered as Bolingbroke crossed the field with six warhorses in tow. It seemed even the King's presence could not oppress the will of the commoners, they loved Bolingbroke and when he bent his head to their acknowledgement, a faint smile played at the corner of his mouth. Argyle glanced at the King on his dais but if he was upset, he did not let on.

The Duke of Surrey, Thomas Holland, first announced Bolingbroke, who opened his visor and looked directly at the King. 'I have come to prosecute my appeal in combating Thomas Mowbray, Duke of Norfolk, who is a traitor, false and recreant to God, the King, his realm and me!' Bolingbroke sat strong and proud in the saddle, showing his shield with the arms of St George.

Once Surrey acknowledged Bolingbroke's arms, he rode straight for his pavilion, which was decorated with red roses, to the sound of more cheering and blessings. The people's prince, Argyle thought as he watched Bolingbroke vanish into his tent, but would they still have a prince at the end of the joust? He shuddered at the thought, a brief scream from the past slashing through the expectations of the current day. So much might happen on a battlefield, and was not the same true of a duel? Who was to say who Lady Fortune would support? Argyle shuddered in the clammy September air and banished the memory of a splintered lance spilling noble blood unto dirt and sand. Memories were useless - the past was the past.

Thousands of faces turned to see Thomas announce himself to Surrey and the King. Thomas paused only long enough to swear his oaths; for once this great courtier seemed to have lost his eloquence. He turned his horse towards his pavilion and looked out over the crowd of spiteful faces.

'God speed the right!' Thomas' words rang through the air, as he charged past the barriers, his head held high, staring into the distance. He was already clad in his armour, his helmet pinned beneath his arm, the red plume pushed back. Argyle closed his eyes.

There was nothing left to do but go to battle.

Once their lances were measured and accepted, the two great nobles mounted their horses once more. Their squires uncapped the lances and almost synchronously pushed the weapons into their masters' hands. Argyle noticed that Thomas fumbled to get his hold. Bolingbroke slammed down his visor, advancing at once on Thomas who did not move. Argyle held his breath waiting for the first blow to fall.

'HO! HO!'

With all eyes on the field, no one had noticed that the King was now standing. Bolingbroke reigned in his horse, pushing up his visor and giving the King a shocked glance when his lance was taken from him. Thomas dropped his lance at once, the sound of wood on grass dull, and looked relieved.

'I ask the Dukes to return to their tents. I must deliberate!' the King declared and retreated to the sound of thousands of disappointed voices. This was unheard of. The crowd had been promised a battle, and it would not be happy until that promise had been fulfilled. Left behind, the Queen stared around, fear painted on her face at the angry shouts from the spectators and the spreading confusion when some of Bolingbroke's men broke through the barrier and ran onto the field.

Argyle was torn between going to the Queen to protect her and following his brother who rode towards his tent, some of his own men waiting to grab the reins when Thomas climbed off the horse and disappeared through the tent-flaps. When four White Harts appeared along with some of the Queen's ladies-in-waiting and escorted her to a nearby carriage, Argyle was relieved.

He made his way to Thomas' tent and slid in. 'Brother.'

Thomas was seated on a low chair still in full armour. He looked equally perplexed and relieved. 'What is happening?'

'I do not know. Maybe the King has had a change of heart.' Argyle struggled to believe his own words.

'Yes, well … But the King himself ordered this joust.' Thomas pointed towards a pitcher, and Argyle went to pour a cup of wine for his brother.

Handing it over, he gave Thomas a concerned look. 'What do you think we may expect?'

'How am I to know? How is anyone to know what goes on in that head?!' The cup shook violently in Thomas' grasp.

'Thomas! You know more of court and games than I ever care to. Has this ever happened before?'

Thomas gulped down the wine. 'No. And I meant it. No one

understands our King anymore. The court has been turned upside down, and no one is safe.'

Argyle rested a hand on Thomas' shoulder. For the first time since they were children, Thomas did not push him away. Fear and terror flowed in Argyle's veins and he only hoped that it did not seep from his trembling hand into Thomas' skin.

ꟸ ꟸ ꟸ ꟸ

Time dragged on, noon came and went and Argyle kept peering out through the opening in the pavilion to see if the King had returned. The grumbling crowd was hissing and shouting, several fights had broken out, and the King's White Harts forced many rowdy bystanders from the field.

Finally, the Duke of Brittany mounted the herald's stand and unfurled a long roll of parchment. Thomas and Bolingbroke were summoned by some of the royal guards and now sat on their horses, their backs turned to the crowd facing an empty dais.

'My Lords!' the Duke of Brittany shouted, a slight quiver in his voice. 'I must inform you by order of the King that Henry of Lancaster, Duke of Hereford, appellant, and Thomas Mowbray, Duke of Norfolk, defendant, have both appeared here valiantly and that each was and is ready to do his duty as a brave knight.'

The thousands of people assembled began to voice their irritation once more, and some of the White Hart archers strung their bows to subdue the discontented masses.

'Nevertheless,' the Duke of Brittany continued, the parchment fluttering in the breeze, 'our lord the King, considering the reason for the battle is so high, that is to say treason determined by Parliament, and the Dukes of Hereford and Norfolk being so close in blood to the King and of his arms, our lord the King, as one who has always trusted in the worth and honour of all those of his blood and of his arms, and grieving in his heart, as a good and gracious Lord.'

Argyle's mind went blank. Although the field was ringed by thousands of people, the echoing silence was inconceivable and the Duke of Brittany looked rattled.

'To avoid complete dishonour befalling one of the said Dukes …' The roaring crowd once more drowned out the Duke of Brittany, and Argyle saw Thomas lean forward on his horse to hear the Duke's words.

'... Of his special grace has taken the battle into his own hand. Our said lord the King, with the full advice, authority and assent of Parliament wills that the said Henry of Lancaster, Duke of Hereford, should quit his realm for ten years!'

The assembled people screamed profanities and more archers strung their bows, aiming them at the unruly masses. The Duke of Brittany glanced about with bulging eyes. 'And that he should be outside the said realm before the day of the octave of St Edward the Confessor, upon pain of incurring the penalty for treason by authority of Parliament!'

Bolingbroke looked almost paralysed. When he finally moved, his eyes prowled the King's empty dais, perhaps looking for his father, but Gaunt was nowhere to be found. Even from afar, Argyle could see shock and terror racing across Bolingbroke's face, his horse seemed to sense his state and began moving restlessly, the cloth covering it flapping around its hind legs. Two of Bolingbroke's men grabbed at the reins to try and calm down his steed, when it became obvious to them that Bolingbroke was too stunned to act.

Thomas tightened his grasp on the reins, and Argyle swallowed sour spit. So far only Bolingbroke's sentence had been read.

'Our said lord the King,' the Duke of Brittany yelled, turning towards Thomas, 'with the full advice, authority and assent of Parliament wills that the said Thomas Mowbray, Duke of Norfolk, should quit his realm for the remainder of his life and forfeit his title as Duke of Norfolk and Lord Marshal!'

Argyle saw Thomas teeter in the saddle; his horse tossed its massive head and scraped the ground. Two of Argyle's men stepped forward, but something in Thomas' face made them stop. An iron taste spread in Argyle's mouth.

Just as Thomas looked at Bolingbroke he turned to leave and gave Argyle an inscrutable glance before spurring his warhorse on. The green and blue velvet fluttered as Bolingbroke, the favourite of the people, galloped away, his men falling in behind him in a confused hurry.

Eleanor ran across the field, her dress billowing behind her, and Argyle willed his feet to move too, making for Thomas' horse. He grabbed the bridle and held out an arm for Eleanor to cling to.

'Oh, Thomas!' Eleanor gasped. 'I am so sorry!'

CHAPTER 38

17 September 1398 - Kenilworth Castle, Warwickshire

'Majesty, I beg a moment of your time if you would grant it?' Argyle asked humbly biting back his contempt for the King whom he had once loved without question.

The dark rooms of Kenilworth had reflected Argyle's sense of foreboding when he crossed the inner court, the curtain wall teeming with White Harts. Thomas was now housed in rooms near the gatehouse while Bolingbroke occupied his usual apartments in his father's castle although a royal guard had replaced his own men outside his doors. Argyle had seen them when walking along the outside walkway on his way to the King's magnificent royal apartments in Leicester's Building.

'Come to ask me to forgive your brother?' The King's voice was toneless.

'Yes, Majesty.'

'Well go on then, Sir Argyle.' The King looked around the room. 'Let us hear your plea.'

Argyle regretted not having asked for a private audience, although he was convinced that the King would not have granted it. The room was packed with the sycophants the King surrounded himself with these days, most of the noble families not represented in the sea of gossip-starved faces. Most of the courtiers had always loathed Thomas, and now their greed seemed to ooze down the high wooden panels; it was almost more than Argyle could bear, but he had come to ask the King's forgiveness, and he would not be cowed or shamed out of his mission.

'We are waiting, Sire.' The King bathed in the bellow of spiteful laughter from the men in the room.

'Majesty, I know you have doubted my brother's loyalties at times.' Laughter erupted once more, forcing Argyle to raise his voice. 'But I come pleading on my own honour. For the love you know that I bear you. For the loyalty, you have demanded and that you have always found in me. I pledge upon my honour and that of your beloved friend, who believed in me, that Thomas is innocent of treason.'

The King nodded gravely, his face stiff at the mention of La Fontaine, stifling the laughter and leaving the room quiet as a tomb.

'I besiege your Majesty to have pity on my poor, misguided brother - for my sake if not his own.' Argyle's voice trembled and he had to look down to continue. 'And for the sake of his family. Thomas can be difficult that I freely admit, but he loves your Majesty beyond doubt.'

'That is enough, Sir Argyle,' the King interrupted. 'Quite enough.'

Argyle bit back the rest of his speech. He had prepared to say much more, but the King was always in a changeable mood these days, and Argyle was convinced that if he misspoke he would quickly be named a traitor along with Thomas.

'The rest of you can leave us,' the King said, standing on the dais to see his court cower backwards through the great, oak doors that had been thrown open by the guards.

Argyle noticed a fair few Cheshire archers in the King's livery inside the great hall and wondered, once more, what exactly the King was afraid of since he kept so many close at all times. Although this time it had been prudent, their presence yesterday on the jousting field had kept most of the spectators at bay after the Duke of Brittany had delivered the King's decision to abandon the joust. Argyle pondered if Coventry had survived the angry masses last night, cheated out of bloodshed on the field it was easy to imagine that once in the drink, many men would not be able to resist a good brawl.

When the room was empty, the King stared down at Argyle. 'Kneel, Sir Argyle!'

Argyle reluctantly obeyed. The old timber floor creaked slightly under his knee.

'Have you gone mad?' the King asked, his voice barely more than a whisper.

'No, Majesty, I know you did what you did to spare blood being spilled, but …'

'WHAT?!' The King's famous temper flared up. 'ARE YOU CALLING OUT YOUR KING'S DECISION?!'

Argyle kept his eyes on the floor, the massive planks shone for decades of wear, in some places there were deep grooves in them filled with dirt and grime. He had heard that Gaunt had done much to improve the castle since it was given to him as a wedding present many years before, but today it only reeked of the King's vengeance.

'ANSWER ME!!'

'Your Majesty, I am your most humble servant. I would never presume to grasp your Majesty's decisions, only that they must be difficult indeed.' Argyle stared at the floor; ice had supplanted the angry fire inside. 'I plead for a brother hoping he might one day be allowed to return. I only ask that your Majesty, in your infinite wisdom, offer a humble servant some hope.'

'And what would my most humble servant do to prove his belief in my wisdom?' The King's quiet voice echoed around the empty room.

'Anything, your Majesty.' Argyle threw himself upon the poison tip of the King's words. He knew he had just signed his own death warrant and that his desire to save his brother was worth more than his life, but was it worth robbing a child of his father? Or a wife of her husband? Those were questions he had laboured over all night, and yet here he was committing himself to a vengeful King. How to choose between one family member and another? Argyle did not know.

'Hard proposition to turn down, Sir Argyle, although it is no more than I am entitled to,' the King said, crushing Argyle's concerns as dead leaves underfoot. 'And you of all men should know that I might just ask anything of you! Let us then strike this bargain; if you will truly obey me in any command and never waver in your service, I shall reconsider my sentence on your brother.'

Argyle knew this was as much as he could have ever hoped for, and quite possibly, more than the King had initially felt inclined to offer. 'Thank you, Majesty, for your most gracious offer. I live to serve you.'

'Let us hope that your brother understands the sacrifice, you have given in his place, and that one day he will thank you for it.' The King swept a grand gesture at the empty room.

Argyle knew that Thomas would never thank him. He was a proud and infuriating man, but Argyle loved him for the brother he had been and for the blood they shared. He had asked as much for the sake of their sisters as for himself, and more so for Thomas' family. He knew that if anyone would thank him it was more likely to be Thomas' wife Elizabeth, but Argyle was not waiting for a heartfelt letter of gratitude from her either.

'Get up, Sir Argyle,' the King said and descended the dais stairs. 'You look a fool. I have a favour to ask of you, now that we are on good terms again.'

On good terms, Argyle thought, was overreaching, but you never argue with the King of England. He wiped defeat from his brow and fell in behind the King. 'Majesty?'

'It is the Queen, she is quite beside herself,' the King admitted leading the way out of the throne room and into his private apartments. Argyle was struck by the difference between the dark, ominous reception hall and the sun-kissed room with its opulent bed and golden and soft furniture, which he now found himself in. The King's state bedroom had a clear view of the surrounding countryside and the moat far beneath Kenilworth's walls. But for the cause of his visit, he would have found the view magnificent and the room beautiful.

Argyle recognised the King's private throne from his apartments in Westminster, he never left court without it. The King sat down, caressing the golden armrests. 'She cried all day yesterday. I had to send her back to Windsor. I thought that my decision to spare the lives of two great noblemen would leave her happy, but she is not. You must go to her and find out what ails her. Let it be the first act of good faith you do for me.'

'Yes, Majesty.' Argyle did not want to be away from Thomas, not be sent off to comfort a child, even if it was his Queen. Reluctance bit at his heels, and he felt the floor heave beneath his unsteady feet.

'And you will continue to be your brother's gaoler until he is shipped off to exile. He will leave from Plymouth. I want him sent off in shackles.' The King gave Argyle a hard stare. 'He must know that what he has done is unforgivable.'

'Yes, Majesty,' Argyle said averting his eyes. You do not ask much, he thought.

'And finally, you will see off Bolingbroke,' the King commanded. 'I must have a trusted man present when my cousin sails from Dover. I have given him a month to get his affairs in order. You will receive an order of when to appear in Dover, and you will make your report to me afterwards.'

Argyle nodded unable to voice his consent, feeling what little freedom he had left splinter and dance away as dust in the streaming sunlight. He knew now that the King would never be satisfied.

'Those are my orders. Do not disappoint.'

Visit the Queen. She will have her revenge. Argyle bowed his way out of the King's presence, his mind ringing with Eleanor's voice. *Celeste is carrying the King's child.*

26 September 1398 - Windsor

The Queen's ladies-in-waiting glanced uncomfortably at Argyle when he entered the room, which looked much the same as ever, low stools placed near the windows, flowers on every table. The Queen sat on her red throne staring out of the window, Lady Mortimer trying to engage her in conversation.

'Sir Argyle is here, Majesty,' Lady Mortimer said in a soothing voice, but the Queen kept staring out into the garden. 'Majesty, will you not greet your visitor?'

The Queen turned her head slowly. 'Sir Argyle, what brings you here?'

'I heard you were unwell, Majesty,' Argyle said kneeling before her dais. 'I came to offer what comfort I might.'

'How kind.' The Queen gestured for him to stand and turned to whisper to Lady Mortimer, who looked uneasy when she ushered the ladies from the room, leaving Argyle and the Queen alone with just a few royal guards. 'Come sit with me. The King sent you?'

Argyle weighted his words. 'Yes, Majesty. He is concerned for your health.'

'Then he is a fool!' She gave a shrill laugh, grasping the armrests tightly, they seemed to have been picked at, the red paint gone in some places. 'My health is just fine!'

'I see that now, Majesty.' Argyle noticed one of the guards glaring at him. 'The King told me you had been crying after …'

'Oh, it has nothing to do with the joust. I am not such a fool as to cry over a wasted day.' There were dark circles around the Queen's eyes, making her look years older than she was. She gave Argyle's hand an apathetic pat. 'Not that I am not sorry for your brother, but in all fairness, did he really expect to survive a joust of war against Lord Bolingbroke? I had always thought him more clever than that. And Eleanor pleaded with me for so long to interfere and try to persuade the King to be lenient.'

Eleanor! Of course it would be his sister's doing that Thomas had been spared. He had been right to expect that she had influence at court, but Argyle knew from Eleanor's tears on the field that she had not thought herself successful - and neither had Thomas. Perhaps he would have preferred the uncertain outcome of a joust to a life in exile.

'I am grateful, Majesty.' Argyle paused. 'Might I ask what has distressed you so if not the joust?'

The Queen pulled Argyle to a tall window overlooking the woods. 'Celeste,' she whispered, tears forming in the corner of her eyes. 'She is with child.'

Argyle did not know what to say. Did he admit that he knew and let the Queen know that all of England was buzzing with the news? Or did he lie and tell her it was a great surprise?

'You knew, of course.' The Queen wiped her wet cheeks, her movements stiff and erratic. 'Everyone knows. Her husband is dead, did you know that too?'

'No, Majesty,' Argyle said, suddenly out of breath, surely this was what foreboding felt like. He had to clear his throat before continuing: 'Was he sick?'

'Old age. He was just old. And probably stupid!' The Queen turned from the window. 'I shall walk with Sir Argyle, fetch Mistress Prudence and have her bring my cloak and gloves!' The Queen gestured to one of her guards and whispered to Argyle. 'We will speak outdoors.'

The guard returned shortly after with Prudence carrying the Queen's clothes, a quiet smile on her face. She kept stealing glances at Argyle while she dressed the Queen and when he gave a non-committal smile it brought a little colour to her cheeks; he still had some power over her, but what use was that?

'Will you join us, Mistress Prudence?' Argyle caught a haughty look from the Queen. 'Or perhaps not?'

'It is cold!' the Queen said and tore her gloves from Prudence's outstretched hand. 'Mistress Prudence will stay indoors. My guards will suffice, they know how to keep their ears and mouths shut.'

Prudence coloured deeper and scuttled away, most likely to report the slight to Lady Mortimer. Argyle thought the Queen was playing a dangerous game, all but alone in a court that was by all accounts loyal to the King - or at least, the King's family. She was still a stranger.

'Was that wise, Majesty?' Argyle asked as the door closed behind them. It seemed that all life had been drained from the Queen's pretty garden, the only sound was the gravel crunching under her boots as she stomped along a path leading away from the castle. Argyle walked beside her; two guards following at a safe distance.

'Certain matters came to light when Celeste's husband died.' The Queen's voice betrayed no emotion. 'It seems she is not quite the woman we all thought she was. Not quite as desolate and sad, not exactly to be pitied.'

'Majesty?'

The Queen stopped and picked a solitary red rose from a withering bush. 'It reminds me of Bolingbroke's tent. Did you not think it was a wonderful spectacle? Two Dukes of the realm poised for mortal combat, and my husband all that stood between them and blood spilled?'

Argyle winced at the slap of her cold voice. 'Yes, Majesty.'

'Well, I did not think so!' The Queen threw the rose down and crushed it with the heel of her little boot. 'I know now it was a lie! All a lie! Bolingbroke should be happy I did not tell the King what I am about to tell you, Sir Argyle. Or he would most certainly face the executioner tomorrow!'

Fear stole up Argyle's spine, chilling him to the core. Before he could stop himself, the question spilled out; 'Of what are you speaking, Majesty?'

The Queen gestured for the guards to stop and pulled Argyle behind a hedge, almost concealing them from view and certainly from any curious eyes watching from the castle. 'What do you know about Celeste? About her childhood, her parents?'

'They were poor nobles, offered her to her husband for a handsome sum that allowed them to live as they preferred,' Argyle said, the words came out in hard blows. 'She once said that she would do almost anything for her family, and that she thought of you as her family.'

The Queen's laugh caught in her throat. 'Then she has a very strange sense of family and duty. When her husband died, her mother wrote to me, as well she should. It seemed Celeste's father - or who she thought to be her father - had died around the same time. Now, Celeste's mother felt that she might freely admit that Celeste was not his daughter, but rather the daughter of an English nobleman. With close affinity to the Crown.'

'Who?' Warm drips of fear ran down Argyle's back despite the cold wind, the drum of his blood was deafening.

'The Duke of Lancaster.' The Queen picked up a handful of pebbles and threw them into the shallow basin in the centre of the little rotunda, droplets of water catching the weak sunlight. 'She is Gaunt's brat!'

Argyle fumbled for the bench standing a little off to the side. Although he knew that he must not sit in front of the Queen without her permission, he slumped on it. She went to sit beside him. 'Ah, you feel it too? The utter betrayal!'

Gaunt's daughter? Bolingbroke's sister? Was that what they had been whispering about so long ago? Gaunt had not just sent a spy into the King's bedroom; he had sent a member of his own family, a woman whose child could throw the entire succession to the throne! Images of the King and Celeste flickered before his eyes, Bolingbroke hiding behind curtains and Gaunt laughing in his sick chamber. Cursed be all of them!

The Queen grabbed his hand. 'You must tell no one! I have not even told the King, although I feel I should. That I must. And yet, I have delayed it for so long. When the King spared Bolingbroke - and your brother - I thought he would sentence him to exile for good. But he did not! FOOL!' The Queen shook from anger. 'Now, I have no choice but to tell him.'

'If you do, Majesty,' Argyle found his voice, 'you condemn her to death.' The Queen shook her head, but Argyle saw that she knew it to be true. 'Majesty, you know the King will never forgive Celeste her betrayal; he will punish her and all that ever knew her. He will think the whole French court has plotted against him. All that you have to offer will pale against his desire for revenge.'

'But they did not! We knew nothing!' the Queen said, her eyes desperate.

Are you sure, your father did not know? Argyle thought and continued his plea. 'Majesty, please reconsider!' Too often he had experienced the King's infamous temper, and he was sure a child Queen would be not match to it.

'What if he finds out that I knew?' the Queen asked, the wind drying the tears on her cheeks. 'He will not dare accuse my father, he needs his truce with France!' Her words were those of a woman far older than her nine years. Was it her royal upbringing that made her speak this way, or was it perhaps some secret ambassador from her father's court, whispering in her ear?

'Maybe so, but what about Celeste and the child?' Argyle tried to penetrate the Queen's armour, but his words fell useless to the ground.

'She should have been honest!'

'If she knew before your marriage, and she had told you, you would both be in danger.'

'Celeste made her bed, let her sleep in it,' the Queen said, her words bitter. 'She could have claimed sanctuary from me! I could have sent her home under some pretext or other. But she decided to bed my husband. The ultimate deceit made even worse by her mother's revelation.'

'When will you tell the King?' Argyle's mouth was laced with sand.

'I shall be gracious and let your brother and Lord Bolingbroke go to exile before I tell him. Lord Gaunt is old and ill, not even my husband would punish him by sending him to the block. He may reconsider his sentence on Lord Bolingbroke, but he must know.' She spoke with an adult's conviction.

'You have to save yourself,' Argyle said. 'I understand.'

'I am only sorry, I had to involve you, Sir Argyle,' the Queen said and squeezed his hand. 'I had hoped to stay here secluded until word reached me that the Dukes were sent away. Now, I throw myself at your mercy that you will not tell the King before I do.'

How could I, Argyle thought, when you have condemned me too?

CHAPTER 39

2 October 1398 - Plymouth

Thomas looked lost. Argyle was holding the fetters that had just come off Thomas' wrists and looked around the crowd assembled to see the great Lord Mowbray being put forcefully on a ship bound for exile. He wondered where his sisters were. Margaret had been suspiciously quiet throughout the whole debacle from Thomas' allegations against Bolingbroke, through the gut-wrenching wait for the joust that never was, and until this very moment. Eleanor ought to be here, she had sent word that she and her husband would attend and offer what little comfort they might. Joan was as ever unpredictable, she might come or not depending on which way her husband leaned that particular month.

Hooves on the wooden dockside announced the arrival of Elizabeth's carriage, her two sons on horseback flanking her. The Mowbray livery looked bloodied and terrible on her servants and guards.

'John, Thomas,' Thomas said when his sons dismounted and came to greet him, their faces solemn and their heads bare. They only stayed by their father for a moment before John went to help Elizabeth out of the carriage. Her dress swirled about her body, the silk so dark red it was almost black in the low October sun.

'Husband. Who would have thought it would ever come to this?

Thomas bowed and kissed her fingertips. 'Not I, wife, not I.'

Argyle, who had heard their raised angry voices last night, was impressed by their ability to look the part. He was convinced that nothing had come from their screaming match, but now that they were out in public they seemed determined to put on a show.

'Sister,' Argyle said when Elizabeth turned to face him. 'I hope you have said your farewells?'

'You were kind to let us have one last night together,' Elizabeth said with a stiff smile. 'Now, John and Thomas will say their goodbyes.'

'Of course,' Argyle said and stepped aside to let the two boys approach. The glances they gave their mother were filled with regret and fear.

'Come, let me look at you one last time,' Thomas said, and the boys obeyed. 'John, be a good brother and a shoulder for your mother to lean on. Thomas, keep at your training and be obedient.'

The boys knelt for their father's blessing and then hurried back to stand behind Elizabeth. 'Husband, be safe.'

Thomas just nodded at her, his gaze fixed on someone or something else that Argyle could not see in the throng of people on the dock.

'It is time,' Argyle said as two White Hart archers approached.

Thomas flinched at the sight of them and turned to Argyle. 'This is not over! It cannot be over. Hear me now, brother. Whatever came between us, this cannot be it, plead my case to the King, have him at least concede that I return after ten years, just as Bolingbroke will do. Promise me that!'

'You know as well as I do that the King will not be swayed,' Argyle said stopping the two archers with a commanding gesture. 'He gave you life when Bolingbroke would have given you death. Take what is offered and be content.' Argyle had decided not to tell Thomas of his deal with the King. It was unstable at best and there was no reason to give Thomas false hope when he might still die penniless in exile if Argyle failed to change the King's mind.

'How am I to be content?' Thomas' voice rose. 'Do not let me die far away from my home and my family!'

'Where you live and die is not for me to choose,' Argyle said, as the White Hart archers came forward and forced Thomas up the gangway. 'God be with you, brother!'

'He will return,' Elizabeth said at Argyle's elbow. 'He must.'

'It is in the hands of God and the King.' Argyle echoed words that had already been said a thousand times.

'One of which you know intimately.' Elizabeth stared at her husband lost on the deck of the ship while the sailors hurried about hoisting the sails and winding in the massive anchor chain. Thomas looked down at his hands, dismay on his face.

'He has little love for me,' Argyle said.

'But the Queen does, and so does his whore - the fair Celeste.' Elizabeth whispered and pinched his arm. 'God help me, Argyle, you will bring him back to me!' She held her head high and walked away, her sons trailing in her wake.

Argyle turned and saw Eleanor standing on the far side of the dock, her cheeks white and glistening with tears. The wife sheds no tears for her husband, Argyle thought, but then neither do I.

The two White Harts pushed past Argyle, one of them hitting him on the shoulder and grinning broadly. 'One pest out of the country, and soon another will follow,' he said. 'Oh, the King sent this for you.' He pressed a letter into Argyle's hand. 'Best read it right away, Sire!'

13 October 1398 - Dover

Argyle let the salty wind whip around his body. He remembered being here all but three years ago, sailing back to the white cliffs, wondering what might happen once he stepped foot on English soil. If he had known then what he knew now, he might have chosen a watery grave. He had gone back to save his family and look at it now; Margaret was gone from court and Eleanor had not spoken to him since the day of Thomas' exile; nothing could remedy the deep cracks in the Mowbray mortar.

'Lord Bolingbroke is coming!'

The streets of Dover were lined with people who cheered for Bolingbroke as he slowly wound his way down towards the large ship that lay waiting for him.

Argyle had ridden hard to get from Plymouth to Dover in time to see Bolingbroke off. The King had kept his word that Argyle was to witness the exile of the two greatest noblemen in the realm, just as he had ordered when Argyle had pleaded for his brother to be spared. A big carriage followed Bolingbroke towards the docks. It was adorned with Gaunt's crest.

'They say he was cheered on by thousands of Londoners,' Stephen mumbled. He had come from Beauworth with thirty men to join Argyle's party at Dover, and he had done nothing to hide his resentment. Stephen grabbed the high pummel of his saddle and stared straight ahead. 'They treated him as a hero. Some even say that England won't be safe until he returns.'

'I hope they did not say it too loudly,' Argyle grumbled. 'That would be unwise.'

Stephen rolled his shoulders. 'How do you think he'll be received in France?'

'Well enough, I presume. They say he has already sent envoys to King Charles to ask that he might stay in Paris for a while.'

'Quite a party he's taking,' Stephen looked around. 'How many men'll he bring?'

'No more than 200.' Argyle saw Bolingbroke stop to accept a bouquet of late blooms from a fair-haired girl. The crowd cheered him on. 'The King sent word that I am to ensure he does not bring more, and that Beaufort is not among them. Nor too many knights, the King wants them to remain in England.'

Stephen turned his face to the wind. 'Does the King expect them to be loyal to him?'

'Most likely,' Argyle said and gestured for his men to move Bolingbroke's retinue along. 'But he would be a fool.'

'Now who's being unwise?' Stephen met Argyle's eyes for the first time that morning. 'You look beat to death.'

'Being the gaoler of two Dukes will do that to a person. I shall be pleased when Lord Bolingbroke is well on his way across the Channel and I on my way home.' Argyle heard the hollow ring of his words and looked away.

'Ah, home … Now that's something to look forward to.' Stephen turned his horse around and began making his way back towards Dover Town, scattering the assembled crowd as he went. 'I'll wait for you at our lodgings, M'lord.'

Bolingbroke trotted past, and Argyle let his massive, black steed fall into step. 'Ready to leave, my Lord?'

'I knew my cousin would send some fool to see me off,' Bolingbroke said, smiling at the crowd. 'What does he expect? That I would turn around and thunder back to London? That I would break exile before I even went into it?'

'He merely wants to make sure you have all you need.' Argyle did not care to pick a fight with Bolingbroke, and secretly blessed the cheering crowd. Bolingbroke would not be seen to lose his temper when he had fervent spectators all around him. Argyle continued; 'All your provisions were carried aboard yesterday, my Lord. Will you be bringing your horse?'

Bolingbroke considered Argyle for a while. 'You are not here by choice.'

'No.'

'Yes, I will be bringing my horse. You may ensure it is taken aboard while I say my farewells to my father.' Bolingbroke rode ahead, and Argyle thought he gave him a little smile before he did.

'Sir Argyle.' Grenteville rode up alongside Argyle. 'I did not know you would be here.'

'Nor I you, Master Grenteville.'

'I go where my Lord Gaunt asks me to. Though I am sure you will not ferry across with Lord Bolingbroke to Calais? The King might worry that you would not return.' Grenteville winked, and Argyle graced the hilt of his sword.

'Will you be joining Lord Bolingbroke?'

'Oh no, Lord Gaunt has use for me here,' Grenteville said companionably. 'He too does not trust that I will return if I go abroad.'

'What does that make us, Master Grenteville?' Argyle asked.

'Fools.' Grenteville spurred on his horse, and Argyle watched him career towards Gaunt's carriage where Bolingbroke was helping his ailing father out onto the dock. The two clasped hands and Gaunt gave Bolingbroke a purse, probably containing a large part of his annual sum. Bolingbroke would have to learn to make do.

When Argyle arrived at the dock, Gaunt stood alone, watching Bolingbroke scale the gangway, two of Argyle's men walked behind him trying to keep his horse in check.

'Sir Argyle,' Gaunt said without looking over.

'My Lord Gaunt. I am here to …'

'I know why you have come. I asked the King to send you.'

CHAPTER 40

24 November 1398 - Beauworth

Lost in thought, Argyle leaned back in his great chair, La Fontaine's chair, and closed his eyes. Lately, La Fontaine had haunted him day and night, and today was no different. It felt as if the knight had come back from the dead, not unlike his former friend Coxcombe, except Argyle did not expect to fight La Fontaine at every turn. His head swam from exertion and lack of sleep.

'Husband?' Isobel's voice crept across the room, and Argyle opened his eyes slowly to find her hovering in the doorway.

'Wife.' His mild voice seemed to soothe her, and she closed the door behind her.

'You are busy?'

'Never too busy for you,' he said though part of him wished her away. 'What is it?'

Isobel stood in the middle of the room with an indecisive look on her face. 'You ... I ...' her eyes glistened. 'I am with child again.'

Argyle jumped up, the legs on his chair screaming against the stone floor. 'Oh, Isobel, what good news!'

Her face broke with a smile. 'I have known for a while, but I wanted to be sure ...'

'You are well?' Argyle asked, he held his arms out to her, and she nodded against his shoulder. Argyle reached down and turned her face to his giving her a kiss. What solace she had bestowed upon him.

'I am glad, you are happy,' Isobel said. 'You have been in such a state since you came back.'

Argyle heard her complaint in her voice but let it slide. 'I know. It was a hard time.'

And of late, I constantly wonder what Eleanor is up to, and when the Queen will tell the King about his mistress, Argyle added in thought.

'I wish we could forget about court, about the King and Queen and all of them,' Isobel said, her voice a little shrill. 'They bring nothing but heartache and pain.'

'This time they brought each other heartache,' Argyle said, a little surprised at his own confession. It was not often he confided in Isobel although he did not know why. When she turned a questioning face up at him, he had no choice but to continue. 'The King's mistress is pregnant. The Queen is furious.'

'What is that to you?'

'She has few friends in England, and ever fewer at court,' Argyle said with regret. 'The Queen is anxious.'

'Is that why they plan to visit?' Isobel's cheeks burned. 'Because she wants to visit her friend?'

Argyle took out the letter from court announcing their Majesties' visit. 'I have only this letter and it does not say, you know this as well as I, wife. The King rarely visits the south; he is not beloved here. But he is determined to make a tour of the southern estates to see if perhaps the Queen can tame the people and draw them to him.'

'God help her,' Isobel said. 'Has he visited before?'

'Not that I can remember. He may have visited Beauworth as a boy or before La Fontaine took me in, but since then there has been nothing but turmoil in the land.' Argyle sat back down. 'And I was away for quite a while when I first inherited the estates, as you well know.'

'Yes, you have been a great friend to the King.' Isobel's voice was leaden. 'And now you are a great friend to his wife. Beware, husband, that you do not value friendship higher than your own family.'

25 November 1398 - Beauworth

'You are far away, M'lord.' Stephen's voice yanked Argyle from his sinister thoughts. 'I'd ask what's bothering you, but I know that'd be fruitless.' Stephen dragged a platter of meat and sweet carrots towards him.

'What a relief,' Argyle said. 'Have you seen Isobel?'

'M'lady's driving the kitchen staff mad with her preparations,' Stephen said wiping his greasy chin. 'Bessie's threatening to get with child again just to get away from the stoves.'

Argyle smiled, Bessie was one of the most loyal women in the kitchen, and he would be hard pressed to replace her. 'I shall have a word with my wife.'

'Please do, though I doubt it'd change her mind.' Stephen reached for the ale. 'What's spawned this sudden interest from the King to visit Beauworth?'

'I cannot say; all the time I was in La Fontaine's service the King did not visit once.' Argyle tried to hide his worry. 'Perhaps he is just interested to see how we train the men.'

'Perhaps,' Stephen said, not weighing in further.

'Perhaps the Queen is behind the plan.' Argyle pushed away his full bowl; everything was tasteless these days. Stephen glanced up briefly then concentrated on his stew. Argyle looked around the hall, his soldiers and squires talking, shouting and laughing, making the room ring with noise. He leaned towards Stephen. 'Time for honesty, I think.'

Stephen nodded, grabbed his cup and led the way from the great hall and across the hallway to Argyle's study. He closed the door quietly behind him, shutting out the noise and bustle.

'I think the Queen wants the King away from court and away from a certain lady.'

'French by any chance?' Stephen returned Argyle's stare. 'You came home in a foul mood. It didn't take much adding up to guess what might've happened. It's one thing to be your brother's gaoler, but another to guard secrets that aren't yours.'

Argyle cursed how easily Stephen read him. 'What have you heard?'

'Whispers,' Stephen said and shrugged. 'I've kept in touch with some of my old friends.'

Sometimes I wonder who these friends are, Argyle thought and asked, 'Have you told anyone here?'

'News travels fast, M'lord. All of England knows of the mistress, but no one talks about her openly.'

Argyle picked a little meat from his teeth. 'Glad to hear it.'

'I favour loyalty more than you might think. They say the lady's with child?'

'The King should have known better than to choose the Queen's friend for his sport.' Argyle tried to ignore Stephen's question. 'When their Majesties reach Beauworth, I would prefer that she is not mentioned.'

Stephen looked out the window. 'We're speaking of the same lady that …?'

'Yes.' Argyle looked around his always-cluttered study; there was no place for the eyes to rest. 'We are.'

'M'lady knows?'

'Of the situation at court?' Argyle knew full well that Stephen was hinting at something else.

'That too.'

'She knows that the King has a mistress who has set the royal household on edge, and that the Queen is looking for this visit to divert her husband's attention.' Argyle leaned back in his chair, running his hands through his hair. 'She does not know it is the same lady that I once courted.'

'Wise. But can you trust the King to keep silent on the subject? Or the Queen for that matter?'

'The Queen wishes to forget the whole unfortunate affair,' Argyle said, hoping more than believing the truth of his words. 'The King, however …'

Stephen offered some more ale. 'Although I've only met him a few times, I find the King has little sense of situation or feelings.'

Argyle briefly reflected on how Stephen still managed to surprise him. 'Too true. You are trying to advise me, Smith?'

Stephen smiled, and for a moment, he looked like the youth, Argyle had met many years ago right here at Beauworth. Their balance between friendship and master and servant relationship was ever a hard one. 'Better to tell M'lady in advance than have her surprised by the King,' he said.

Or both of them, if the Queen should be fool enough to choose this place to tell the King about Celeste's secret, Argyle thought.

10 December 1398 - Beauworth

'I am sure their Majesties will be well entertained throughout their stay,' Argyle said looking around the parlour, which was brimming with decorations and smelling of fresh pine and faint incense. 'You have planned and procured for weeks. They will only stay a few days at most.'

'How can you be so callous?' Isobel stomped her foot angrily. 'It may be a trifling matter to you, but all of court has their eyes on us, and I would rather …'

'That they did not come?'

Isobel wiped her face. 'Yes!'

'I agree, my dear,' Argyle said and tried to catch her into an embrace, but she skirted him. 'However, they are coming, and I am sure you have everything in hand.'

'What if the King wants to visit the villages?' Isobel broached a subject they had both been avoiding. 'What if some fool tells them what my sister was …'

'I will make sure that does not happen.'

Isobel finally sat down, and Argyle went to put his hands on her shoulders. 'I am terrified, Argyle.'

'There is no need. The Queen …' Argyle did not know how to proceed. 'They will enjoy their stay. I will show the King some of La Fontaine's favourite hunting grounds, and we will be back every day before dark.'

'And what will I do with the Queen?'

'She brings her ladies-in-waiting. You can set the minstrel playing and they may dance, or sing or whatever you prefer.' Argyle drew a chair up next to hers and sat down. The trinkets on the tables and little cushions scattered around the room gave the parlour a warm, womanly touch.

'What minstrel?' Isobel asked with a snap.

'I have summoned musicians to entertain their Majesties, and a minstrel to tell tales.' Argyle did not understand why Isobel was so annoyed. 'You asked me to.'

'I asked for music, not a minstrel,' Isobel said, and Argyle noticed how full her breasts were against the cut of her woollen dress, once more her body was changing with the pregnancy. 'Where does he hail from?'

'I met him in Dover. He was entertaining in the tavern we lodged in,' Argyle scratched his cheek. 'Smith liked him.'

'Smith likes all things bawdy!' Isobel released the cushion she was crushing between her hands. 'Will he be appropriate for the Queen and her ladies?'

'I will have a word with him and make sure that he only tells tales that are fit for the ears of ladies,' Argyle promised and Isobel seemed a little appeased. She plumped the cushion and straightened a jewelled box on the small table beside her.

'I will be happy when they are gone again,' she said before opening the door. 'Ah, Smith, I hear you have been put in charge of our entertainment?'

Stephen entered the room perplexity wiping the smile from his face. 'M'lady?' But Isobel slammed the door shut on his question.

'She thought a minstrel was a bad idea,' Argyle said. 'What is it, Smith?'

Stephen laughed. 'Thank God, I thought I had forgotten something important. I just wanted to ask you if perhaps we should move some of our horses to stables in the villages? There are some empty near here, and it would make room for the horses in the royal entourage.'

'Yes, do that.' Argyle went to the fire. 'We have enough wood to warm all the rooms?'

Stephen quickly listed the most important provisions, and Argyle was soon satisfied that all was ready. Now they could but wait for the royal messenger to announce the arrival of the King and Queen.

12 December 1398 - Beauworth

Horses and carriages were cramming through the gate and filling up the courtyard, and more were blocking the road and bridge leading from the countryside into Beauworth. Isobel stood on the stairs, staring at the commotion in the freshly decorated courtyard. 'They are here,' she whispered and Argyle bent to hear her. 'They actually came …'

'Yes.' Argyle brushed down the fur lining of his cloak, he had wondered if they would change their minds, Christmas was fast approaching, but the Queen must have insisted. Now there was nothing for it but to receive the royal party and make merry. The King would surely never have agreed to come, if the Queen had let slip her secret. 'They will stay but two days. We shall survive.'

'Do you think so?' Isobel straightened her necklace and tucked at her hairnet, Argyle had seen her maid fuss over her all morning and the result was very pleasing.

Before Argyle could compliment her, a herald announced the arrival of the royal party and the King rode into the courtyard while everyone knelt. The Queen's carriage came rumbling across the bridge, the sound of the wheels a strange whirr on the cobbles. The sound jumped around the courtyard, and the dogs in the kennel barked madly at the unfamiliar echoes of strange voices. Argyle held Isobel's hand in his, irrationally afraid what might happen to their unborn child if she exerted herself. Her icy grasp and short breaths pierced his skin and ears, and he felt the cold wind and icy surface of the stairs seep through his warm clothes. He should have told her to stay inside by the fire.

'Sir Argyle!'

'Majesty, how good to see you! I hope you had a pleasant ride?' Argyle rose and helped Isobel to her feet, she brushed her skirt before cupping her swollen belly and together they walked down the stairs to receive their guests.

The King was helped from his saddle and looked about. 'We did. I cannot remember ever setting eyes on Beauworth before, can it really be that I never visited La Fontaine even once?'

'Not while I was in his service, Majesty,' Argyle said and bowed before the Queen. 'Majesty, a pleasant trip?'

'A little cold,' the Queen said and looked at Isobel, 'Lady Mowbray, how well you look.'

Argyle noticed her blue-tinged lips, but Isobel curtsied deep and mustered a smile. 'Thank you Majesty.'

The King drew Argyle to one side. 'Already pregnant again, Sir Argyle? You do not dawdle.'

'As the Queen said, it has been cold,' Argyle admitted, and the King smiled. 'Shall we go inside, Majesty?'

The King grabbed the Queen's hand and tucked it under his arm, then he reached out and grabbed Isobel's hand and tucked it under his other arm. 'Lead the way, and I shall bring the ladies.'

Isobel looked stiff and uncomfortable so near the radiant King, but she smiled politely at him, briefly meeting his gaze before she looked down. He gave her a lingering look, and the Queen tugged at his arm. 'I am freezing, husband, let us go inside before Lady Mowbray catches a cold. You would not want our hostess fall ill because of us.'

'No, my dear, you are quite right,' the King said and dragged the two women past Argyle into the hall where a roaring fire greeted the guests.

ℬ ℭ ℬ ℭ

'We will not stay long,' the Queen said to Argyle later that evening. 'He is in a foul temper.'

Really, Argyle thought and looked at the King who was eating and laughing on the dais, with Isobel next to him, only picking at her food. Tables and benches were set up along the walls creating a large open space in the middle of the great hall where the floor had been swept clean.

'He seems in high spirits,' Argyle said. They were standing off to one side watching the Queen's ladies-in-waiting dance, their jewellery glittering in the candlelight. None was dressed more magnificently than the Queen herself, her deep purple silk dress was elaborately decorated with gold and silver thread, gemstones and pearls. Isobel had commented earlier that the Queen's seamstress must be very clever because the dress alluded to a cleavage that was not there yet, and now that he stood so near her, he saw the truth of Isobel's words. The Queen's dress did indeed seem to be made for a young woman and not the girl who wore it.

'A show.' The Queen caught the King's eye and smiled widely, clapping in tune to the music, her large ruby ring sparkling. 'He hates that I dragged him from court and … well … he also hates the south. Although I could not say why.'

'He has had bad experiences come from the south,' Argyle said remembering the tales of the peasants revolting in the early years of the King's reign. 'Perhaps he thinks it is a dangerous place. I think he has only been happy in the south the few times he has stayed at Porchester.' Argyle had secretly wondered why the King had favoured coming to Beauworth rather than stay at his own royal palace.

'Not nearly as dangerous as court.' The Queen nodded when Mistress Catherine went flying by, her yellow skirt billowing. 'Your wife looks uncomfortable.'

The King had turned to Isobel and tried to engage her in conversation, and Argyle saw her staring desperately around the room. 'I may have to go and save her soon.'

'First, I would have a word.' The Queen walked to a table laid out with mulled wine and warm ale. 'I will never understand your desire to boil wine.' She sighed but accepted a glass of mulled wine nonetheless. 'It ruins the flavour.'

'But warms the belly. What does her Majesty want?'

'Have you found out more about Coxcombe?' Argyle had to bend towards her to catch her words, and worry ruined the mulled wine for him. 'Did you ever speak to him?'

'He seems to have vanished,' Argyle said with at grudge. 'There has been no word of him since the trials.'

'Be in the passageway near my chambers at first light tomorrow,' the Queen said and turned to face the great hall. She smiled when some of the other guests inclined their cups to her. 'Mistress Catherine will have some news for you.'

Just then, Catherine danced by, her yellow dress glowing in the candlelight and her dark hair flying behind her in the quick dance. Her bright smile was serene and honest and her cheeks were flushed from the exertion. Argyle followed her around the floor, acutely aware of her fine figure and elegant movements; she was by far the most beautiful of the Queen's ladies but seemed unawares. When the musicians finished, all the ladies curtsied deep before the dais and the King applauded them making some remark or other to Isobel. Catherine accepted the hand of a courtier for the next dance, but when she entered the line, her eyes lingered on Argyle.

࿇ ࿇

'Sir Argyle,' Mistress Catherine's voice sounded muffled. 'Is that you?'

'Yes, Mistress, what …'

She stepped out of the shadows and held out a warning hand. 'The King is lurking. The Queen and he had a terrible row last night.'

As we all heard, Argyle thought and let Catherine lead him from the passageway and into the small chamber adjoining to his study. She peered around before closing the door softly, only then did she remove the thick scarf that she had wrapped around the bottom half of her face and her neck. At winter, Beauworth was as cold a house as any other and there were no hearths in the passageway to warm the bare stones. 'The Queen asked that I speak to you. About a certain man.'

Argyle nodded and beckoned her closer to the fire. She went a little reluctantly but relaxed when the warmth reached out and caressed her skin, wrapping a blanket of golden light around her. 'Please, Mistress, tell me all.'

'He had courted my sister.' Catherine's hair glistened black in the firelight, today she was wearing a demure dark blue dress a stark contrast to the yellow silk of last night. Even so, she looked oddly out of place in the distinctly masculine room; and Argyle realised that no woman had ever been in here before - not even Isobel. 'He tried to get his way, but she would not give in.'

'Wise girl,' Argyle said and sat down on an old chest. There was hardly any furniture in the room, which functioned almost solely as an archive, but he had never considered putting a chair or table in there, it would only get in the way. The walls were naked, the fire rarely lit but in the dead of winter, and even then it was only to keep the damp from corrupting the documents.

'Stupid girl to get involved with the fallen knight in the first place! Everyone knows what he is, but she was ever a sap for a flattery and stolen kisses.' Catherine glanced at Argyle but looked away when he caught her eye, perhaps the lingering look from last night was all in his imaginings. 'It never went past that, but I think he wanted it to.'

Most men do, Argyle reflected but said nothing. Coxcombe was not a terribly attractive man, but with the right kind of flattery many women were still easy marks, and some were prone to prefer the dangers that came with a fallen knight.

'I think he let his mouth run away with him to get her to spread her legs.' Catherine blushed, causing Argyle to speculate about how old she might be; he had never really paid any attention to her before last night when the Queen had singled her out. For a brief moment, he considered whether the King had noticed her too; now that his mistress was with child, he might well be looking to find someone to replace her.

'I had already told her to turn him down.' Catherine's voice brought him back to the present. 'But she was amazed at what he had to say. The stories he could tell. About deceit, changing loyalties, deadly whispers.'

'That is all good and well, Mistress Catherine,' Argyle said and saw her tremble a little at his harsh tone. 'But what do you know that I might be able to use. Do you know where he is?'

'I know that he had a hand in the death of the knight who lived here before you.' She rubbed her hands together and held them out towards the low flames. The small room offered little space between them. 'Though not exactly why.'

Argyle reached out and grabbed her hands. 'Where is he?' He could hear footsteps in the corridor and lowered his voice. 'All I need to know is where he is.'

'Still in London. He left with the White Harts after the trials and he has been gone these many months, but now he is back in London, and he sought out my sister.' Catherine looked terrified but did not draw back from his touch, rather she returned his grasp. 'He warned her to keep quiet or he would …'

'Kill her.' Argyle saw tears spill from her eyes. He reached out and wiped one of them off her smooth cheek. Did she lean in a little at his touch? Argyle continued, 'he is dangerous, you are right to be afraid for her.'

'Shoe Street, he lives in Shoe Street.' Catherine glanced over her shoulder, and Argyle saw a shadow under the door. They both tensed, her hands still in his, the sleeve of her dress tickling his wrist.

'You can leave by this panel,' he whispered and opened a door hidden in the crude panelling on the back wall. 'It leads off to a narrow walkway. If you turn left, you will get back to the Queen's rooms. Go quickly.'

Catherine slid from the room, reluctantly letting go of his hand as she went, and he pushed the panel shut just as the other door opened.

'What are you doing here?' Isobel asked while her eyes darted around the small room. 'The King is up, roaring for breakfast!'

'I was looking for some papers, I promised Smith to find.' Argyle opened the chest and took out a random batch of papers secured by a wide band, all the while despising how easy it was to lie to her. 'But it can wait.'

'It had better, you cannot keep leaving me alone with that man!' Isobel was angry and desperate, her hands clutching each other, the woollen sleeves falling down before her pregnant form. 'He keeps looking at me as if the can see inside my head! As if he knows what I am!'

Argyle grabbed for her, pulling her tight and stroking her hair. 'He does not know. He is just a man - he may be a King - but no one can read the mind of others.' Although if Argyle was to make a wager, he would be more inclined to believe the King able to read minds than any other man he had ever met.

'Promise me that they will leave today,' Isobel said to his chest. Her breath cooled his skin where he had forgotten to tie the collar.

'Promise!'

'Judging from their raised voices last night, they cannot wait to be back in London.'

ꟷ

CHAPTER 41

4 February 1399 - Beauworth

'M'lord.' Stephen walked across the hall to hand a note to Argyle, the thick plank door swinging shut against a crisp February day. 'A messenger just arrived with this.'

Why can we not be left alone? Argyle thought heavily, it felt as if a new messenger arrived every few days and it was beginning to wear him thin. Since Thomas had been sent into exile, the King had simply substituted him with Argyle, and now more than ever, he wanted Thomas back at court. No wonder he had sometimes been bad tempered and difficult to get along with.

Argyle took the letter and began walking towards his study. 'Which livery?'

'White Hart. He's still here.' Stephen's footsteps rang against the barren stone floor in the outer hall. The servants were cleaning the house from top to bottom on Isobel's orders and every scoured inch smelled of vinegar.

'Have him fed,' Argyle broke the King's seal. 'Sometimes I wonder if …'

'If what, M'lord?'

'Tell the messenger to stay, I have an answer for him to take back.'

Argyle let his faint hope of a quiet day float away. Once more dark clouds came down from the north. 'That damned FOOL!'

Stephen stepped into the study, the door half open behind him. 'Bad news?'

'It is worse, it is … insanity!' Argyle fought to keep his temper under control. 'The King has decided to revert Gaunt's lands and wealth to the Crown! To exile Bolingbroke for life! What in the Devil's name has possessed him to think this is a good idea?! It is utter MADNESS!'

'Not the first time …' Stephen said. 'Not the last …'

'I saw a rider on the road.' Isobel appeared in the doorway, and Stephen bowed to her. She ignored him completely. 'What news?'

'A letter from court.' Argyle watched Isobel close the door. The study instantly grew warmer. 'The King has taken possession of Gaunt's estates.'

'Oh?' Isobel looked away. 'Is that bad?'

'It means that no nobleman's lands are safe.' Argyle put the note down on his cluttered table. Lately, Isobel had not been in to tidy up the stacks, and it showed. Argyle found he missed her desire to keep even his own sanctum neat. 'Most likely it means trouble.'

'Trouble that takes you from here?' Was that spite in her voice? For some reason Isobel seemed to despise the entire royal family, and the more Argyle had thought about it the more he was convinced that she had overheard him speaking with Mistress Catherine and had somehow misunderstood their whispered conversation.

'Not yet, but yes, I think so. The King is acting in ways that no man can accept.' Argyle leaned back and Stephen stepped to the window, turning his back to them.

'No nobleman. It is not the same, Argyle. I do not see, what it has to do with you,' Isobel said, her face set. Her thick woollen dress could not hide the swell of her belly or the curve of her full breasts.

'My lands are endowed to me by the King. If one day, he wakes and decides that Beauworth or indeed any other part of England should be his, all he has to do is rescind, and we will be homeless! You married a nobleman.' Argyle bit back his resentment. She must have known that when Thomas was exiled the King's focus would shift to the younger Mowbray; after all, their family had ever been close to the rulers of England.

'But we are all at the mercy of the King.' Isobel slid into a chair near the hearth drawing the fur collar on her dress close around her neck. 'He can take estates, men or lives. We are worthless to him.'

Argyle gave her a sharp look, but Stephen's presence stopped him making a vicious reply. Instead, he reached for a piece of paper. 'We will discuss this later. Smith, tell the messenger …'

'That you wish to send word back with him.' Stephen turned from the window. 'What'll you write?'

Isobel glanced at Stephen displeasure coursing across her face. Argyle was certain it irked her that he would share concerns and make arrangements with Stephen and not her. But when Stephen returned her look, the whisper of a smile played in her eyes.

'I told the King that I would do anything for him. I am sworn to him.' Argyle heard Isobel drum her fingers on the armrest. 'If he commands me to come, I must. Perhaps this will prove my undying devotion, perhaps it will even soften the King's decision on Thomas' exile …'

'But you doubt it.' Stephen paused at the door.

'Yes, I doubt the King will ever be moved to do anything by anyone no matter how dedicated, loyal and devoted they are. However, I have to try.' Stephen gave a concerned look before he left Argyle and Isobel alone.

'You never told me about your pledge to the King.' She leaned closer to the fire.

'It is no more than he is entitled to,' Argyle said wearily. 'But it was all I had to offer in return for the King's benevolence. I was hoping …'

'That you might bring back your brother.' Isobel turned her head, a few locks of her auburn hair swinging lightly across her shoulder, she always wore her hair down when there were no visitors staying at the house. 'Why would you do that?'

'He is family. I had to try. When the King's declaration was read …' Argyle still remembered Thomas' shocked look and Eleanor's tearful apologies on the field, her blue dress snapping around her legs in the wind. 'It affected more than just Thomas and Elizabeth, it affected all of us.'

'How so? What has he ever done to help you?'

Short of getting me out of house arrest and back in favour? Argyle thought and had to agree with Isobel's unsaid meaning. What had Thomas ever done? Argyle ran a hand through his hair. 'I did it as much for my sisters as for him. Eleanor was distraught.'

The mention of Eleanor stifled any angry words from Isobel; the two of them liked each other, although what they could possibly have in common, Argyle did not know.

'I am sorry for her.' Isobel got up. Even though she had been sitting before the fire, her lips had a blue tint. 'I shall leave you to make your reply, but I suppose I will soon be sending you off to London?'

Argyle crossed the room and grabbed her arm lightly. 'I do not want to …'

'But you will leave your pregnant wife again,' Isobel said thinly. 'Is this to be our life?' She left before he could offer any kind of answer.

Argyle sighed, bent over the piece of paper and jotted down a few words. Beneath the pile of papers next to him lay another message that he had yet to answer. A plea from a dangerous woman.

CHAPTER 42

10 February 1399 - Westminster

Celeste was shivering; her thin dress no shield against the cold draft in the walkway. When he had sought her out in her humble lodgings just off the palace, she had pushed him out of the door and into a small orchard around the back of the house. Now they were standing opposite each other, both of them intent to keep the other at bay. Argyle flexed his hands.

'How is the Queen?' Celeste hugged herself, revealing her pregnant frame. She had not even a cloak to protect her against the wet piercing February wind.

'Well,' Argyle said in a measured tone, his blood boiled in his veins almost rendering his thick woollen cloak unnecessary. 'Why did you ask to see me?'

'The King has spurned me of late, I wondered if you knew why?'

Argyle ignored the plea in her voice. 'I am not in favour with the King.'

'Oh,' Celeste took a trying step forward and stopped when she caught Argyle's eye.

'You really cannot imagine why his Majesty does not want to see you?'

'Perhaps my condition has changed his heart,' Celeste said, she shifted a little, her delicate shoes pushing around the withered leaves in the walkway. 'He no longer calls for me or even comes to visit. He used to.'

'Some physicians say that you should not disturb a pregnant woman. His Majesty is bound to be happy that you are with child.' His voice was flat.

'Is he?' Celeste made a wry face, her teeth clattering. 'He has a strange way of showing it.'

'Why did you ask me here?' Argyle had never replied to the letter she had sent to Beauworth, hoping she would be insulted and not contact him again. When, upon arriving in London, Argyle had received her second letter, he had been tempted to burn it without reading it. Now he wished that he had.

'I heard you were in London and …' Celeste reached out and his hand smarted at the touch of her icy fingers. 'I have never been this lonely!'

'What is that to me?' Argyle battled mixed feelings of anger and pity. He wanted to rip his hand away from her grasp and yet part of him was relenting, remembering the promises of the past, the ease of being in her company.

Celeste drew Argyle further down the walkway, glancing around. 'Remember when I said we would both do amazing things for our family?'

Argyle nodded, he had an inkling that Celeste was about to confirm the Queen's news about her family ties. He hoped that she would not. It was bad enough if the King caught wind that the Queen had confided in him, but if he knew from two sources and still chose to keep it from the King, Argyle would be for the block. 'Please, say nothing you will regret, my Lady.'

'You pleaded for your brother, a brother you do not even like!' Celeste's shrill voice bounced off the stone walls and she bit down hard to compose herself. When she spoke again, her voice was soft. 'Why will my brother not do the same for me?'

'Your brother?' Argyle turned away wondering how he might keep her quiet. He did not want to be the one to hurt a pregnant woman but desperate times … He turned back to her. 'You mean Lord Bolingbroke?'

Celeste clapped her hands over her mouth, her sky-blue eyes almost purple in the weak light. 'Oh, no! How?'

Argyle grabbed her by the arms. 'How long have you known?'

'Since before the King chose my Princess,' Celeste said, tears spilling down her cheeks. 'Long before. My mother met Lord Gaunt when they were both young, shortly before she married the man who thought he was my father and that I just came early. Maman never told him, but just before my marriage she revealed her secret to me. I think she hoped that I could make something of my knowledge, although she had already promised me to ...'

'Your aging husband,' Argyle finished her sentence when she could not.

'I think she believed that he would not last long.' Celeste dried her cheeks with the long, flowing sleeve. The soft peach colour looked faded. 'When I told her that I would accompany the Princess to England, she told me to seek out my Lord Gaunt and make myself known. She told me that he knew of me and that he might be able to protect me in the poisonous English court.'

Argyle swallowed back bile; she had known all this when she first approached him in the camp outside Calais. He fought not to drown in her deceit and dug his fingers into her arms, making her gasp. 'What the Hell were you thinking!! Why did you not tell the Queen?! Why did you engage the King?! Are you mad?!!'

Celeste shook her head at his every question; her body limp in his grasp. Argyle let her go and she staggered away. 'Only my father and brother know. I could not …'

'The Queen knows too.' Argyle was savagely satisfied to see Celeste totter. 'She is threatening to tell the King! You have hurt her so deeply that she is prepared to make you pay for your betrayal with your life.'

'How do you know? Who told you?' The soft rustle of leaves dancing in the walkway almost drowned out Celeste's questions. She was paralysed from fear; her sky-blue eyes stared blankly at him.

'The Queen received word from your mother that your husband had died.' Argyle gave her a vicious glare. 'She also told the Queen what you really are. She was devastated! But it also offered her a chance at revenge.'

Celeste sobbed, her breath shaking. 'What will I do?'

'Leave England! You can never come back, but you are a widow now and the estate is yours,' Argyle said. The solution was clear as day; she had to disappear, vanish into oblivion never to be heard from again. 'Go there and raise your bastard child.'

'Will she tell the King?' Celeste tried to get her bearings. Perhaps she too saw a way out of the mess she was in.

'I may be able to persuade her that she need not tell him, IF you leave!' Argyle wondered if it would be enough for the Queen to know that Celeste had left in disgrace and would not return, nor claim anything for her unborn child. He was far from certain.

Argyle was startled when Celeste laughed. 'Ah, I had heard you had won the Queen's little heart.'

'What?!'

'You may be married now but when you spend that much time with the Queen, sneaking off to steal moments alone,' Celeste said with triumph in her sky-blue eyes, 'the whole underbelly of court begins to whisper! Everyone knows you can seduce almost any woman - why not the Queen? Why would she be immune to your advancements when no one else is?!'

His heart sank. All those glances from the ladies-in-waiting, from Mistress Prudence and Lady Mortimer, and he knew that one of the Queens ladies' younger sisters waited on Celeste. But the Queen was a child! He took a step forward, closing the gap between them. 'You speak out of turn!'

'I have nothing left!' Celeste stood her ground, her hands protectively covering her belly. 'If you tell the King my secret, I will tell him about your sordid dealings with his sweet, little wife! And if she tells him, I shall expose you both as disgusting lovers!'

'And if I promise that we will both keep your secret?' Argyle heard his words as an admission of the horrid allegations she had just thrown in his face.

'I will leave for France,' Celeste said with a cruel satisfied smile. 'I will never come back, and we will be tied to each other in a web of deceit until the day we die. If I should ever want for anything, you will provide it - of course.'

To think I once believed that you loved me, Argyle thought as he considered her proposition. That I thought you loved the Queen and would never deceive her. He turned from her to hide his defeat. 'Very well. The Queen and I will keep your secret. But I know that once you are in France, you are free to see your brother, the terms of whose exile the King has changed. I want your promise in return that your brother will never tell anyone.'

'How am I to promise that?' Celeste grabbed his arm, and he shook off her hand, his back still turned to her. 'I do not even know where he is!'

'He is at the French court.' Argyle heard her take a step back, leaves crushing under her feet. 'When you are back in France you will visit him and get his sworn word, and you will send word to me that it is done.'

'What will I write?'

Celeste's touch made him turn and in the pale light of winter, Argyle finally noticed that she had lost all her beauty to him; for the first time he saw her for what she was. 'That the child's uncle has visited and blessed him. If Bolingbroke has taken others into his confidence about your secret, I cannot vouch for that.' Argyle rested his hand on the hilt of his sword, fingering the ornate silverwork.

Celeste seemed to consider her options. 'I understand.'

Argyle's breath caught; at least one other person knew of Celeste's whereabouts. If Coxcombe knew everything, he would have the upper hand and a bargaining chip that Argyle could not match. 'One more knows. The same man who told me where you lived. I will deal with him.'

11 February 1399 - Cheapside

Argyle tried to run as silently as possible through the dirty, crowded streets of south London, an early onset of thaw had lured many from their hearths to haggle over what scant goods were available. He shouldered his way through a crowd that had assembled to listen to a passing preacher who stood on the top of a small staircase leading to a brothel. His voice rang clear through the air as he condemned all those inside the building and, as far as Argyle could tell by the shocked faces, all those outside it too, to an eternity in Hell.

Looking behind to see if his pursuer was still on his heels, Argyle barged into the side of a low wagon carting vegetables to the nearby market. He grunted and rolled sideways across it, landing unsteadily on his feet. Argyle could hear someone shouting, perhaps a guard, but in the increasing darkness it was hard to make out how many had joined the chase.

The next turn of the street revealed an alley leading off to the right. Argyle sprinted for cover in the winding alley and ducked into a gate.

Only now did he notice that he was gripping the hilt of his sword tightly, and he slowly released it, his fingers burning when blood rushed into them. Argyle crouched when two figures approached the gate, but it was just two apprentices walking to or from their master's yard debating which tavern to visit that night. Leaning heavily against the mud wall, Argyle's mind began to race. He had chased down Coxcombe to get him, once and for all, to promise to keep quiet about Celeste. In return, he was prepared to make a genuine offer to let up on his enquiries about La Fontaine's death. A fair deal.

But somehow Coxcombe had caught wind of Argyle's frantic attempt to find him and had disappeared. Argyle wondered where he had gone and who might have tipped him off. Had Celeste been honest with him when she said, no one else knew her secret?

In any event, rather than being the one looking for Coxcombe, Argyle was the one being chased. Coxcombe or whomever he was working with was scouring every alleyway and street, and Argyle knew that it was just a matter of time before they found him hiding here. He had to think fast. He was caught in a part of town that he rarely visited.

He jerked upright. The two apprentices had talked about taking a wherry to Southgate later on. Argyle knew he was close to the river; why not distract his pursuers and head for the river, hire a barge or better yet a wherry to his house and come back later for his horse and the truth?

'Pox on that!' he cursed under his breath. The order from the King's secretary that he was to appear in Westminster on the morrow had spooked him. But Argyle had sent a note to the Queen begging her to keep quiet until they had a chance to speak, and he refused to believe that she would act rashly when she had kept the secret for months.

Celeste must be making arrangements to leave, Argyle thought and carefully slid into the darkened alley, she will be safe in France. He hoped that if the King found out about Celeste, he would be wise enough not to send a regiment of White Harts to France to fetch her back. It would risk his alliance with King Charles and threaten the fragile peace between the countries that England, at least, desperately needed to preserve.

Argyle turned the last corner of the alley, and the smell of the Thames jolted him back to the present just a moment too late. Though his hand was still on the hilt of his sword his move was not quick enough. A tip of hardened steel floated inches from his throat, the blade glittering in the weak moonlight.

'Thought you were safe?' Coxcombe grinned. 'Thought that the King did not watch your every move?'

Argyle stepped back and felt another blade at his back. He resisted the urge to turn around and kept his eyes on Coxcombe. The narrow passage moved in on him, the walls blocking out the weak sunlight. The faint sounds of the crowded street on the other side of the dingy houses seemed miles away. If he did shout for help, most likely no one would hear him.

'Whatever drove you to seek me out, it must have been serious! Perhaps you wanted a secret kept?' Coxcombe rasped.

'No,' an oddly familiar voice chimed in behind Argyle. 'It must be the lady. Everyone seems willing to risk their lives for the lady.'

'Perhaps Sir Argyle should have a care, he has too many ladies in his life. I wonder what his wife will think of his French whore - or his little Queen?' Coxcombe lowered his sword to point it at Argyle's heart. 'Something rotten in there, I think.'

'Think what you like,' Argyle said trying to decide whether he could fight his way out. What choice did he have?

'Oh, I do, though I don't have to.' Coxcombe smiled to whoever was standing behind Argyle. 'I have my orders.'

'To do what?'

'Sadly, for the time being, to keep you alive,' the man behind him said. 'Although after tomorrow who knows what our orders be?'

'And you are?'

'Unimportant,' Coxcombe said and quenched any protests from his companion with a cold stare. 'We'll take you to your house. Best you do not tell the King that you were out and about tonight, he might ask who helped you find your way home.'

The man behind Argyle grunted and poked him in the back. 'Move!'

'This must be the second time you are cheated out of killing me, Coxcombe,' Argyle said, his shoulder brushing against the raw wall, clearly they were staying in the shadows. 'It cannot sit well with you. I should not wonder if you are still half frightened that I might have found out more than is good for you and your master about La Fontaine's death.'

'We made a deal!' Coxcombe's voice almost broke. 'I led you to the lady, and you let up your enquiries.'

'Now where would the fun in that be?' Argyle baited Coxcombe and heard the other man clear his throat. 'Are you afraid of your friend?

Perhaps he is here to make sure that you do not act rashly?'

'I am here to take you home,' the man said, finally stepping into view. He slipped Argyle's sword from its scabbard and slid it into his own belt. 'Coxcombe will fetch your horse and deliver it to your stables.'

Argyle could not see the man's face beneath the hood, but the voice sounded familiar, and he could see Coxcombe's face flash with anger. Here perhaps was his way out. 'Still taking orders, Coxcombe?! Not able to make your own decisions? How tiresome that must be!'

'I get by.' Coxcombe fastened the grip on his sword and glanced at the hooded man. 'Some day, it'll just be the two of us, and I shall hunt you to the ends of the Earth if I have to.'

'For what? Revenge? What did I ever do to you?'

'You got in my way! La Fontaine's lands were supposed to go to me upon his demise, not some nobleman's brat!' Coxcombe's face split in an ironic grin.

There it is at last, Argyle thought, the real reason why Coxcombe hates me, land. How could he ever have thought that La Fontaine's estates would end up in his lap? The hooded man pressed his blade against Argyle's side. 'What a friend you were!'

'What a friend I WAS??!' Coxcombe exploded. 'What about him?! What it all came down to in the end was not friendship or chivalry it was COWARDICE!! And I made sure a coward died that day!'

Argyle stepped towards Coxcombe and winced when the hooded man's blade bit into his side. 'Truth at last!'

'La Fontaine was dangerous.' Coxcombe sheathed his sword; his leather gloves creaked when he balled his fists. He gave Argyle a dirty look. 'He would have dragged down everyone with him. Ask yourself; if he was such a hero then why did no one try to help him in the end?'

The hooded man stepped between them and grabbed Argyle by the arm. 'On the wherry! NOW!'

Coxcombe was still breathing heavily when Argyle and his gaoler stepped on board. The hooded man pushed a fat purse of coins into the wherry-man's hand, and he turned to steer the wherry into the current.

'La Fontaine is dead, let it die with him,' Coxcombe's voice floated across the black Thames water thick as a fog. 'Forget him. Forget me.'

CHAPTER 43

12 February 1399 - Westminster Palace

'I will not have that filthy whore at MY court a moment longer!' the King shook with fury, his eyes burning in his pale face. 'She is a disgrace, she is contemptuous, and she has deceived us all! Take her AWAY!'

Two of the King's guard grabbed Celeste and pinned her arms behind her back, her face twisted in agony and desperation. 'Will no one speak for me?'

Argyle had been pulled out of bed at first light, forced across London to Westminster by four White Harts and pushed into the great hall, brimming with people looking as perplexed as he. The longer they had waited the more Argyle feared that the worst had happened. Although all the hearths were roaring, the hall was freezing, animosity and distrust trickling down the walls and sticking to the wall hangings, distorting their bright colours.

When the big oak doors had finally been thrown open, his worst fears had come to life. Celeste had been cast down on the floor below the dais, her dress was torn and she bled from several scratches on her cheek. She had sought his eyes for just a moment and recognised Argyle's dread. She must know that he had not revealed her secret.

'PLEASE!' Celeste now screamed. 'PLEASE, your Majesty, for the love …'

One of the White Harts hit her hard across the face, and her head jerked back. The room was quiet, everyone holding their breaths to see who would be foolish enough to come to her aid. Argyle noticed Bolingbroke's son Henry of Monmouth shift slightly at the King's right side, but the young man kept staring vacantly into the dusty air, his face betraying no emotion. Surrey and Kent were staring at the ceiling while other noblemen, courtiers and knights looked at their boots and the floor.

Argyle saw a couple of the Queen's ladies-in-waiting standing in a corner, Mistress Prudence among them. He caught her eye, but she turned her flushed face from him, and Argyle's sense of dread deepened. Where was the Queen?

The guards pulled Celeste up and marched her through the throng of people. In the doorway, the captain turned towards the King. 'Where shall we take her, Majesty?' his thick Cheshire accent rolled through the air.

'The Tower, YOU FOOLS! I shall decide her fate later!' the King said and turned to the room, his face all at once complacent and alive. 'Now that this sad business is at an end, shall we return to more pleasant matters?'

The side door opened and the Queen entered, splendid in blue and silver. She glanced around the room and looked briefly at Argyle before her gaze wandered on. He thought she looked taut and afraid although she managed to hide it reasonably well. Mistress Prudence joined the Queen's train, stepping in behind Lady Mortimer, the two of them exchanging a single look. Mistress Prudence leaned in and whispered something that made Lady Mortimer jerk.

'Sir Argyle.' Surrey slid up beside him. 'What make you of that?'

'Nothing, how about you?'

'A show for the Queen?' The Duke of Exeter appeared next to Surrey, nodding to his relative.

'Then it was a poor show, the Queen was not even here,' Argyle said certain that both the King's half-brother and his nephew knew that Argyle had been fetched by the White Harts. 'I wonder what the lady has done that would make the King send her to the Tower? In her condition.'

'Come now, it has been long since your dalliance with the fair Celeste, surely you do not care for her? You did not speak in her defence.' Exeter tried to make light of the situation, but his eyes betrayed his merry tone.

Argyle balled his fist so hard, his nails bit into his palms. 'She is pregnant by the King, for God's sake!'

'Some say it is not his,' Surrey said. 'That she has kept a lover.'

And who might that be, Argyle thought staring at Surrey. But he forced himself to ask, 'Is it true?'

'There are few secrets at court,' Exeter said. 'Take for instance the rumours about the Queen.'

Surrey nodded. 'She is full young to have taken a lover, but all young girls fall in love with someone older, is that not so, Sir Argyle?'

'I have heard nothing about the Queen.' Argyle tried to keep calm. Surely, Celeste would not have betrayed their agreement? But he also knew that brute force had been administered and would not blame her if she had been broken.

'Well, you have been with her much,' Surrey said, looking about the room with a disinterested air. The courtiers and ladies tried to put on happy faces, but apprehension made them clumsy and stiff. 'Perhaps you are not the right one to ask about the Queen. Perhaps …'

Exeter laughed. 'Oh no, I have known Sir Argyle for a long time, and he would never …'

They shrunk back when two White Harts appeared. 'Sir Argyle, the King wishes to see you.'

ꕤ ꕤ

'DID YOU KNOW, SIRE?!' the King screamed, lunging for Argyle. He felt all blood drain from his face, and did nothing when the King punched him hard in the ribs. 'GAUNT'S!! THAT IS WHAT SHE IS!!' The King's hands closed around Argyle's throat. 'A FUCKING WHORE - AND THE DAUGHTER OF A WHORE! A FRENCH WHORE AND BASTARD!! YOU KNEW!!!'

A couple of the King's guards interfered and pried the King's hands from Argyle throat. He fell to his knees coughing. 'No, Majesty. I knew nothing!'

'LIAR!' the King shook off his guards' hands. 'FOOLS! How dare you touch your King?!'

The guards returned to their posts by the presence chamber's side door. Although they were in all likelihood used to seeing much and more, the King's assault had made them anxious. Now they struggled to assume their usual vacant stares.

The King knelt before Argyle who was still on his knees, bringing them at eyelevel. 'You had her first, and you knew nothing?' he whispered. 'She turned your head with her lying body and flaunted herself before all the lords of England, and they knew nothing? You fucked her day and night, and you will have me believe that you knew nothing?'

Argyle bowed his head in submission. The bright colours of carpet beneath his hands and knees were moving in an unsettling way.

'IDIOT!' the King seethed. 'Be thankful I sent for you to come here! Though perhaps your humiliation would have been to more use had it been publicly known.'

'I am thankful, Majesty.'

'She is a snake!' The King got up and brushed his knees. Argyle could only see the toes of his subtle leather boots. 'Fetch me the Queen.'

One of the guards slipped out of the door and in the wait, Argyle felt the rushes stab at his knee through the carpet. The King had returned to his throne, waiting for the Queen to arrive, and Argyle dreaded what might happen next. 'How did you find out, Majesty?' His throat burned with every word.

'I have my ways!' the King said, and Argyle could hear that he was rustling with something on the dais, but he dared not look up. You certainly have, he thought, but why did you not use your ways sooner? She has been with the Queen since before your marriage.

Argyle was sure that it had been Coxcombe who had finally told the King and considered what punishment the King had doled out on Coxcombe.

'Isabella, my sweet,' the King said in a strange seemingly happy tone and stood. 'Come sit by me.'

The Queen walked past Argyle, her hand, hidden in its long, flowing sleeve, brushed his shoulder. 'My Lord,' she said sweetly. Argyle could tell that she tried to keep her voice light. 'The whole court is in uproar; they say you have sent Lady Celeste to the Tower? Whatever might she have done?'

'Oh, I think you know, my dear.' The King's words crept around the empty room. 'I think you may have known for some time.'

Argyle glanced up and saw the Queen give a contorted smile; the King was crushing her hands in his. 'What are you talking about, husband?'

The King threw her down on the dais. 'YOU WILL CALL ME

MAJESTY!!' One of the guards by the door moved ever so slightly, but looked down when the King glared at him. No help would be issued for the Queen who now cowered before the King's feet.

'You have harboured Gaunt's bastard girl in your entourage!' the King spat. 'Paraded her around the court and let her slip between my sheets! YOU DISGUST ME!'

'I did not …' The Queen fell back when the King hit her, splitting her lip and making her nose bleed. Argyle thought he saw a glimmer of defiance cross her face. 'Majesty, I knew nothing …'

'Oh, is that so?' The King brushed the blood from her face, leaving a streak of shocking red across her white cheek. 'You see, I think the two of you,' he pointed past the Queen to Argyle, 'knew all along and conspired to put her in my bedchamber!'

The Queen got up and stood before him, pushing his hand away. 'Oh really?' she said coldly, anger flashing in her eyes, making her tiny frame shake. 'And how might I have done that? You sent me from court and kept her here, against my will. I lay this at your door - Majesty.'

The King looked momentarily surprised at her behaviour; suddenly she was no longer a child to be easily subdued. 'You will be quiet!'

'No,' the Queen said, blood slowly trickling down her chin. 'You will not treat your Queen in such a despicable manner! I am of royal blood, I am the only thing holding back a French invasion, and you WILL treat me with respect!'

'NEVER THREATEN ME!' the King screamed but the Queen stood her ground.

'NEVER HIT ME AGAIN!' she screamed back, balling her small fists. 'If you wish for me to speak, simply ask me for the truth.'

Argyle watched the power struggle with increasing wonder and panic, did the Queen not know that she was treading dangerous ground, and that once she managed to send the King into a rage, he would stop at nothing to punish her? Had her father told her nothing about the English King's reputation? Then he remembered her mention how she often had visits from French ambassadors and thought, she is not alone at court - she has many friends and allies who will rally to her side.

The Queen swept a shallow curtsey clearly meant to insult her husband and sat down on her chair on the dais. 'Why is Sir Argyle kneeling there?' Her voice trembled a little, betraying her calm face.

'You were conspiring with him.' The King's words were weak and deflated. 'You both knew, you have been whispering about it for months. Do you deny that you told him the truth about Celeste? That you dote on him and often see him alone?'

'No,' the Queen said staring into the back of the room. 'I rely on him.'

'So he knew?'

'You sent him to me. You said I should trust him.' The Queen stole a glance at Argyle probably meant to be reassuring. 'You were the one to say that the most honest and loyal man in England was Sir Argyle, and that I would find in him a friend that would never falter.'

The King looked appalled. 'You are saying …'

'I took him into my confidence only because you sent him to me after the joust.' The Queen's face was an immovable mask. 'I had just learned about Celeste, and I did not know what to do. Sir Argyle was kind to offer his support. I swore him to secrecy.'

The King looked at Argyle. 'Stand, Sir Argyle! Is this true?'

'Yes, Majesty.' Argyle was astounded at the Queen's stealth; she seemed determined not to be treated as a child. 'Until her Majesty told me, I knew nothing.'

'You told her to keep it from me?' the King asked and owned a livid stare from the Queen.

'How dare you?!' Her voice quivered with fury. 'No one - except you - can command me.' The Queen took her husband's hand. 'I told him to keep it quiet. I did not know how to tell you that a woman you thought highly of was a liar and an imposter. What would you have me do? I was in shock! I thought perhaps Lord Bolingbroke or Lord Gaunt had …' She shook her head. 'Sir Argyle did my bidding.'

'Gaunt's brat!' The King snapped his hands from the Queen's grasp. 'You would have kept it from me that I had bedded my own cousin?'

'No,' the Queen said and earned a confused look from the King. 'I wanted to use it for revenge. When you were bobbing a boy you had off her on your knee, I would tell you what you had done and who she really was.' The cold passion in her voice made Argyle wince. 'Even he did not know what I intended to do,' the Queen nodded towards Argyle, 'no one knew. Until I told Sir Argyle who Celeste was, he thought that she had had an affair with Bolingbroke before ending up in your bedchamber.'

The King roared with wild laughter. 'Bolingbroke must have known right from the offset and sent her Sir Argyle's way. He must have thought that if Sir Argyle would fuck her, I would too! Gaunt must have known she was his, after all how many French women has he bedded?! She was but a pawn in Gaunt's attempt to secure the throne for the Lancastrians … one way or another! If I would not name Bolingbroke my heir, Gaunt would have his bastard daughter bed me until she was with child. Or have someone else put a baby in her belly and pass it off as mine!'

Argyle's mind refused to believe the King's ramblings. If that had been Gaunt's final bid for the throne, it was not only a massive gamble, but also foolish beyond belief. How could the old man know that the King would not go on to make heirs on the Queen when she came of age? The thought was too terrible to finish …

'What will become of her?' Argyle asked, the blood in his veins running cold.

The King shot him a dark look. 'What do you think? She is of his blood.'

Argyle flinched, the King's words woke the dormant snakes in his stomach and they wormed about, hissing and biting.

'What choice do I have? The woman is a threat to the kingdom, to the Queen.' The Queen winced when he grabbed her hands. 'And to ME! She must be wiped out, history shall not remember her; she will not have existed. Her heritage will be her undoing.' The King's voice turned surprisingly soft and sad. 'No one will know what she was or who she was, only that she displeased the King and endangered the Queen. That is enough to send most people to the chopping block, why not her?'

'Her life?' Argyle saw black spots. 'You will have her life?'

'No, I will take it.' The King's mad smile took the air out of Argyle's lungs, and out of the corer of his eye, he saw the Queen grasp the armrest of her chair to steady herself. 'And both of you will watch.'

Argyle could tell by the Queen's pained looks that the King was once more putting force into his grasp. Her eyes welled up and she looked at Argyle with pleading eyes but terror pushed forward only one word. 'When?'

The door behind the dais opened and Celeste appeared between two hard-faced White Hart guards. She hung limp between their hands, and for a moment, Argyle thought she was already dead. But then she looked up, her face swollen and bruised. 'How have I offended your Majesty?' she asked in a thick voice.

'How do you think, lady?' The King walked slowly towards her while the guards forced her to her knees. 'What could you possibly have done?'

'I know not, Majesty,' Celeste insisted, her sky-blue eyes brimming with tears, the left was half-closed by a bruise. 'I would do anything to change it.'

'Not to worry, you will soon enough, my Lady,' the King rested a hand on her head, stroking her thick honeyed hair. 'Is that not so, my sweet? She will soon redeem herself.'

Celeste caught sight of the Queen sitting on the dais. 'Majesty, please forgive me for what I have done, please …'

'You led me on,' the Queen said thinly. 'You were a spy in my chambers, and you went from my bedchamber to my husband's. I shudder to think what secrets you have passed on to your father and your brother. We are all shocked to find what you are and what you have done. Is that not so, Sir Argyle?'

Argyle swallowed hard, his mouth was so dry that no words would come. How could the Queen sit there and pass judgement over her former friend? Did she not know that playing into the King's hands was dangerous? The King wanted blood spilled, was she willing to let that happen?

'Argyle?' Celeste turned her head a little in his direction, wincing when the guard drew her arm up hard. 'You are here?'

'Oh, yes, Sir Argyle, the Queen and I have had a very interesting conversation, my Lady,' the King said in an informal tone that made Argyle's skin crawl. 'He is convinced that you want nothing from me. But then, he has his own troubles to contend with. He has all but seduced the Queen.'

Argyle started and the Queen once more grabbed her armrests tightly and glared at the King, while Celeste began crying. 'Please, Majesty, for the love I bear for you, I know nothing of …'

The King struck her with the back of his hand so hard that spittle and blood flew from her mouth. 'SHUT UP, SLUT!'

Argyle instinctively tried to stand and felt ironclad hands grab his arms. He glanced at the guard to his right, dressed in chainmail, his sword at the ready. The Queen too flinched but kept her seat; she seemed to have made up her mind that Celeste would have to be sacrificed.

'Majesty, please,' Argyle's words seared his throat as he tried to change the King's mind. 'Not here! Do not sully the royal halls with the blood of a traitor …'

'I am NO traitor!' Celeste screamed, blood pouring from her mouth. 'My father was the lord Gaunt, uncle to the King of England, lord of …'

The King struck her again, and Celeste fell sideways. Argyle began struggling, but a second guard pushed him down, his knees smashing hard against the stone floor underneath the beautiful carpet. Anger surged from the pit of his stomach to his head, turning his gaze red.

'Majesty! She was your friend!' Argyle tried to call upon the Queen's mercy but she turned her face from him.

'A dangerous woman,' the King was stroking Celeste's hair again, so much like a child with a kitten - a cruel child. 'She would have put her own bastard on the throne of England if she had the chance. She would have claimed her Lancaster inheritance in due course, thinking herself safe as my mistress! I can scarce imagine what she might do to my beloved Isabella …'

'Majesty, please!' Argyle shouted, he had seen the unadulterated malice on the King's face. 'The Queen …' One of the guards struck him with the butt of his sword and Argyle's head jerked left. His vision blackened, and he fought to throw aside the sticky cloth of unconsciousness.

'The Queen, the Lady …' the King walked slowly towards Argyle. 'They are women! What do they know?! What does anyone know about being King, but the King?' The King crouched beside Argyle and turned his face towards him, a fragment of wonder in his eyes. 'What do you know?!'

'That it is in your power to be forgiving, Majesty,' Argyle heard his slurred speech and tried to clear his head, feeling the King's fingers dig into his jaw. 'Let her live her life in the Tower, she will be forgotten.'

'I think not! Too many times others have acted on my behalf, I believe it is high time I act for myself and see this witch to her grave,' the King said smiling slightly. 'You know about witches, do you not, Sir Argyle?' Argyle snapped his head back and narrowly escaped a blow to the face; the King's hand struck his throat instead, the impact sent a bolt of pain flashing in front of his eyes. 'Get him up!'

The two guards heaved Argyle to his feet; he shook his head and a rain of stars clouded his vision. Celeste was trembling on the floor and the Queen's face was white, the clotted blood on her cheek glittered in the candlelight as uncut gemstones.

'What a great King you serve, Sir Argyle!' Celeste said defiantly. 'What a valiant King! And what a gracious and kind Queen he has!'

The King's lips were wet with spittle when he marched back to her, kicking her in the face hard enough for Argyle to hear her nose break. Celeste fell backwards but the guards pushed her roughly forward. 'BITCH!'

'She is right!' Argyle said, and the King stopped dead in his tracks.

'Right?'

I have his attention; I have to keep it on me, Argyle thought. He struggled to continue, his brain was slow to react. 'What kind of man …'

'Oh, Sir Argyle, I am no mere man, I am a KING!' the King drew a sword from the scabbard of one of his guards and looked lovingly at it. 'And a King can do as he pleases!'

The King swung the sword down, blade flashing, and thrust it hard into Celeste's creamy neck. Life sighed out of her and she slid sideways, blood spilling down her gown. Graceful, even in death, Argyle thought irrationally. The Queen drowned a scream with her sleeve and looked away.

The King drew out the sword, wriggling it lightly when it caught in Celeste's bones. He looked at her body with something like compassion and caressed her swollen belly, where Argyle thought he could see movement. He retched and the guards that held him pushed him forward.

The King's boots were soaked in Celeste's blood, leaving marks on the steps when he walked across to where Argyle was crouching. The Queen was sobbing on the dais. 'What to do about you, Sir Argyle?'

'Kill me too,' Argyle croaked, the gauntlet hand that forced him to the floor seemed to tear away his voice.

'Now why would I do that? I have no need for French whores, but a sworn and loyal knight? I can never have enough of those,' the King said, Argyle thought he heard malice and mockery in his voice. 'And you want your brother back some day, do you not? You will want to keep your family safe. That pretty wife of yours. Your heir. Your unborn child …'

'You cannot think I will be loyal after this!'

'I not only think it, I know it! I have an armed guard riding for your home to fetch your boy and your pregnant wife!' the King retorted. 'Do not doubt that they will obey my order, if I thought you could not be trusted. Their blood will be on your hands! You OWE your allegiance to ME! Who else is there, Sire?!'

Argyle hung his head, even though he did not truly love Isobel, he loved his boy more than anything in this world; too much was at stake. The King had dragged the Queen with him from the dais and the two of them stood before Argyle. 'What will it be?' The King rested the bloody sword in front of Argyle. 'Loyalty or betrayal?'

When Argyle did not answer, the King slowly slid the sword up the front of his shirt, letting the bloodied tip rest in the hollow of his throat. 'Well?!'

'Loyalty, Majesty,' Argyle said as his skin was pierced. But not to you, he added in his mind, loyalty to my blood, my family, and the Queen - you deserve no more of my loyalty.

'I thought as much,' the King removed his sword and the guards pulled Argyle roughly to his feet. 'Well done, Sir Argyle! Your brother said your loyalty would never be swayed - I almost thought that for once, he had got it wrong and that your loyalty could be thwarted by a filthy whore!'

Argyle grit his teeth and followed the King's pacing with his eyes, the guard holding him upright squeezed his arm. He refused to look at the Queen who remained standing before him.

'Thank God it takes more than a wet woman for you to break! Now I know it takes at least two - and a baby in its swaddling! Still, I cannot simply let you go …' The King looked around and grunted. 'Get that out of here!'

One of the King's men heaved Celeste over his shoulder and walked off, her head dangling against his shoulder, blood dripping on the rushes. Another went to the door to call for a servant but the King stopped them. 'No, I want no more witnesses. I want her wiped from existence - and that will never happen if even a single servant sees this! Find somewhere to hide it where no one is bound to look. In the filth beneath the kitchens if needs be.'

'How prudent, Majesty.' Argyle earned a singing slap for his insolence and relished it. He felt more alive with the pain than he did when he looked at the pool of blood on the floor.

'Be quiet,' the Queen whispered, her hand once more held in the King's iron grip.

'I will have my men at Beauworth even before you are in the Tower! They will seize your boy and bring him here if, God willing, nothing happens to him on the way.' The King snorted when Argyle flinched. 'Do we have an understanding, Sir Argyle?'

The two guards tightened their grip, but Argyle bowed his head nausea washing over him. 'Yes, Majesty.'

'Best not let him loose in the palace just now. Put him on a barge and see he gets to his London house. There he can sit in house arrest until he is ready to come to court and pay homage to me,' the King said. 'On his knees!'

Two guards grabbed hold of Argyle and began dragging him from the room, but the King stopped them. 'There is one more thing, Sire. The small matter of my young wife's heart.'

Argyle's blood curdled, and the Queen stomped her little foot. 'You are out of line, my Lord!'

'Am I now?' the King asked. 'Lady Mortimer tells me you steal off with Sir Argyle whenever you can. Truly, Isabella, did you think I would suffer such insolence?'

'You have just killed one of my friends,' the Queen shook with anger, any sign of despair or sorrow wiped from her face, 'after you bedded her and got her with child - would you strip me of all my friends?!'

'Only the one who seems to have an unnatural relationship with his child Queen,' the King said in a quiet, threatening voice. 'I need your reputation pure and intact. What would your father say if I told him that I let one of my knights have his way with you?!'

The Queen turned on the dais steps and slapped the King across the face his eyes bulging at the insolence. 'What is to say I have not already told my father all about your mistress?! Do you think he will keep to his end of the bargain, if he thinks you are slighting me?! Sullying my reputation?! I am all of nine years old, Majesty - you had best remember that!'

'WHAT?!' The King raised his hand, but something in the Queen's eyes made him waver. 'You dare threaten me?'

'Let him go to house arrest, what do I care?!' the Queen spat. 'But if you announce him my lover, I will bring the whole of France down upon your head!' She spun around and left.

'Take him away!' the King growled and kicked Argyle. 'I cannot bear to look at him anymore! Take him to his house and post a guard!'

Argyle hung limp between the guards when they dragged him from the room. He did not doubt that the King had indeed dispatched White Harts to Beauworth even before he had called Celeste out in public. The King knew that Argyle would intercede but not if he could be stopped by mere words; collateral was needed. At this point, he was left to wonder if he could trust the King to call back his men. The Queen's final words rang in Argyle's head; *I will bring the whole of France down upon your head …*

The guards finally tired from half-carrying him along, and one of them used the flat of his blade to slap Argyle to his feet. He walked grudgingly between them through the back ways of the castle to the river, his head was aching and every time he blinked, sparks flew before his eyes. The Thames was flowing rapidly, filled with dirt and grime, dead animals bobbing along in the current. The guards commanded a royal barge to furl its standards, and all three of them stepped on board.

'You will be home soon,' one of the guards said.

'Best to forget, what happened here today,' the other chimed in.

'Best you let me go, now that we are on the water,' Argyle said but the guards kept hold of him and he was too groggy to struggle. The barge navigated the crossing currents and moved quickly along the bank. 'How long will I stay under guard?'

'You heard our orders,' one of the guards said. 'You will stay at the King's pleasure.'

CHAPTER 44

2 March 1399 - London

Argyle was going mad. Since his return from the King's presence chamber he had hardly slept, for every time he closed his eyes, Celeste's bloodied body floated before him, and the Queen's words cut through his mind. His London house was a sickening prison, the ground floor occupied by a royal guard and the upper rooms had been stripped of their good furniture, only a few chairs and a cot left. The King was determined to make his stay as miserable as possible and every day, Argyle expected that the guards would escort him to the Tower, but no royal order came.

He had tried to send word to Beauworth, but his letter had been intercepted and returned to him, the guard holding it out as if it was poisoned. It was clear that Argyle must be kept in the dark about his family's fate.

He pushed his meagre meal away and clutched his cup. He had nowhere left to turn, no one to plead his case. Thomas was in exile, unable to wield his usual, if never quite comfortable, influence; Margaret was nowhere to be found. Only Eleanor still lingered at court. Argyle had seen her on the day of Celeste's death, but he doubted she would be able to get to him.

'A visitor, M'lord,' a servant announced and the guard opened the door reluctantly. It was clear to Argyle that he had no instructions about what to do, if someone showed up asking to see the master of the house.

'Oh, brother!' Eleanor flung herself into his arms, her big hood falling back.

'What are you doing here?' Argyle held her tight for a moment.

'I come from the Queen.' She stepped back and waved at the guard by the door. 'Leave us!' The man glared, but Eleanor would not be disregarded. 'Are you hard of hearing? I said leave us!'

He stepped outside, giving Argyle a knowing look before he closed the door. 'This will get back to the King,' Argyle said and offered Eleanor a seat by the fire. 'How did you get past my guard?'

Eleanor held the Queen's seal up triumphantly. 'I come armed!'

Argyle laughed despite himself. 'You are resourceful, dear sister. But the Queen is playing a dangerous game if she thinks the King will accept that she sends visitors to me.'

'I am not just any visitor,' Eleanor said and warmed her hands over the flames looking around the bleak room. 'I am family! And you will be pleased to know that Isobel and Edmund are safe at Beauworth.'

Argyle said a silent prayer. 'Thank you!'

'Oh, it is not my doing.' Eleanor shrugged off her cloak. 'Whatever happened that day? The Queen came back to her chambers in a fit and declared she would leave for Windsor immediately. She instructed Mistress Prudence to stay behind and that I take her place. Lady Mortimer protested, but the Queen silenced her with a threat that she would be replaced by another if she did not do as she was commanded.' Eleanor accepted a cup of wine. 'Have you any food? I am starving! Walking through London at night is hungry business!'

Argyle offered her his plate and she took it eagerly, finding an uncomfortable seat on a low stool near the fire. 'Well?'

'I cannot tell you.' Argyle began pacing the room. 'If the Queen has told you nothing then neither can I.'

'You were in there so long, and then the herald simply announced that you were to be kept in house arrest at the King's pleasure.' Eleanor picked at a piece of chicken. 'Something dreadful must have transpired?'

Argyle turned his back to her. 'Yes. I put my family in danger.'

'But they are safe?' Eleanor realised what he was not saying. 'Oh … Is that why the Queen has been housing me these last weeks?'

Most likely, Argyle thought, but rather than pursue the subject he asked, 'What are they saying at court?'

'For all I know absolutely nothing! The Queen turns away all the King's presents and courtiers.' Eleanor drank deep. 'But I have had a letter from Margaret.'

'Margaret?'

'She writes that you are in grave danger and she sent word for me to visit you. To give you this.' Eleanor handed him a little letter, sealed with the Mowbray crest.

Dangerous to use, Argyle thought and broke the seal. The words on the paper danced in front of his eyes.

'What does she say?' Eleanor tried to look over Argyle's shoulder but he crumpled the letter and threw it into the flames.

'Better that you do not know, sister,' Argyle said. 'You should not linger. The King is bound to know that you have come - even if you bear the Queen's seal. It is not safe for you to be here.'

Eleanor looked at him for a long moment, equally disappointed and upset, and Argyle grabbed her hands. 'I am thankful that you came, you do not know how I have longed for a familiar face, another voice in my rooms and for news of Isobel and Edmund. But you must go.'

Eleanor's eyes shone with tears when she threw on her cloak and drew up the hood. 'Stay safe, darling little brother.' She kissed his cheek lightly and let herself out.

As soon as she left, his guard entered, looking around the room as if he thought that Eleanor had smuggled in a small army. 'The King will hear of this.'

'It was just a sister worried about her brother.'

'Or it was a messenger from the Queen to her lover. That's what they're saying at court, Sire, that you've turned the little Queen's head.' Argyle looked long and hard at the guard, and he shrunk back a little. 'Well, that's what they say!'

Argyle sat in the chair, his back turned to the guard who settled on his stool beside the door. Looking into the flames, Argyle re-read Margaret's note in his mind.

- You were betrayed by a man called Grenteville. Old Fish Street. Burn this. -

Grenteville, Argyle thought. If he was working for Bolingbroke, perhaps he would had known the truth about Celeste, but then what would have inspired him to tell the King about her? If he was working for the Lancaster clan, he should have protected her. Argyle leaned forward, the fire warming his face. He had to get to Old Fish Street to see Grenteville. His eyes caught the glimmer of the poker.

ꕥ ꕥ ꕥ ꕥ

2 March 1399, midnight - Old Fish Street, London

The guard had kept his blade sharp, but had been too slow to defend himself against a desperate man with a poker. Argyle relished the soothing sound the sword made when he pulled it from the hardened leather scabbard. He swung it around and narrowly escaped Grenteville's lunge; his sword fell through in the air inches from Argyle's ear. Ducking to avoid the back swing, Argyle thrust forward, feeling steel sink into flesh.

Grenteville grunted when blood gushed from a deep wound in his right thigh, and Argyle darted forward, his sword raised for the final strike. Grenteville turned with uncanny speed, slipping a dagger from his belt and burying it in Argyles left shoulder. The sharp, burning pain spread from his shoulder blade to the upper arm. Grenteville's grip on the dagger was so strong that he yanked the blade free when Argyle pulled away, his blood pumping from the wound. He gritted his teeth, never missing a step.

Circling each other, Argyle sought out Grenteville's weak spot, it was eerie how he managed to ignore the wound in his thigh. In a sudden rush, Grenteville struck out, slashing his knife across Argyle's neck and he felt the skin split sending a torrent of blood down his chest. Argyle lunged and thrust his sword at Grenteville, forcing him to sidestep; Argyle spun around and felt his knee impact with Grenteville's wounded thigh. For the first time, he let out a guttural scream, sliding sideways, his knee smashing into the cobbled street and when he looked up, his eyes shone with malice.

In a fluent motion, Argyle pulled out his dagger, slid behind Grenteville and grabbed his hair with his left hand, pain seared through his shoulder threatening to paralyse his arm, but he held on tight and pulled Grenteville's head backwards pressing the dagger to his throat.

Wheezing from pain and exertion, Argyle growled. 'No more lies! Who sent you?'

Grenteville fought to escape, pushing Argyle's dagger into his own throat in his efforts. 'Your enemies linger close to home …'

Argyle let go of Grenteville's hair and grabbed his arm, forcing it up behind his back. He snarled but continued to struggle to get to his feet, and Argyle felt his dagger slip, his hand slick with blood. 'Who sent you?!'

Grenteville wrenched free, blood gushing from the wound on his neck. He threw his dagger at Argyle, the tip grazing his cheek before he could move out of the way. The furious fighting continued, but Grenteville was losing momentum, and Argyle kicked him in the knee, forcing him to his knees. 'I ask for the last time - who sent you?!'

'I serve England.' Grenteville coughed up blood. Argyle heard his dagger clatter on the cobbles; he had not even felt his hand let go of it. A moment of inattention was all Grenteville needed, he got up, his thigh pulsing a steady stream of blood when he crept backwards. 'What did you expect?'

Argyle grabbed his sword tight, his left arm completely useless. 'If you truly serve England, then what do you want with me?'

'I want you dead!' Grenteville lunged with extraordinary speed the scream caught in his throat.

Argyle raised his sword just in time to fend off the attack, Grenteville spun to his right, striking Argyle's wounded shoulder with a fist. Grunting, Argyle staggered backwards trying to escape his opponent for long enough to deliver the final blow. Grenteville was cursing and spitting blood, Argyle could see a white glimmer of bone through Grenteville's ragged wound. His shirt was dyed a deep, dark red from the wound on his neck, which was gushing blood, but he fought on possessed by mad fury.

Argyle stepped back once again, parrying Grenteville's blows, which fell ever more fiercely and desperately. As their swords crossed, their bodies impacted and Grenteville grabbed for Argyle's left shoulder and hit his mark, pushing two fingers deep into the wound. Argyle roared and ducked to get away from the pain, kneeling on the cobbles just long enough to feel the tip of a dagger under his knee. Grabbing it he pulled Grenteville close and thrust the dagger deep into his side. The blade slid easily through flesh and sinew, and Argyle felt bones break, as he forced the dagger through the ribcage.

'I plan to send your master after you, Grenteville! Be sure to give him my regards, when you meet in Hell,' Argyle whispered in Grenteville's ear.

'You would kill a King?' Grenteville croaked before sliding from Argyle's grasp and collapsing on the cobbles. Argyle let go and staggered backwards, the burning pain from his neck and shoulder momentarily forgotten. A King?

The sound of hooves shocked Argyle back to the present. Turning from Grenteville's bloody corpse, Argyle picked up his dagger and ran towards a high wall; he had to scale it before they arrived. With a massive effort, Argyle hauled himself up over the wall, feeling his left shoulder give way and send a sticky warm river down the arm. He threw himself down the other side, rolling to his right and felt his shoulder impact with grass. The sensation was such sweet relief that he almost cried out, but there was no time to waste, he had to get away. Looking around the small garden, Argyle found nowhere to hide; he would have to scale another wall without knowing what was behind it.

Argyle heard men shouting and ducked as he ran along the wall, pausing in a corner to catch his breath. Sprinting towards the opposite wall, he heard a man shout at him just when Argyle jumped and heaved himself up. This time, he did not spare his aching left shoulder when he tumbled down the other side. Searing pain shot down his arm, as Argyle rolled around, and he got to his feet gingerly staring at the dark surroundings. He was in a narrow street and could just about make out the river, so he ran for the water. At the sound of angry voices he looked back, seeing hands on the edge of the wall, and then he slammed face first into a massive horse that screamed and reared. He fell backwards, his wounded shoulder taking the brunt of the impact when he hit a wall and landed on the filthy cobbles.

'When you are commanded to stop in the name of the King, you STOP!' roared the haughty voice of Thomas Holland, the Duke of Surrey.

Argyle struggled to get up and tried to ignore the searing pain in his shoulder and the black spots dancing before his eyes. 'I was attacked.'

'Let me be the judge of that!' Surrey snapped his fingers at two White Harts. 'Throw this villain in the Tower. Give him one of the damp cells near the river - he seems to yearn for water.'

The soldiers laughed and seized Argyle roughly, the pain forcing him to his knees.

'You are far from home, Sir Argyle. Imagine my surprise when your guard came to me, his face a bloody mess!' Signalling to the guards, Surrey added. 'Have no fear, I shall inform the King immediately - of your deed and your insubordination. I am sure that the King will be most interested to hear what I have to say.'

'Be sure that you do - it may well be the last thing you say to his Majesty.' Argyle hissed, the raw pain in his shoulder clouding his mind and slurring his speech. 'And send a physician to my cell.'

Surrey laughed. 'You think you can make demands, Sire?'

'Even a prisoner can demand to be seen by a priest or a physician - I choose the latter.'

Surrey considered Argyle's words for a little while. 'Very well, a physician it is. But do not kid yourself, the King will not rush to your aid, I rather think he will forget your plea if he can, and that should be a small feat!'

Argyle grunted when a guard pulled him to his feet and tied his hands behind his back, the pain blurred his vision. Another guard hailed a barge, and paid the bargeman for transport to the Tower. Surrey turned in his saddle, looking coldly at Argyle. 'I am sure, we will not meet again.'

'And I am sure, we will.' Argyle winced when one of the soldiers punched him with the butt of a sword.

'Best you keep quiet, prisoner!'

Argyle rattled the guard with an evil smile and let himself be dragged towards the Thames.

So close, Argyle thought, I was so close. Stepping onto the barge, he looked back to see Surrey vanishing down the alley, calling for the guards to fall in. Grenteville's body hung across one of the horses.

ꕥ ꕥ

CHAPTER 45

2 March 1399 - London

'What the Hell were you thinking?!!' A lean, hooded man slammed the cell-door shut on the stunned warden and proceeded to push Argyle up against the damp stonewall. 'Have you lost your mind?!'

Argyle marvelled at how familiar the stranger sounded.

'Answer me!!' The hood slid back revealing Thomas' tense face.

'How …?' Argyle did not even know what to ask his brother's ghost; for surely this was a ghost. He was exiled, he left; Argyle had put him on the ship himself. He had sworn to the King that Thomas was gone.

'There is no time!' Thomas' ghost said, pulling Argyle close. 'I repeat, what the Hell were you thinking?!'

He tightened his grip, and Argyle instinctively tried to fight back, but Thomas had the upper hand; Argyle's shoulder was raw and sore, and he fell back clumsily. 'I was ridding the King of an enemy.'

'An enemy? Grenteville an enemy to the King?!' Thomas drove his fingers into Argyle's wounded shoulder, clapping a hand over his mouth when he tried to scream the pain away.

'He attacked me, sword drawn - should I simply have let him chop me to pieces?' Argyle mustered enough strength to push back into Thomas' hold; he finally let go, the tips of his fingers bloodied.

'This is madness!' Thomas dried his fingers on his cloak. 'Grenteville has never had cause to turn against the King, has never even wavered no matter what orders the King gave him. And now you would have me believe that he has turned his coat?'

Argyle sat down, trying to ease the pain in his shoulder, little sparks of pain shot around in his head whenever he moved. 'I must see a physician.'

Thomas snorted. 'And who would provide one? Surely you cannot think I can fetch one? The whole of London would know I am here …'

'Surrey promised me a physician.' Argyle's head was swimming. 'How did you come to be here?'

'Never you mind!' Thomas prowled the floor. 'I should not have come, only … If you must know, Eleanor sent for me as soon as word reached her that you were arrested. It seems that our dear sister has quite a few informants of her own.'

'Eleanor?'

'Perhaps you should sue her for help.' There was true hurt in Thomas' voice. 'She is as thick as thieves with all the right people at court these days. I never imagined she would learn so easily, but learned she has! She wields power as if she were born to do so. The King or someone close to him might even allow her to send a royal physician to you. The London hacks cannot be trusted, why just last week, I saw a man chop off a perfectly good arm of a young man, just because it had gone a little black! Turned out the boy was shifting coal, but by then he was an arm short - now London has another beggar to feed.'

'Las week?' Argyle leaned back and closed his eyes, hoping Thomas' ghost might disappear or, at the very least, shut up. 'But I put you on the ship, I saw you sail out.'

'And I turned back, once you had gone,' Thomas said. 'There were things to be done, masters to serve and orders to carry out. Do not pretend to understand me or my situation, and do not for one moment think to tell Elizabeth or my boys that I never left!'

Argyle opened his eyes again; the ghost was still there. 'What masters?'

'None of your business! I have worked hard to keep you safe - you and our sisters - and you go and shit on all of my efforts by breaking the King's house arrest.' Thomas scratched his patchy beard; it looked very unkempt and distinctly unsuitable on the face of his brother's ghost. 'Why were you put in house arrest in the first place?'

'I thought there were no secrets to ghosts.' Argyle mumbled and his mind drifted. Thomas' slap jerked him upright. 'What the HELL?!'

'Oh I assure you, I am NO ghost! Now tell me all!'

Argyle felt his cheek burn, but the blow had cleared his head a little. 'The King killed his mistress.'

'Lady Celeste?' Thomas sounded confused. 'But she …'

'Was pregnant by the King, though sadly for her, also Bolingbroke's half-sister.' Argyle was giddy from pain and almost burst out laughing at the sight of Thomas' disbelief. 'A Lancaster spy with a King between her legs.'

Thomas fell down on the only chair in the cell, a rickety old thing, anger crumbling on his face. 'What?'

'The King stuck a sword in her throat and killed her, the babe still kicking in her womb. Right before the Queen. Grenteville told the King about Celeste's affinity. It was not I or the Queen, but we knew.' Argyle was babbling and noticed Thomas' livid stare. 'And now, I have gone from house arrest to the Tower. But none of that matters … What does matter is this: how did you come to be here?'

'Is that what matters most to you? Not what punishment the King will serve up? For rest assured you will not be let off with exile.' Thomas sounded uncertain. 'He will have your head.'

'I expect no less. Her death had to be avenged, and if I could, I would have driven my sword right through the King himself.' Argyle winced when Thomas jabbed two fingers into his wound once more.

'Take that back,' hissed Thomas. 'Even these walls have ears.'

'You would know. Although, if they do, then you too are in danger, brother,' Argyle said trying to focus on one of the two Thomas' sitting across from him. It seemed vital to find out why Thomas had come back and how Eleanor knew. Argyle just did not know why.

He was about to ask, but Thomas spoke first. 'He knows.'

'Who knows?'

'You really are a very stupid man!' Thomas fingers left red marks on the chair. 'The King.'

Argyle stared avidly at the ghost.

'Did you think he would let me go and have to do his dirty work himself? Or that he might find anyone else who would do it for him? Then you know very little of the King of England!' Thomas rose. 'But you do need a physician. I shall ask Eleanor to provide one, she may want to visit but do not tell her anything you do not want repeated in the King's ear.'

'Eleanor?'

'Has her own agenda,' Thomas said and turned to knock on the cell door for the warden to let him out. He slid up his hood, once more to conceal his face.

'Thank you.'

'Do not thank me; this may be the last time we meet. Best we say goodbye.' The door opened and slivers of flickering light specked the walls for a moment.

'Goodbye then and God's speed.' Argyle let the sticky cloth of oblivion take hold of him. With any luck, he would sleep forever all his pain comforted by the sweet relief of death.

On the fringes of his conscious the echo of a child crying resounded and a pair of bright blue eyes floated before him, glittering with tears.

'Edmund …?'

HISTORICAL NOTE

The reign of Richard II Plantagenet is perhaps best known for the Peasants Revolt in 1381, a moment in history that proved beyond a doubt what kind of king, Richard II was to become.

When Richard II lost his beloved queen Anne, he was for a long time inconsolable and became a volatile king. Without her kind and calm guidance, Richard II descended upon a path of revenge. His long harboured hatred towards the Lords Appellant would finally be satisfied.

A first sign that Richard II was openly defying former arrangements was his decision to bring back the corpse of his beloved friend Robert de Vere with whom he had grown up. When the Lords Appellant forced Robert de Vere into exile and later forced Richard II to make this decision permanent, he must have felt both powerless and betrayed. To send for Robert de Vere's body to be exhumed and returned to England to be entombed much as a royal prince would be is sure to have offended and appalled many of the English noblemen.

Deciding to take several of the Lords Appellant prisoner appears to have been a well-planned action. According to historians Richard II did indeed take charge in the imprisonments, aided to some extent by Robert FitzAlan's brother Thomas, who urged Robert FitzAlan to surrender to Richard II's mercy.

During the trials that condemned the Lords to their deaths, it is generally believed that Richard II took but little advised. However, his uncle John of Gaunt seems to have managed to stay on Richard II's good side as a constant and unwavering supporter and advisor.

What some historians find strange is that two of the Lords Appellant, namely Richard II's cousin Henry of Bolingbroke, son of John of Gaunt, and Thomas Mowbray came away from the trials without a blemish. This perhaps suggests the power which John of Gaunt still wielded.

Another explanation why Thomas Mowbray was spared might be found in the strange death of Richard II's uncle Thomas of Woodstock. While incarcerated in Calais, he was rumoured dead several weeks before Thomas Mowbray went to collect the prisoner for his trial. The false proclamation of the death of Thomas of Woodstock might have fuelled Richard II's desire never to set eyes on his uncle again and avoid an open spectacle of a trial for a member of the royal family. Whatever the reason, most historians agree that Thomas of Woodstock did not die of natural causes but rather was killed before he could return to defend himself at trial. It is likewise generally believed that Thomas Mowbray had a hand in the death, possibly that he smothered Thomas of Woodstock with a pillow. If Thomas of Woodstock did confess his guilt is a less certain matter.

Historians generally agree that Richard II doted on his French child bride Isabella. Though deemed an entirely unsuitable match by contemporaries, after all Richard II desperately needed an heir to secure his line, by all accounts Richard II and Isabella were happy companions. During the marriage negotiations, he is rumoured to have said that her young age would be remedied by each passing day, perhaps suggesting that unlike others, Richard II believed that in time she would bear him children. Another appealing quality in Isabella was her nationality. By marrying a French princess, Richard II managed to secure what looked to be a permanent peace in his lifetime. An end to the wretched war for the French crown that his grandfather had begun many years ago. Richard II was a lover of peace and would, by all accounts, go to great lengths to secure it.

For dramatic purposes, I have chosen to introduce a grown woman into Isabella's entourage. It is quite possible that she brought with her French ladies-in-waiting, and not entirely inconceivable that one or more might have proven an exotic novelty in a court starved for fresh blood. That Richard II took a mistress would be seemly for a time when kings wee expected to prove their fertility and worldly appetites beyond all others. While queens did not enjoy the same liberties, for a king to take one or more mistresses would be quite normal. Though posterity would remember Richard II as a pious king, he might well have acted as a king of the day would. Likewise, his temper is recorded as that of a true Plantagenet, indicating that he could go from calm and levelheaded to terrifying in a matter of seconds. Furthermore, as the Lords Appellant trials indicate, Richard II was at times a vindictive and spiteful king.

The dispute between Thomas Mowbray and Henry of Bolingbroke has many more facets than those described in this book.

It is generally believed that both sides thought themselves in the right, and that Thomas Mowbray did indeed steal from the Crown to line his own pockets. What Henry of Bolingbroke might achieve by pointing this out to Richard II is less certain other than if he felt threatened and decided to put someone else in the King's line of fire.

Thomas Mowbray did indeed encounter Henry of Bolingbroke on the road and attempt to warn him that the King was plotting to kill both his father John of Gaunt and himself. The plot was never proved but given the strained relationship between the royal cousins and John of Gaunt's decreasing power over Richard II it is not impossible to believe he was working to rid himself of what he most likely found to be two very impossible noblemen.

It would not be out of reach to assume that Richard II was very happy to take the feud between Henry of Bolingbroke and Thomas Mowbray as a means to an end. He did indeed proclaim that the duel between the two was an idea inspired by a divine vision. It is also a fact that he ended the joust of war before it began and went away for hours to deliberate the decision that he eventually came to.

To send his own cousin into exile might seem extreme, but by now, Richard II might have realised that his position of power was weak and that the people and most of the English nobility harboured more love for Henry of Bolingbroke than they did for Richard II. Sending Henry of Bolingbroke away was a perfect solution to a difficult situation.

The lifelong exile of Thomas Mowbray was quite possibly forged by the same desire; to rid himself of a tiresome nobleman who had become a liability to Richard II. It is commonly believed that Thomas Mowbray left England and never returned. However, for the purpose of this book, I have left open the possibility that Thomas might not have left right away. After all, Richard II had until this time relied heavily on Thomas Mowbray in many ways and might have been reluctant to let him go.

Most of the knights and soldiers in this book are dreamt up for this particular occasion. We know for a fact that Richard II was the first English king to have his very own army, and that he called for his White Harts to be present at the Parliament during which the Lords Appellant were tried and sentenced.

Coxcombe who becomes Argyle's nemesis in this book is likewise completely fictional. That some knights did fall from grace is not unheard of for the age and it is quite possible that knights in positions similar to Coxcombe would take bribes and change allegiance to promote their own interests.

The timeline of this book spans some of Richard II's most difficult years. He attempted to resume autonomous power and to get back his beloved friends. He attempted to settle old debts and rid himself of his most ardent enemies.

Did he succeed? That is a question to be answered in another book. Sufficing to say that to many historians the reign of the Plantagenet Kings ended with Richard II.

ABOUT THE AUTHOR

Mette Holm is a writer of historical fiction focusing on last of the Plantagenet rulers beginning with Richard II. The Mowbray family caught her eye when she was first researching the age and especially Thomas Mowbray was so fascinating, she simply had to write about him and the Mowbray family. The decision led to her first book: At the King's Command. In this sequel, she once more delves into the vipers' nest that was the English court.

Mette Holm has been telling stories all her life, be it in school, at university or even in her day-job as an independent business owner and copywriter. While historical fiction holds a special place in her heart, a yet unfinished fantasy manuscript occupies her top drawer and rumour has it that it will in time be dug out and finished. As a quirk despite her Danish heritage, she knows more about medieval England than she does about Danish medieval history.

For more information and to sign up to her newsletter (ensuring you get first dips on all new releases) please visit: metteholmbooks.com

Follow Mette Holm on Facebook: @MetteHolmBooks and Instagram: @authormetteholm

FOLLOW ARGYLE MOWBRAY ON HIS NEXT QUEST IN BOOK 3: WEB OF LIES

'To survive, we must sometimes make choices that are unsavoury.'

Argyle Mowbray wakes up bludgeoned and bloody. He has no idea where he is or how he got there.

Slowly, the pieces of Argyle's nightmare puzzle fall into place, revealing an unravelling King, an enemy returned to claim more than what is his by rights, and a royal secret that threatens to tear England apart.

Determined that, this time, he will learn the truth, Argyle turns his back on England to honour a promise made twice. Once on his sister's deathbed, and once to a woman whose husband was notorious for his double-dealings.

When Argyle is dragged to Paris in shackles, he has but one choice if he wants to earn his freedom and protect his family:

Retrieve King Charles' beloved daughter or die trying.

Web of Lies is based on historical events and is the third volume of the Mowbray Chronicles. The book is set in and around the medieval English court, spanning the tumultuous years of late 14th and early 15th centuries.

ALSO BY METTE HOLM

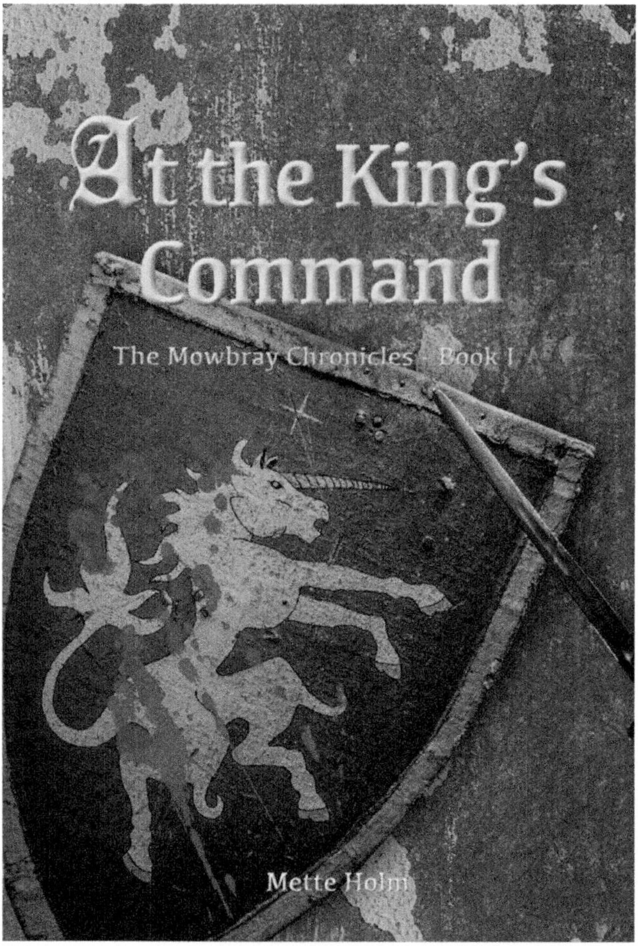

At the King's Command

Court of Deadly Whispers

Web of Lies

Printed in Great Britain
by Amazon

42863225R00219